The Slave King

Peter Darman

Contents

List of characters

Those marked with an asterisk * are Companions – individuals who fought with Spartacus in Italy and who travelled back to Parthia with Pacorus.
Those marked with a dagger † are known to history.

The Kingdom of Dura
Aaron: Jew, royal treasurer at Dura Europos
*Alcaeus: Greek, chief physician in Dura's army
*Byrd: Cappadocian businessman resident at Palmyra, formerly chief scout in Dura's army
Chrestus: commander of Dura's army
Claudia: daughter of Pacorus and Gallia, princess of Dura, Scythian Sister
Eszter: daughter of Pacorus and Gallia, princess of Dura
*Gallia: Gaul, Queen of Dura Europos
Kalet: chief lord of Dura Europos
Lucius Varsas: Roman, quartermaster general of Dura's army
*Pacorus: Parthian, King of Dura Europos
Rsan: Parthian, governor of Dura Europos
Scelias: Greek, head of the Sons of the Citadel
Talib: Agraci, chief scout in Dura's army
Zenobia: commander of the Amazons

The Kingdom of Hatra
*Diana: former Roman slave, now the wife of Gafarn and Queen of Hatra
*Gafarn: former Bedouin slave of Pacorus, now King of Hatra

Other Parthians
Akmon: King of Media, son of King Spartacus
Atrax: prince of Media
Cookes: Governor of Mepsila
Joro: commander of Media's army
Parmenion: High Priest of the Temple of Shamash at Irbil
†Phraates: King of Kings of the Parthian Empire
Soter: chief lord of Media

<u>Non-Parthians</u>
Lusin: Armenian, Queen of Media
Rasha: Agraci, Queen of Gordyene
Spadines: Sarmatian, close ally of King Spartacus
Spartacus: adopted son of Gafarn and Diana, King of Gordyene
Titus Tullus: Roman, former tribune in the army of Quintus Dellius

Chapter 1

Rsan, now in his early seventies, had served the city of his birth diligently during his tenure, first as a minor official and then as its governor, replacing his friend Godarz when the latter had been basely murdered. Rsan was a curious individual: abstemious, reserved and a stickler for rules and regulations. He was also averse to war, which I explained on numerous occasions was a view I too held. But I also believed in the maxim, 'if you want peace, prepare for war', and so under my guidance men such as Lucius Domitus, Kronos and now Chrestus created and maintained an army that not only defended Dura but also the Parthian Empire. Despite his dislike of all things military and the chaos and destruction of warfare, Rsan was also a stern disciplinarian, urging the city magistrates to clamp down ruthlessly on crimes of violence and theft. Murderers, rapists and thieves were hanged outright, minor transgressors were whipped, and blasphemers lost a body part, usually an ear or finger, or had their tongues bored if their words were particularly disrespectful. This ensured Dura remained a law-abiding city, which in turn resulted in a happy citizenry and made Rsan a popular governor.

It was testament to that popularity that he walked from his mansion the short distance to the Citadel for council meetings and other business either alone or accompanied by a clerk or manservant. He always refused Chrestus' offer of an armed guard wherever he went in the city, declaring he had lived to a good age without guards and saw no reason to enlist them now. In weekly council meetings he always sat next to his friend Aaron, the city treasurer, who was now a grandfather. Apart from Chrestus, my muscular, shaven-headed general, all of us who gathered round the table in the Headquarters

Building were over sixty. It would soon be time to introduce fresh blood to the administration of Dura.

After the usual round-up of affairs in the city and kingdom, the usual bickering began between Chrestus and Aaron regarding finances for the army. My treasurer was querying why soldiers in training damaged so many javelins, shields and shot so many arrows, when I held up a letter from Claudia.

'This arrived earlier from Princess Claudia. She and the Exiles are returning to the city, my daughter to attend her sister's wedding.'

The clerk taking notes scribbled furiously to record my words, though who would read the dozens of papyrus sheets stored in the archives – the record of Dura's council meetings going back years – I did not know. Aaron and Rsan nodded their heads.

'At least we will have the Exiles back where they belong, instead of acting as Phraates' personal bodyguard,' grumbled Chrestus.

Following the Battle of Ctesiphon, the Exiles had stayed in the marching camp south of Phraates' palace to enforce security in the Kingdom of Babylon, the city having rebelled against him during Tiridates' insurrection. A thousand had garrisoned Babylon itself, though following the crushing of the revolt the city's nobility were eager to reaffirm their loyalty to Phraates, especially after the high king had executed the entire Egibi family and other prominent Babylonians who had supported Tiridates.

'Ctesiphon has reimbursed Dura handsomely for the loan of your soldiers, general,' remarked Aaron. He was perusing a parchment in front of him, running a finger over a list of figures. He looked up at me.

'I was wondering, majesty, if I we might loan out Dura's soldiers in the future, as the recent experience has proved most beneficial to the treasury.'

'We won't be doing that,' insisted Chrestus.

Aaron smiled at him. 'Surely, that is for the king to decide.'

Chrestus gave him a dark stare but I discounted the idea.

'The loan of the Exiles was an exception, Aaron. Dura's soldiers are not mercenaries to be hired out to the highest bidder. They exist first and foremost to protect this kingdom.'

But Aaron had the bit between his teeth.

'Forgive me for being pedantic, majesty.'

'But you are going to be anyway,' complained Chrestus.

'But you despatched commanders Azad and Sporaces to Ctesiphon with their horsemen,' continued Aaron, 'for a campaign that may last perhaps a year, in the process incurring considerable costs.'

'It is in Dura's interests to do so,' I stated.

Aaron was going to probe me with more answers but Chrestus had had enough.

'It's quite simple,' he hissed. 'If the Kushans breach the empire's eastern frontier they will swarm west like a plague of locusts, just like Tiridates did recently. It is in Dura's interests to keep war as far away from its walls as possible. I would have thought you would appreciate that strategy, Rsan, as you tremble at the mere hint of conflict on the horizon.'

Rsan turned his nose up at the general and Aaron mumbled something under his breath.

'The Kushans will be far worse than Tiridates,' said Gallia, 'and he was difficult enough to deal with.'

None at the table aside from me knew about her part in his downfall and I preferred to keep it that way. I changed the subject.

'Princess Claudia will be journeying with the Exiles, as will Phraates himself.'

My announcement at first did not register, the clerk merely recording my words, but then a look of alarm spread across Rsan's face.

'The king of kings, visiting Dura?'

'That is correct, Rsan,' I said. 'The recent rebellion against him has made Phraates determined to spend less time at Ctesiphon so he can visit the capitals of the kingdoms he rules over, or so my daughter informs me.'

Rsan was stunned. 'In all my time serving Dura I never thought the high king of the empire would visit this city.'

His eyes began to moisten, much to Chrestus' amusement.

'For more years than I care to remember, Dura was regarded as a city of outcasts, a place where the empire's unwanted were banished to. The Euphrates was not only a river but also a dividing line between what was decent and what was barbarian, and Dura was on the wrong side of that line.'

His voice was now shaking with emotion. 'But now it will be blessed by the person of the king of kings himself, and his visit will proclaim to the whole world that Dura is no longer a despised backwater but a loyal and trusted ally, first among equals.'

They were heartfelt words and made me realise just how much the visit of Phraates would mean to him.

'That it has become so is due in no small part to your unstinting efforts, Rsan,' smiled Gallia. 'You are the rock upon which this kingdom has been built.'

9

'Absolutely,' I agreed, 'and I will be sure to inform Phraates of that when he arrives.'

Rsan dabbed a tear from his cheek and Aaron put an arm around his old friend's shoulders. But then my governor's eyes filled with apprehension. He rose to his feet and bowed.

'The city is not ready to receive the high king. If you will forgive me, majesties, I must speak with Ashk as a matter of urgency.'

'There is plenty of time,' I reassured him.

Rsan shook his head. 'The whole of Parthia will be watching, majesty. I must attend to my duties.'

He bowed and hurried from the room, prompting Chrestus to roll his eyes.

'Let's hope Phraates is not too much of a disappointment to Rsan when he finally meets him.'

'Well, it is high time he did so,' said Gallia. 'Dura has spilt much blood and lost too many valued friends keeping Phraates on his golden throne for the high king to ignore us.'

'How long will he be staying?' asked Aaron, no doubt his mind already turning to the expense entailed in playing host to the king of kings.

'That will depend on how agreeable he finds Dura and its kingdom,' I told him.

'Not long, then,' grinned Chrestus. 'Dura is a poor relation compared to Ctesiphon, Babylon and Seleucia, places where the high king is accustomed to spending his days. He will want to be away from here as quickly as he can.'

'I am surprised you think so little of this kingdom, general' remarked a disapproving Aaron.

'On the contrary,' said Chrestus, 'I prefer a Dura without rich trappings, fawning courtiers and armies of priests. We keep things simple here and I prefer it that way. Phraates, on the other hand, is used to drinking out of gold rhytons, eating off silver plates and reclining on luxurious couches.'

I stared at the wooden cup before me on the table and knew Chrestus was talking the truth. But I smiled when I remembered that during his 'exile', Phraates had been living in a simple stone hut in the Alborz Mountains, hundreds of miles away from the opulence of Ctesiphon.

'The high king will take us as he finds us,' I said, 'though I think we might all be surprised by a change in him since the recent rebellion. If not, then I am certain he will not dally in Dura.'

But I had to admit the fact he was even visiting Dura marked a radical change in the official policy of the king of kings. When I had been a boy and the empire had been ruled by Sinatruces, my only memory of Dura, and a fleeting one at that, was of a wild place where the empire's unwanted were exiled to. The River Euphrates marked the Parthian Empire's physical western boundary and it was no coincidence Dura was on the river's western side. It was apart from the empire, different, desolate and separated from civilised society by a wide river. It was a place no self-respecting Parthian would ever visit, and that had included my father and mother who had never blessed Dura with their presence even after I had been appointed its king. And even Orodes, though he had spent a good portion of his life here at Dura, had never made an official visit to my kingdom when he had become high king, though that was due to his insistence on visiting every other kingdom in the empire as a means of promoting good relations between Ctesiphon and the rulers of those

11

kingdoms. I often wondered if the constant travelling the length and breadth of the empire had worn him out and led to his premature death. I refused to believe his son had poisoned him.

Aaron was less impressed by the prospect of Phraates visiting Dura; aware as he was of the financial strains such a visit would place on the kingdom.

'Having been paid by Ctesiphon for the services of our soldiers,' he complained, 'it would appear the high king is intent on Dura reimbursing him said gold.'

'Phraates is visiting to attend Eszter's wedding, Aaron,' I told him, 'not to get his gold back.'

An evil glint appeared in Gallia's eye.

'You might be interested to know, Aaron, that the king was offered a thousand talents by Phraates as a reward for his services in crushing the late rebellion. The king refused the offer.'

Aarons' eyes opened wide in astonishment. 'A thousand talents?'

'Gold plundered from the House of Egibi,' I informed him. 'I wanted no portion of riches stolen from a murdered family, even if its leading members were traitors.'

'Such an amount would have bolstered the treasury's reserves,' said Aaron.

'The treasury is full, is it not?' I queried.

'The word "full" has a number of interpretations, majesty,' began Aaron.

'That means yes,' said Chrestus.

'Perhaps I should send you to Vanadzor, Aaron,' I suggested. 'You and King Spartacus appear to hold the same views when it comes to extorting money from the high king.'

'Majesty, I would never seek to…'

I held up a hand. 'And I would never accuse you of doing so, Aaron, but the treasury will be bearing the cost of Eszter's wedding and the visit of the high king. I will not have it said that the King of Dura skimped when it came to his daughter's wedding.'

'Will the King of Gordyene be attending, majesty?' enquired Chrestus.

'He will be invited,' answered Gallia, 'though I doubt he or Queen Rasha will be gracing us with their presence, not after the business at the king's sixtieth birthday celebrations.'

'That is a great shame,' said Aaron, behind him the clerk recording every word uttered on papyrus.

'And what of King Akmon and Queen Lusin?' asked my treasurer. 'I assume an invitation will be extended to the new rulers of Media?'

'That should stir up a nest of vipers,' said Chrestus. 'If King Spartacus discovers his estranged son and the Armenian, what did he call her, whore? If he discovers they are coming there will be hell to pay.'

'I will not be dictated to by my nephew concerning who will and who will not be attending my daughter's wedding,' I said.

'It is yet to be decided if an invitation will be extended to the new rulers of Media,' announced Gallia.

After the meeting I walked back to the palace with Gallia, the courtyard largely devoid of activity as the midday sun roasted Dura from above. There was no wind and the heat was oppressive, sweating legionaries pacing the walls of the Citadel and others standing to attention in the shade of the palace porch. They snapped to attention as we passed, rivulets of sweat running down their necks

13

to soak their tunics. In the heat of summer guards were replaced at hourly intervals to stop them collapsing due to dehydration. Even in the shade, temperatures could rise to high levels and sap the stamina of men wearing mail armour, helmets and equipped with shields, swords, daggers and javelins.

It was warm inside the porch and entrance hall, the doors to the throne room open to allow what little air there was to circulate.

'It would be politic not to invite Akmon and Lusin to the wedding,' suggested Gallia, 'it is not as if they are close relations, after all.'

I nodded. 'That is true, though an invitation would be a way of showing Dura's support for the new rulers of Media.'

'And a way of insulting Gordyene.'

I stopped to look at her. 'Do you know, I am getting heartily sick and tired of having to tiptoe around Spartacus. He acts like a petulant child but expects everyone to treat him as a mature adult.'

'Perhaps if he learns Phraates is attending, Spartacus might put aside his animosity towards you.'

'Me? What about your machinations, plots and schemes, together with your fellow female conspirators?' I asked her. 'I was not the one who engineered Akmon and Lusin becoming Media's rulers.'

'No,' she agreed, 'that was Rasha. But you did threaten Spartacus when he intimated he would seize Queen Parisa and her children. And you did invite Akmon and Lusin to your sixtieth birthday feast. And we all know how that ended.'

After a morning in the Headquarters Building in the stifling heat, my head was beginning to throb and I had no appetite to argue with her.

'My head tells me to invite Spartacus and Rasha and not his estranged son and daughter-in-law, not that Gordyene's rulers will come.'

'Probably for the best,' she said, 'we don't want an incident at the wedding, especially as Phraates will be there. Claudia must hold great influence at Ctesiphon to persuade him to come here.'

I continued walking into the palace. 'Everything has come full circle. Dobbai's protégé has taken her place beside the high king, just like she did when Sinatruces ruled Parthia'

I stood in the doorway to the throne room and stared at the griffin banner hanging limply on the wall behind the two thrones.

'I have no son.'

'Pacorus?'

'Who will rule Dura when we are gone?'

I suddenly felt very old. Sensing my despair, she gripped my arm.

'There are a few years left in you, yet. Besides, if Eszter and Dalir have a son, he will be the heir to the throne.'

I sighed loudly. 'That would see the kingdom bankrupt within a generation and the gods alone know what would happen to the army.'

She jabbed me in the ribs and walked into the throne room.

'I know who you really want as your successor, though you will not say it.'

I followed her. 'Who?'

She spun and rolled her eyes. 'Your namesake, of course, the living demi-god who is satrap of Elymais, though doubtless he could become that kingdom's ruler if he desired it. Not that he would, of course, his manners and character being beyond reproach. Well, I hate to disappoint you but Prince Pacorus is the heir to Hatra's throne, not Dura's. I did not realise our daughters were such a disappointment for you.'

'They are not,' I insisted, 'but I must confess Dalir being the crown-prince does not fill me with relish.'

She frowned. 'How you underestimate Eszter, Pacorus. I have no doubt she will be the power behind the throne, just as Isabella is in Sakastan and Claudia is at Ctesiphon.'

'And Gallia at Dura?' I teased.

She winked and grinned. 'Naturally.'

We walked to the door at the rear of the chamber giving access to the palace's private quarters.

'Well, then, I would welcome your assistance with negotiations regarding the marriage contract between Dalir and Eszter.'

'That should be straightforward enough.'

I laughed. 'You forget who I am negotiating with.'

As in all societies, marriage was of vital importance because it not only ensured the continuation of the family, the bedrock of all civilisations, but also contributed towards social stability. What was society but a vast collection of families, each operating according to a framework of rules and regulations passed down from generation to generation? Good citizens were not created and raised by kings but by husbands and wives. Marriage was therefore one of the most important institutions in the civilised world.

The marriage process itself could be rather torturous and in the more traditional parts of Parthia, such as Babylon and Seleucia, negotiations between families could drag on for months and were usually conducted by third parties, who invariably took the opportunity to line their own pockets. The marriage contract between Dalir and Eszter would be simpler and quicker, or so I hoped.

Kalet, Dura's chief lord, roisterer, raider, loyal warlord and a man who could be sadly lacking in the social graces, arrived that afternoon. As usual he was dressed in black flowing robes, his head covered with a *shemagh,* half a dozen men similarly attired accompanying him when he trotted into the Citadel's courtyard. He was a frequent visitor to Dura and well known among the army's senior commanders, as well as the city's inns and brothels, his wife having died when Dalir had been a but a boy. The duty centurion ordered the visitors' horses to be taken to the stables before escorting Kalet to the palace terrace, his companions being shown to the barracks in the courtyard.

Ashk, the palace's chief steward, showed him to his chair beneath the large awning that provided welcome shade. Kalet gave me a slight bow of the head and a wink at Gallia before flopping down into the chair and snatching a cup of water proffered by a servant. He whipped off his *shemagh* and tossed it on the floor before emptying the cup.

'Your sword, lord,' said Ashk.

'What?' snapped Kalet.

'You must surrender your weapons,' I told him.

Kalet groaned, stood, unbuckled his belt and handed it and the scabbard attached to it to Ashk. He also took a dagger from his boot and another from inside his robe, handing both to my steward.

'How long have we known each other?' asked Kalet.

We took our seats opposite his.

'Rules are rules, Kalet. How are you?'

17

He flopped back down in the chair and clicked his fingers at the servant to indicate she should refill his cup.

'Hot. Any wine?'

'Perhaps we should leave alcohol until after the contract is agreed,' I offered.

He came straight to the point. 'Bride price still tent talents of gold, then?'

I nodded. I had demanded the bride price of ten talents of gold, the equivalent of a ton of the precious metal, in the aftermath of our victory at Battle of Ctesiphon. For a desert lord it was a huge sum and though Gallia had pressed me to lower the amount, I had stuck firm. Whatever Eszter was, and she was certainly a wild child of the desert, she was still a royal princess and should command a bride price commensurate to her position.

'It's on its way,' he smiled.

I looked at him and then Gallia, both of us wondering how he had acquired such a tidy sum.

'Never thought you were the type to judge a man by his appearance, lord,' he grinned. 'Just because I don't wear fancy clothes, don't mean my purse is empty.'

'Well, subject to the bride price arriving safely at the Citadel, we are happy for the marriage to proceed,' I said.

'What about the dowry?' he shot back. 'No marriage will take place until I am happy with the dowry.'

'You are unhappy?' quizzed Gallia.

'No offence, princess, but business is business.'

Ever since the days of Spandarat, my desert lords had nicknamed Gallia 'princess', owing to her days fighting for Spartacus when she had been a princess of the Senones tribe. Her forthright

18

manner and usefulness with a variety of weapons had immediately endeared her to Dura's wild lords and their feral retainers, and she had reciprocated their affection and respect.

'Five hundred camels,' I offered.

It was perhaps overly generous, but such a number would allow him to sell them on and recoup some of the gold, which he had probably stolen anyway.

'I was thinking of the same number of horses, lord.'

'Five hundred horses?' Gallia was stunned.

'Can a price be put on a daughter of Queen Gallia?' Kalet said nonchalantly.

'It can,' I told him, 'and that price is two hundred horses or five hundred camels.'

'Don't suppose you would throw in one of your fancy swords on top?' he said casually.

'You are right,' I replied, 'I would not. Those fancy swords, as you call them, cost a gold bar each, though I dare say I could arrange for one to be made for you if you paid Arsam, my chief armourer, the required amount of gold.'

'It would take many months to make one,' said Gallia. 'The metal to create an ukku blade comes from India, and we would have to negotiate with the Satavahanis to acquire an ingot.'

Kalet had already lost interest. 'Two hundred horses it is. I can pick them out myself, of course?'

'I will notify the head of the royal stud farms you will be paying him a visit.'

Kalet rubbed his hands, spat in his right palm and held out his arm. Gallia laughed when I spat in my own palm and shook his hand to seal the deal. Thus was Eszter officially betrothed to Dalir.

19

'What shall we call each other?' asked Kalet, a servant pouring wine into his goblet. 'Now that we are family, I mean?'

'You can carry on calling me "lord",' I told him.

He downed the wine in one and held out the goblet to be refilled.

'Always bear in mind the old saying, Kalet,' I said, 'you can choose your friends, but you are stuck with your family.'

'But we will welcome Dalir as a son,' smiled Gallia, 'and will look forward to greeting our grandchild in the near future.'

I asked Aaron to come to the palace terrace when a score of burly warriors arrived at the Citadel that afternoon, as Kalet had promised, with a dozen camels in tow. The saddlebags of the beasts carried gold coins – ten talents' worth – which Aaron could not stop grinning at when the saddlebags were dumped at his feet on the terrace. My treasurer had brought two clerks with him, who immediately set up a pair of scales and began recording the number and weight of the coins. Kalet's men, bored and thirsty, were escorted to the banqueting hall where they were watered and fed. As they departed the master of horses arrived, a man with a long nose and narrow neck to give him an equine appearance. I told him to take Kalet to the royal stud farm, located some twenty miles south of the city, where he was to select two hundred horses, the bride price for Princess Eszter. After they had departed I queried Aaron on the provenance of the gold.

He picked up one of the coins, a beautiful piece showing the bust of my friend Orodes on the obverse side, wearing a tiara, the reverse showing a beardless archer wearing a cloak and seated on a throne. Around him was the inscription: *King of Kings, lord of all Parthia*.

'Judging by their pristine condition, majesty, I would say they have never been in circulation, at least not until now.'

'Kept in a vault somewhere, then?'

He turned the coin over in his hand, admiring the metal and rubbing his fingers over the engraving.

'The vault in Ctesiphon?' I asked.

Aaron placed the coin back in one of the chests he had ordered be brought to the terrace.

'Difficult to say with certainty, majesty.'

'Indulge me.'

'Most probably,' he said.

Gallia smiled at the row of chests.

'Will you be able to find room in the treasury vault for all this, Aaron?'

'There is always room for more gold, majesty,' he replied sternly, 'though the kingdom will need every ounce to pay for the princess' wedding, and the visit of the high king, of course.'

'I don't want the Kingdom of Dura to be perceived as parsimonious, Aaron,' I said. 'The eyes of all Parthia will be studying us while the high king is here. For forty years Dura has let its army do all the talking. But now I want the world to know this kingdom is not the abode of barbarians and gruff soldiers; rather, it is a place where civilisation and learning have also taken root.'

How I was to regret those words.

Chapter 2

With three months to go before the wedding and visit of Phraates, Dura became the centre of much activity. The guest list took on a life of its own and I worried that the banqueting hall, which could seat up to five hundred people, would prove inadequate to host the small army that had been invited, to say nothing of the entourage of the high king that would inevitably follow Phraates to my city. Rsan and Aaron, usually so parsimonious and careful when it came to official costs, suddenly became much more relaxed about royal expenditure. I found myself signing authorisation papers to purchase banners, lots of banners. Banners showing a red griffin on a white background, the horned bull of Babylon on a purple background and other banners showing an eagle holding a snake in its talons. They were the symbols of Dura, Babylon and Susiana respectively and were to be flown throughout the city to welcome Phraates, who was the ruler of Babylon and Susiana. He had also been the ruler of Persis but that was now the domain of King Silani, formerly the commander of the high king's bodyguard.

Chrestus baulked at the suggestion all legionaries on duty should wear red and white plumes in their helmets, though he acquiesced when Aaron promised he would not quibble over his quartermaster's demands up to and immediately after the high king's visit. Chrestus got his replacement weapons and armour and Rsan got his plumed soldiers.

Dura was built as a frontier outpost, its ochre mud-brick walls, towers and Citadel constructed with strength in mind, not beauty. That strength had withstood Agraci war bands, Roman legions and Parthian armies with ease, the siting and construction of the city

22

entirely functional, with no regard for aesthetic qualities or ornamentation. It was above all a military stronghold that proclaimed strength and endurance from its position atop the rock escarpment by the side of the Euphrates. It was a far cry from the ornate palaces and their gardens found in such cities as Babylon, Seleucia, Hatra and Susa. Or so I thought.

Equine training always took place in the early morning, just after dawn when the air was fresh following the cool of the night, the sun still rising in the east. The training fields to the west of the city became hubs of activity, though the absence of Sporaces and his horse archers and Azad and his cataphracts meant they were unusually quiet, save for the Amazons. By the time the sun was warming the earth to herald another blisteringly hot day, both riders and horses were making their way back to barracks to enjoy a hearty breakfast.

I pulled up Horns and dismounted from his saddle, Gallia beside me, as the Amazons trotted into the courtyard behind us. On the palace steps the palace steward was nodding his head as the tall, olive-skinned man beside him was pointing to the four corners of the courtyard. A stable hand took Horns and Gallia's mare and we walked up the steps, the two stopping their conversation and bowing their heads.

'This is Adel, majesty,' Ashk informed me, 'sent from Hatra by your brother, King Gafarn.'

Adel reached inside his tunic and pulled out a papyrus scroll, which he handed to me.

Pacorus

As you are to be blessed with a visit from Phraates himself, I thought Dura could do with brightening up. This is Adel, one of my most talented gardeners. He can work miracles, which is just as well as Dura is an arid wasteland. We look forward to seeing the fruits of his labours.

Gafarn

I handed the note to Gallia.

'Dura is not Hatra, Adel. There are no springs here to bring forth water to nourish greenery.'

The gardener scratched his beard and nodded.

'I was warned by the king that conditions might be challenging, majesty.'

'But Adel has some interesting ideas, majesty,' said Ashk, 'and Lord Aaron has agreed to release funds for the additional staff.'

'What staff?'

'Two hundred gardeners, majesty,' answered Adel.

I was astounded. 'Two hundred, for what?'

'To turn your Citadel and palace into an oasis of green, majesty,' he informed me.

I knew the rudiments of garden design from my youth at Hatra, which had some of the most impressive royal gardens in the empire. But Hatra was fed by underground springs that brought cool water from the earth to fill ornamental ponds, create fountains and waterfalls and nourish the trees, flowers and shrubs all year round. Dura was blessed to be next to the Euphrates, a river that never dried up and gave life to the kingdom. But the city sat atop a rock escarpment and water had to be fetched from the river below. Water carriers were employed by the crown to ensure a constant supply of the precious liquid to the city, but no provision was made for the

24

watering of trees and shrubs, which were considered a waste of precious resources. So the city and Citadel were devoid of foliage. That changed with the arrival of Adel and his gardeners.

He set about his task with gusto and soon the Citadel's courtyard was bursting with wooden tubs and terracotta pots filled with small cypress trees, which were associated with the mythical Life Tree and were assumed to have healing powers. I must confess I found Adel an interesting character, a man who had devoted his whole life to creating paradise on earth, or at least a manmade interpretation of that blessed place.

I estimated him to be in his late fifties, his face and arms turned dark brown by years spent outdoors in the sun, which had made his skin leathery and his face deeply lined. I had to admit the addition of greenery to the courtyard, far from being intrusive, was a welcome contribution and pleasing to the eye. We stood at the top of the palace steps as his small army of gardeners watered the ornamental junipers, cypress, rowan, pine and aspen, sweating under a merciless Mesopotamian sun.

'I will have to organise watering rotas to ensure the plants do not wither in the heat. Still, at least your palace now has the four elements, majesty.'

'Four elements?'

'Since earliest times man has sought to create paradise on earth by harnessing the four elements: sky, earth, water and plants.'

He pointed to the heavens. 'We have sky, the earth we stand on and now water and plants.'

'It is very different from Hatra.'

He nodded. 'Hatra is a living paradise on earth, an oasis of greenery and life in the middle of a barren desert and yet Dura is closer to the gods.'

'In what way?'

'In all palaces, it is traditional to construct a large pool in the front space of a royal garden to reflect the image of the palace and the sky,' he told me, 'to cement the realm of the earthly to the heavenly. Here at Dura, the Euphrates, the great giver of life created by the gods themselves, fulfils the function of binding the realm of the earthly to the heavenly. That is why this city is beloved of the gods.'

'My father did not think so when he first learned I had been made its ruler,' I remembered.

'I never knew your father, King Varaz, majesty, though I was privileged to speak to your mother on occasion. She was a keen gardener.'

An image flashed through my mind of my mother kneeling on a cushion with a small trowel in her hand as she planted flowers in her beloved garden at Hatra. How long ago that seemed.

'She certainly was.'

'You have visited the royal gardens at Ctesiphon, majesty?'

I thought of the pools filled with fish and fountains, and peacocks strolling around the grounds.

'They are most impressive.'

Dura would never rival Ctesiphon for wealth and opulence, but Adel worked hard to make the city pleasing to the eye. Foliage appeared on the main street that led from the Palmyrene Gate to the Citadel, though Chrestus complained he had to post extra guards to prevent the plants and shrubs from being stolen. The general was in a testy mood in the period leading up to Phraates' visit, not because the high king was gracing Dura with his presence, but because he wanted to be in the east with Azad and Sporaces. He was commander of the army and half that army was hundreds of miles away, which sat ill with him. But he was able to take out his frustrations on the Durans and Exiles, organising long route marches in the desert and punishing battle simulations with the aid of Kalet and his lords and Malik and his warriors. When he had returned from one such exercise he came to the Citadel to make his report, meeting me at the armouries where I was making my weekly rounds of Arsam's hot hell on earth. Afterwards I walked back to the Citadel with Chrestus, a party of Exiles providing an escort.

'When will the high king be arriving, majesty?'

'Within the month, you will be pleased to know.'

'And then we can get back to normal?'

'I sincerely hope so.'

We entered the Citadel and paced towards the palace, walking up the steps to enter its porch, to be accosted by a young man. He jumped out from behind a large terracotta pot holding a flowering acanthus shrub. 'Armed' with a lyre that he held in the crook of his left arm while he plucked at the strings with his right hand, he was suddenly before me, singing a song in a most harmonious voice.

'Behold, behold, Pacorus of Dura.

'When enemies do threaten, he declares you go no further.

'Though outnumbered and bereft of allies he did not falter or fear,

'Riding towards the barren plain of Carrhae.'

Now his voice hit the high notes as he sang the name of the battle over and over again.

'Carrhae, Carrhae, Carrhae.'

A horrified Chrestus had had enough.

'Guards!' he shouted.

Two sentries standing next to the stone columns of the porch rushed forward with swords drawn, stopping the singer who threw up his hands.

'I meant no offence, majesty. I arrived this morning on the orders of Lord Byrd.'

I waved the guards back, Chrestus eyeing the young man suspiciously and ominously tapping the vine cane he was carrying against his thigh. Always a bad sign.

'Byrd?' I said. 'Put down your arms. Who are you.'

He flashed a smile to reveal a row of even white teeth.

'Nicias, lord.'

'You are Greek?'

Another smile. 'Yes, lord. Originally from Thebes but now resident in Damascus where I make my living composing and singing songs.'

There was a disapproving sigh from Chrestus beside me.

'I often sing for the governor of Syria,' Nicias informed me, 'who is a great friend of Lord Byrd. The governor suggested I come to Dura to compose songs about Parthia's great warlord. Lord Byrd has kindly financed my trip here, lord.'

'How generous,' groaned Chrestus.

'You travelled alone from Damascus?' I asked.

'No, lord, I am part of a group sent here by Lord Byrd for your entertainment.'

'Oh?'

'Poets, dancers, musicians and costumiers, lord.'

28

'Costumiers?' bellowed Chrestus. 'The king doesn't need anyone to dress him, boy. Byrd has more money than sense, if you ask me.'

With mounting trepidation, I walked from the porch into the reception hall and through to the throne room where Gallia was being entertained by a poetry recital. She sat on her throne listening to a young man with a soft voice reciting a tale of Remus, my old warhorse. Behind me Nicias plucked gently at his lyre until Chrestus turned on him.

'You continue to play that and I will shove it up your arse.'

'Chrestus,' I rebuked him mildly, 'don't be a barbarian. Don't you know Dura has become a place of beauty, civilisation and learning?'

'Quite right.'

I saw a beaming Alcaeus standing near the dais and an equally happy Scelias next to him. I had never seen so many Greeks in the throne room, all enjoying the soft voice of the handsome young poet who was coming to the end of his recital. His voice became tremulous as he told the story of the death of Remus and my horse's journey to the afterlife. I stepped on to the dais and sat beside my wife as the poet's head dropped and he wiped a tear from his eye.

'That was most moving, Agis,' smiled Gallia, 'you must return to the palace this evening so the king may hear your poem in full.'

The young Greek bowed deeply to Gallia, who tossed him a gold coin. Agis caught the coin, knelt before the queen and spread his arms.

'I will write a poem about the Queen of Dura and the Amazons, which will rival the *Iliad* and the *Odyssey* when it is finished.'

'Bravo,' shouted Alcaeus. 'The queen is worthy of such epics.'

Gallia, delighted that a handsome Greek poet had heard of her and the Amazons, stood and held out her hand.

'You shall by our guest at Dura for as long as it takes, Agis.'

The Greek sprang forward and planted a dainty kiss on my wife's hand.

'Your beauty and fame inspire me, majesty. I shall waste no more time but will away to start my work.'

'Hopefully back to Greece,' said Chrestus loudly.

Agis gave the general a disparaging glance and skipped from the throne room.

Alcaeus stepped forward. 'Heard of the *Iliad* and the *Odyssey*, Chrestus?'

'No.'

'They are epics from ancient history,' Alcaeus told him, 'written by a Greek named Homer and tell of the war between the Greeks and the Trojans. They are required reading for anyone who purports to consider themselves civilised.'

'I've never read them,' I confessed.

'Me neither,' added Gallia.

Alcaeus looked at Scelias who rolled his eyes.

'We live in a cultural wasteland,' lamented the head of the Sons of the Citadel.

'Culture doesn't stop foreign armies burning your home or killing your friends,' said Chrestus.

'No, indeed, general,' admitted Scelias, 'but it does save one from a slow, lingering death.'

Chrestus pointed his cane at him. 'Whenever I hear the word "culture", I reach for my sword.'

He pointed the cane at a rotund man with a neat beard and bald crown who was dressed in a white, knee-length tunic with red boots and fingers adorned with gold rings. Draped over his left forearm was a blue cloak, which was fastened to the tunic at the left shoulder by a gold clasp. He stepped forward and bowed to Gallia and me.

'Pontius Cinna at your service, dresser to Marcus Tullus Cicero, Governor of Syria.'

'I thought Lucius Didius was the governor of Syria,' I said.

'Cicero the Younger is newly appointed, majesty,' Cinna informed me. 'And is eager to meet you when your daughter marries the son of Lord Kalet.'

I had extended an invitation to the governor of Syria following Gallia corresponding with Octavian concerning the return of the eagles lost at Carrhae and Lake Urmia. This had prompted a discourse between Phraates and Octavian that was leading to lasting peace between Parthia and Rome, or so it seemed and so I hoped. In the climate of improving relations between the empire and Rome, I thought it appropriate to extend an invitation to the governor to travel to Dura, not least because he could have a face-to-face meeting with Phraates.

'Cicero the Younger is high in Octavian's favour?' I probed.

'Very high, majesty,' replied Cinna. 'He took an active role in the defeat of Mark Antony, the *triumvir* having killed Cicero's father. Both the governor and indeed Octavian himself are mindful of your own part in the defeat of Mark Antony.'

I was surprised. 'My part?'

'You alone were responsible for defeating Mark Antony before the walls of Phraaspa and later when the *triumvir* formed an alliance with Queen Aliyeh. The governor is in no doubt his defeats in Parthia contributed towards his eventual crushing at Actium.'

'Are you a poet, too?' asked Chrestus.

Cinna smiled. 'I am the personal tailor to Governor Cicero, sent to Dura to fit the king's new clothes.'

'What new clothes?' asked a bemused Gallia.

'The ones ordered by Lord Byrd, majesty, and currently stored in his mansion in the city.'

I wasn't really interested in a new set of clothes but I was eager to quiz the Roman on the whereabouts of Tiridates, who had sought and been granted sanctuary in Syria. I had gifted Byrd a mansion in the city in the hope he and Noora would make it their home. But they were happy living in a tent in Palmyra, albeit a large tent. So the mansion was unoccupied for most of the year, though Byrd did pay staff to maintain it and prevent it falling into disrepair. The building itself was an impressive mud-brick structure, built in the Greek style like all the buildings in Dura, specifically according to Hippodamian principles, named after the Greek architect Hippodamus of Miletus. A two-storey building, the first floor contained bedrooms and a library, the ground floor an entrance hall, kitchens, study, dining room, entertaining lounge and colonnaded garden. We availed ourselves of the study when I had my fitting, Cinna overseeing a young male apprentice who took my measurements. Gallia reclined on a couch sipping wine as Cinna studied my attire.

'Are they your working clothes, majesty?'

I looked down at my simple white tunic, tan leggings and leather boots.

'This is my normal attire.'

Cinna's brow creased into a frown. 'Oh, dear.'

He clapped his hands to prompt the appearance of another young assistant, also male, young and attractive. The youth was carrying a white silk robe, upon which were stitched red griffins.

'Try this on, majesty. Lord Byrd gave me your approximate measurements but the robe can of course be adjusted.'

I unstrapped my sword belt and handed it to Gallia before putting on the robe, which was as light as a feather. It had long, loose-fitting sleeves and was open at the front to facilitate ease of fitting. The boy handed me a red silk sash that Cinna informed me was to be used as a belt to keep the robe closed.

'What about my sword belt?' I asked.

Cinna tutted. 'No weapons to be worn with this robe, majesty. Presumably you have guards to keep you safe?'

Gallia laughed. Half a dozen Exiles had escorted us to the mansion but I felt naked without my *spatha*.

'Is Tiridates still in Syria?' I asked.

A servant handed me a chalice of wine, proffering another to Cinna.

'Yes, majesty, I believe he is.'

'Where?'

His confident manner disappeared as his piggy eyes darted between Gallia and me.

'Near the coast, majesty, or so I am told.'

'Have no fear, Cinna,' Gallia reassured him, 'the king has no intention of sending assassins to kill him, though we cannot vouch the same for King of Kings Phraates.'

The boy tied the sash around my waist.

'The high king will not try to kill Tiridates while his son is in Rome,' I said.

'The governor informed me the child is under the care and protection of Octavian himself,' said Cinna.

The tailor stepped back and admired his creation, his gaze concentrating on my boots. More tutting.

'They will not do, not at all. Bring the boots.'

The youth with the tape measure disappeared and reappeared moments later with a pair of beautiful red leather boots. Cinna saw my admiring look.

'You'll not find a finer pair in the whole of Mesopotamia, majesty. They are made from ox leather prepared by a vegetable tanning process that takes two years to complete. They are more comfortable than a pair of slippers yet very durable for outdoor wear.'

The youth placed the boots on the floor. I removed my own footwear and slipped my feet into them. Wide straps that passed under the feet and crisscrossed up the lower leg secured the soft leather uppers. They were certainly comfortable and as a nice finishing touch were adorned with silver griffins. I liked them. I stepped back and faced Gallia.

'What do you think?'

'Very kingly.'

'I have more robes in blue, red and purple, majesty, with corresponding complementary sashes. I assume you will be taking them all?'

'He will,' smiled Gallia.

'Lord Byrd has also paid for a number of dresses for yourself, majesty,' Cinna told Gallia. 'Perhaps you might send your female dressers to collect them later.'

'I have no dressers,' Gallia told him.

Cinna was perplexed. 'Then who dresses you, majesty?'

'I dress myself,' she told him.

'No slaves, majesty?'

'No slaves.'

Cinna was shocked. 'But I have seen slaves in your palace.'

'They are paid servants,' I said, 'free men and women who are hired for their services.'

'Has Tiridates indicated he will stay in Syria?' I asked, changing the subject.

'I am not privy to that information, majesty,' said Cinna.

'Does he have any supporters around him?' queried Gallia.

'Again, majesty, you must forgive my ignorance but I do not know.'

Afterwards, wearing my new robes, I walked back to the Citadel with Gallia.

'When the Roman governor arrives we can question him more closely about the whereabouts and motives of Tiridates,' she said.

'It seems strange he is lingering in Syria. I suspect he is biding his time until conditions are right.'

'To return to Parthia?'

I nodded. 'He has had a taste of being high king and I doubt the prospect of being an exile in Syria holds much allure.'

'We should get Byrd to locate him,' she said. 'He has offices and contacts throughout Syria.'

'To what end?'

'To kill Tiridates, of course.'

I stopped to look at her.

'If we kill Tiridates, Octavian might retaliate by murdering the son of Phraates.'

'Not if we are careful.'

'Careful?'

'A pretty girl could infiltrate his household easily enough.'

My blood ran cold. 'I was not aware the Daughters of Dura were being trained as assassins.'

She continued walking back to the Citadel.

'They are trained to be loyal to their king and queen and their homeland. Or I could send one of the younger Amazons. It makes no difference.'

'And when your girl or young woman has slit Tiridates' throat, what then? She will be far from home and alone. You would be condemning her to death, a slow death nailed to a cross.'

We walked into the Citadel, guards at the gates snapping to attention as we passed by. I dismissed our escort and the duty centurion coming from the office just inside the gates instructed them to return to barracks. He looked surprised to see me in such rich attire but composed himself and saluted us both.

'She would not be alone,' said Gallia. 'Some of Kalet's men would be her escort, or Malik's warriors if we asked him. Tiridates deserves to die.'

I could not argue with her logic, though I would not sanction an assassination attempt.

'We do nothing until after the wedding.'

She shrugged. 'As you wish.'

We walked up the palace steps.

'Promise me you will not take matters into your own hands,' I beseeched.

She raised a well-manicured eyebrow. 'Not until after the wedding. You have my word.'

The presence in Syria of the man who had been responsible for igniting a civil war in Parthia, in addition to causing the deaths of Nergal and Praxima, meant he could expect no mercy from Gallia still bent on exacting revenge. But the crushing of Tiridates' rebellion, combined with the negotiations that were ongoing between Octavian and Phraates, had resulted in the prospect of a lasting peace on the empire's western border. I saw no reason to endanger the blossoming relations between Rome and Parthia, not least because there existed a very real danger in the east. Kujula had recovered from his battle wounds and his gaze was once again focused on expanding the Kushan Empire at the expense of Parthia. Fortunately, the arrival of King of Kings Phraates focused Gallia's attention on Dura and her daughter's wedding rather than on murdering the former King of Aria.

Dura suddenly seemed small and overcrowded as the guests and their entourages began to arrive. The Governor of Syria, Cicero the Younger, arrived in the company of Byrd, Noora, Malik, Jamal and Riad, his son who had recently returned to Palmyra. We greeted them in the palace, Byrd complimenting me on my new clothes and Malik asking if I had lost my sword. The governor, in his late thirties, his hair receding, reminded me of one of Aaron's clerks but was most courteous and softly spoken. Byrd had thought it prudent for him to be lodged in his mansion for the duration of his stay, which made sense as he and my former chief scout were friends and the governor was also familiar with Malik and his family.

The next to arrive were Gafarn and Diana, though without Prince Pacorus who was ruling Elymais while Queen Cia concentrated on giving birth to the kingdom's heir. It seemed strange not to see the prince at the head of Hatra's Royal Bodyguard, though nothing could diminish the happiness we felt at the arrival of our oldest friends. When he had finished chiding me about my new apparel and complimenting me on the greenery in the Citadel, Gafarn had some interesting news from Hatra. We were sitting on the palace terrace, enjoying a vivid sunset of a white sun dropping in a red western sky, the heat of the day yet to leave the earth.

'Atrax has left Hatra,' announced Gafarn.

'I'm amazed he was able to summon the strength to leave his bed,' remarked Gallia, noticing Gafarn was rubbing his right leg. Diana saw her stare.

'He tripped and fell in the palace a few days ago and cut his leg.'

'Wretched thing won't heal,' complained Gafarn.

'You should see Alcaeus,' I said.

He rolled his eyes. 'I've seen a small army of physicians, plus a host of priests, sorceresses and faith healers, all of whom got word of my ailment and beat a path to the palace. Their wittering and wailing were an excellent cure for insomnia but did nothing for my leg.'

'So what are you taking for it?' asked Gallia.

'Keeping it clean and fresh bandages every day,' he told her. 'It's only a large cut. I've suffered worse.'

'But you were younger then,' I said. 'You must take care of yourself.'

'Yes, father,' he grinned.

'So, Prince Atrax survived his wounds,' I said.

The son of the late, unlamented King Darius of Media had been grievously wounded during Darius' abortive invasion of Hatra, which had resulted in the king's death. His son had made it back to Irbil but was expected to succumb to his wounds. He was still on the

38

verge of death when he, his mother and sisters left Irbil in the aftermath of Aliyeh's suicide to seek sanctuary in Hatra.

'It was a miracle,' said Diana. 'Prayers were said day and night for the prince and the high priest of the Great Temple had been planning for his funeral. But the gods smiled on Atrax and he slowly recovered.'

Gafarn nodded. 'He made a full recovery, and as soon as he was able to walk declared his intention to leave Hatra.'

'And go where?' enquired Gallia.

'Zeugma,' he replied.

The city on the Euphrates had formally been part of the Parthian Empire but its ruler, the debauched King Darius, had defected to the Romans for a large bribe. Darius was long dead, but his city thrived under Roman rule, being on the Silk Road and benefiting from its riches.

'Another penniless prince,' said Gallia.

'Not so penniless,' her friend informed her. 'When they left Irbil, Atrax's two sisters took the crown jewels with them, along with a substantial amount of gold.'

I remembered the two young women at Aliyeh's funeral. Darya and Setareh had appeared vulnerable and lost.

'They have their grandmother's propensity for scheming,' said Gafarn bluntly. 'Unlike their mother who has joined the Sisters of Shamash.'

The Sisters of Shamash was a religious order dedicated to the care of unfortunates, its female devotees living lives of chastity, poverty and obedience to the Sun God. My own sister Adeleh was a member and now it seemed Queen Parisa had joined the order.

39

'Of course, Parisa will have to serve two years as a novice before she becomes a fully-fledged member of the Sisters,' said Diana.

'The death of her husband was the final straw,' remarked Gafarn, 'but Adeleh informs us she is happy living the simple life of a servant of Shamash.'

'That's the last we will see of Atrax and his sisters, then,' I surmised.

Gafarn looked at me. 'I hope so, because his character leaves a lot to be desired. He hates you, of course.'

I sipped at my wine. 'Me? Why? What have I done to wrong him?'

'You underestimate yourself, Pacorus,' smiled Gafarn. 'You killed his uncle, Prince Alexander, was responsible for his grandfather walking with a limp, and caused his grandmother to take her own life. Or so young Atrax believes.'

I was most disappointed. 'I saved his life, and those of his sisters. If Spartacus had had his way, they would be rotting in cells in Vanadzor by now, or worse.'

'Talking of Spartacus, can we assume he will not be attending the wedding?' asked Gallia.

Diana avoided her friend's eyes and Gafarn's head dropped.

'He is stubborn,' said the King of Hatra, 'I apologise on his behalf.'

'He seems to hate the world and everything in it,' lamented Diana.

'Parthia is fortunate to have him guarding its northern border,' I said, 'but we have to accept Spartacus is a man who does not

40

forgive or forget. I assume he has not visited the new King and Queen of Media?'

Gafarn laughed. 'He holds you responsible.'

I was not amused. 'Me? As I seem to remember, it was Rasha, cooperating closely with our wives, who instigated Akmon becoming the ruler of Media.'

Gafarn winked at Gallia. 'We know that, but Spartacus, for all his faults, loves his wife dearly and so refuses to believe she was the progenitor of the plot to make Akmon ruler of Media. He loves and respects his mother, of course, and so believes she is blameless in all things. He respects his aunt greatly and though he accepts Gallia *was* responsible for Akmon's elevation, he also accepts she was grieving deeply for the loss of Nergal and Praxima, so in his own way he has absolved her of any blame.'

A wicked grin spread across Gafarn's face. 'So that leaves you, Pacorus, to be the focus of my son's wrath.'

'There are no words,' I replied.

In truth Spartacus did not occupy my mind at all as the wedding drew nearer. Ashk showed me the seating arrangements for the wedding feast, Chrestus accompanied me as we walked the route the newlyweds and their guests would take from the Temple of Shamash, located around half a mile from the Citadel, back to the palace, and Aaron briefed me on the expected costs of the ceremony and entertaining Phraates and his entourage. Chrestus had requested, and had been granted, money for new mail tunics and helmets for the soldiers lining the wedding route, as well as those who would be fulfilling the role of guard of honour when the high king arrived. Hundreds of plumes had also been purchased to decorate the helmets of legionaries.

41

I waved the papyrus scroll at Aaron. 'I did not realise red and white plumes could be so expensive.'

'The colours of Dura, majesty, to symbolise the red griffin on a white background.'

'Yes, of course.'

'Can I say we are all very excited about the high king's visit, especially Rsan. He is like a man reborn.'

I had to admit Aaron was right and for that reason alone all the expenditure and inconvenience was worth it to see my governor truly happy. For him Phraates' visit was the culmination of a lifetime's dedication to Dura and the empire. I just hoped Phraates treated his visit to Dura as a privilege and not a chore.

The high king arrived on a searing hot summer's day, his great pavilion taking shape on the eastern side of the Euphrates, the sun sitting high above it in a cloudless sky. I sent Chrestus and a mounted party to the sprawling encampment of multi-coloured tents, wagons, camels, horses and soldiers. Gafarn sent the commander of his bodyguard to accompany him, as the land across the river was Hatran territory, though I had declared Dura alone would pay for the upkeep of the high king and his followers for the duration of their stay. Due to the temperature the high king would rest in his pavilion before journeying to the city on the morrow, but as was custom I sent an official party to his residence to inform him the requirements of his entourage would be provided for by the Kingdom of Dura. It was a mere formality because as soon as the royal party was within sight I had ordered supplies to be sent across the river.

Lucius Varsas, Roman, graduate of the Sons of the Citadel and the army's quartermaster general, had been given the responsibility of supplying Phraates' encampment. He had spent weeks preparing the logistics of such an exercise, liaising with the deputy head of the camel corps, who had remained in the city in Farid's absence, concerning supplying the high king's compound. Water for men and beasts would be provided by the Euphrates, but the hundreds of camels and horses also required fodder. The soldiers and servants of the high king also had to be fed, which meant a steady stream of carts leaving the city each morning loaded with bread, cheese, beer, wine, freshly caught fish, fruit and vegetables. Cattle, goats, chickens and pigs would be transported alive across the river, to be slaughtered, butchered and prepared for consumption by imperial cooks. Feeding the high king's entourage was like preparing for a military campaign and fortunately Lucius was up to the task.

I invited Rsan, Alcaeus, Aaron and Scelias to the palace terrace the night before Phraates entered the city, the high king's camp across the river being illuminated by dozens of burning braziers and campfires.

'Everything is ready?' I asked Rsan.

'All is ready, majesty,' he replied, gazing in wonder at the great camp on the other side of the Euphrates.

Alcaeus gently laid a hand on his friend's shoulder.

'He's just a man, Rsan, and is subject to the same bodily functions as all of us.'

'The more so if his diet is excessively rich,' added Scelias.

'The richest if the daily requirements of his court are anything to go by,' said Aaron.

But nothing could detract from the sense of awe and wonder Rsan was experiencing as he gazed upon the camp of Phraates, son of Orodes, grandson of another Phraates and great grandson of Sinatruces. The high king was more than just another ruler, he was the living embodiment of the idea of Parthia – an empire of disparate kingdoms, races and religions – the thread that bound those differences together. And after an unsteady start Phraates was finally becoming the high king we all wanted him to be.

'Tomorrow will be a great day for Dura,' I told them. 'For the first time in its history, Dura will receive an official visit from the king of kings of the empire. It will be your day, Rsan, for you above all have been the steadying hand that has guided this kingdom through both prosperous and perilous times.'

He bowed his head. 'Thank you, majesty.'

Gallia stepped forward and planted a kiss on his cheek.

'We are in your debt, Rsan.'

The governor, a stickler for protocol, stiffened slightly at such familiarity but his eyes were moist with tears of gratitude and joy.

'Let us hope, now that the time of adversity has passed,' said Scelias, 'Dura does not enter an age of decadence.'

I looked at him. 'Decadence?'

He returned my gaze. 'Rich apparel, extravagant expenditure. These are the outward signs of decadence, which invariably corrupt a kingdom as sure as a plague of locusts strips the land bare.'

'I can assure you,' I informed my stoic Greek, 'the change of clothes is a purely temporary measure, as is the current, admittedly high, level of expenditure. We don't want Phraates to think Dura is an impoverished backwater, Scelias.'

'If Phraates has a brain,' he said, 'he would have realised years ago that Dura is the brightest jewel in his crown, whose army has saved his hide on numerous occasions and lately restored him to his throne.'

'Well said,' remarked Alcaeus.

'Not all that glitters is gold,' continued Scelias. 'Only a fool mistakes displays of opulence and wealth as indicators of real power.'

He made a great sweep with his arm. 'Real power can be found in the most modest of places, forged by keen minds and determined spirits. I hope you will show Phraates the Staff of Victory, lord, because such a simple totem speaks volumes concerning real wealth and power.'

Real wealth and power were on display the next day when Phraates entered the city. The Exiles and Durans, plumes and all, lined the route from the pontoon bridges that spanned the Euphrates all the way to the Palmyrene Gate, and from there to the Citadel. In the Citadel itself an honour guard stood to attention and Kalet and his lords stood behind Gallia and me at the foot of the palace steps. Flanking us were Malik, Jamal and Riad, Byrd and Noora, Gafarn and Diana, and Eszter and Dalir, my daughter actually attired in a dress, her arms bare, following a heated argument between father and daughter in which I suggested she might like to try looking feminine for once instead of a desert raider. To one side stood Chrestus, his senior officers, all sporting large crests in their helmets, Lucius Varsas, Rsan, Aaron, Alcaeus and Scelias. All were dressed in their finery, including the lords and their wives who lived in the city, mostly former merchants who had lived in Dura for many years and had been ennobled as a reward for their services to the city and kingdom.

The morning was warm and getting hotter as we waited for the arrival of the high king. The courtyard was full of soldiers and civilians, and behind them, near the stables, stood stable hands, farriers, veterinaries, servants, smiths, bakers and armourers, all craning their necks to get a glimpse of the demi-god who ruled the

Parthian Empire. We heard his arrival before clapping eyes on him, the cheers of the crowds lining the main thoroughfare growing in volume as he neared the Citadel. I smiled when I heard cries of 'Phraates, Phraates', and glanced at Rsan who was bursting with pride. I was glad his friend Alcaeus was standing next to him because when Phraates appeared he might pass out.

The irritating sound of kettledrums, a low rumble that I had come to loathe on the battlefield for its intense annoyance, reached my ears, heralding the arrival of Phraates. Before the pair of mounted kettledrummers appeared, young girls carrying baskets of white petals from the lotus flower appeared at the gates, scattering petals on the ground to create the image of a white carpet. The lotus flower was associated with innocence and holiness and the petals symbolised the sacred nature of the high king's visit. The girls emptied their baskets as the kettledrummers rode into the foliage-adorned courtyard, their incessant thumping mercifully drowned out by a fanfare of trumpets from the musicians beside the colour party. And then Phraates himself appeared, dressed in a rich purple tunic and purple leggings, his boots white leather adorned with silver clasps. Behind him rode his Babylonian Guard – men in purple uniforms wearing shimmering dragon-skin armour cuirasses: a thick hide vest covered with overlapping silver plates that protected the chest and back. Their burnished open-faced helmets sported huge purple plumes, their swords were carried in purple scabbards and their purple saddlecloths were decorated with golden bull symbols. The bull, symbol of Babylon, was also a totem of strength, power and rage.

Beside the mounted guards walked Scythian axe men: big men with broad shoulders who cradled their massive war axes menacingly. Shields were strapped to their backs and wicked long knives dangled in sheaths attached to their belts. Looking out of place among such fearsome individuals was a slave who dashed forward to stand beside the high king's horse. The royal stool bearer's job was to ensure Phraates never dismounted from his horse without the aid of a step.

'Perhaps we should hire one of those,' whispered Gafarn, Phraates dismounting from his horse and walking towards us.

As one we bowed our heads to him, the fanfare ceased and the kettledrummers desisted their din.

'Welcome to Dura, highness,' I said, 'please avail yourself of our hospitality.'

Phraates smiled and looked around at the courtyard, guards standing to attention on the walls and at the top of the steps, where normally we would have stood to greet guests. But protocol dictated that no king or queen should stand higher than the king of kings and so we stood at the foot of the steps.

'I am glad to be here,' smiled Phraates, 'for too long I have been confined within Ctesiphon's walls.'

He held out his arm. 'Claudia, you will be my guide to your home.'

My daughter, as ever dressed in black robes, had dismounted from her horse and now walked up to Gallia, embracing her mother and then Diana, leaving Phraates' arm in mid-air. She kissed me on the cheek.

'Introduce him to Rsan,' I said quietly, 'it would mean a lot to the governor.'

She took the high king's hand and whispered into his ear. Phraates turned and walked towards Rsan, the old man gulping and staring in wonder at the tall, now athletic young man before him, the gleaming golden crown of Babylon on his head. He bowed deeply to

47

Phraates, causing me some concern his back might lock. But it did not, and he raised his head to look at Phraates but two paces away.

'Governor Rsan, Princess Claudia informs me it is you who has been the bedrock that has allowed King Pacorus to provide such sterling service to the empire. On behalf of myself and the Parthian Empire, I thank you for your services.'

'You, you are most kind, highness,' stammered Rsan.

Phraates smiled, turned and walked up the steps beside Claudia, the rest of us in tow. Rsan, not believing the high king had taken the time to speak to him personally, stood rooted to the spot, awe-struck.

I thought Phraates would make some condescending remark about Dura being tiny compared to Ctesiphon, or indeed Babylon and Seleucia, but he was all smiles and polite conversation as we strolled through the entrance hall into the throne room, the commander of the high king's guard falling in behind his lord. Phraates stopped when he spotted my griffin banner hanging above the dais, pointing at the flag.

'Is that it?'

Claudia nodded. 'Yes, lord.'

He walked forward to step on the dais, peering up at the banner.

'It looks freshly made and yet it is how old?'

Claudia looked at me.

'It was gifted to me forty years ago, highness,' I told him.

'And it has been carried in every battle you have fought in?' asked Phraates.

'Yes, highness.'

'And yet it does not have a mark on it. It was given to you by the sorceress Dobbai, your daughter informs me.'

'Yes, highness.'

'And where did she get it from?'

'I never asked, highness.'

He turned to look at me. 'The gods themselves must have forged it; for it is well known the army of Dura has never tasted defeat. Who is entrusted with its care when you go to war?'

'The commander of my Amazons, highness,' Gallia told him.

'A woman?'

'An Amazon,' she shot back.

'Yes, of course.'

On the terrace we enjoyed refreshments under the large awning to shade us from the sun. There was a slight breeze blowing from the east that made the terrace pleasant enough as we reclined on soft couches and Phraates rested his feet on his footstool. Only the kings and queens were in attendance, plus Byrd and Noora. My former chief scout had made an effort with his attire and was dressed in a fresh robe, Noora looking delightful in a white dress complemented by gold rings on her fingers and a gold tiara. I chuckled when I compared Byrd's modest attire to the gold and silver jewellery and silk clothes on display. He was probably wealthier than all of us put together following his reward for financing the campaign that put Phraates back on his throne.

I beckoned Eszter and Dalir forward as Phraates nibbled on a slice of melon.

'This is my daughter Princess Eszter, highness, and her future husband Dalir, son of Kalet, Dura's chief lord.'

They both knelt before the high king and bowed their heads.

49

'Princess Claudia informs me it is the custom for Dura's lords to build their own desert strongholds.'

Dalir nodded. 'Yes, highness.'

'As a wedding gift, you will be given fifty talents of gold so you can construct your own home in the desert.'

Eszter, unused to palace protocol at the best of times, looked up and gave Phraates a dazzling smile.

'You are most kind, lord, and when it is finished you will be our first guest.'

She then went to embrace him, prompting the commander of Phraates' bodyguard, a strapping individual in his early forties, to step forward gripping the hilt of his sword.

'You are dismissed, Eszter,' I said quickly. 'To touch the body of the high king means death.'

Dalir grabbed her arms and bundled her away, bowing his head as he did so. Claudia rolled her eyes and Eszter gave her a withering look.

'You are too generous, highness,' I said, the officer stepping away from his lord.

'I owe a great debt to Dura,' said Phraates, 'as I do to you, Lord Byrd.'

Byrd smiled and bowed his head, looking happy because the high king had finally mastered the correct pronunciation of his name.

'The Roman governor of Syria is at Dura?'

'Yes, lord,' said Byrd. 'He good man.'

'That remains to be seen.'

After half an hour of polite conversation about nothing in particular, Phraates declared he wished to visit the legionary camp outside the city. It was approaching midday now and the summer

50

heat was intense, but he was not to be dissuaded and so we left the terrace. Gafarn, using his aching leg as an excuse, declared his intention to stay in the palace, while Byrd, who had a permanent limp, also declined to accompany us, citing his affliction.

'I hope you are not going to abandon me as well, King Malik,' pleaded Phraates.

'It will be an honour to journey with you, lord,' replied Malik.

I looked at Gallia who smiled with satisfaction. We had lived to see the day when the ruler of the Parthian Empire was treating the leader of the Agraci people like an old friend. In that moment, I felt great happiness that all the years toiling to convince Parthians that the Agraci could be valued allies had seemingly paid off.

Phraates walked from the terrace beside Malik.

'It is good to see you again, majesty.'

I turned to see the commander of Phraates' bodyguard before me, helmet in the crook of his arm. He looked vaguely familiar but I could not place him.

'Forgive me, but my memory fails me as to our last meeting.'

'This is Commander Adapa, father,' said Claudia beside me, 'you last met him when he was about to escort the high king from Seleucia.'

The gravity of her words struck me like a punch to the stomach. Adapa, the former soldier of Babylon. Adapa the leper.

'By the gods.'

Before I knew it, I was recoiling from him, tripping over a couch to land on my back. Everyone turned to see what the commotion was about as I lay on my back staring up at the man who had once been a leper. *Was* a leper, and yet did not have a mark or blemish on his face. Gallia rushed over.

51

'Are you hurt?'

'What? No.'

She helped me up, Gafarn finding it most amusing.

'Too much wine on an empty stomach, Pacorus.'

I ignored him. 'How can this be?'

'Simple enough,' said Gallia, 'if you don't look where you are going you will end up flat on your back.'

'Not that,' I snapped. 'This is Adapa.'

She looked at me with a blank expression.

'The leper leader, at Seleucia.'

Her jaw dropped as she beheld the living miracle before her. Claudia walked over and took my arm.

'It is rude to stare, father,'

I looked back at the blushing Adapa.

'That is Adapa,' I said.

'Commander Adapa, father, that is his official title.'

'You cured him?'

She shook her head. 'There are blessed pools in the Alborz where afflictions can be washed away.'

'It is a miracle,' said Gallia.

We followed Phraates and Malik who had resumed their amble, Adapa rushing past us to catch up with his lord. The two Scythians who had been waiting in the hall adjacent to the terrace fell in beside him.

'You remember the lepers who were with Adapa?' Claudia asked.

I nodded, their disfigured limbs and faces filling my mind.

'They were in the courtyard earlier.'

'Lepers in the palace?' I said loudly, Diana and Gafarn turning to stare at me.

'As they are members of the high king's bodyguard, they can hardly be lepers, father.'

'They were all cured?' I was astounded.

Claudia gave me a malicious grin. 'They were given life to replace the living death they were enduring. Such a gift means they will be absolutely loyal to Phraates.'

'How so?' asked Gallia.

'Because I said the gods would make them lepers again if they were disloyal, mother.'

'Is that true?' I queried.

'The gods give and they take,' she shrugged.

In the courtyard Phraates' horse was brought to him, along with our own. Adapa mounted his own horse and I scanned the riders of the Babylonian Guard for the other lepers but saw only men in their prime. We trotted from the Citadel, flanked by Scythians on foot and a large detachment of legionaries led by Chrestus. The searing heat had dispersed the crowds and the road to the Palmyrene Gate was largely free of traffic, sensible people seeking shade during the hottest part of the day. In front of us Phraates chatted to Malik and behind trotted five hundred Babylonian Guards.

'You possess a great gift,' I told Claudia beside me, 'for you have the power to cure diseases that have plagued man for centuries.'

'You think I should announce the presence of the healing pools in the Alborz to the whole world?' she asked.

'Naturally.'

'I would rather slit my own wrists,' she scoffed, 'mankind is inherently corrupt and diseased, father, that is why the gods punish us with ailments and disfigurement.'

'That is harsh.'

She threw back her head and laughed, which turned into a malevolent cackle.

'You are a dreamer, father, a man who longs for a world that will never exist. Like a small child chasing a rainbow, you seek to find a pot of gold, except your dream is to see the world free from war, want and corruption. But it is a dream, and not a desirable one, for what would men such as you do if there was no war in the world?'

The legionary camp was, as usual, half-empty when the Durans and Exiles were in residence. A substantial number of soldiers were manning the mud-brick forts spaced at five-mile intervals north and south of the city. Others were garrisoning the city itself, and some centuries were conducting desert marches. Outside the camp new recruits were learning how to use wooden copies of the *gladius* against wooden posts sunk in the ground, under the watchful eyes of centurions armed with vine canes that they used liberally on the trainees when they failed to obey instructions.

Phraates was genuinely interested and halted his horse to watch the trainees sweating profusely as they wielded training shields and wooden swords.

Phraates pointed at the recruits. 'They are wooden weapons and shields?'

'Yes, highness,' I said, 'though heavier than the real things to strengthen the recruits' arms.'

A recruit nearest to our party slashed at the post with his sword, prompting the centurion behind him to whack him on the arm and berate him loudly.

Phraates was confused. 'He hit the target.'

'He hit the target, highness, yes,' I said, 'but Dura's foot soldiers are taught to stab, thrust, feint and lunge with the short sword. There is no place for wild slashing in the ranks.'

'Where do you recruit your soldiers from, majesty?' enquired Adapa.

'Any male who presents himself at the recruitment office in the city will be considered, irrespective of his status, subject to certain conditions.'

'Which are?' asked Phraates.

'They must have all their limbs, be of average height or above, and possess good eyesight.'

'What if they are runaway slaves?' asked Adapa.

'We make no distinction in Dura between freemen and women who volunteer for service in the army,' said Gallia, 'and those who have escaped from bondage.'

'Their former owners do not seek compensation for their lost property?' asked Phraates.

Gallia bristled at his words. 'In such a situation, highness, the court of trial by combat will decide.'

'I do not understand,' said Phraates.

'The former slave turned soldier and his former master are given the opportunity to fight each other to decide the merits of the claim,' replied Gallia. 'Curiously, fat, indolent masters are reluctant to try their luck against a trained soldier.'

Claudia laughed and Malik grinned, though Phraates said nothing but nudged his horse forward. We entered the camp and rode to the three tents positioned to the rear of the commander's tent in the centre of the huge compound. The trio of tents woven from goat's hair as used by the Agraci, housed the semi-religious totems of the Durans and Exiles and the army's Staff of Victory.

Each tent housed a single emblem and Phraates wished to see them all. The first tent contained the Durans' golden griffin, fashioned years before by a testy Greek named Demetrius. Each tent was guarded by a detail commanded by a centurion, who insisted all visitor weapons were surrendered before entry, though only Adapa was forced to give up his sword as the rest of us were unarmed. Phraates admired the gold griffin before walking to the middle tent that housed the Staff of Victory, a simple *kontus* shaft decorated with silver discs, each one commemorating a military triumph.

For the army the staff was a source of immense pride; for me, a reminder of friends and family I had lost over the years. At Susa I had lost my father; at Hatra, when the Armenian hordes had been destroyed, I had seen Lucius Domitus slain by a slingshot; at Carrhae, Vagharsh, my faithful banner man, had met his end; and recently at Ctesiphon where my dear friend Silaces had fallen. Blood is the currency of war but I had paid a high price for glory over the years.

Phraates was bedazzled by the Staff of Victory, insisting I inform him of the significance of every disc; Gallia pointing out the battles his father had taken part in. His head dropped when she had finished.

'I have never been victorious in battle,' he said softly, almost apologetically.

'You are still young, highness,' I said, 'besides, the empire has a chance to be free from Roman aggression. Negotiation is always better than fighting.'

'Tell me, King Pacorus, if you were me, would you surrender the captured eagles to Octavian?'

'Yes.'

'Even though it would cause discord within the empire.'

'Discord?'

He sighed. 'There would be many who would view such a gesture as a slight to the pride of the empire.'

'Only those who took the eagles residing in your Hall of Victory have the right to decide whether giving them back to the Romans is a dishonourable act,' I told him. 'Of the ones taken at Carrhae, only I, Queen Gallia and King Spartacus should be consulted, if you wish to solicit opinion. Similarly, of the two taken at Lake Urmia, only King Spartacus and Queen Rasha should be consulted.'

We walked from the cool of the tent into the searing heat of the sun.

'King Spartacus is an implacable enemy of Rome,' said Phraates, 'he will never agree to giving the eagles back.'

'Then don't ask him.'

He gave me a curious look. 'And risk offending him?'

'King Spartacus is capable of starting an argument in an empty room, highness, though if he should take exception to your decision you can remind him you are high king, not he.'

We entered the tent housing the Exiles' silver lion, guards eyeing us to ensure those they did not recognise did not get too close to the sacred totem. Phraates studied the lion, which in truth was not as inspiring as the gold griffin, but was intoxicating nevertheless.

'Spartacus is useful to secure the empire's northern border,' he said, 'especially as he possesses a very capable army. I admit I have indulged him, but the gold I have gifted him is spent on that army. He also keeps Armenia in check.'

I was surprised. 'I thought Artaxias is now an ally of Parthia.'

He strolled from the tent. 'For the moment, yes, but the heirs of Tigranes the Great do not take kindly to being subservient to Parthia, or Rome.'

I remembered Tigranes; a big man with big ambitions who thought Parthia was his toy. He had died mysteriously at the height of his powers and my mind went back to a strange ceremony Dobbai had conducted to enlist the aid of the gods to safeguard the empire. The price for the assistance of the immortals had been a heavy one and of those who had taken part in the ceremony, only I had survived. But Tigranes had died and the power of Armenia had been broken, so much so that the Sarmatians – allies of Spartacus – now occupied the Armenian city of Van and the surrounding land.

The next day my youngest daughter married Dalir in the city's temple dedicated to Shamash. A far cry from the Great Temple at Hatra, it was nevertheless a lavish affair, both the bride and groom wearing white robes in honour of the Sun God. Again, cheering crowds turned out to wish the newlyweds well as they walked from the temple to the Citadel after the ceremony, Phraates in a nice gesture walking behind Eszter and holding a parasol over her head as a defence against the sun. Gallia walked beside him and behind them strolled Diana and Gafarn.

Eager crowds surged forward to get a closer look at the newlyweds, as well as the high king, Chrestus and his men ensuring they did not get within ten paces of the wedding party. Phraates was caught by surprise when the air was suddenly filled with red, purple, pink and white desert roses, thrown by well-wishers to create a carpet of petals in front of Eszter and Dalir. Unfortunately, many hit the couple, Phraates and Gallia. I was walking beside Claudia, behind Gafarn and Diana, and grinned when I saw the parasol momentarily waver.

'Phraates is unused to the love of the people.'

She gave a smirk. 'He finds such closeness to commoners disconcerting, though he will lap up the increase in popularity that comes with it.'

'He has changed.'

'Has he?' she retorted.

'I remember a cynical, malicious, pale young man surrounded by sycophants when I first met Phraates. In looks and mannerisms he is far removed from that individual.'

She laughed. 'Oh, father, after all these years you still look for the best in people. Like a drowning man clinging to a fragile piece of ballast, you latch on to the flimsiest evidence to support your hopes and dreams.

'Phraates is the same as he ever was, father, though the rebellion of Tiridates and the desertion of so many of those he believed to be allies shook him to the core. For the moment he is malleable, vulnerable even. But it will not last.'

'And you decided to take advantage of his vulnerability.'

She looked disappointed. 'Naturally. Far better to have the Scythian Sisters influencing Phraates than men such as Timo and

Ashleen, and let us not forget the sycophants Osrow and Dagan. No, the empire is in safer hands now.'

'How long will you remain at Ctesiphon as Phraates' adviser?'

'Until you and mother die,' she answered matter-of-factly, 'then I will return to rule Dura.'

'What?'

'Now that Eszter is married, any sons she gives birth to will be the heir to Dura's throne when you and mother have left this life.'

'That is the custom.'

'However, in return for saving his life, his reign and the empire,' she said, 'Phraates has pledged to support my elevation to Dura's throne.'

'You will not harm your sister or any children she might have,' I told her sternly.

'You think I would kill my own sister? I hope she and Dalir enjoy many happy years together. But Dalir is the son of Kalet, a glorified horse thief who would oversee the ruin of what you have built over four decades. I cannot allow that to happen and the empire cannot tolerate a weak Dura.'

'What if I and your mother outlive you?' I teased.

'Then Dura's future will be yours to safeguard. In your heart, you must know Eszter and Dalir will make poor rulers. At least at Ctesiphon I will be a part of trying to ensure the smooth running of the empire.'

I was unsure. 'So Dura will be subject to the whims of the Scythian Sisters, for surely you take your orders from them rather than Phraates.'

We were nearing the Citadel now, the crowds having been ushered away by Chrestus' men. As a result the streets were quiet and

60

largely deserted, aside from a few curious onlookers peering at us from tiny first-floor balconies.

'You are wrong, father. The sisters do not exercise control like some sort of secret society. They seek harmony within the empire, so a united Parthia can defeat external enemies. We serve the gods, good kings serve the gods, and in turn the gods give their support to those who respect and serve them.

'Dura is high in the favour of Phraates and the gods.'

'It is?'

'You are too modest, father. You have lived an honourable and pious life. Few men can make such a boast.'

'I do not make such a boast.'

'My point exactly.'

The feast was a testament to the organisational skills of Ashk and Rsan; five hundred guests being fed a variety of different meat and fish dishes, washed down with an unending supply of wine and beer. For most the dishes were just food, but those of a more discerning disposition would have recognised they had been carefully chosen to bless the union of Eszter and Dalir. The number seven is sacred and so the feast included the seven elements that were regarded as particularly auspicious. First was *sabzeh* – sprouted wheat, which symbolised rebirth. Next was *samanu*, a creamy sweet dish that was associated with affluence. The simple apple signified health and beauty, and garlic was incorporated for general good health. *Senjed* – fruit of the wild olive – symbolised love. *Sumac* spice encouraged fertility and, finally, vinegar symbolised health and beauty in old age.

Such symbolism was lost on Kalet and his lords, who got roaringly drunk, as did Dalir, Claudia catching my eye and frowning disapprovingly at her new brother-in-law. Dalir was brave and loved Eszter, but Claudia was right in believing he would make a poor king.

Phraates left Dura two days later in the company of Gafarn and Diana, the high king intent on visiting Hatra as part of his grand tour of the empire, or at least the western half of it. After Hatra he would be calling on King Silani in Persis, the former commander of his bodyguard now the ruler of one of the largest kingdoms in the empire. Life at Dura quickly returned to normal, though a letter from my brother was a cause for concern.

Chapter 3

After the wedding and Phraates' departure, the poets, musicians and entertainers also left Dura. I gave a feast for Byrd and Noora to thank my old friend for his mischievous generosity. To indulge him I dressed in a red silk robe emblazoned with white griffins, a gold sash and my red boots complementing the ensemble. I must admit I found the luxurious clothes comfortable to wear and had relished the approving stares and glances from Phraates and his courtiers. But like the entertainers hired by Byrd, who had made us laugh with their clever wordplays, my interpretation of an ancient Persian satrap was only temporary.

When the magic had gone I returned to being the plain, no-nonsense King of Dura, and dressed accordingly. I even sent Adel and his small army of gardeners back to Hatra. I gave away the plants and trees in the Citadel, and allowed those lining the city's main thoroughfare to be taken by whoever wanted them. It was time to concentrate on less frivolous matters.

The Roman world had its excellent roads – marvels of engineering that criss-crossed Rome's territory like a giant spider's web. But Parthia had its post stations: mud-brick stables, stores and living quarters surrounded by a mud-brick wall spaced at thirty-mile intervals throughout the empire. It was over a thousand miles from the Euphrates to the Himalayas, and five hundred miles from the Caspian Sea to the Persian Gulf. It was a curious thing that despite the years of civil strife that had often plagued Parthia, not one post station had been plundered or destroyed. This was because whoever made a grab for power recognised that a functioning, empire-wide communications system was essential to the smooth running of

Parthia. Information is power and the quicker it is transported and disseminated the better; reaction times can be shortened accordingly.

It was around eighty miles from Dura to Hatra as the raven flew and so a letter penned by Gafarn in the early morning could reach Dura by the evening. And a missive bearing a horse head seal was presented to me by Ashk as I relaxed with Gallia on the palace terrace in the early evening, the sun a huge red ball in the west as it began its rapid descent. We were expecting the arrival of Cicero the Younger, who had remained in the city after Phraates' departure following my request for him to do so. I had had no chance to talk to him, playing host to Phraates, the wedding and feasting having absorbed all my time. He and the high king had spent a morning in discussions, which had gone well judging by the relaxed body language of all parties afterwards.

I broke the seal on the letter and read my brother's words, passing it to Gallia after I had finished. I looked at her as she perused the words, her hair loose around her shoulders, her attire, and mine, having returned to normal following the departure of the high king. She tossed the letter on the low table between us.

'So Spadines has been ejected from Van,' she shrugged. 'It was only a matter of time.'

Gafarn, fearing Spartacus would use it as a pretext for launching a war against Armenia, had asked us to accompany him and Diana on a journey to Vanadzor to plead with the King of Gordyene to refrain from any aggression against his northern neighbour.

'I don't know why Gafarn wants me to accompany him,' I said, 'Spartacus will not listen to anything I have to say. You, perhaps.'

'Phraates must have departed Hatra just before the news of the fall of Van reached Gafarn,' she surmised. 'He will be on his way to Persis by now.'

'Phraates will be unconcerned by events in Armenia,' I said, 'unless they threaten the security of the empire.'

'And will they?'

I shook my head. 'Armenia is a minnow compared to the military might of Gordyene. But if Spartacus launches an invasion of Armenia, then it could de-stabilise the empire's northern border. And with King Ali away in the east, any conflict could spread into Atropaiene.'

'We go, then?'

I nodded. 'At least it will be good to see Rasha again.'

Ashk reappeared and bowed. 'Governor Cicero is waiting in the throne room, majesty.'

'Escort him to the terrace.'

To make the governor feel at home the kitchens had prepared a Roman meal, the first course consisting of eggs, salad with asparagus, and salted fish. The portions were small and Cicero was a picky eater, but his manner and conversation were convivial enough. Dressed in a white toga, Byrd had informed me he was aged around forty, though his slightly gaunt face and thinning hair made him appear older.

Reclining on a couch, he sipped at his wine and dabbed his thin mouth with a napkin.

'I wanted to thank you personally for expediting the talks between Octavian and High King Phraates, majesty.'

'In what way?'

'The high king is desirous to secure the return of his son to Parthia,' said the governor, 'and to hasten this he has agreed to return the eagles currently held at Ctesiphon to Rome.'

'He has?' Gallia was surprised.

Cicero took a sip of wine. 'Such a gesture will be greatly appreciated by Octavian and the Roman people. In return, I informed High King Phraates that Octavian has agreed to make the Euphrates a permanent border between Rome and Parthia.'

'What of Tiridates?' I probed.

Cicero put down his silver cup. 'I can assure you, majesty, that Rome will give him no financial or military aid in the future, though Octavian has granted him sanctuary in Syria.'

As the light began to fade and servants lit torches around the terrace to illuminate the scene, the second course was served, a mixture of cooked meats ranging from chicken, mutton and beef, to goat and pork. Most of the dishes were returned to the kitchens largely untouched, Cicero picking at his dish and eating very little. We too ate sparingly, partly because we had over-indulged during Phraates' visit, which had occasioned lavish feasts every evening.

'Your father was killed by Mark Antony.'

Gallia's words shocked Cicero and for a brief moment I thought I detected genuine sorrow in his eyes. But the diplomat in him returned and he nodded his head sagely.

'Murdered would be a more accurate description, majesty. That was some sixteen years ago, and afterwards I joined my father's allies Cassius and Brutus in Greece, who were fighting Julius Caesar, Octavian's uncle.'

Gallia was confused. 'If you were fighting Octavian's uncle, how is it you now serve his nephew?'

66

Cicero smiled, a gesture that was alien to him judging by the lopsided shape his mouth assumed.

'Cassius and Brutus were defeated by Octavian and Mark Antony at the Battle of Philippi in Macedonia, which resulted in their deaths. I was pardoned afterwards and soon there appeared a division between Octavian and Mark Antony and I was more than eager to join the former's supporters.'

'You might be interested to learn that Mark Antony was once our prisoner,' said Gallia.

Cicero was surprised. 'I did not know that, majesty.'

'It was a long time ago and his imprisonment lasted for one night only,' I told him. 'He was exchanged for a young Agraci princess we were very fond of.'

'My husband admired the *triumvir*, governor,' said Gallia, 'seeing him as a worthy adversary.'

'He had many skills,' conceded Cicero, 'but his inflated view of his own importance and insatiable ambition resulted in the needless spilling of an ocean of blood. Not only Roman but also Parthian.'

'I'm glad he is dead,' said Gallia.

Cicero raised his cup to her. 'As am I, majesty.'

The third course, consisting of nuts, pastries and fruit, was served but again was mostly returned to the kitchens intact, a great shame for the cooks had spent hours preparing our meal.

'There is one matter I wished to discuss with you, majesties, a delicate matter.'

'I'm sure it cannot be more delicate than the return of the eagles,' I replied.

He tried to smile but his face adopted a somewhat severe countenance.

'The issue of the return of the eagles is now well underway, majesty,' he said, tipping his head to Gallia, 'thanks in large part to the intercession of Queen Gallia. I have no doubt that in the atmosphere of goodwill and mutual respect that currently exists between Rome and Parthia, it will be resolved to the satisfaction of all parties. But the matter I speak of concerns your nephew, King Spartacus.'

My heart sank and I looked at Gallia, who rolled her eyes.

'Please elaborate, governor.'

Cicero took another sip of wine. 'Pontus is a client kingdom of Rome, and as such is under the protection of Rome.'

Gallia inhaled deeply but said nothing. There was a time when she would have launched a vicious tirade against him, stating Pontus was but a slave kingdom under the heel of Rome. But the fierce Gallic warrior had been tempered by pragmatism so she kept her emotions under control.

'King Polemon is its ruler, I believe,' I said.

Cicero nodded. 'Correct, majesty, and it was King Polemon who complained to Octavian concerning the activities of Gordyene and its king.'

Gallia raised an eyebrow. 'Activities?'

'Raids launched from northwest Gordyene into Pontus, majesty. The Pontic villages along the border have been plundered and their inhabitants either killed or carried off into captivity. Now the raids are penetrating ever deeper into King Polemon's realm and it is only a matter of time before he retaliates.'

'Has he sent an official complaint to my nephew?' I asked.

'Alas, majesty, the raids are carried out by Sarmatian horsemen, but it is well known that King Spartacus is an ally of the Aorsi tribe.

68

Gordyene may deny it has anything to do with these raids, but we are not so naive to believe that the Aorsi are acting without the blessing and indeed encouragement of Gordyene.'

Cicero leaned in closer. 'If King Spartacus does not muzzle his Sarmatians, Pontus, with the support of Rome, will be forced to retaliate. This would lead to war between Pontus and Gordyene, which would draw in the allies of each kingdom. Octavian does not want that, Phraates does not want that and I am sure you above all, majesty, wish to avoid such a scenario.'

'You are right, governor,' I told him.

'Then can I urge you to impress upon your nephew that his actions imperil the delicate peace that has been established between Rome and Parthia. I think we are at a crossroads, majesty, whereby said peace may either flourish and grow or wither and die.'

'Your visit is fortuitous, governor,' I said, 'for I and the queen are about to depart Dura to travel north to Hatra and on to Vanadzor.'

He seemed genuinely pleased. 'I shall notify Octavian immediately, majesty.'

Afterwards, following the governor's departure, we sat drinking wine and pondering what Cicero had told us. We had said nothing about the possibility of Spartacus waging war against Armenia, which was under Parthian influence in any case.

Gallia voiced my fears. 'Spartacus is playing with fire by threatening war against Armenia and goading Pontus. If he carries on, Rome will seize the chance to wage war against Gordyene and occupy Armenia.'

'It was always a mistake inviting the Sarmatians to live in northern Gordyene,' I fumed. 'They are like a weed that has taken root. It would be best if they were evicted and sent back to their homeland.'

'Spartacus would never agree to that,' she said.

'He might, if he realises no one will support him if Rome and Pontus attack him.'

'We would never abandon Gordyene, surely?'

'I will merely remind him that Rome conquered Gordyene once and if he continues to act as he does, it may happen again,' I replied vaguely, though she was right: I would never abandon Spartacus.

Cicero left Dura the next day, with a promise that he would return to the city in the near future. I liked him and even Gallia found his company agreeable. With Phraates having confirmed he was returning the eagles and Octavian eager for peace with Parthia, I found the prospect of Spartacus wrecking a bright future intensely irritating. The King of Gordyene was becoming like a toothache and often the best remedy for such an ailment was to yank out the bad tooth with a pair of pliers.

With Azad and Sporaces away with King Ali, I wanted to ride north with more than a hundred Amazons, so I called Chrestus to the palace and made an unusual request.

'I want a hundred men drawn from the Durans and Exiles who can ride. I assume there are some among the legions that can ride?'

He was taken aback. 'Horse archers and cataphracts ride, majesty, and foot soldiers march on foot.'

We were in the Headquarters Building, which was airless and hot despite the shutters of the room where council meetings were held being fully open. I poured him a cup of water and filled another cup for myself, then told him about the trip to Gordyene.

'King Gafarn and Queen Diana will be accompanied by Hatra's Royal Bodyguard and I want more riders than a hundred Amazons.'

He was far from convinced. 'A legionary on horseback rather defeats his purpose.'

'It will be purely for show,' I assured him. 'If I had the time I would march north with the legions.'

He emptied his cup. 'It's that serious?'

I explained how Spartacus was threatening Armenia with war as well as using his Sarmatian allies to raid Pontus, which threatened to ignite a conflict between Rome and Parthia if his activities remained unchecked.

'It would seem the rulers of Gordyene are cursed. Didn't Orodes defeat and kill Surena before the walls of Vanadzor?'

'Sadly, yes, and before Surena liberated Gordyene it was under the control of the Romans. It really does seem to be a cursed kingdom, but I do not believe it is inevitable that Spartacus will suffer the same fate as Surena.'

'I will call for volunteers, majesty,' he said, 'we should be able to find a hundred. Who had you in mind to command them?'

I had given the matter no thought. He saw my vacant expression.

'Lucius Varsas would be more than adequate,' he suggested. 'And he will be delighted to study Vanadzor's fortifications. Oh, and he can ride a horse.'

Dura's quartermaster general was now thirty years old, married and living in the former home of his relation and mentor, Marcus

Sutonius. In appearance he resembled a Roman with his clean-shaven face and close-cropped hair, but he had married a Parthian woman and their two young children were very much natives of Dura with their olive skin and long black hair. As a high-ranking Duran officer he had a life of prosperity and privilege, his children having private tutors and his wife servants to keep their house in order. But his lifestyle did not corrupt his character and he jumped at the opportunity to travel with us to Gordyene.

It took two days to reach Hatra, our column of one hundred Amazons, the same number of Varsas' mounted legionaries, and fifty Daughters of Dura leading an equal number of camels. Because it was still summer we left the city before dawn, riding for two hours before dismounting and leading our horses on foot for another hour before resting. By mid-morning it was already hot, the desert horizon turning to liquid in the heat haze and all of us squinting as we journeyed east towards my brother's city. We avoided the road because it was choked with camel caravans travelling east and west on their way to and from Dura, the highway enveloped in an unbroken dust cloud as a result of the hundreds of camels and horses using it. For the owners of the caravans such activity meant wealth, for the drivers and guards days filled with dust, grime and heat.

Away from the road the terrain is barren and flat with only traces of plant and animal life. Often blasted by fierce desert winds, it is a hard, merciless landscape where the unwary can perish with ease. Normally we would have brought civilian servants with us to erect our tents and attend to the mounts of the legionaries, Dura's foot soldiers receiving no training in the care and maintenance of horses. Gallia had insisted that the Daughters of Dura would fulfil those duties, though I felt uneasy about fifty teenage girls accompanying a hundred battle-hardened legionaries.

First formed during the recent war against Tiridates, whose army I feared might attack Dura, they were all orphans who had been recruited by Gallia and trained by the Amazons in the use of a bow. In the event Tiridates did not attack the city and the emergency passed, but Gallia decided not to disband the Daughters of Dura but rather use them as a recruitment pool for the Amazons, akin to the male squires of the cataphracts.

I had to admit the girls, all aged between eleven and sixteen, went about their tasks diligently, their enthusiasm and pride at being selected to accompany their queen resulting in them tackling rubbing down and feeding horses with gusto. For their part the legionaries mounted sentry duty around our camp, their commander liaising with Zenobia, the leader of the Amazons, concerning shifts pairing legionaries with female archers. His name was Bullus and if ever there was a man who resembled what his parents had named him it was he. He had a large head decorated with scars, broad shoulders, thick neck and muscular arms. I invited the centurion to dine with us in our tent that evening, along with Zenobia and Lucius Varsas. We were served bread baked in Dura, dates, yoghurt and goat freshly slaughtered by teenage girls dressed in leggings, leather shoes and white tunics. Bullus shook his head when a smiling girl placed a wooden plate heaped with bread and cooked goat in front of him, taking a sip of wine when another young female filled his wooden cup.

'Food not to your liking, centurion?'

He tore off a chunk of bread. 'Food is excellent, majesty.'

'Then what? Speak freely.'

His dark brown eyes glanced at the queen. 'No offence, majesty, but it is a bad idea bringing all these girls along.'

'Why is that?' asked Gallia. 'Are your men not disciplined?'

'They are under tight control well enough, majesty, but men are men, not slabs of stone, and fifty teenage girls are an unwelcome distraction.'

He stuffed some meat in his mouth. 'No offence meant.'

'The Amazons have been part of the army for years,' remarked Zenobia, her dark locks hanging freely around her shoulders, 'and there have never been any problems.'

'That's different,' said Bullus.

'In what way?' I asked.

He swallowed the meat. 'The whole army knows it is death to lay a hand on a member of the Amazons, and in any case they are always around the king and queen, so detached from the rest of the army. But if the army is going to have teenage girls running around camp, that will be a recipe for trouble.'

'All those girls are under the same protection as the Amazons,' said Gallia in a low voice.

'Besides, this is not a campaign, centurion,' I said in an effort to lighten the mood, 'merely a visit to Gordyene. Ever been there?'

'No, majesty.'

'A land of hills, mountains, fast-flowing streams and wild valleys,' I told him, 'quite beautiful in summer, bleak in winter.'

'King Gafarn and Queen Diana will be joining us on our journey north,' said Gallia.

'I am looking forward to seeing Hatra again, and Vanadzor,' stated Lucius, 'I was impressed by Hatra's one hundred and fifty towers along its perimeter wall.'

'And a moat,' I said, 'in front of the wall around its circumference.'

He nodded. 'A moat in the middle of the desert, quite extraordinary.'

'Hatra is extraordinary,' I waxed, 'an oasis of green and life in the middle of a barren desert.'

I noticed Bullus had a grin on his face as he tucked into his evening meal, a girl filling his cup with more wine after he had emptied it.

'Something amuses you, centurion?'

'No, majesty, ignore me, I'm just a low-born soldier.'

'When you sit at this table, centurion,' said Gallia, 'your opinion is as valid and worthy of being heard as every other diner. So, I will hear what amuses you.'

Lucius nodded to him. Bullus inhaled deeply and took a gulp of wine.

'Good man King Spartacus, your nephew, majesty, a no-nonsense soldier at heart. We were glad to have him beside us at the recent Battle of Ctesiphon. But I don't think you and his parents are travelling to Gordyene to wish him well.'

'So why are we going to Gordyene?' I asked.

'I'm just a soldier who obeys orders, majesty.'

'But you have an opinion, surely? I would hear it.'

'If I was a betting man,' he said, 'I would hazard we are going to Gordyene to prevent conflict breaking out.'

'We are not here to interrogate our king and queen, Bullus,' said Lucius sternly.

'You have a keen mind, centurion,' I complimented him. 'And you are right, we journey north to prevent a war, a war that might spread to provoke a clash between Rome and Parthia.'

Lucius was surprised. 'It is that serious, majesty?'

'It is that serious.'

'Hopefully, with the assistance of King Gafarn and Queen Diana,' said Gallia, 'war will be averted.'

But when we reached Hatra we discovered that our friends would not be accompanying us north. Gafarn's leg ulcer had worsened, with the result he was confined to the palace and forbidden to ride until it had healed. A concerned Diana hovered around him like a mother hen, overseeing the ulcer being cleaned and dressed on a daily basis, much to the annoyance of Gafarn.

'I am not an invalid,' he complained as the court physician, a fussy, irritable individual examined the ulcer before a fresh bandage was applied to it, Diana peering at it beside him.

'Of course, if you had journeyed to Dura in a cart instead of on a horse,' said the physician, 'you would not have exacerbated the wound. And you failed to keep it clean and dressed. Most unacceptable.'

'Will it heal?' there was concern in Diana's voice.

'If the king follows my instructions,' replied the physician, 'then yes.'

He stood and gestured that the waiting assistants should begin cleaning the wound. He observed Gallia and me coolly and stroked his neatly trimmed beard.

'The king requires rest and recuperation.'

'I have to go to Gordyene,' said Gafarn, watching as one of the medical orderlies applied a honey-coated dressing directly to the ulcer.

The physician's nostrils flared. 'Out of the question. I assume you wish to keep your foot?'

Diana went pale. 'His foot?'

The physician's forehead creased into a frown.

'Ulcers are notorious for developing into more serious afflictions. Should the infection worsen, the entire limb might be in danger. Naturally, I would act before this occurred.'

'Act how?' demanded Diana.

The physician gave me knowing look.

'I'm sure King Pacorus is well acquainted with the procedure, being a skilled practitioner of war. I would remove the foot by first using a scalpel to cut the skin, followed by a long, double-edged knife to cut through any muscle, followed by the swift application of a sharp saw to carve through the bone. This should take no more than three to four minutes, after which hot oil would be applied to the seal the wound.'

Gafarn, usually never wanting when it came to a sarcastic quip, stared at the physician with worried eyes.

'You will stay here, in the palace, until the ulcer heals,' commanded Diana sternly.

'As ever, my queen,' smiled the physician, 'you are the voice of wisdom among fools.'

The orderlies finished cleaning and dressing the wound and escorted the physician from our presence.

'Is he always like that?' I asked.

'He has a curt manner,' agreed Diana, 'but he is an excellent physician. You two will have to go to Vanadzor alone.'

The thought of confronting Spartacus had hardly infused me with excitement when it had involved Gafarn and Diana. Without them its appeal was diminishing by the second.

'He won't listen to me,' I said bluntly, 'especially after our altercation concerning giving sanctuary to Parisa and her children.'

The wife and children of the late King of Media had fallen into Spartacus' hands following the surrender of Irbil in the aftermath of Aliyeh's suicide. Spartacus had wanted to retain them, their fate to be decided by him alone. But I told him in no uncertain terms that they were to be allowed to go to Hatra, making it clear I was prepared to back up my demand with force.

Gafarn looked at us both. 'You two are the only ones that stand between peace and war.'

'There is something else you should know,' said Gallia, nodding at me.

I told him and Diana about the meeting we had with Governor Cicero and his concerns regarding the Sarmatian raids against Pontus. As peacocks strolled in the royal gardens outside the intimate reception room and gardeners trimmed lawns and pruned bushes, Gafarn, his injured leg resting on a footstool, leaned back on his couch and closed his eyes.

'It is even more imperative that you travel to Gordyene, Pacorus. The last thing we want is another war with Rome, and I have no desire to see Armenian soldiers outside the walls of Hatra again.'

'Very well,' I said without enthusiasm. 'We will go.'

'I have written to my grandson, King Akmon, requesting safe passage through Media,' said Gafarn. 'He agreed, of course.'

'How is he faring?' asked Gallia.

'He rules a land laid low by years of war and plunder,' replied Gafarn.

'But at least Media is now at peace, thank the gods,' added Diana.

'He knows he can call on us for aid at any time,' said Gafarn.

'Can he make the same call on his father?' said Gallia.

'They are still estranged,' Diana told us, 'though hopefully in time, and with Rasha's persuasion, father and son will be reconciled.'

We would have liked to stay longer in Hatra, sharing the company of our old friends, but I felt the momentum of events bearing down on me and so we left the city the next day, striking east to head for the ford across the Tigris at the city of Assur. Before we left I visited my sister Adeleh in the retreat of the Sisters of Shamash located near the Great Temple where the Sun God was worshipped. She was now head of the all-female holy order, though she dressed and lived exactly the same as the other sisters who dedicated their lives to Shamash. She said she would pray for the intercession of the Sun God to ensure my mission to Gordyene was a success, replying I said I needed all the help I could get. In our hurried conversation and tearful goodbye, no mention was made of the presence of Parisa, former Queen of Media, among the holy sisters. Nor did the topic of Parisa and her children arise during our time with Gafarn and Diana. Once part of Media's most ancient and august family, they had become a mere footnote in Parthia's history.

Sixty miles to the east of Hatra was Assur, a city that guarded the east of my brother's kingdom. Sited on the western bank of the

Tigris, which was low and slow moving following the end of the spring melt waters weeks before, Assur was a formidable stronghold. It had been originally constructed so that the Tigris protected the city on two sides, with a moat that covered the other two sides. A double wall, the space in between filled with buildings to house troops of the garrison, surrounded the city on the landside. On top of the outer wall was a parapet protected by battlements, the latter containing narrow slits from where archers could shoot down on attackers below. There was no bridge across the river to link the Kingdom of Hatra with Media on the other side, but there was a ford that was passable throughout the year, though in spring the current could be dangerous to travellers.

We stayed one night in the city; the governor informing us clearance had been given by the Medians for transit through their territory. General Herneus, now the commander of Hatra's army, had been the governor for many years and the current occupant was his nephew. Unlike his uncle, he had thick black hair, a bushy beard and a talkative character. As we reclined on couches in his mansion sipping wine served in silver chalices, he briefed us fully on affairs across the river.

'By all accounts King Akmon is mounting a great effort to make himself and his queen popular amoung their subjects, though it may take a while.'

'Why is that?' I queried.

'Akmon is the son of King Spartacus, your nephew, who has spent the last few years raiding northern Media,' he replied, 'and he butchered a fair few when he defeated the late King Darius at Mepsila.'

80

'You think the lords of Media will rise up against Akmon?' asked Gallia.

He shook his hairy head. 'No, majesty, not with Hatra pledging its support to King Akmon, that and the fact many of Media's lords are dead. Media is crying out for peace after King Darius' series of disastrous wars.'

'Were you here when he invaded Hatra?' I asked.

He laughed. 'He was a fool, bringing his army across the river with no means to reduce this city or indeed Hatra itself.'

He suddenly realised Darius had been a distant relation.

'I meant no offence, majesty.'

'You are right,' I told him, 'Darius was a fool and a fool leading an army will invariably bring about the destruction of that army.'

'You go to Mepsila, majesty?'

I nodded.

'The governor there is the one weak link in Akmon's armour, a scheming, duplicitous character who has turned self-preservation into an art form.'

'You think he might foment rebellion?' I asked with concern.

'The only thing Governor Cookes foments, majesty, is the beer that he consumes in great quantities,' he replied. 'But he attained great wealth and position under King Darius and Akmon effectively banished him to Mepsila.'

'He should have banished him from Media or executed him,' said Gallia.

The governor raised his chalice to her. 'Therein lies King Akmon's problem, majesty. He cannot act ruthlessly for fear of alienating Media's surviving lords, but he needs to get rid of any seditious elements to cement his reign.'

'Now that there is peace,' I said, 'he has a chance to win over the people of Media.'

The people of Media had suffered greatly during the wars involving Mark Antony. King Spartacus and the recent conflict saw the armies of Hatra and Gordyene marching across their land. We saw for ourselves the consequences as we journeyed north after crossing the Tigris and riding along the eastern riverbank of the waterway. Many villages alongside the river were deserted, their fields untended and their livestock long gone. As we journeyed to Mepsila we came across many settlements that had been torched, probably by the soldiers of Spartacus. It saddened me greatly to see such devastation, especially as Media was not for nothing termed the 'breadbasket of the empire'. The capital Irbil was located in a great plain blessed with fertile alluvial soil, fed by underground water and thousands of natural springs. Those villages sited near the Tigris used its waters to grow their crops and maintain their livestock, as well as catching fish in the river.

Inland from the Tigris, the hundreds of villages on the great plain, enjoying the blessing of an abundance of water, grew a host of crops, including barley, wheat, flax, onions, figs, grapes, turnips, lentils, dates, pomegranates and olives. Of these, barley was the most valuable food source because it could be ground into flour for bread, made into soups, or fermented and turned into beer. But to grow barley required between forty and fifty days of moist soil, a blessing deprived most kingdoms. As a result, Media was able to export great quantities of flour to neighbouring kingdoms, along with wine, beer and flax, which was used to produce cloth, netting and linseed oil.

As we neared Mepsila, my spirits rose when I saw thriving settlements filled with healthy villagers, animal pens holding sheep and goats, and irrigated fields, orchards and vineyards. We were met by a party of mounted spearmen five miles from the town, every rider wearing a blue tunic and grey leggings, protected by a helmet, leather cuirass and a round wooden shield faced with leather sporting a white dragon emblem.

The commander pulled up his horse and bowed his head to Gallia and me.

'Governor Cookes is expecting you, highnesses.'

Mepsila was a dingy place; a small town next to the Tigris surrounded by a mud-brick wall urgently in need of repair and filled with single-storey mud-brick homes packed tightly together. The governor's mansion was a two-storey building faced with cracking plaster in need of a renovation, the nearby barracks surrounded by a wall that was at least well maintained. Before we entered the town the commander of our escort requested that the Amazons and legionaries remain outside Mepsila because the barracks was too small to accommodate them.

The words 'too small' could not be applied to the governor, who stood in front of his mansion to greet us when we rode into the small courtyard in front of his home. He was a grotesque figure, a portly man with an enormous gut encased in a gold robe with a huge red sash around his mid-rift, gold rings on nearly all his fingers. On his feet were a pair of red boots and a slave held a parasol over his head as a defence against the sun that was roasting Mepsila and its inhabitants. Despite this his bald crown was beaded in sweat, as was his bloated, puffy face, another slave rushing forward to dab his enormous fat head when a steward ordered him to do so.

83

We dismounted and the fat governor bowed his head, waving forward more slaves to take our horses to the stables.

'Welcome, King Pacorus and Queen Gallia' he said.

He walked forward and extended an arm to an over-painted, plump woman on his left.

'May I introduce my wife, Hanita?'

'It is an honour to meet you, majesties.'

I estimated them both to be their fifties, though the wife had so much makeup on her face it was difficult to determine her age. She wore almost as much jewellery as her husband, though at least her skin was in a better condition than Cookes'. Obsequiousness dripped from them in greater quantities than sweat and I felt instantly uneasy in their company. Judging by the false smile on my wife's face so did Gallia. Lucius Varsas was diplomacy itself but Bullus made no attempt to disguise his contempt for our hosts, though he did appreciate the meal laid on by Cookes that evening.

He may have been the governor of a drab backwater of a town, but Cookes lived like a king. He deprived himself of nothing and neither did his wife. What a repulsive pair they were, gorging on meat and fish as they entertained me, Gallia, Lucius Varsas and Centurion Bullus in the dining room of their mansion. We sat at a huge table with feet carved to resemble dragons, with more dragons painted on the walls and stucco dragonheads decorating the ceiling above us. Cookes devoured great portions of meat, the juices running down his face and beard on to the napkin he had tucked into the top of his robe. The napkin caught most of the meat juices but failed to prevent the beer that dribbled from his mouth staining his clothes. I had never seen anyone drink so much beer, a slave standing behind him with a jug of the beverage ready to refill his rhyton when it had been drained. In an effort to halt his ferocious consumption of alcohol, I endeavoured to engage him in conversation.

'How long have you been governor here, Lord Cookes?'

He shoved a piece of bread in his mouth, muffling his reply.

'Too long, majesty.'

His wife cackled like a hyena, holding out her rhyton so it could be refilled. Cookes belched.

'It was a punishment dished out by our new king. He doesn't like me.'

My estimation of Akmon rose.

'I was a loyal friend of King Darius, you see,' spat the governor bitterly, small pieces of bread leaving his mouth.

'You fought for Darius at Mepsila?' I asked.

Cookes drained his rhyton and slammed it down on the table, making the slave behind him jump.

'I was organising the defences of Irbil.'

'I do not recall seeing you in the palace when Irbil fell to my nephew.'

'I was away at my estate at the time.'

'Organising its defence?' said Gallia caustically.

Hanita, who was now quite drunk, gave my wife an unamused look, before hissing at a slave that her rhyton was empty.

'King Akmon wants to have a care,' she slurred, 'there are many who wish to see the true king placed on Irbil's throne.'

Cookes emitted a nervous laugh. 'You must forgive my wife, majesties, her tongue has a life of its own when she has had too much to drink.'

'Akmon *is* Media's true king,' said Gallia slowly and forcefully, 'placed on the throne on the orders of Phraates himself.'

Cookes belched loudly and raised his rhyton. 'A toast to King Akmon and his lovely queen, Lutin.'

'*Lusin*,' I corrected him.

He grunted and took another gulp of beer, wiping his mouth on the back of his sleeve.

'Your northern border is quiet?' I enquired.

He nodded. 'With the son of King Spartacus on Media's throne, he is hardly going to raid Media. We thank the gods for that, at least.'

'Peace means prosperity, governor,' I said, 'and I firmly believe King Akmon will endeavour to preserve that peace, irrespective of him being the son of King Spartacus. If he succeeds, then you will find he will become a popular king in Media.'

'He is not Parthian,' slurred Hanita, whose cheeks were aglow as a result of the prodigious amount of alcohol she had consumed.

'What does that matter?' I snapped.

Surprisingly, Cookes appeared to sober up instantly, putting down his rhyton and staring at me with his bloodshot eyes, his beard wet with beer, and his double chin wobbling.

'King Akmon is half Thracian and half Agraci,' he uttered the last word with barely concealed contempt. 'He has no claim on the throne of Media, which is one of the oldest and most revered kingdoms in the Parthian Empire, whose royal family's great strengths were its continuity and heritage.'

'That royal family invited Romans into the empire,' stated Gallia, 'and invited the rebel Tiridates to use Media as a base from which to depose the rightful high king, which allowed Tiridates to plunge Parthia into a civil war. The end result is that Media is now laid low, many of its villages either torched or half empty due to their menfolk having died in Media's ill-judged wars.'

While his wife continued to drink heavily, Cookes remained subdued and picked at his food, occasionally glancing at Lucius and Bullus. He clapped his hands to bring a troupe of dancers into the room, accompanied by musicians holding lyres, flutes and drums. The dancers were a mix of young men and women wearing very little clothing, their bodies oiled so they glistened as they began a frenetic routine that I found most tedious. But I put it down to my age and so tried to give the appearance I was enjoying myself. Hanita was an embarrassment, whooping with joy and trying to grope any male dancer that came within arm's reach. I uttered a silent prayer when the entertainers had finished that we could retire to our beds. Fortunately, as Hanita was on the verge of passing out due to her over-indulgence, Cookes brought the evening to a merciful end.

As we had eaten and drank little we were not tired when we retired to our bedroom. I sat on the bed staring at the cracked plaster on the walls.

'It is madness Spartacus is estranged from his son. If Cookes is anything to go by, Media has fallen into decay and is administered by gross incompetents.'

Gallia sat in front of a small polished bronze mirror and began brushing her hair.

'Cookes is certainly gross, though whether he is incompetent I'm not sure.'

'Oh?'

'He survived the great bloodbath of Mepsila where Spartacus butchered a high number of Media's lords. And he managed to wriggle his way out of the siege of Irbil, despite being a close ally of King Darius.'

'We have only his word for that.'

She stopped brushing to turn to me. 'You look at him and see a fat, beer-soaked fool. But I would not underestimate him. Beneath the blubber and bluster is a schemer. Akmon should get rid of him.'

'I'm sure Akmon has…'

I was going to say that the young King of Media was sure to have good advisers around him, but his father had effectively culled Media of its lords, or at least a great many of them, and I worried about the calibre of those that were left. If Cookes was anything to go by, Media was now sadly lacking in sage counsellors.

'Has what?' she asked.

'It all hinges on convincing Spartacus not to retaliate against Armenia and stopping his Sarmatians from raiding Pontus,' I said. 'If we succeed, then that will buy Akmon time to put his kingdom in order.'

She turned back to the mirror and recommenced brushing her hair.

'Phraates himself should be journeying to Vanadzor to prevent Spartacus attacking Armenia.'

I pulled off my boots. 'Phraates is clever. Of all the kings, Spartacus has proved the most useful to him, so he will not risk alienating the King of Gordyene. To be fair, Phraates is unaware of the danger of Rome being dragged into a war with Gordyene over Pontus.'

'What about Armenia?'

I flopped down on the bed, staring up at the cracked ceiling.

'Phraates is happy for Armenia to be a lamb to the lion of Gordyene. If Artaxias is absorbed with containing Spartacus, he will not be sending his armies south across the Araxes River. And, happily for the high king, because the Romans killed most of his family the King of Armenia will not be seeking the friendship of Rome in the foreseeable future.'

We left Mepsila the next day, Cookes and his wife looking remarkably bright and fresh despite their gluttony the previous evening. He asked if I would pass on his compliments to King Spartacus, which surprised me somewhat considering his ramblings the night before against Akmon's lineage.

'As you wisely stated, majesty, Media needs peace to prosper.'

I smiled as he tried to fool me into thinking he was pleading on Media's behalf. But the reality was he knew Mepsila would be the first town Spartacus would assault should he send his army into Media once more. Having avoided one battle at Mepsila, Cookes clearly had no desire to be present should there be a second.

'I cannot speak for the King of Gordyene,' I told him as a slave held Horns' reins to allow me to gain his saddle, 'but I can state with some certainty that he is not planning any aggression against Media. Not unless he is provoked.'

'I would advise against leading any raids into Gordyene,' said Gallia, adjusting her floppy hat. It was threatening to be another hot day.

Cookes brought his hands together and bowed his head, which was beaded with sweat despite the slave holding a parasol over him.

'I would never lead a raiding party, majesty,' stated the governor.

'Not even against a caravan transporting beer?' she said dryly, turning her horse to ride from the crumbling mansion.

Chapter 4

If a bird flew from the ramparts of Irbil to the black stone fortress in Vanadzor, a distance of one hundred and twenty miles, it would take it less than a day. But we had no wings and our journey would be more convoluted as we left the Tigris and headed northeast towards the border with Gordyene. There were no signs to denote the dividing line between Media and Gordyene, no great fence to delineate where one realm ended and another began, not even forts to mark the territories of King Spartacus and his son. But as we travelled north the terrain slowly changed to become hillier and wooded, heralding our entry into Gordyene. In the near distance were the high mountains that ringed Gordyene. Inside the ring the land was filled with rivers bloated with raging waters in spring, seemingly endless forests of beech and oak and wind-swept mountain steppes. I had travelled this route many times during the past four decades and knew it better than many scouts, though Spartacus obviously believed we might get lost for on the second day after leaving the tatty, rundown Mepsila, we ran into a patrol of the King of Gordyene's soldiers. Or more likely he did not like the idea of any parties of foreign soldiers roaming his kingdom unaccompanied.

We had been riding along a narrow track that cut through a vast forest of oak, the trees filled with birds – eagles, kites, harriers and goshawks – and their noisy calls. But suddenly the birds became silent and an oppressive atmosphere began to press down on us. Horns became nervous and flicked his ears.

I turned to Zenobia. 'Order your women to have a care.'

Bows came out of cases and arrows were nocked in bowstrings. Though the legionaries' shields and javelins were loaded on camels, Lucius ordered his men to draw their swords, though if it came to a fight I wondered how effective a hundred mounted foot soldiers would be. I too nocked an arrow in my bow, as did Gallia beside me, our eyes darting left and right to detect any movement among the trees flanking us. We slowed our horses as we entered a curve in the track, around which was a party of horsemen blocking our path. Gallia gave a muted laugh.

I held up my hand. 'Stand easy.'

'King's Guard,' hissed Gallia. 'I hope that oaf Shamshir is not among them, otherwise it will be a very long journey to Vanadzor.'

There were around a score of them, immaculate in appearance, the coats of their horses shining in the summer sun lancing through gaps in the forest canopy. One of their number nudged his horse forward, a man with dark eyes, beard as black as night and hair of the same colour showing beneath his burnished helmet. He halted his horse in front of us and bowed his head.

'Greetings, King Pacorus, Queen Gallia, welcome to Gordyene. I am Commander Kuris, assigned to escort you to Vanadzor.'

At least he was not Shamshir, the thuggish commander of the King's Guard, the élite soldiers in Gordyene's army and Spartacus' bodyguard. Like the Vipers, the female horse archers who protected Queen Rasha, the King's Guard numbered five hundred men. But unlike the Vipers every man was armed with an ukku blade. I glanced at Kuris' hip and smiled when I saw a sword with a silver lion's head pommel.

'Thank you, commander,' I replied, 'I trust your king and queen are well?'

'Very well,' he said, looking past us to peer at the column behind.

'King Gafarn and Queen Diana are not with you?'

'Alas, no, the king has a leg wound that needs rest to heal,' Gallia told him.

'It is nothing serious,' I assured him, 'but for the moment King Gafarn is confined to Hatra's palace.'

He fell in beside us and his men formed a vanguard as we continued our journey through the forest teeming with red deer. The air was warm but not excessively so, the forest canopy shielding us for the most part from the sun. Kuris was attired like the others in his party: black leggings, red tunic, burnished helmet and stunning scale armour cuirass of alternating steel and bronze scales sewn on to a thick hide sleeveless vest. Additional protection was provided by thick leather *pteruges* – leather strips – covering the thighs and shoulders. A bow was attached to his saddle on the right side and a full quiver on the left. His men carried round wooden shields faced with red-painted hide and embossed with a white lion's head, but Kuris' shield dangled from the rear of his saddle. Beneath the saddle was a beautiful red saddlecloth with silver lion motifs stitched in each corner. No money had been spared to clothe and equip the King's Guard. I noticed Kuris' saddlecloth also had three gold arrow motifs stitched into it. I pointed at them.

'Do they denote your rank?'

'No, majesty, they denote my winning Gordyene's annual archery competition three times.'

'It is a competition among the army's soldiers?' asked Gallia.

'No, majesty, it is open to everyone, regardless of sex, rank or civilian or military status. The only exceptions are the king and queen because if they were beaten it would damage their authority. The winner is awarded a golden arrow.'

'How many people have won the competition three times?' I said.

'Just me, majesty.'

'Well, then, perhaps we could put your skills to use by hunting some deer to fill our bellies tonight.'

We established a camp early, away from the track a short distance, so parties could be despatched further into the forest to hunt game. A dozen parties were organised, each one comprising two archers and two more individuals to tend to the pair of horses that would haul the game back to camp. In an effort to find out more about Spartacus' plans, I teamed up with Kuris, two of his King's Guard leading their horses behind us. The forest was an ancient one, the canopy open in places where birch, maple and hazel trees grew. Shafts of sunlight reached the forest floor to illuminate blueberry and laurel shrubs, the air heavy with the scent of foliage.

After we had walked for perhaps ten minutes, threading our way through and around shrubs and trees, Kuris ordered his two men to halt and wait for him, before carrying on into the forest. Like me he had shed his helmet and armour, being armed only with a bow and long knife. He squatted and picked up an acorn.

'The forest is rich in food for wildlife, majesty, and there are lots of not only deer here but also bears and squirrels.'

He stood and looked around at the greenery that surrounded us.

'We will find a place and wait for the prey to come to us.'

He moved deftly, lifting his boots high before stepping forward and being careful where he placed his foot. I stepped on a dry small branch and snapped it in two, the sound inordinately loud. Kuris froze and gave me a disapproving frown.

'Have a care, majesty,' he whispered.

We moved very slowly, quivers slung on our backs and arrows nocked in our bowstrings. The forest was full of noise – birds, the rustling of the wind through the forest canopy and the scurrying of squirrels through the undergrowth – but we were silent after crouching beside an ancient oak tree towering above us, its trunk thick and gnarled.

'What do you know of your king's intentions regarding Armenia?' I whispered.

'Nothing, majesty, I am a soldier and am not privy to the king's intentions.'

'All soldiers hear rumours about forthcoming wars and campaigns, Kuris, and I'm sure those of Gordyene are no different.'

He placed a finger to his lips to silence me. Clearly he would not divulge any information to me, not willingly anyway. His eyes narrowed as he scanned the terrain ahead, shards of sunlight making it difficult to spot anything moving. But Kuris had spotted something and so we crouched in silence, sweat running down my neck, a combination of the stifling heat in the forest and the anticipation of downing a deer.

I heard the beast before I saw it, the mere hint of dry leaves under a hoof as the beast approached. Then I spotted it, a magnificent male Caspian deer with huge antlers, its coat a dark brown, blending in perfectly with its surroundings.

The Caspian deer was indigenous to a great swathe of territory from the shores of the Caspian Sea, from where it got its name, to the alpine meadows of the Alborz Mountains, being plentiful in the oak forests it favoured. Subsisting on a diet of plants, shrubs, acorns and berries, Caspian males could grow to become magnificent specimens, and this particular one was a big beast. I estimated it to stand at least four feet at the shoulder and weigh well over five hundred pounds. It would feed many mouths. If Kuris could drop it.

'There are more behind,' he said in a barely audible whisper.

I peered ahead and saw he was right. I could see two, no three, other deer. Females, smaller but their flesh would taste just as good. He gave me a sideways smile and then forgot me as he went about his business. The male was leading his harem, which meant he was blocking any shot I might take against a female. Regardless of the animal being hunted, an archer strove to make a clean, fast kill, ideally by putting an arrow through the chest cavity. It was much the same on the battlefield against humans, though complicated by the 'prey' wanting to do the same to you.

The tension in the air was palpable as the stag stopped and looked directly at us. Had he spotted us, was he about to bolt? He was around thirty paces distant and Kuris had a clean shot. But he did not take it. Instead, he waited until the stag walked forward a few more paces, reducing the range to around twenty-five paces.

Twang.

The arrow hit the stag in the chest, causing him to lunge sideways. A second arrow was already in Kuris' bowstring when the male bolted away and the females followed. But not until he had hit another in the flank and I had put an arrow into the rump of a third. Kuris placed two fingers in his mouth and whistled to signal the two men with the horses to come forward, stringing another arrow in his bowstring before dashing forward. I followed, running through the undergrowth to trail the wounded animals. We found the male a mere

96

twenty paces or so from the place where he had been shot, blood oozing from the wound around the arrow, its lifeless corpse on the ground. We left him to pursue the two females, finding the one Kuris had hit collapsed and dying by the trunk of an oak. He slit its throat and followed me as I searched for the one I had shot.

We found it limping badly further on, grunting and having difficulty breathing. I put an arrow through its heart to end its misery. The other parties enjoyed similar success and after the Daughters of Dura had collected a great quantity of fallen branches for firewood and Bullus' men had skinned and butchered the carcasses, everyone ate their fill of venison. I sat with Gallia in front of one carcass being turned on a spit, the fire hissing when meat juices fell into the flames.

'I got nothing out of Kuris,' I complained, 'Spartacus has trained him well.'

Gallia smiled when one of her teenage protégés handed her a wooden bowl filled with sizzling meat.

'Gordyene is surrounded by hills and mountains to keep it remote, apart from other kingdoms. Its people are by their nature suspicious, distant.'

'Like their king,' I remarked.

She chewed on a piece of meat. 'It seems the fate of Gordyene is to either suffer invasion or strike first, with no third way. Of the two, I prefer the latter.'

A girl bowed and handed me a bowl of meat. 'You would, though I worry that now Gordyene is a major power in the north, Spartacus will be tempted to strike without provocation. After all, Van never belonged to Gordyene; it was always Armenian. I cannot criticise King Artaxias for taking back one of his cities.'

'Spartacus is not a fool,' she said, 'he knows that as much as we do. I'm sure with our gentle persuasion, war with Armenia can be avoided.'

We were both to be disappointed.

It took three days to ride through the mountain passes to reach Gordyene proper, and another day to enter the Pambak Valley where Vanadzor was located. The ancient city, nestled in the narrow vale, straddling the river of the same name, was once a small settlement on the west bank of the river, no more than a collection of wooden huts protected by a stake fence. But in time the wood had been replaced by stone as trade with Armenia and its southern neighbours had brought a degree of prosperity to the kingdom. That had been over a hundred years ago. Now the city was a great fortress and Spartacus had filled the Pambak Valley with other stone strongholds to guard the approaches to his city, all constructed from the dour, black stone used to build Vanadzor itself.

The Pambak Valley was a beautiful sight, full of flowers, the rivers and streams filled with ice-cold water from the mountains no longer capped with snow, their lower slopes basking in the warmth of the summer sun, though in Gordyene the heat never reached the heights found in the deserts to the south.

We followed a track that hugged the eastern bank of the river and then crossed a wooden bridge over the waterway. It was not wide at this point, around forty feet or so, the water below blue and crystal clear. I smiled to myself.

'Many years ago, commander,' I said to Kuris beside me, 'I rode along this track with my young squire, intent on insulting the occupants of Vanadzor and goading them into sending out a patrol to kill us. The city was occupied by the Romans at the time.'

'My grandfather once told me of that time, majesty,' he said.

I suddenly felt very old.

'Well, the Romans obliged and sent out a party of horsemen to apprehend us,' I continued, 'but we had arranged an ambush and wiped them out not far from this spot. You may be interested to know that the name of my squire was Surena, who later wore the crown of Gordyene.'

Kuris nodded approvingly. 'My father also once told me that Surena was a good king, majesty.'

'He was,' said Gallia, 'though a little hot-headed.'

'And killed by outsiders,' said Kuris, which also killed the conversation.

I was still smiling, thinking about that time when we had been bandits in the forests of Gordyene fighting the Roman occupiers. My smile disappeared when we came within sight of the city.

What is in a word? When is a legionary not a legionary? The simple answer in Gordyene was when he was an Immortal. As I rode towards the city a wondrous sight greeted me: ten thousand Immortals arrayed on parade to welcome us to Vanadzor. A neutral observer would have assumed the soldiers arrayed in perfect order were identical to Roman legionaries. But the King of Gordyene hated the Romans and so it was forbidden to call the ten thousand foot soldiers that marched, dressed and fought in a similar fashion to Rome's legions, legionaries. Cruel tongues remarked that Spartacus hated not only the Romans but also the whole world and everything in it. That was not quite right: he loved his wife, his children and his kingdom, though Akmon's 'betrayal' meant it would be a long time before his oldest son was forgiven. Claudia had once told me Spartacus was a brooding menace best left alone, an apt description of the former prince of Hatra. And if he had been content to sit in his palace in Vanadzor and ruminate then he could indeed be left alone. But he had been raised at a time when the empire was at war, both fighting external enemies and ripping itself apart in civil strife. He had seen at first hand the army of Dura training and fighting, and he himself when no more than a boy had fought at Carrhae, taking an eagle from the Romans so he could marry his beloved Rasha. Orodes had made him King of Gordyene, an appointment some frowned upon, but the former high king and my great friend saw huge potential in the angry young man who raged against the world. And Spartacus fulfilled that potential, turning Gordyene into a major power in the empire.

The instrument that transformed Gordyene's fortunes was drawn up in the Pambak Valley – the army that Spartacus had created and had used so effectively to establish his power in the north of the empire and win the favour of Phraates. Spartacus had an interesting relationship with the high king, seeing him as a source of gold to finance the equipping and services of his army. Phraates in turn was happy to hire the services of that army for it supported his strategic aims. To date, Spartacus had extorted or had been gifted, depending on one's point of view, thirteen hundred talents of gold – the equivalent of one hundred and thirty tons of the precious metal. Many kings would have used such a sum to dress themselves in rich clothes, decorate their palaces with fine works of art and hire poets, artists and sculptors to indulge their every whim. But Spartacus lavished his wealth on his army.

As Horns walked slowly along the lines of Immortals, I could immediately see changes in their uniform. Gone were the spears, leather cuirasses and leather greaves protecting their lower legs. In their place were javelins and mail armour, their heads still protected by helmets with large cheek and neck guards. At their hips were short swords, identical to the Roman *gladius*, though to even infer it risked a fine. The shields of the Immortals were also identical to the design of the Roman *scutum*, being large, curved and oval, faced with leather painted red, though with a silver lion's head design around the central boss. And now they had scorpion bolt throwers, a line of the wooden weapons deployed beyond the front ranks.

The Immortals formed a corridor through which we rode, at the end of which, a huge red banner bearing a lion billowing in the wind behind them, were Spartacus and Rasha, both seated on black horses. Nearby the rulers of Gordyene were the King's Guard and Vipers, a thousand professional riders, all highly trained and superbly equipped. Less highly trained, though effective enough if employed correctly, were Gordyene's lords and their retainers: men and women wearing little or no armour and equipped only with a bow and a dagger, a lucky few armed with swords.

A similarly ragtag group were the Sarmatians drawn up behind the Immortals. Members of the Aorsi tribe, they had first been invited to Gordyene by Surena, who had hit upon the idea of securing his northern border by populating that region with the Aorsi who in return for lands in northern Gordyene sent a portion of their plunder to Vanadzor. The Aorsi raided Armenian lands and had until recently been based in the city of Van, which had fallen to Spartacus following a brief war with Armenia. The Aorsi presented a sorry spectacle: a scruffy lot dressed in a myriad of different colours and wearing a mixture of mail and leather armour or no armour at all. They carried a mix of weapons, ranging from bows, spears, swords, maces and axes. They had poor discipline and were notorious for

101

brawling among themselves, though an observer would have noticed that every horse was well fed, groomed and looked in peak condition.

As we neared Spartacus and Rasha I saw with disappointment that the leader of the Aorsi, Spadines, was beside the king. He may have been the Prince of Van but he still looked like a horse thief, his thin face framed by wild hair and beard. I also saw the tall, dark and ugly figure of Shamshir in front of the King's Guard.

We halted our horses in front of Spartacus and Rasha, trumpeters on horseback sounding a fanfare as Rasha grinned at Gallia.

'Welcome, uncle, aunt,' said Spartacus after the trumpets had fallen silent, 'where are my parents?'

I pulled out a letter carrying a horse head seal and handed it to Spartacus.

'King Gafarn has a leg ulcer that prevents him from travelling,' I said, 'he asked me to give you this.'

Alarm showed in Spartacus' brown eyes and his square jaw locked.

'It is nothing serious,' Gallia reassured him, 'just a leg ulcer that requires rest and daily treatments.'

'I will pray for him,' said a concerned Rasha.

'You waste your time,' scoffed Spartacus, 'the gods are a mere fiction, invented by men to control other men.'

'Perhaps you could visit Hatra,' I suggested, 'my brother would be delighted to see you both, and you too, young princes.'

'We have to punish the Armenians first.'

It was the first time I could remember hearing Prince Castus speak, though no doubt as a child he had made his voice known on the occasions when we had been in his presence at Vanadzor, Hatra or Dura. As the second son he was given scant regard by those other than his parents, though now Akmon had departed Gordyene he was the heir to the throne and a young man of some importance. I studied him momentarily, this tall, handsome prince with a severe countenance not unlike his father's. But unlike his father, or mother for that matter, he had blue eyes and long dark blonde hair, setting him apart from his younger brother, Haytham, whose hair was as black as night.

'Punish them for what, Prince Castus?' I asked, already knowing the answer.

'Now is not the time to discuss such matters,' said Spartacus, 'our guests will be tired after their journey. Please, aunt and uncle, avail yourselves of our hospitality.'

To be fair he appeared to be in a convivial mood as he and Rasha rode beside us the short distance to the city gates and on to the palace. Shamshir and his King's Guard, Kuris and his men joining them, rode into the city to clear a path through the curious crowd that had gathered to see the King and Queen of Dura. There was no cheering, shouting or waving of hands, for the people of Gordyene are a dour lot, their land subjected to extremes of weather, especially in winter when high winds from the north bring blizzards and thick snow. But they are also hardy and with the right training and weapons can be turned into formidable soldiers.

The buildings in Vanadzor were squat and ugly, words used by unkind individuals to describe the people who inhabited them. The city walls and buildings were constructed from local black limestone, giving the city a rather bleak and forbidding appearance, especially in winter when the Pambak Valley became a dour, cold and snow-covered place. No thought had been given to making the city's palace an attractive place, its high, black walls, round towers at each corner, and its three-storey gatehouse having no grace or beauty, though at least the latter had been decorated with red lion banners to lessen its ugliness. The city walls and palace projected strength and power, as did the gates to the palace, constructed as they were of thick oak reinforced with iron spikes and bars.

A welcome bath and change of clothes brought relief to our tired limbs, and that evening Spartacus and Rasha were the perfect hosts as they laid on a lavish feast, Lucius and Bullus joining us at the top table, the palace's hall filled with the city's nobility and the army's senior officers. Spadines also sat at the top table, a score of his senior officers, if such posts existed among the Aorsi, gorging themselves on food and drink on a nearby table. The Sarmatian said nothing to me and I in turn ignored him. I saw him as the spark that might ignite a war between Rome and Parthia, and I'm sure he in turn regarded me as an unwelcome restraint on his friend and lord, Spartacus.

He was also present the next day when we met in the same hall to discuss the reason for our arrival in Vanadzor. The previous evening had been a riotous affair, the Sarmatians drinking too much and making fools of themselves, with their endless toasts to Spartacus and Rasha and pledges to die in their service. Despite the burning of incense to banish the unpleasant aroma of sweat, leather, meat juices, spilt drink and vomit, the chamber was still slightly rank. At least Spartacus was relaxed as he sat next to his wife, his two sons flanking them.

'So, uncle,' he said, slaves nearby scraping dried vomit off the stone tiles, 'I assume you have come to Gordyene to deliver sage advice.'

I gave Spadines a disparaging look.

'I will come straight to the point. I assume the army arrayed in front of the city yesterday was not for our benefit. Your father is of the opinion, as am I, that launching a war against Armenia is a mistake.'

Spartacus poured himself a cup of water.

'Armenia has attacked Gordyene's most valued ally. As such, I have no choice but to support Prince Spadines, for it was agreed long ago that an attack on either the Aorsi or Gordyene would be considered an assault on both.'

'How convenient,' I said, 'though how can the liberation of an Armenian city by King Artaxias be considered an act of aggression.'

'Van is an Aorsi city,' insisted Spadines angrily, his spittle showering the table.

I sighed. 'We all know it has nothing to do with the Sarmatians, who I believe have traditionally inhabited the lands around the Caspian Sea, over two hundred miles from Van.'

'Armenia insults us,' said Castus, 'and insults must be answered.'

Spadines roared his approval and slammed his fist on the table. Gallia rolled her eyes.

'How did the Armenians retake their city?' she asked Spadines. 'I have heard it has strong defences.'

'There is no point picking over the past, aunt,' said Spartacus. 'I will march against Artaxias for his discourtesy in attacking my Aorsi allies.'

'The same allies that are attacking Pontus?' said Gallia.

I noticed an exchange of glances between Spartacus and Spadines, but the latter said nothing.

'Allow me to expand on what my wife has said,' I smiled. 'The governor of Syria was recently at Dura, a charming man who is facilitating the improvement of relations between Parthia and Rome.'

Spartacus was staring into space, seemingly uninterested. Rasha looking concerned and her two sons bored.

'The governor informed me that if these raids against Pontus continue, then Octavian will retaliate, as Pontus is a client kingdom of Rome.'

'Slave kingdom, you mean,' grunted Spartacus.

'It is as you say,' agreed Gallia, 'but that does not change the fact Rome will strike against you if these raids continue.'

I confronted Spadines. 'What do you have to say, *prince*?'

'The strong prey on the weak,' he grinned.

'Is this what Gordyene has become,' I said in exasperation, 'a kingdom that inflicts misery and war on its neighbours for sport?'

'Gordyene is the northern shield of the empire,' stated Spartacus.

'It gives the impression of being more of a spear,' said Gallia.

'You must desist the raids against Pontus,' I said bluntly. 'Parthia does not want another war with Rome, especially one caused by the depredations of a bunch of vagrant Sarmatians.'

Spadines jumped up. 'You insult me.'

'Is it possible to insult a Sarmatian?' I asked.

Spartacus calmly indicated Spadines should sit down, leaning back and bringing his hands together.

'I am a reasonable man, uncle, and have no reason to provoke a war between Parthia and Rome. I will make you this bargain. The raids against Pontus will cease, you have my word.'

'I must object, lord,' protested Spadines. Spartacus ignored him as his gaze held mine.

'In return,' said Spartacus, 'Dura and Hatra will support my punitive campaign against Artaxias of Armenia.'

'Our best horsemen are in the east,' I replied, 'and my legions are three hundred miles to the south. There is no way I or your father can reinforce your army.'

A mischievous glint appeared in Spartacus' eye.

'I do not need your soldiers, uncle, or those of Hatra for that matter. What I need is your assurance you and my father will support Gordyene when King Artaxias goes whining to Phraates.'

'Only if you guarantee not to annex any Armenian territory,' I shot back.

'Van is mine,' bleated Spadines.

'The Armenians must make restitution for the distress they have caused Prince Spadines,' said Spartacus.

'You are intent on war, then?' I asked.

'I am.'

'As am I,' said Spadines.

'And is it a war of conquest?' asked Gallia.

'No,' said Rasha firmly. 'I will not lose another child.'

Claudia had told me how she had 'cured' Prince Haytham after he had fallen ill, though her remedy was to convince Spartacus to abandon his plans to absorb Media into his own realm. I seemed to remember her talking about the legend of Gordis but my memory was not what it was and I could not recollect the precise details.

'We will not offend the gods,' she said.

Spadines gave her a quizzical look but I noticed Spartacus just stared at the table top, saying nothing.

'Armenia is currently beholden to Parthia for freeing it of Roman subjugation,' I said, 'but if you embark on a campaign to humiliate and plunder his kingdom, Artaxias might be tempted to rethink his relationship with Rome.'

'The Romans murdered his family,' said Castus. 'Why would he side with them?'

'You are only half-right, prince,' I told him. 'The family of Artaxias were taken hostage by Mark Antony and transported to Alexandria where they were murdered. Mark Antony is dead and Octavian, a leader who is radically different from the *triumvir*, now rules the Roman world. For one thing, he does not murder the family members of rivals.'

'Then he is weak,' sneered Spadines.

His mere presence was irritating me immensely but I kept my temper in check.

'Acting like an uncivilised barbarian is not strength, prince. You may think that Pontus is your plaything, but if you provoke a Roman response you will find Octavian will marshal the full strength of the Roman world against you. Remind me, how many men do you command? Four thousand, five? The Romans can raise one hundred thousand soldiers with ease.'

Spadines grinned, to reveal stained, uneven teeth. 'But behind the Aorsi stands King Spartacus, and behind him all Parthia.'

'Parthia will not support a war of aggression against Armenia,' I told him, 'especially as Armenia is an ally of High King Phraates. If Armenia threatened Gordyene then Parthia would indeed come its aid, but this campaign is nothing more than one of retribution.'

'You are right, uncle,' agreed Spartacus. 'Dura is fortunate to have friends and allies for its neighbours, but Gordyene only has the Aorsi and I will not abandon them.'

It made sense. For years Media had raided Gordyene when Darius had been its king, and when Armenia had been strong it had posed a threat to Gordyene's northern border. But now it was weak and I worried Spartacus would take advantage of that weakness to plunder Armenia and leave a legacy of lasting animosity towards Parthia that Octavian, despite him favouring diplomacy over war, would take advantage of.

'All I would ask,' I said, 'is that any campaign is of a short duration, for the longer you occupy Armenian territory the more lasting damage you will do.'

'We go to clip the wings of King Artaxias, uncle,' stated Spartacus, 'nothing more.'

'Why don't you come with us?' said Castus. 'Our victory would be assured with the famous King Pacorus by our side.'

Gallia laughed and reached over to squeeze his arm in congratulation and Spartacus looked at me expectantly.

'A most inviting offer, prince,' I replied, 'but my army is not here and besides, your father is younger and more able then me. I would just slow you down. However, be assured that if Armenia violates Gordyene's border, then Dura's army will march north to support its king and queen.'

'You are becoming an adept diplomat, uncle,' said Spartacus, 'is that what happens to old soldiers?'

'Old soldiers thank the gods they have reached their autumn years,' I replied, 'and are most reluctant to embark on unnecessary wars. You should all remember that most wars are started by old men but fought by young men.'

I looked at Spadines. 'How old are you, prince?'

He thumped his chest. 'Fifty-eight and still capable of bedding a maiden all night and fighting a battle the next day.'

Gallia sighed disapprovingly and Rasha shifted uncomfortably in her chair.

'My point exactly,' I said.

Gordyene's army set out the next morning, the Immortals marching six abreast as they headed north, Spartacus' scouts having left before dawn with Spadines and his Aorsi to reconnoitre the route the army would take. It was more an exercise in logistics, to plan how twenty thousand soldiers and hundreds of packhorses and carts would negotiate the mountain passes in northern Gordyene. This would mean dividing the army into separate parts, thus increasing its vulnerability, though I doubted there were any Armenian troops anywhere near the border lands.

Kuris was left as commander of Vanadzor's garrison, which comprised the unit that was responsible for the induction and training of new recruits into Gordyene's army. At Dura it was called the replacement cohort but at Vanadzor such Roman terminology was banned and so the formation was called the replacement battalion. As in the famed Immortals who guarded the Persian kings before Parthia even existed, ten men formed a company; ten companies formed a battalion, ten battalions a division, and ten divisions a corps. Kuris could also summon army veterans from the city and outlying towns and villages to the colours if need arose, though that scenario was highly unlikely.

We rode with Spartacus and Rasha from the city towards the track we had taken to reach Vanadzor, the King's Guard following and behind them the Vipers. Red lion banners billowed in the wind as the Immortals tramped north. The vast collection of tents around the city had disappeared, the swathes of flattened grass the only evidence of their presence. Castus and Haytham chatted with the brooding Shamshir as they waited for their father to say his goodbyes.

I extended an arm to him. 'Keep safe and return with all your family.'

He reached over to clasp my forearm. 'I will keep my word about preventing the Aorsi from raiding Pontus. I have no desire to see Roman soldiers marching against Parthia.'

Gallia embraced Rasha and I kissed the Queen of Gordyene on the cheek.

'Try to act as a restraint on him,' I said, looking at Spartacus embracing his aunt before wheeling his horse away.

'On *them*,' she said. 'Castus and Haytham are eager to share in their father's glory.'

'I remember when I thought like them,' I smiled, recalling the time I had captured a Roman eagle in my youth. Then the memory of my capture in Cappadocia and subsequent enslavement flashed through my mind. 'It resulted in me becoming a Roman slave. Youth is like a sword blade that has yet to be tempered.'

'I will try my best to ensure Armenia is not humiliated,' she said.

'The gods be with you, Rasha.'

She turned her horse and galloped to catch up with her husband, the King's Guard and Vipers following. I smiled to myself.

Gordyene would try not to humiliate Armenia. How times had changed. Once Armenia was a major power and Gordyene was an insignificant kingdom on its southern border. Now, thanks to the efforts of Spartacus, the army of Gordyene was the power broker in these parts. I took comfort that he had kept his notorious temper in check and appeared to be more considered in his opinions. Perhaps he was finally maturing into a well-rounded ruler.

'Let's hope so,' I said to myself.

I sat with Gallia watching Spartacus and Rasha grow smaller and smaller as they headed north with their escort, the last of the Immortals forming the rear of a huge black and red column that snaked through the Pambak. I stared up at the sky dotted with puffy white clouds. It was pleasantly warm with a nice breeze – ideal campaigning weather. The gods seemed to be smiling on Gordyene.

'Time to go,' I said.

I nudged Horns ahead. Lucius sitting on his horse nearby gave the signal for our own escort to move, and we began the journey back to Dura.

Chapter 5

The forests of Gordyene are beautiful in the summer, the air filled with the woody scents of pine, juniper, spruce and fir. Honeysuckle clambers up trees, white dog roses illuminate the forest floor, and oak moss, a greenish-silver lichen, clings to oak trees. By streams and rivers grows mint, and between the trees are stretches of camomile, which when trampled on by horses' hooves emit a sweet, fruity apple-like scent that is most pleasing to the senses.

The sun shone through the forest canopy to warm our faces, the air was sweet and the streams filled with crystal-clear water, and yet I felt dejected. I had failed to persuade Spartacus to refrain from attacking Armenia, though at least he had promised to halt the raids against Pontus. But while his wretched Aorsi allies still inhabited his northern borderlands, the threat to Pontus still existed, and with it the possibility of it causing trouble between Parthia and Rome.

We moved slowly through the landscape, as there was no rush to reach Hatra to inform Gafarn and Diana of my failure.

'What did you expect?' said Gallia, reading my thoughts.

We had camped near a wide stream in the middle of an ancient and large oak and beech forest, the camp alive with the sound of activity as horses were unsaddled and rubbed down, camels corralled and tents erected. I was rubbing Horns down with a brush; having examined his hooves to ensure none of his shoes was loose. Gallia was doing the same with her mare, Daughters of Dura erecting temporary stables with poles and canvas around us. Bullus, having established a perimeter of guards, prowled the camp like a wolf hunting for prey, berating anyone who appeared to be idling.

113

'In truth, nothing, but I had hoped our presence might have sowed the seeds of doubt in his mind.'

She took a nosebag from a waiting female squire and attached it to her mare.

'There is no doubt in Spartacus' mind. His world is black and white. You are either for him or against him.'

I finished brushing Horns and fitted his nosebag containing fodder.

'It would help if he was not surrounded by those wretched Aorsi.'

'Those "wretched Aorsi" are the only people Spartacus truly trusts, Pacorus. It will not be lost on him that when Orodes marched against Surena, only the Sarmatians stood by him.'

'That was a different time,' I said dismissively.

'They have long memories in Gordyene.'

One of the Amazons had downed a large stag that morning and Zenobia had gifted the carcass to the queen to enjoy as an evening meal. So we invited her to dine with us, along with Bullus and Lucius, the former ill at ease in the company of royalty and so once again said almost nothing as we took our seats. The night was warm and pleasant, the air filled with the delightful aroma of pine, juniper and cooking meat.

'We have a guest,' said Gallia sitting opposite, looking past me.

I turned to see a boy, no more than ten years old, his feet bare, standing behind me. In the light of the oil lamps in the tent he had golden hair and piercing blue eyes.

Lucius jumped up. 'Are your sentries asleep, centurion?'

Bullus rose and drew his sword.

'No, no,' I commanded, 'stand at ease and put your sword away. We do not murder children.'

Gallia smiled at the boy, who was dressed in a white tunic fringed with silver. He smiled back at her.

'Greetings, Queen Gallia, King Pacorus. My master invites you to dine with him tonight. His camp is just a short distance from here.'

Bullus gave a low chortle. 'Be on your way, boy, before I take my cane to you. There's no camp within a mile of our own.'

The boy ignored him. 'It will require only a short walk, majesties.'

'What is the name of your master?' asked Zenobia.

'The lord of justice,' came the reply.

Bullus guffawed. 'He is obviously mad, majesty. Let me beat him out of camp.'

'My lord has information about Irbil, majesty,' he said to me, his voice full of authority despite his young age.

I grew concerned. 'What do you know about Irbil?'

'I know nothing, majesty,' he replied calmly, 'only that Irbil is in danger, son of Hatra.'

A chill danced down my spine. There was something odd about this boy and his last three words confirmed it. I looked at Gallia who wore a severe countenance. The look in her eyes told me all I needed to know.

'You say your lord's camp is near?'

'No more than five minutes away, majesty.'

'Impossible,' snapped Lucius, 'we would have seen the campfires and heard the sounds of men and horses.'

Gallia nodded to me.

'Then lead on,' I said, to the astonishment of our guests.

115

'I will organise an escort,' said Lucius.

The boy rounded on him. 'No escort, Roman, the king and queen will be safe in my lord's care.'

How did he know Lucius was Roman?

'We will be quite safe, Lucius,' I said.

Despite further protestations from Zenobia and Bullus, we followed the boy from our tent, walking through the camp seemingly invisible. No one noticed their king and queen following a barefoot boy among them. We reached the perimeter where Bullus' legionaries patrolled, passing through them like ghosts, unseen. There were no sounds in the forest as we followed our young guide through trees illuminated by silver moonlight flooding through gaps in the canopy above. We carried no weapons but I sensed no threat; indeed, I felt very at ease. The air was sweet and the ground soft underfoot. I could see no camp ahead, though, and as we ventured deeper into the forest I wondered if we were the willing victims of dark sorcery. I started to panic and grabbed Gallia's hand, ready to turn around and race back to camp, cursing myself we had brought nothing to defend ourselves with.

'We are here,' said the boy.

Seemingly out of nowhere a camp materialised. A fire burned in front of us and beyond it were five tents, each one of a different shape and colour. One was round, another square, the one nearest to us was rectangular and a fourth had an arched roof. The largest tent was like a miniature royal pavilion with a central entrance and a high roof.

'Welcome, welcome.'

A figure appeared out of nowhere on our left, a tall man with a long face carrying a spade, a snake dragon motif on his robes that would not have looked out of place on a king. He smiled at us and bowed his head.

'Please accept my apologies, camp duties, you understand.'

The spade he was carrying appeared to have a silver blade and looked as though it had never touched any dirt.

'You must be famished,' he smiled, 'please avail yourselves of our hospitality.'

Whoever he was he had an amazing ability to put people at ease, his eyes filled with kindness, his voice soft and warm. So calming was his effect on us that we never asked him his name as he led us towards the pavilion, passing his spade to a handsome young man in a pure white tunic.

We followed him into the tent, the interior of which was lavishly decorated with plush carpets on the ground, silver oil lamps and large, luxurious couches, upon which sat four individuals. They all stood when they saw us, three of them smiling and the fourth viewing us with angry eyes. My own eyes were drawn to the only female in the group, a stunningly beautiful woman with a voluptuous body. Her skin-tight robe barely concealed her large breasts, though despite her ample chest there appeared to be not an ounce of fat on her. Her light brown eyes lit up when she saw Gallia, gliding over to grip my wife's hands.

'It is so good to meet you at long last, warrior queen.'

Gallia had always been a striking woman, and she could still turn heads, but against this beauty she paled. Not into insignificance but certainly into a distant second place.

'Forgive me, but I do not know your name,' said Gallia.

'Her name is Ishtar.'

The man who spoke was the oldest in the group who wore a horned headdress. He stood tall, aloof from the rest, his long robes white as the driven snow, his skin a dark olive brown. There were flecks of grey in his neatly trimmed beard and he wore a large gold signet ring on the smallest finger of his right hand. I could not see the crest carved on it. Before either Gallia or I could respond he beckoned us over to the two vacant couches.

'Drinks for our guests.'

'About time,' said the stocky man with a short, wide face who was wearing a curved sword at his waist. 'I'm starving.'

'You must forgive Erra,' smiled his companion, 'his temper is shorter than his height.'

I sat myself on a couch. 'Erra? You are named after the God of Death, War and Destruction.'

Erra frowned at me. 'Named after?'

His companion, a man with pure white hair and light skin, giving him the appearance of an albino, rolled his pale eyes.

'Hurry with those drinks.'

Young men with perfect skin and pristine white tunics served us wine in gold chalices. I wanted to stare at the one named Ishtar but my eyes were drawn to the albino's armour. I was well acquainted with dragon-skin armour but this was unlike any I had seen before. Every scale on his cuirass shone like a thousand suns, the colour alternating between silver and gold. It must have cost a large fortune to produce such armour.

The elderly man retook his couch and shook his head disapprovingly.

'I hope you are not going to get drunk, Erra.'

I sipped at the wine, or at least I think it was wine because it was unlike anything I had tasted before. The beverage was sweet and red in appearance, but when I swallowed a warm, tingly sensation went down my throat and into my stomach. It was not unpleasant, far from it, more invigorating and I took a large gulp. It was as if my insides were being cleaned and renovated at the same time. I could feel my limbs being energised and my senses heightened. The only other time I had felt this alive and enthused with energy was in the midst of battle. I glanced at Gallia and saw her blue eyes sparkling. She too was obviously benefiting from the drink.

'This is a fine wine,' I said.

'It is not wine,' said Ishtar, 'more an elixir.'

'More for our guests,' roared Erra, emptying his cup in one gulp.

Our cups were refilled and I drank the strange elixir once more. Any aches and pains in my leg disappeared and I felt ten, twenty, years younger. I caught the eye of the pale man.

'Fine armour.'

'Would you like one like it? I will make you one.'

'Girra is very skilled with his hands,' said the leader of the group.

I took another gulp. 'Girra, the God of Light and Fire? I do not appreciate taking the names of the gods in vain.'

'Nor do we,' remarked the man with the snake dragon motif on his robe.

'Don't tell me,' I said, 'you are Marduk, the deity of Babylon, whose symbols are the snake dragon and spade.'

'He is,' said the elderly man with the horned headdress.

I guffawed loudly and Gallia giggled like a little girl. We had obviously been the victims of a tawdry deception, but such was my intoxicated, or exhilarated, state that I did not take offence.

Gallia pointed at the elderly man who had a tolerant, generous bearing. Her cheeks were flushed and she could not stop smiling.

'And you must be Shamash, the Sun God.'

'And I am very pleased to meet you, Queen Gallia,' he said without a trace of sarcasm.

Gallia looked at me and we began laughing, followed by the others. It was a monstrous joke and high sacrilege but such was our state of mild delirium that we only saw the humour in their deception. Beautiful young women, scantily dressed with taut bodies, green or blue eyes and wearing a scent that could only be described as divine, served the food. Silver trays loaded with fruit, pastries and sweet meats were proffered, the pastries melting in the mouth, the fruit sweet and nourishing and the meats mouth-watering.

'I told you this would be a waste of time. What do you expect of mortals?' sneered Erra.

'These are not just any mortals,' said Ishtar. 'They have rendered great service to us and should be treated with respect. King Pacorus saved my temple from being plundered in Babylon.'

She gave me a dazzling smile. 'For which I am eternally grateful.'

A servant refilled my cup with the elixir. I drank greedily and felt my very soul being refreshed.

'You ride back to Dura?' asked the man masquerading as Shamash.

'Stopping off at Hatra on the way,' I told him.

Erra flashed an evil grin. 'Let me tell him.'

120

'No,' said the elderly man, his voice powerful and stern.

'How many soldiers are with you, King Pacorus?' Shamash asked.

'A hundred Amazons and the same number of mounted legionaries,' I told him.

'Plus fifty female squires,' said Gallia.

'They don't count,' sneered Erra.

'Why?' snapped Ishtar. 'Because they are women?'

'Because they are *girls*,' he replied.

'Girls who can all use a bow,' said Gallia.

'And an arrow shot by a girl can kill just as effectively as one shot by a powerful man,' said Girra.

'Marduk' looked glum. 'It is not much of an army.'

The elderly man stared directly at me, his brown eyes boring into me. I suddenly felt naked and uncomfortable.

'An army approaches Irbil, King Pacorus, do you know this?'

'No, lord.'

I do not know why I called him 'lord', but it seemed right that I should do so.

'What army?' asked Gallia. 'We have peace with the Romans and the Armenians are fully occupied with Spartacus, or will be.'

Girra clapped his hands. 'You are among the best generals in Parthia.'

'In the world,' smiled Ishtar.

'You are correct in what you say, Queen Gallia,' said the elderly man, 'but this army is neither Roman nor Armenian. It is a mixed force of mercenaries and rebels and seeks to depose and kill King Akmon and Queen Lusin.'

'Who leads this army?' I demanded to know.

'The man you should have killed months ago,' said Erra.

'Prince Atrax,' Marduk informed me.

'The one Claudia warned you about,' added Girra.

'Prince Atrax is a landless prince,' I told him dismissively, 'who is living a dissolute life in Zeugma.'

The elderly man wagged a finger at me. 'He left Zeugma weeks ago to journey north to the court of King Artaxias, there to lobby the ruler of Armenia for troops to support his legitimate claim to the throne of Media.'

I stood, spilling my drink on the carpet.

'Atrax has no claim on Media's crown. King of Kings Phraates personally made Akmon the ruler of Media, and as such has the full backing of Ctesiphon and the rest of the empire.'

'Sit down, Pacorus,' hissed Gallia.

'You have a choice, both of you,' said 'Shamash' as I sat back down on the couch. 'You can ride back to Dura via Hatra and abandon Akmon and Lusin to their fate, or you can ride directly to Irbil and warn them of the approach of their executioners.'

'Or ride to the nearest post station and despatch letters to Hatra, Atropaiene, Babylon and Susiana to send horsemen to Media,' proposed Gallia.

'The letters will not reach their destinations,' said Girra, 'for Atrax's allies have agents in all the post stations along Media's border and watch all crossing points over the Tigris.'

'Then we will ride directly to Hatra and marshal the strength of that kingdom to save Akmon and Lusin,' I said smugly.

Shamash nodded sagely. 'That would be the most logical course of action, but if you implement it the cost will be the death of King Gafarn.'

'He will not be swayed in his determination to ride with you,' said Marduk.

'His leg wound will worsen,' Ishtar told me, 'and the infection will spread throughout his body and death will surely follow.'

I caught the eye of our host. 'The decision lies with you two.'

'Only Hatra's strength can save Irbil,' announced Erra. 'What is the death of another king weighed against the stability of the empire?'

I looked around at the plush surroundings and immaculately dressed servants.

'Easy to say when it is not your life in danger.'

He bristled at my words. 'Have a care, mortal, you might not live to see the end of this night.'

'I've never fought a god before,' I replied caustically.

He leapt from his couch in a lightning-fast fashion, to stand over me with his sword drawn, the cool blade at my throat. I had never seen a man move so quickly. But Gallia was also not tardy, tossing aside her cup to stand, rush over, pull the dagger hanging from Erra's belt and hold the blade to his throat.

'You fight my husband, you fight me.'

'Halt!'

He may have been the oldest among us but our host's voice hurt my ears as his command shot through the air. The dagger seemed to leap from Gallia's clutch and Erra winced in pain as he dropped his sword. Ishtar came forward to escort Gallia back to her couch.

'He is such a bully, the result of being the lord of war and death, I suppose.'

'Are you unhurt, King Pacorus?' asked the pale man.

123

'Yes, thank you.'

Erra picked up his sword and returned to his couch, rage etched on his face. Marduk gave me a reassuring smile.

'May I ask your intentions?' asked our host, his voice calm once again.

'To think on what you have told me,' I replied, 'for there is no proof that what I have heard is the truth, no disrespect intended.'

'Feisty mortal, isn't he,' growled Erra.

'You are right to be sceptical,' smiled Marduk, 'but why would we invent such a story, King Pacorus?'

'Let me ask you a question, then,' said our host. 'Do you think the loss of Van hurt Armenian pride?'

'Yes.'

'That being the case, its recapture has greatly increased the popularity of King Artaxias among his own people. They are united behind him, which Spartacus will soon discover. But the resentment felt by the Armenian people towards the King of Gordyene meant Prince Atrax's plan met with a receptive ear.'

'Will Spartacus be hurt?' asked Gallia with concern.

'It will take more than King Artaxias to kill the lion of Gordyene,' Ishtar reassured her.

'But he can be wounded,' said our host, 'and what better way than to kill his oldest son? Quite clever, really.'

They all looked at me. The leader with the horned headdress, the voluptuous woman, the angry bull, the man we had seen with a spade, and the white-haired man with shining armour.

'Only you can save him,' said our host.

'If you have the courage,' Erra taunted me.

124

'Or the inclination,' remarked Marduk. 'For if any man deserves to see out his autumn years in peace it is you, King Pacorus.'

'He will go,' smiled Girra. 'He is a man of honour.'

A servant refilled my cup and I sipped at the liquid, glancing at Gallia who looked ten years younger. Clearly the drink had a high alcoholic content because my eyes were playing tricks on me.

'It is no trick,' said our host.

This was getting mildly alarming. How did he read my mind? Did I imagine what he had just said?

'We will go,' announced Gallia.

Ishtar gave a triumphant laugh and our host nodded approvingly.

'Your wife speaks for you?' snapped Erra.

'Apparently,' I replied dryly. 'It is getting late and we now have a hard ride tomorrow. I do not suppose you have any information on the strength and disposition of the force approaching Irbil?'

'You will know soon enough,' smirked Erra.

I stood and held out my hand to Gallia, who rose and took it.

'Then I thank you for your hospitality and bid you all good evening.'

Our host clapped his hand to bring forth the boy who had escorted us to the camp.

'The king and queen are leaving.'

Ishtar rose from her couch to embrace Gallia and plant a kiss on my cheek, my nostrils filling with her alluring, intoxicating perfume.

'Because you saved my temple in Babylon from being plundered, I had Girra make you both a gift,' she told us.

'You will both benefit from the beverage you have been drinking,' remarked our host as we left the pavilion, 'for a while, at least.'

My head swirling, we left their company to walk into the warm night air. The forest was alive with noise, crickets sounding very loud and the nocturnal animals crushing dried leaves as they moved. I heard and saw everything and smelled all. Gallia grabbed my arm and looked around the camp.

'There are no horses,' she said.

She was right. There was no sign of a horse or a camel. The fire was still burning but there was no one to tend it. Indeed, there were no signs of human life at all: no guards, no squires and no servants.

'Follow me, please,' said the boy.

We retraced our steps back to our own camp, the boy stopping and pointing to the flicker of flames among the trees.

'Your camp, majesties.'

I turned to thank him but he had disappeared into the blackness of the forest. Gallia shrugged and we carried on the short distance, to be halted by a curt voice.

'Step forward and identify yourselves.'

The soldier had his shield in front of his body and his javelin held at the ready. We raised our hands and walked slowly out of the darkness.

'Pacorus, King of Dura,' I said.

'Gallia, Queen of Dura.'

The soldier went down on one knee.

'Apologies, majesties, I did not recognise you.'

'Get up,' I ordered, 'there is no need to apologise for diligence.'

The legionary turned and bellowed at the top of his voice.

'The king and queen have returned.'

In moments Lucius and Bullus were before us, the latter with *gladius* in hand scouring the forest behind us.

'Do you want me to send out a patrol to hunt down the little bastard, majesty? He is obviously mad.'

'Why do you say that?' demanded Gallia.

The centurion stared at her in disbelief. 'For leading you on a wild goose chase, majesty.'

'Did he run off the moment you left camp, majesty?' asked Lucius.

Had they been drinking?

'Why do you say that?'

'Because you have only been gone about ten minutes.'

I was going to tell him he was a fool because we had been gone for at least two hours, perhaps longer. But Gallia caught my eye and shook her head.

'It is late and I am tired,' she said, giving a false yawn.

Lucius escorted us back to our tent and bid us goodnight, leaving Bullus to stalk the perimeter looking for an inattentive guard to strike with his cane. But we were not tired, far from it, and so I ordered wine to be brought to our tent as we mulled over the evening's experience. We both skirted around the meat of the subject, until Gallia grabbed my arms and stared into my eyes. Despite the lateness of the hour her eyes were a sparkling blue, bluer than I had ever seen them.

'They were gods, Pacorus, or was I dreaming?'

127

I grinned like a naughty child. 'There can be no other explanation. But they looked…'

'Just like us?'

I nodded. The guards at the entrance called that the wine had arrived, a legionary entering the tent to place a jug and two wooden cups on the table. I filled them and handed one to Gallia.

'To our good fortune in the war to come.'

I took a sip and spat it out. It tasted like vinegar. Gallia grimaced but refrained from such an unladylike gesture.

'It tastes disgusting,' I moaned.

'Compared to what we were served with earlier, yes.' She giggled. 'I feel strange.'

'Sleepy?'

'Not a bit.'

I felt my loins stir. 'Then we must think of something to pass the time.'

She pulled me to her and kissed me hard on the lips, pressing her thighs into mine.

'Excellent idea.'

We pulled and ripped at each other's clothing as we stumbled to the sleeping area, which was separated from the main compartment by a curtain. We laughed as we tried to keep our lips locked together while removing our boots, failing miserably. We tumbled onto our cot and both leapt from it in alarm.

'What in the name of the gods is that?'

Something large, wrapped in a soft leather cover, lay on the cot. I went to touch it.

'No,' cried Gallia, 'it might be a snake.'

Half-naked, I rushed back to retrieve my sword, pulling it from the sheath and jabbing the leather with the point. There was no movement.

'If it was a snake, it would have moved by now.'

'Then what is it?' she said.

I used the point to lift up the leather, to reveal something metal beneath. Forgetting all about a snake, Gallia ripped open the leather cover and picked up an armoured cuirass, which was identical to the one Girra had been wearing earlier.

'Dragon-skin armour,' she cooed.

There were two suits, each as light as a feather and covered with metal scales. Normal dragon-skin armour comprised a thick leather vest covered with overlapping silver plates that had been stitched on to protect the chest and back. Like all scale armour it was bulky and heavy, but these cuirasses were light to hold, the leather soft as a baby's skin and thin, the metal polished but unlike silver. We admired our gifts and tried them on. They were a perfect fit, Gallia's shaped perfectly to accommodate her breasts.

'A gift from the gods indeed,' she beamed.

We made love in the armour, our bodies contorting into shapes not seen since the heady days of Italy when we had been young and free but always within a hair's breadth of being captured and crucified. The threat of imminent death made us live life to the full and sharpened our survival instincts. Afterwards we had faced dangers and travails aplenty, it was true, but in Italy we were young and had no ties. Over the years our lust for each other had given way to a deep love and mutual respect. But after our strange meeting our minds and bodies were once again flushed with youthful lust and energy. We did not sleep at all, wiping each other down with towels after our exertions. Just before dawn we donned our clothes and new armour and walked around the camp, which was coming to life as a new day was being born. Guards were being relieved and breakfast prepared. Men stretched their limbs, women brushed their hair before platting it in preparation for the day's ride, and Bullus still stalked the camp.

'Do you think he was given some of the gods' elixir,' grinned Gallia.

I felt my chin, which needed a shave. 'No, his power comes from the vine cane he carries. Power and authority are powerful stimulants.'

After breakfast I called him and Lucius to our tent, which was being dismantled as we spoke outside the pile of collapsed woven goat's hair.

'We are riding to Irbil,' I told them.

'It is in danger,' added Gallia.

'We are only two hundred, majesty,' said a concerned Lucius. 'Would it not be better to ride to Hatra and gather King Gafarn's forces?'

'That is not possible,' I said.

Bullus raised an eyebrow but kept his counsel.

'You have something to say, centurion?' I asked.

'We could send a rider to Dura to fetch General Chrestus and the rest of the army, majesty.'

'I will be frank, centurion. That fat drunkard Cookes controls all the post stations and the river crossings over the Tigris. Any courier I despatch I will sending to his or her death.'

Lucius was perplexed. 'How did you obtain this information, majesty?'

'From friends,' Gallia told him.

'Do they have any troops we can borrow?' queried Bullus.

Chapter 6

We rode directly to Irbil, passing deserted villages and fields overgrown and choked with weeds. Many of the mud-brick buildings were scorched and without roofs, the result of Spartacus' invasion and the subsequent plundering of the country. He had defeated Darius at the Battle of Mepsila and then laid siege to Irbil when Darius had declared war on Gordyene and Hatra. But he had been manipulated into that disastrous decision by my wife, Diana and Rasha, much to Media's cost.

We trotted through a deserted, plundered village, its inhabitants either fled, butchered or taken and sold into slavery. The dozen or so huts and two warehouses were burnt-out husks, the animal pens empty and the well in the centre of the settlement destroyed. Like hundreds of other villages in Media, it was sited to take advantage of the underground water sources that blessed the kingdom. I glanced at Gallia as we trotted through the forlorn village.

'Do you regret bringing about the war between Media, Gordyene and Hatra?'

She stared ahead. 'No.'

'It is a shame to see so much devastation,' remarked Lucius riding behind us.

We left the settlement and followed the track through a large apple orchard, now sadly neglected. Like many other villages in the kingdom it was surrounded by orchards and a vineyard, plus small gardens to the rear of huts.

'Media's wealth is derived from its rich soil, which makes it the breadbasket of the empire,' I told him. 'Unlike at Dura, Media is blessed with seasonal rains and an inexhaustible supply of underground water. This village should be filled with healthy, happy people and the fields should be brimming with crops turned bronze by the sun and waiting to be harvested. It is a tragedy.'

'And now more tragedy is to be visited upon the kingdom,' lamented my quartermaster general. 'May I compliment both you and the queen on your new armour, by the way. Arsam has excelled himself.'

'Indeed,' I said sheepishly, while Gallia grinned.

We sent riders ahead to scout out the stronghold of the local lord, a sprawling two-storey mud-brick building with its own lake, our intention being to relay our compliments and ask permission to ride through his territory. But they returned with news that the residence was empty and had been thoroughly looted.

'The lord and his retainers are probably dead,' said Gallia, 'either killed at Mepsila or during Spartacus' invasion.'

Only now did the stark reality of the devastation visited on northern Media dawn on me. It would take years for the kingdom to recover, though if it were true that another army was about to invade it, any recovery would be more a distant hope than a certainty.

After two days of riding past deserted villages and seeing no one on the road to the capital, it was a relief to see Irbil in the distance as we approached it from the north, the same direction the army of Prince Atrax would follow. I sent a rider ahead to announce our approach, it being bad manners for a foreign king to appear in another ruler's city unannounced. It was midday, the sun at its midpoint in a clear blue sky and the air hot and dusty, when we sighted a column of riders approaching from the city, a large banner billowing at its head. I ordered Zenobia to remove the wax sleeve that covered my furled griffin banner to display the emblem of Dura as the Median riders slowed to a walk, at their head a tall man wearing an open-faced helmet, his beard pure white. I called a halt as he did likewise and both he and we walked our horses forward until we were around ten paces apart.

'Greetings, King Pacorus, Queen Gallia, the king and queen send their compliments and look forward to speaking with you.'

His name was Joro and he had commanded Media's army for many years. He had been a senior officer when my friend Atrax, the husband of my sister Aliyeh, had been Media's ruler, and a junior officer under Farhad, and when Media's army had been a force to be reckoned with. Now that army had been bled white and I wondered how many men Joro would be able to summon at short notice.

'The king and queen are well?' I asked him as he rode beside us back to the city.

'Yes, majesty.'

His voice contained not a shred of emotion, but then Joro was a traditionalist, the scion of an ancient lineage that could be traced back to the time of the Persian Emperor Darius. Many of Media's ancient families also had proud heritages and I wondered what they thought of the son of the hated King of Gordyene and an Armenian woman being appointed to rule them. Media, after all, had been the progenitor of the policy of 'Parthian purity' that I and others had ridiculed. But in Media where customs and age-old practices were strictly adhered to, such a policy had seemed entirely appropriate.

'The city has a wall.'

Lucius' voice interrupted my musings. So busy had I been fixing my stare on Irbil's citadel in the distance — a yellow-ochre walled stronghold atop a hundred-foot high circular stone mound —

that I had not seen the wall that now surrounded the hundreds of homes, shops and warehouses around it.

'How fortunate,' I said, 'and long overdue. My congratulations on your foresight, general.'

'The idea was not mine, majesty, but the king's. When his father besieged Irbil, he erected an earthen rampart around the city. King Akmon retained the earth bank, strengthened it and built a wooden wall on top of it, with four gates giving access to the city.'

I estimated the earth rampart to be approximately twice the height of a man, the wooden wall on top of it ¬— made from horizontal timbers interlocked between grids of wooden posts – to be around the same height. To add strength to the rampart and wall, there was a wide ditch in front of them, which meant an attacker would have to traverse the ditch before attempting to clamber up the rampart and scale the wall. In addition, there were wooden towers at regular intervals along the wall: nothing more than simple two-storey structures really, but they gave defenders using bows and slings extended range and allowed archers and slingers to make cross-shots at attackers approaching the walls.

The population of the city had swelled since the last time I had been in Irbil, many tents being pitched between the new perimeter wall and the mud-brick buildings ringing the citadel. Joro saw my look of concern as we rode through one of the gates.

'Refugees, majesty, who have fled from their villages in the north of the kingdom. The king feeds them and paid them for their labour during the construction of the city wall. But now they have no work and drain the royal granaries.'

There was disapproval in his voice but he would never openly criticise his king. Men like Joro believed in the natural order of things.

Kings were appointed by the gods, or in Akmon's case by the high king acting as the mortal vessel of the gods. The king sat at the top of a pyramidal society, beneath him the lords who carried out his wishes, enforced the laws throughout his kingdom and provided soldiers in times of war. Priests also enforced the law and cemented the legitimacy of the king by reminding worshippers that flocked to their temples that the gods had appointed their ruler. At the bottom of the pyramid, or more accurately the pile, were the commoners who worked the land to produce food to fill the bellies of the king and his family, the kingdom's lords and the appetites of the gods, who demanded vast quantities of food daily to keep them appeased. To men like Joro, feeding homeless commoners did not form any aspect of kingship.

'The city prospers, general,' said Gallia as a huge press of people, camels, donkeys and handcarts near the city bazaar slowed our column.

'Clear a path,' ordered Joro.

His horsemen used their beasts to try to move people out of the way but short of using their swords, there was nothing to be done except remain patient.

'There is no rush, general,' I said. 'It is good to see Irbil on the mend.'

The bazaar was a sprawl of self-contained, two-storey buildings packed tightly together, bisected by alleyways. The latter were lined on both sides with rows of small shops, workshops on the ground floor opening on to the alley, the rooms on the upper floor being used mainly for storage. The smell of spices, animals, their dung and the excited chatter of individuals haggling and arguing reached our nostrils and ears and made me smile. Life had returned to Irbil and I was determined it would not be snuffed out by Prince Atrax.

Things were quieter near the ramp that led to the citadel. The long, narrow slope had been cut into the rock and led to a huge southern-facing gatehouse from which flew a giant black banner showing a white dragon. Guards at the gates stood to attention as we entered the citadel, an oasis of calm and order compared to the mad bustle below.

The citadel was around a quarter of a mile in diameter and in the centre stood the walled palace, around which were temples and the homes of the richest lords, all built of brick and surrounded by a maze of narrow alleyways. I wondered how many nobles remained in the citadel after the costly wars of King Darius.

When we entered the palace compound a guard of honour stood to attention, trumpets and kettledrums sounding a fanfare. Horns grunted at the noise and a few of the horses flicked their tails in annoyance but desisted when the din stopped. The guard of honour comprised around fifty mounted cataphracts and a hundred foot soldiers.

'I thought Media's professional foot soldiers were wiped out at Mepsila,' I said to Joro as slaves came forward to take the reins of our horses. We dismounted and the beasts were led to the stables.

He removed his helmet and adjusted his blue tunic.

'The replacement unit remained at Irbil during the march to Mepsila, majesty, and King Akmon has recalled some veterans to the colours in an attempt to rebuild the army.'

Akmon himself, resplendent in a blue silk tunic, white leggings and black boots, took the hand of his wife and led her down the palace steps to greet us. Queen Lusin, her heart-shaped face framed by lustrous chestnut curls, wore a flowing blue dress and both wore gold crowns. They were both slender, tall and in their prime, which was just as well as they were about to face a stern test. They came forward and embraced us, both Akmon and Lusin kissing Gallia on the cheek. Akmon noticed our shining cuirasses.

'Fine armour, lord.'

'I am not your lord, Akmon,' I told him, 'merely your friend and ally.'

'Would you like to inspect the honour guard?' he enquired.

We did so, the cataphracts immaculate in their burnished scale armour, the men sweating as they paraded on horses encased in armour, each holding a *kontus* vertically. The foot soldiers were as I remembered them from the time of my friend Atrax, the grandfather of the man who was marching on the capital. In appearance, they resembled the Roman legionaries they had been created to fight: helmets with large cheek guards and neck protectors, short-sleeved scale armour tunics, and thick leather greaves over leather boots. Their large oval shields were faced with hide painted black and sporting a white dragon motif. Their primary weapon was a mace, originally a short length of wood topped with a spiked iron head, the latter now replaced by a more effective head with iron flanges. They were also equipped with short swords, by the size and shape of the scabbards at their hips, weapons identical to the *gladius* carried by Dura's foot soldiers and Spartacus' Immortals.

Afterwards we took refreshments in the palace garden, which due to the limited amount of space in the citadel was small in comparison to the ones at Hatra and Ctesiphon. Nevertheless, because the citadel was blessed with abundant underground water sources, there was a pond full of goldfish in the front space of the garden and numerous fountains among the apricot, peach and apple trees and the lush green lawns.

As at Hatra, in the middle of the garden was a gazebo painted white where we sat down on couches with gold feet in the shape of dragons and were served wine in silver rhytons in the shape of a crouching dragon. We toasted Akmon and Lusin, the austere Joro standing like a sentry beside his king.

'Sit down, general,' smiled Akmon, 'you are making us all feel nervous.'

He did as he was ordered, refusing the offer of wine and looking like a sentry perching on the edge of a couch. But he looked every inch the general when I revealed the purpose of our visit.

'We have been reliably informed that an army is heading for Irbil, Akmon, advancing from the Araxes River and intent on storming this city and taking your crown.'

Joro jumped up. 'What army?'

'The army of Prince Atrax, eldest son of the late, unlamented King Darius,' Gallia told him.

Akmon, to his credit, remained calm.

'Do you have any information as to the strength and composition of this army, lord?'

I shook my head. 'I do not.'

The worry lines on Joro's face appeared to increase by the second.

'I thought Atrax was at Hatra, grievously wounded.'

'He underwent by all accounts a miraculous recovery and left Hatra weeks ago,' I informed him.

'We must send riders north at once, majesty,' advised Joro.

Lusin looked frightened but her young husband maintained his resolve.

'See to it.'

He bowed his head to his king and marched briskly back to the palace.

'One more thing, general,' I called after him, 'you should know that Governor Cookes is a traitor who has secured all the post stations along the Tigris, and perhaps in other parts of Media.'

He took in the information, frowned and left our company.

'Cookes has betrayed me?' said Akmon in a faltering voice.

'We will deal with him later,' promised Gallia.

'I will send a rider to Dura to fetch my army,' I said.

'What of Hatra's army?' he asked.

'It has been committed to the east,' I deceived him.

Gallia selected one of the Amazons, an Agraci by birth, who was known for her endurance in the saddle. She carried with her a letter for Chrestus ordering him to bring the Durans and Exiles to Irbil, together with Kalet and his lords, but leaving the siege engines behind. To avoid Hatra I ordered the army should use rafts to float down the Euphrates for around fifty miles before striking east across the desert well south of Hatra and crossing the Tigris on a pontoon bridge. Thereafter he was to march to Irbil with all haste.

I stared at the papyrus map, the oil lamp flickering on the table beside it. Gallia sat opposite, staring at me. The shutters were open to allow a pleasing breeze to enter our bedroom.

'It will take your woman five days to reach Dura, even with her two fresh horses. Another two days for Chrestus to organise the army and a further fifteen to get to Irbil. Just over three weeks.'

'Well, then, we had better put our newly gifted energy to use.'

'Impossible!'

Soter was indignant.

The head of an ancient Median family, he had vast estates in the south of the kingdom and a house in the citadel itself. Like many of his fellow nobles he had been an avid supporter of Darius' and my sister's Parthian purity policy. As in many Parthian kingdoms, Dura's included, the lords of the realm elected one of their own to represent their interests at court. The very first king of Media had elevated his closest friends to the nobility, bequeathing them land to farm and administer, in return for which they were permitted to accrue personal wealth on condition they paid a share to the crown. That was generations ago and the ties between the king and his nobility were now not as tight, especially in the wake of Darius' disastrous reign.

'I can assure you, Lord Soter, it is very possible,' I shot back.

Akmon had assembled a council of war in the palace the following morning, the attendees including Pogon, the harassed commander of the city garrison, Joro, the high priest of the citadel's Temple of Shamash, an aloof individual named Parmenion, Lusin and Gallia.

'May I enquire as to the source of your information, majesty?' asked Soter.

Gallia shot me a glance.

'From a very reliable source,' I replied.

'Scouts left the city earlier,' said Joro, 'they will provide detailed information on the location and size of any army approaching from the north.'

'How many of your fellow lords are still loyal to Prince Atrax?' I asked Soter.

141

He bristled at the suggestion of treachery.

'Media's lords have always been loyal to the crown,' he replied.

I looked at Akmon. 'I would advise summoning them all to Irbil, together with their retainers, to muster an army to confront Prince Atrax.'

Soter looked at Akmon. 'Highness, we have no evidence an army is approaching Irbil, and the suggestion Media's nobility would betray you is thoroughly scurrilous.'

Parmenion examined his well-manicured hands.

'High King Phraates himself appointed King Akmon to rule Media, King Pacorus. Why would Media's lords betray their king and high king for a landless prince?'

It was a fair point and one I would normally agree with, but not even the high priest of Shamash's temple in Irbil had broken bread with immortals.

'He has foreign backing,' declared Gallia, 'Armenian, most likely.'

'King Spartacus, in retaliation for the Armenian recapture of Van,' I told them, 'is marching with his army to invade Armenia.'

'Then I would have thought King Artaxias has enough to contend with rather than supporting Prince Atrax,' said Soter. 'We all know Gordyene is the major power in these parts. I doubt Armenia has enough soldiers to contain the Thracian…'

He stopped mid-sentence, realising he was no longer in the company of Darius and Aliyeh but rather the son and uncle of Spartacus.

I smiled. 'Please continue, Lord Soter.'

'I was merely trying to emphasise that the Armenians will be hard-pressed containing the king's father,' he replied, 'and will not have the resources to support a wild scheme in Media.'

'It is a valid point, majesty,' said Joro.

The general had kept his counsel but now supported Soter. It was an astute move. Soter represented Media's nobility and Akmon would need the kingdom's nobles if his reign was to prosper.

'I will summon my lords,' stated Akmon. 'It would be unwise not take precautions after King Pacorus has provided us with timely and valuable information.'

Soter was unimpressed but said nothing, preferring to stare into space.

'Governor Pogon,' said Akmon, 'is the city prepared to repel an assault?'

He began shaking his head immediately, running a hand through his thinning hair and exhaling loudly.

'The city is filled with refugees, highness, all from the north when Spartacus, that is King Spartacus, invaded and laid waste the land.'

'I am quite aware of the damage done to this kingdom by my father,' said Akmon tersely. 'I have spent the past few months trying to repair it.'

'The refugees should be expelled, majesty,' suggested the governor, 'to save our food supplies.'

'Where would they go?' asked Lusin.

Pogon shrugged and Soter gave an evil leer.

'You should not concern yourself with the welfare of commoners, majesty. If I have discovered anything it is there is an

143

inexhaustible supply of them, but not an inexhaustible supply of food in Irbil to feed them.'

'How large is the city garrison?' I asked.

Pogon took a large gulp of water. 'How small would be a more accurate question, majesty. At present I can muster one hundred cataphracts, three hundred horse archers, two hundred heavy foot and two hundred spearmen. Eight hundred men in all.'

'How many men marched with you, majesty?' Soter asked me.

'One hundred men and one hundred women,' Gallia replied frostily.

'A thousand in all,' remarked Joro, 'who will be hard pressed if the city is attacked.'

'*If* being the operative word,' said Soter. 'But surely the King of Hatra, your brother, King Pacorus, can reinforce us if indeed Irbil is attacked.'

I shook my head. 'My brother is ill and will not be able to aid us.'

'But his large army…'

'Did you nor hear me?' I shouted. 'Hatra's army will not come to our aid.'

Soter, unused to being spoken to in such a manner, regarded me coolly. No doubt my outburst confirmed what my sister had told him about me.

'It might be wise to send appeals to Atropaiene, Babylon and Susiana,' suggested Joro.

'That would be wise,' agreed Gallia, 'though Babylon, the nearest, is two hundred and fifty miles from Irbil.'

'It would be best to advance to meet Prince Atrax with however many men we can muster before he reaches Irbil,' said Pogon.

Joro toyed with a ring on the finger of his right hand.

'To march against an enemy without knowing anything about that enemy is madness. Besides, the king is summoning the lords and their men to Irbil, which means we have to wait for them.'

'At least allow me to expel the refugees,' pleaded Pogon.

'No,' said Lusin firmly, 'to do so would condemn them to certain death.'

She looked at Parmenion.

'When I was at the Temple of Anahit, we often distributed food to the poor and deserving from the temple's warehouses. Perhaps Irbil's temples could do the same.'

Parmenion's round eyes nearly popped out of his head. Temples were the abodes of the gods they were dedicated to, watched over by priests and priestesses who lived in and around them. And just like mortals, the gods had to be fed every day to keep them pleased and appeased. As part of daily rituals, therefore, the gods were offered the best cuts of meat, as well as great quantities of bread, dates, fruit, fish, honey, milk and beer. Such quantities of food would certainly alleviate pressures on the city's food supplies, but at the risk of offending the gods.

'This is not Armenia, majesty,' smiled Parmenion. 'To do as you suggest would be to anger the gods, whose help we will need to defeat the forces of Prince Atrax.'

Lusin toyed with her lustrous locks. 'Perhaps you and your priests might make any food left over at the end of each day's sacrifices available for the relief of the refugees, then. After all, if the

145

population of Irbil is slaughtered there will be no one left to give offerings to the gods.'

I smiled. 'Well said.'

'The city will be placed on a war footing,' announced Akmon, 'and we will make more definite plans when General Joro's scouts return.'

It was around two hundred miles to the Araxes River, the traditional boundary between southern Armenia and northern Media and Atropaiene. Like all borders within the empire, there was no fence or wall to mark a precise boundary and people who lived in the borderlands criss-crossed different kingdoms at will and considered themselves residents of one realm or another depending on their point of view. If they thought about it at all. But any army marching towards Irbil would follow a certain path: cross the Araxes, head south to hug the eastern side of Lake Urmia before striking southwest towards Media's capital. A force composed wholly of horsemen would be able to make the journey in six days; with foot soldiers that time would increase to two weeks. Longer if those foot soldiers were undisciplined or civilians recruited for the campaign. I prayed it would be so with Atrax's army.

Despite his unkempt appearance and flustered manner, Pogon knew what he was doing when organising the city for a siege. He sent what few horsemen he had into the countryside to collect supplies, requisitioning food and livestock and issuing promissory notes pledging reimbursement from Irbil's treasury once the emergency had passed. Whether the headmen of villages could actually read said notes was a moot point. Normally, the lords whose estates were nearest the city would handle such affairs. But they had either died fighting Spartacus and Gafarn or had fled to join Atrax.

146

I stood on the citadel's battlements atop the gatehouse taking in the magnificent view afforded from such an elevated position. A huge, bronze sea of crops, dotted with islands of settlements as far as the eye could see, surrounded the city. Around the villages were vineyards and orchards, which would be devastated by the arrival of Atrax's army.

'This is first time I have stood on these battlements,' said Gallia beside me. 'I had not realised how rich Media was until now.'

'It was a black day when Aliyeh married Atrax,' I said.

'I remember that day. They were both young and happy. No one could have predicted subsequent events, or indeed how Aliyeh's resentment and malice would grow to poison the empire.'

'Ironic, isn't it?'

She turned her gaze away from the fields of gold. 'What is?'

'Aliyeh became like a poison at the heart of the empire and ended her life by taking poison. A form of poetic justice, I suppose. What do you make of our Median allies?'

'High Priest Parmenion is a pompous ass, Lord Soter is untrustworthy and Pogon looks as though he could drop down dead at any moment. Of them all, I would trust only Joro.'

I laughed. 'Harsh but true. How do you feel, by the way?'

'As though I could take on the whole world,' she proclaimed.

'Which you might have to if our illustrious friends told us the truth.'

'Why wouldn't they?' she asked.

'The gods can be cruel as well as kind.'

A throat was cleared behind us. I turned to see my quartermaster general, who snapped to attention and bowed his head.

'Lucius, you have finished your assessment of the city defences?'

'Yes, majesty,' he bowed his head to Gallia.

Dressed in a pristine white tunic similar to the ones worn by Dura's legionaries, though unlike them he also sported a pair of expensive leather shoes. He was lean and tanned, his face clean-shaven and his hair cropped short in the Roman style.

'I have some suggestions to bolster the city's defences, majesty,' he told me, 'which will require the authorisation of King Akmon.'

Half an hour later we were in the king and queen's company, Joro and Pogon also in attendance. I introduced Lucius to the king and the two senior Median officers and let him give his assessment of Irbil's defences. Because it was the height of summer, the meeting took place in the gazebo in the centre of the palace garden. Lucius stood to attention with his hands behind his back but Akmon told him to recline on a couch.

'You are a general, after all,' he grinned.

I had to admit Akmon appeared to be handling kingship well, considering his young age and the fact he was the son of the hated King Spartacus. But, like many fortunate kings, he had the unbending support of his queen.

'If the city had no perimeter wall to defend the buildings around the citadel,' began Lucius, 'then the chances of the city holding out would have been small to non-existent.'

He tipped his head at Akmon. 'However, your majesty's foresight has increased the chances of Irbil resisting an assault significantly. That said, the perimeter still needs reinforcing to withstand the initial assault, which will be the most powerful.'

'How so?' asked Akmon.

'When the enemy arrives,' said Lucius.

'*If* the enemy arrives,' Joro corrected him.

Lucius smiled. 'Indulge me, general. When the enemy first sights Irbil he will see an earth rampart with a wooden wall on top, with a ditch in front of them both. Prince Atrax, having been born and raised in the city, will know two things. He will know the perimeter wall is a recent addition, and he will know the garrison of Irbil is not large enough to man the whole of that perimeter.'

'Surely,' interrupted Pogon, 'for all he knows Hatra and Dura might have reinforced Irbil.'

Lucius discounted the idea. 'The governor of Mepsila has moved to seize all the post stations along the Tigris, which means he has up-to-date information regarding what forces have crossed the river. Since neither Hatra nor Dura have sent any troops to reinforce Irbil, Prince Atrax will be confident the city is only weakly defended.

'That being the case, he will order an immediate assault on the city with his army, knowing that we cannot defend the full extent of our defences. He will suffer losses, perhaps heavy ones, but ultimately he will succeed in breaching our defences.'

'You do not give much cause for optimism, general,' remarked Joro.

'On the contrary, lord,' said Lucius, 'if we get the enemy to fight on our terms then we can negate any numerical superiority he may enjoy.'

'And how do we do that?' asked Akmon.

'By enlisting the aid of a dead Roman by the name of Julius Caesar, majesty,' he smiled. 'A supreme warlord, he was greatly outnumbered while besieging a town by the name of Alesia.'

149

A row of blank faces and puzzled looks met his declaration.

'Where is Alesia?' asked Lusin.

'In Gaul, majesty, the birthplace of Queen Gallia of Dura, though I believe my queen was actually born in Cisalpine Gaul, which if my memory serves me right…'

'Cut to the quick, Lucius,' I ordered, 'time is of the essence.'

Lucius looked disappointed he was not given the opportunity to wax lyrical about Caesar's achievements at Alesia, or Gallia's heritage.

'We channel the enemy into killing zones when he launches his assault on the city,' he said, 'to reduce his advantages and increase our own.'

'And how do we do that?' enquired an unconvinced Joro.

When Lucius had finished speaking, Akmon gave his consent to his plan.

The king had employed the refugees from the north of his kingdom to construct the ditch and wooden wall that surrounded his city. Mostly farmers and their families, they were used to hard manual labour, which made them an ideal workforce to instigate Lucius' plan. It required chopping down the trees of the orchards that surrounded the dozens of villages within a ten-mile radius of Irbil, the wood being transported back to the city on dozens of carts, where it was chopped and sawed into shape.

I stood on the perimeter wall with Gallia, Joro and Pogon, Centurion Bullus also in attendance as Lucius briefed us on his plan. He pointed to the ground beyond the wide ditch in front of the wall.

'We don't have the time or manpower to supplement the defences already in existence with new obstacles. Therefore, having made an assessment of the extent of the perimeter wall, I intend to strengthen the defences around three-quarters of the wall's length.'

Joro was confused. 'What about the other quarter?'

'That will be left unreinforced, lord,' said Lucius, 'to encourage the enemy to use that space, or rather the four areas that I intend to leave open in front of the wall, to launch attacks into. To channel their forces into killing grounds where our missiles can exact a heavy toll.'

'That is a risky strategy,' I told him. 'The enemy will also have archers and slingers to target our own troops on the wall.'

'We have no choice, majesty,' he told me bluntly. 'We do not have the soldiers to man the full extent of the perimeter wall.'

As well as the farmers among the refugees, Akmon gave Joro authority to impress all males in the city between the ages of fourteen and forty to work on the defences. Lucius and Pogon organised work parties to strength the wall itself and dig trenches and pits beyond it, lots of them. Large branches were hammered into the rampart at the base of the outside of the wall at an angle of forty-five degrees, and then sharpened to present a vicious obstacle to anyone attempting to climb up it. These branches were installed all along the wall. Immediately in front of the ditch rows of trenches were dug, each one narrow, around six feet deep and filled with a row of stakes, which were sharpened when in place. In front of the trenches were small round pits around three feet deep, tapered towards the bottom and containing a single fire-hardened stake. Ahead of the pits were strewn wooden blocks around a foot long, with iron spikes hammered into them and then sunk into the ground, which would incapacitate a man or horse unfortunate to step on them. Ideally, these three belts of obstacles should have protected every part of the wall, but Lucius was right: time and resources dictated they could only cover the majority of the perimeter wall. The four lanes deliberately left open would hopefully be too tempting for the enemy to resist.

I hacked at the earth with the spade, the ground hard and only begrudgingly yielding. Around me hundreds of others were digging trenches and pits and removing spoil in a race against time to complete them before the enemy arrived. It was hot and I was sweating but felt strong and up to the task. I was keeping up with the two legionaries also digging the trench, which was perhaps now four feet deep.

'Move your arses,' barked Bullus, pacing up and down and forwards and backwards as he oversaw the digging. 'The enemy will be here soon enough and I want the trenches dug and filled with nice new stakes to impale the bastards on.'

He stopped at my trench, a frown creasing his broad forehead.

'Are you all right, majesty?'

'Never better.'

He looked up at the sun in a cloudless sky. There were still eight hours of daylight left and many around me, especially the civilians, were wilting in the heat.

'Perhaps you should take a break, majesty, in the palace, perhaps.'

I shovelled earth into a wheelbarrow on the lip of the trench, a teenage boy waiting until it was full before wheeling it further away from the city where it would be spread. I ignored Bullus.

'Bearing in mind your age, majesty.'

I stopped and stared up at him.

'What about my age?'

He looked around. 'You are the only man in his sixties working out here, majesty.'

'You are as old as you feel, centurion, and I feel fine.'

The other two legionaries had stopped their spadework and were using our conversation as an excuse to take a rest. Until Bullus spotted them.

'Get back to work, you lazy buggers, otherwise I will put you on guard duty tonight.'

He tipped his vine cane to me and strode away to torment some other unfortunates.

We worked for the rest of the day trying to complete Lucius' grand scheme, filing back into the city as the sun, a huge blood-red fireball, descended slowly in the west. I drank greedily from a waterskin offered to me by one of the legion of teenage boys who had been tasked with ferrying water to those working on the trenches. Bullus, who had hovered nearby me all day, probably expecting me to faint from exhaustion to verify his concern about my age, marched behind me, my two legionary trench diggers also present. They had donned their armour and helmets, carried their shields and swords and looked fit to drop, despite being a third of my age. The boy was a scrawny article, barefoot and wearing a tunic bleached white from exposure to the sun.

'Are your parents in the city?' I asked him.

'They are dead, highborn, killed by the northern demon.'

'Northern demon?'

'King Spartacus.' He spat out the name with venom. 'Is he coming back to burn Irbil?'

'No, another.'

'Who?'

153

Bullus tapped him on the arm with his cane. 'Watch your mouth, boy.'

'What is your name?' I asked.

'Klietas, highborn.' He pulled out the sling tucked into his rope belt. 'When the enemy comes, I will kill many.'

As we walked to the gates I spotted Gallia and a party of Amazons waiting for me, Gallia's armour dazzlingly bright in the early evening sunlight. Klietas' eyes lit up when he saw her standing by her horse, holding Horns' reins who was next to her mare.

'Who is that?'

'My wife.'

He looked at me with bulging eyes. 'You have a goddess for a wife.'

'Nearly right, Klietas. Where are you sleeping tonight?'

'Wherever I lay my head, highborn.'

'Then tonight it will be the palace.'

He pointed at the citadel, its walls turned pink by the sinking sun.

'In there?'

Bullus grunted in disapproval as Gallia greeted me with a wide grin. She and the Amazons had been assisting gathering in supplies from the countryside.

'How was your day of digging?'

I kissed her on the lips, men around me whistling and whooping.

'Invigorating. This is Klietas, who worked alongside me.'

He stared in wonder at her gleaming cuirass and blue eyes.

'He has given me an idea and will be joining us for the evening meal.'

154

I vaulted into Horns' saddle.

'Do you want me to tidy him up, majesty?' said Bullus, nodding at Klietas.

I nodded. 'I will see you tonight, Klietas.'

As a gesture to the emergency Irbil found itself in, notwithstanding the enemy had yet to be sighted, Akmon had ordered the royal kitchens to cut back on the amount of food served at evening feasts. So instead of six different meats being served, 'only' three were cooked. I sat with Gallia on the top table in the feasting hall with Akmon and Lusin, Joro and his family on the table immediately in front of the dais on which we sat, along with Soter, Pogon and their wives. Only the richest and most influential lords lived in Irbil's citadel, being invited to share the residence of the royal family by the king himself. The majority lived on their estates dotted throughout the kingdom. Inevitably, those who did live in the citadel became the fawning favourites of the king, which would explain why there was a dearth of courtiers. The absentees were probably with Prince Atrax, or perhaps they had been killed during the recent conflicts with Gordyene and Hatra.

The atmosphere was subdued with very little conversation. Akmon picked at his food, Joro and Soter engaged in polite conversation, and Lucius and Bullus said little as they devoured the mutton, chicken and beef on offer. But they lagged well behind another guest who was intent on consuming his own bodyweight in food.

'Slow down,' I told Klietas sitting beside me, 'you will be ill.'

He shoved a slice of beef into his mouth, followed by a chunk of bread.

'Yes, highborn.'

Joro, Soter and their wives had noticed the young boy sitting on the top table but had said nothing, though their disapproving visages spoke volumes. Bullus had done a decent job cleaning him up, had found him a change of clothes and had even cut his matted mane to make him modestly presentable. A servant went to fill his golden rhyton with wine but I placed a hand over the drinking vessel.

'Bring fruit juice for our young friend.'

'Have you adopted the boy, majesty?' asked Soter, a trace of mockery in his voice.

'This is our latest recruit,' I told him, 'a slinger who will augment our forces, he and I hope dozens of others.'

'We recruit children now, lord?' asked Lusin.

'I can fight as well as any man, highborn,' declared Klietas, breadcrumbs tumbling from the corner of his mouth.

'I doubt that,' mocked Pogon.

'How long have you been able to use a sling, Klietas?'

'Since I was five, highborn,' he answered proudly.

'Around a couple of years, then,' said Soter derisively, to the amusement of his and Joro's wives.

'A slingshot can travel over a greater distance than an arrow,' I said, 'and in skilled hands can be deadlier. It would be foolish to ignore the dozens of farmers and their sons who can fight as slingers on the walls. We need every man we can get our hands on.'

'And boy,' said Joro.

I took a sip of wine. It was excellent, though poor in comparison to the magical beverage we had consumed in the tent of our otherworldly friends.

'If the enemy breaches the walls, they will make no distinction between men and boys,' I said harshly.

'Or women and girls,' added Gallia.

Our words soured the atmosphere and conversation died as everyone digested the stark reality of the situation they found themselves in. All aside from Klietas who was blissfully happy to be at a table that contained so much delicious fare. When Akmon and Lusin retired to their private quarters to signal the end of the meal, he began to gather up bread, cheese and fruit before him, intent on taking all he could carry. I laid a hand on his shoulder.

'That won't be necessary. You will sleep in the palace tonight and have breakfast in the morning. We need to put some meat on your bones before the enemy comes.'

The appeal for slingers among the refugees yielded an impressive three hundred volunteers, together with an additional two hundred archers – men who had served as horse archers with their lords during the recent wars, and had been lucky enough to survive the carnage inflicted on Media's armies. We therefore had an additional five hundred men and boys to increase our army to fifteen hundred.

The next day we again laboured on the defences, digging trenches and pits under a blazing sun. As we did so a steady trickle of individuals left the city, mostly foreign merchants but also cowards, those with family outside the city and others who considered their chances of survival to be greater outside Irbil than inside its walls. I was glad to see them go – it meant fewer mouths to feed.

Klietas, in his new tunic and leather shoes, his sling tucked into his new leather belt, sifted through the soil freshly dug from the trench, picking out largish stones to place in his leather pouch. The soil would be put back in the trench when the sharpened stakes had been placed. The four great fields of obstacles around the city were

157

taking shape, in stark contrast to the areas adjacent to them that for an attacker would look very tempting, or so we all hoped.

Klietas picked up a medium-sized stone and examined it.

'How far could you shoot one of those?' I asked him, standing in the trench beside him.

'Four hundred paces, highborn,' he grinned.

'I doubt that,' said Bullus, handing me a full waterskin.

I removed the cork and took two measured gulps before passing it to the centurion beside me.

'It is true,' the boy declared, 'I counted the number myself.'

'What did you kill, boy?'

'A wolf,' he beamed. 'Very dangerous.'

'Not as dangerous as an enemy archer or slinger,' grumbled Bullus.

But Klietas was not to be swayed from the conviction he would reap a harvest of enemy dead when Prince Atrax appeared, which I did nothing to disabuse him of.

'We will be fighting side-by-side, Klietas.'

Bullus said nothing but gave me a sceptical look.

'You and me, highborn?'

'Of course,' I said, 'we are brothers-in-arms now. We will share the same hardships and triumphs in the days to come.'

Bullus glanced behind him.

'Talking of brothers-in-arms, majesty.'

I saw the black banner with a silver dragon motif and the score of *kontus* points glinting in the sun and knew Akmon was approaching. The king was in a gleaming scale armour cuirass, beside him Joro with a great blue plume in his helmet, his blue tunic made of silk and his white leggings also silk. Akmon's open-faced helmet was topped with a gold crown and at his hip he carried his father's sword: a straight, double-edged weapon with a steel cross-guard, grip wrapped in leather, and a silver pommel in the shape of a horse's head. The sword had originally been forged in Hatra and was gifted to Spartacus when he had been a rebellious prince in the city of my birth.

'Make way for the king.'

The cataphracts flanking Akmon and Joro lowered their lances to usher toiling civilians out of the way before halting their horses in front of me. Joro frowned at my dirty appearance and at the spade in my hand. Digging trenches was not how a Parthian King should behave, not at all, but Akmon smiled as I jumped from the trench. Klietas went down on all fours in front of his king. Everyone ignored him.

'The scouts have returned with news from the north,' said Akmon.

I discerned concern in his voice.

I wiped my hands on a cloth. 'I assume Prince Atrax has mustered a large army.'

Akmon nodded. 'Thousands of horse and foot.'

The latter gave me hope we had a few more days yet to complete our task, as the enemy would be forced to march at the rate of the slower-moving foot soldiers.

'How far away?'

'Fifty miles, more or less, advancing from the northeast,' Joro told me. 'They will be here in three days. Media is in your debt, majesty, for without your arrival we would have been in a very vulnerable position.'

I sighed. 'As opposed to merely vulnerable.'

'Lord Soter has left the city with his family,' said Akmon suddenly, 'to rally the lords of the kingdom, you understand.'

I nodded to Akmon and glanced at Joro, whose face was a mask of stone. We were all thinking the same: was Soter a traitor or a loyalist? If the former, I worried that he might attempt to intercept Dura's army as it advanced from the south. But there was nothing I could do about it now. The die was cast.

Bullus kicked Klietas with his boot. 'You will need more stones for your sling, boy.'

Chapter 7

The work on the obstacles was speeded up, men and now women working day and night to complete them before the enemy arrived. The whole city knew it was no longer a game, that the feverish activity sparked by the arrival of the King and Queen of Dura in their magical sparkling armour might just save them. Joro sent out scouts in all directions to ensure our adversaries did not arrive unannounced before the city. Lucius had drawn a plan of the city and its defences on a sheet of papyrus and we now stared at it as he explained the tactics we should adopt. The white-haired Joro watched him like a hawk as we stood round the small table in the king's study in the palace's private apartments. Joro's son was the commander of the king's bodyguard, though it now numbered only one hundred cataphracts, and his wife was still resident in the citadel. He had lost another son at the Battle of Mepsila and despite his loss I knew he was a true professional. It must have taken great resolve to swear allegiance to the man who was the son of the king who had been responsible for his son's death.

'Irbil is essentially a circle,' said Lucius, pointing at the map, 'the sprawl around the citadel copying its round shape. The perimeter wall is thus also circular, with entrances to the city found at the four points of the compass.'

My quartermaster caught Joro's eye. 'You wish to add something, sir?'

Joro shook his head.

'Please continue, Lucius,' I said.

'The fields of obstacles have been constructed either side of the gates,' said Lucius, 'to channel any enemy attack against the four entrances into the city.'

Now Joro spoke. 'There are wooden bridges across the ditch to give access to all four gates, general. We should destroy them before the enemy arrives.'

'That would be sensible, I agree,' said Lucius. 'However, I propose leaving them in place.'

'If the enemy has any sense, he will build four battering rams and use them to smash in all four gates simultaneously,' said Pogon.

'That is the intention,' smiled Lucius.

Joro's blue eyes narrowed. 'Is this some sort of joke?'

'No, lord,' replied Lucius, 'my intention is to present a tempting target for the enemy, so he will throw all his forces against the gates, either side of which will be our slingers and archers. Besides, the bridges will be fired once the enemy is on them.'

Joro was surprised. 'Fired?'

'Yes, lord,' smiled Lucius. 'Beneath every bridge is brushwood, which will be soaked in pitch just prior to the enemy's arrival.'

Joro nodded approvingly. 'Good.'

'How many do the enemy number?' asked Akmon.

'Our scouts indicate an army of between ten and fifteen thousand, majesty,' Joro told him.

'Let us hope nearer the former,' I said.

'Long odds,' remarked Pogon solemnly.

'That is why we must kill as many in the first clash,' said Lucius. 'If Atrax receives a bloody nose in the first assault, he may reconsider launching a second.'

'He will not,' stated Joro. 'He grew up in this palace and I can tell you he will not be diverted from his belief.'

'Which is what, general?' asked Akmon.

'That he is the rightful king of Media.'

'It does not matter what Atrax does or thinks,' I said. 'All we have to do is hold out until my army arrives, then we can crush Atrax and his army.'

'If I may address the issue of dispositions,' said Lucius, eager to move on.

I nodded to him.

'We have just over twelve hundred missile troops to man the perimeter wall,' he informed us.

Joro was surprised. 'That many?'

'Including the squires of your own cataphracts, lord, the Daughters of Dura and the civilian archers and slingers who volunteered.'

'Children and girls?'

It was the first time Lusin had spoken. There were dark rings around her brown eyes and she looked pale and tired.

'If the worst happens,' smiled Gallia, 'even children and girls prefer to have a weapon in their hands before dying.'

To my wife such a view made perfect sense. To a young woman brought up in the confines of Armenian nobility it was an appalling prospect, but even she knew that cities that fell to assault became charnel houses. Lucius tried to provide a modicum of reassurance.

'The reserve will comprise Lord Pogon's city garrison and the palace guard will defend the citadel. If the city falls, there are ample supplies in the citadel to hold out until Dura's army arrives.'

163

'There is not enough food to feed the city population if the perimeter wall is breached, general,' said Akmon.

'No, majesty.'

'Then what will happen to the people?' asked Lusin.

'They will die, most likely, majesty,' stated Pogon bluntly.

'The citadel is strong,' I said, 'and it has its own water supply, so it can withstand a prolonged siege.'

'If the perimeter wall is breached, then the population will be welcomed into the citadel,' Lusin told us.

'I would advise against that, majesty,' said Lucius. 'If the enemy are butchering civilians, it will give us the opportunity to gather our troops and get them inside the citadel.'

She stared, wide-eyed, at my quartermaster-general, appalled at his suggestion.

'No! The people will not be sacrificed to satisfy your theories, general. They and we will triumph, or perish, together. If this condition is disagreeable to our Duran allies, they may leave before the enemy arrives.'

Gallia laughed approvingly and Lucius wore a confused look, but I was delighted by her words. There was obviously steel beneath the charm and looks.

'We have every faith in the diligence and ability of General Varsas,' said Akmon, 'and his plan to defeat the enemy.'

'One more thing,' said Lucius, tipping his head to Akmon, 'when the enemy attacks, endeavour to get the slingers to commence shooting first. Their weapons have a longer range than a recurve bow and it does not matter if their ammunition expenditure is prodigious. There are no shortages of stones whereas there is not an inexhaustible supply of arrows.'

'The armouries are well stocked,' Akmon reassured us. 'The gods be with you.'

It was hot in the palace, the temperature outside oppressive as the sun roasted the city from a cloudless sky. The atmosphere inside the city was also suffocating, everyone weighed down by the prospect of imminent assault. We filed out of the room and a servant immediately accosted Gallia and me.

'Highnesses, your presence is requested in the Temple of Shamash.'

'Who requests our presence?' Gallia demanded to know.

'High Priest Parmenion, highness.'

She rolled her eyes.

'It is just a short distance,' I said.

The beauty of Irbil's citadel was its small size, which meant all points were easily within walking distance. And because it was the preserve of royalty and nobility, it was mercifully absent of crowds, beggars and chaos. In their place was order, calm and quiet, notwithstanding the threat of siege. We walked the short distance to the temple, turning down the offer of litters. As yet the effects of the magical elixir we had been served had not worn off; if anything, our senses, strength and stamina were increasing by the day. The narrow alleyways were largely devoid of life apart from two-man patrols of the royal bodyguard, their orders being to eject anyone from the citadel who had no business being there. Like the other temples dedicated to the Sun God, the main entrance faced east to welcome Shamash as he began his journey across the heavens each day, its white-stone walls and gold-leaf covered double doors presenting a deliberate brilliance to the world. The doors had gold handles and from within came the heady aroma of burning cassia and myrrh,

165

incense being burnt to make Shamash feel welcome and enable mortals to more easily converse with immortals.

We walked through the doors into the temple, sunlight flooding into its interior via the windows cut high in the walls, white marble tiles and columns supporting the arched cedar roof accentuating the light to create a dazzling effect that made us squint.

'Thank you for coming.'

The male voice came from behind us and we immediately spun on our heels. To see a figure wearing a white robe and a belt of silver metal, a hood covering his face. He removed it to reveal a 'man' we had seen before, his skin pale, almost pure white in the temple's brilliant light, his hair white but appearing silver as the sun's rays caught it. Girra smiled at us.

'Time is of the essence, my friends. The enemy draws close and Erra encourages their advance. You will have to endure the wrath of the seven sons of Anu.'

How I wish Claudia were with us at that moment. I wracked my brains trying to remember the *Poem of Erra*, the Babylonian text that was over two thousand years old. A tutor had made me learn it in my early youth but it existed in my mind only as fragments.

'Anu, the king of the gods, sowed his seed in the earth and she bore him seven sons,' I said.

Girra smiled. 'Very good, Pacorus, but do you remember the ordained destinies of those sons, which were also given to Erra?'

Gallia looked at me in anticipation but I failed the test.

'I am ashamed to say I do not.'

'Do not be ashamed,' he said, 'it is a long and tedious piece of writing. But the specific commands given to each of the Seven will be

166

visited on Irbil. To the first Anu said: wherever you go, spread terror, have no equal. To the second, he told him to burn like fire, scorch like flame. To the third he commanded, look like a lion; let him who sees you be paralysed by fear. To the fourth he said: let a mountain collapse when you present your fierce arms. The fifth was exhorted to blast like the wind and scan the circumference of the earth. The sixth was ordered to go out everywhere and spare no one. And the seventh was charged with slaying whatever lives.'

'Are you saying the siege will last seven days?' asked Gallia.

'Seven days of trial,' nodded Girra.

'Are the gods aiding Prince Atrax?' I enquired.

He flashed a smile. 'Shamash has forbidden it, though if I had a choice I would stand beside you both on the ramparts.'

'And Erra?'

Another smile. 'He cares not who prevails as long as there is fire, destruction and death.'

'The gods are cruel,' I hissed, forgetting myself.

A sympathetic look. 'Cruelty, kindness and everything in between are the creations of mortals, whose lives are short and full of fear and uncertainty. What use do they have to those who do not die, grow sick or age? Now I must be away, someone approaches.'

It was High Priest Parmenion, similarly dressed in a long white robe, though without a hood and a belt of silver around his waist.

'It is the high priest,' I said, turning to see Girra had vanished.

'Welcome, majesties,' said Parmenion, 'you have come to pray to fortify yourselves before the coming trial? To ask the forgiveness of the Sun God?'

'Forgiveness for what?' said Gallia sharply.

167

'There are no kings or queens in the sight of the Sun God, majesty, only sinners and weak vessels.'

Gallia looked around the spotless, gleaming temple.

'It is only weak vessels that stand between you and this fine building being turned into dust.'

'Prince Atrax was born and raised in this citadel, majesty,' he replied smugly. 'He would never desecrate the temple where he, his sisters, father and mother prayed.'

'You hope to see him pray again in this temple, Parmenion?' I asked.

'I am a mere servant of Shamash, majesty, I have no opinion when it comes to politics.'

'How convenient for you,' said Gallia, 'to be able to flit from one side to another without any conscience. In the coming battle, will you praying for King Akmon or Prince Atrax?'

'Whatever Shamash commands, majesty,' he said without blinking.

'Thank you, high priest,' I said, eager to avoid a clash between the two, 'we would like to pray alone.'

He bowed in an ostentatious fashion and retreated.

'Can you smell that?' she asked.

'Myrrh?'

'Treachery,' she spat, turning and marching from the temple.

Out of respect or perhaps wishing to avoid further harsh words, Parmenion first ordered his priests and slaves to leave the temple before absenting himself. I walked to the altar, behind which was a large gold disc engraved to represent the rays of sun, kneeling before it and bowing my head.

'Forgive Gallia, Lord of Light. She has always possessed a cutting tongue. Keep her safe in the coming battle and take my life in place of hers if her words have offended you.'

Whether it was the incense or the presence of Shamash Himself, when I left the temple I felt serenely calm, my mind cleared of trivia and focused on the coming fight. That night I enjoyed a deep and peaceful sleep, waking at first light to the sound of a slave banging on our bedroom door.

'Majesties, forgive the intrusion but you must come at once.'

I sprang from the bed, Gallia a split-second behind me, both of us pulling on robes to cover our nakedness before opening the door.

'What is it?'

The slave fell to his knees and bowed his head.

'The army of Prince Atrax has been sighted, highness.'

In fact, it was only the advance scouts that had been spotted, though the news was enough to send a wave of fear coursing through the city. It was a curious thing: before an enemy was seen, people's minds conjured up images of a vast horde of enemy soldiers, all intent on plundering their city, raping their wives and daughters and murdering them all. People flocked to temples to pray to the gods, promising the immortals a life of subservience if only they could be spared. Those civilians who had volunteered to man the walls reported to their muster stations, though many would be cursing their bravado as the reality of fighting enemy soldiers dawned on them.

In the citadel, men went about their business in a sombre fashion. There were a few small armouries in the city below but the majority of Irbil's weapons and ammunition was held in the citadel's armoury within the palace compound. Squat, thickset armourers

169

issued quivers or arrows, of which there appeared to be a great quantity. For the moment I, Gallia and the rest of the Durans would use our own arrows, which equated to four full quivers for each individual, including the Daughters of Dura: a total of six hundred quivers – eighteen thousand arrows.

We attended one final council of war before the main body of the enemy arrived. It was yet again a beautiful summer's day, and though it would be warm on the city wall, the clear, bright conditions were ideally suited to long-range shooting. Before we disappeared into the palace, we inspected Bullus and his legionaries and Zenobia and her Amazons, behind them the Daughters of Dura. I called Bullus and Zenobia forward, the latter dismounting and handing her reins to her deputy, the slim Minu. I caught the sight of Haya, the teenager not yet a woman who was a recent recruit to the Amazons. She gave me a broad grin and I smiled back. Nerves were not affecting her, it would seem.

'Try to restrain our brave civilian volunteers,' I told them. 'They will be tempted to start shooting as soon as they see any enemy soldiers.'

I looked at Bullus. 'Try not to strike anyone, at least not without good reason. Remember, you were once a new recruit.'

There was a blast of trumpets behind us and I turned to see Joro's son leading his cataphracts from the palace courtyard, raising his hand in salute as he did so. I raised my hand in response and admired the hundred armoured horsemen passing by, followed by two hundred squires all equipped with bows. The cataphracts presented a curious spectacle, each man wearing a scale armour cuirass and open-faced helmet, but devoid of arm and leg armour, which would be a hindrance when fighting on the walls where

170

mobility and dexterity were required. They carried no long lances but every man was equipped with weapons ideally suited to close-quarter fighting on the walls: maces and axes.

'Where will *he* be fighting?' asked Bullus, nodding towards the figure of Parmenion striding across the courtyard towards the palace.

'He will be praying for us,' said Gallia.

'Lucius' plan is a good one,' I said to them. 'We hold the walls and we live. The army is on its way. Shamash be with you.'

They saluted and returned to their charges, Zenobia vaulting into her saddle and leading the Amazons and Daughters of Dura from the courtyard, Bullus and his men following on foot.

'Don't say anything to annoy Parmenion,' I said to Gallia as we walked towards the palace.

She gave me an evil grin. 'Who, me?'

In the throne room, the dais flanked by soldiers of the palace guard, Parmenion was holding court when we arrived, raising his arms to the heavens, his aristocratic voice imploring Shamash to shine on Akmon and Lusin in their coming trial.

'We beseech You, great Shamash, to shower the king and queen with your blessings, to cloak them in the armour of your protection and smite their foes.'

Akmon, who as far as I knew worshipped the Horseman like his father, looked very earnest, while Lusin, an Armenian who presumably worshipped the Goddess Anahit, maintained an air of nobility. Joro was fidgeting with his hands, Lucius was like a Greek statue and Pogon was sweating, though to be fair it was warm in the chamber. Akmon saw us enter and used our appearance to cut Parmenion short.

'King Pacorus, Queen Gallia, welcome.'

Parmenion gave us a disparaging look as his arms dropped to his side, Joro smiling with satisfaction. Akmon looked splendid in a dragon-skin armour cuirass and blue plume in his helmet. I pointed at it.

'If I may offer a word of advice, lose the plume. Enemy archers will be looking for such finery. You don't want to attract unwanted attention.'

Lusin rose from her throne, picked up the helmet from the dais and ripped out the plume. She pointed at the fresh goose feathers in my Roman helmet.

'And you, lord?'

'I'm too old to change, lady,' I smiled, 'besides, the enemy does not know I am here.'

Akmon stood, picked up his helmet and embraced his wife.

'Media owes Dura a debt of gratitude, which will not be forgotten.'

He stepped from the dais, Joro falling in beside him.

'Let's get this done,' said the general.

We followed them from the throne room, through the reception hall and into the courtyard where our horses were being held for us. I looked up into the sky and breathed in the sweet air. I felt so alive and free from the aches and pains that had dogged my last few years. Beside me a glowing Gallia put on her helmet and closed the cheek guards, flashing me a triumphant smile. We were so full of life and thirsted to end the lives of our enemies.

Chapter 8

'Look like a lion, let him who sees you be paralysed by fear.'

Lusin accompanied us to the northern gates; a crowd instantly gathering around our mounted column when they discovered the Queen of Media was among them. They crowded round her horse, reaching out with their hands to try to touch her, much to the annoyance of Joro.

'Out of the way,' he bellowed, drawing his sword, prompting Pogon and the score of Palace Guard with us to do likewise.

'Put your weapons away,' ordered the queen, 'they mean no harm.'

They called her 'Mayry,' the Armenian word for 'mother' and it was clear the people loved her, probably because she had organised the distribution of food for the refugees, and had been seen among them handing out blankets, fruit and bread, or so Klietas had told me. I doubted the Queen of Media spent her days administering succour to the poor and homeless, but even if she had done it but once it was a major break with the past. Media's rulers usually never mixed with the lower orders for fear of being attacked or contracting deadly illnesses and diseases. As far as I knew my sister Aliyeh never stepped foot in the city that surrounded the palace, riding through it with a heavy guard to reach the sanctuary of the citadel, which was physically and metaphorically separate and aloof from the general population. But here was Lusin, accepting the adulation of people who appeared to hold her in genuine affection.

The press of people delayed our arrival at the northern entrance to the city, our horses being taken and led away to the stables, formerly warehouses where merchants had stored their goods before fleeing the city, after which Akmon had ordered them to be requisitioned. The entrance to the city had been made by slicing through the earth rampart that encircled it to create a gap, the sides of which were reinforced with logs placed vertically. Then two wooden gates were put in place to create a barrier. This allowed the wall on top on the rampart to run across the top of the gates, allowing soldiers armed with bows, slings and spears to launch missiles down at any enemy crossing the bridge. More earth had been stacked against the inside of the wall to strengthen it and create a platform from which missiles could be shot at an attacker. The wall reached to around chest height for anyone standing behind it, which allowed archers and slingers to shoot at an enemy approaching the walls, but also meant enemy missile troops could aim at the torsos and heads of defenders. It was the same for those manning the towers spaced at equal lengths along the wall.

Lucius had advised standing down those who would defend the walls to deprive the enemy of any intelligence regarding our numbers, or lack of them. I must admit I had not thought of that, but as the enemy's horsemen came into view and rode up and down in front of the walls, I had to admit it was an excellent tactic. There were hundreds of them and they knew what they were doing. I stood with Gallia, Akmon and Lusin watching the riders wearing an assortment of different coloured leggings and tunics carry out their reconnaissance. I smiled when one inadvertently rode into Lucius' field of obstacles, his horse collapsing in pain as it trod on an iron spike. In what seemed like no time at all, the horsemen had identified the iron spikes, sharpened stakes and stake-lined trenches either side of the gates.

'I've seen them before,' I said, wracking my brains trying to work out where.

'They are from Pontus. We encountered them at Lake Urmia,' Gallia told me.

'Of course, the soft caps on the heads, I remember now.'

Akmon was shocked. 'Why would the soldiers of Pontus be marching with Prince Atrax?'

'Your father has attacked Pontus, so for King Polemon supporting Atrax is a way of retaliating against him,' opined Gallia.

'But relations between Media and Gordyene are at a low ebb,' said Lusin.

'I doubt King Polemon cares about that,' I told her.

The horsemen wore no armour and carried only bundles of javelins and round wicker shields for weapons and protection, but they were fast and careful not to stray too close to the walls or towers. Small groups – officers with signallers and standard bearers holding flags bearing a spread-winged eagle, a double-headed eagle and an eagle on the back of a dolphin – stood and observed us. They would see a wall and towers largely devoid of soldiers, though their eyes would be drawn to the richly attired and armoured group staring back at them.

Then I heard it, a distant groaning noise at first, increasing in volume and intensity as more enemy horsemen appeared. A constant droning noise that was as irritating as it was threatening – the sound of kettledrums. They formed the vanguard of Atrax's army: a phalanx of riders wearing bright blue tunics and burnished helmets banging drums sitting either side of the front of their saddles. I had always loathed the sound of kettledrums because for some reason they reminded me of a toothache the way they gnawed at the brain, and it was no different now. From our vantage point we could see a party of mounted spearmen behind the drummers, the sun glinting off whetted lance points, and behind them a group of riders in rich armour, shining helmets, blue plumes and a huge black banner showing a white dragon.

'Atrax,' spat Gallia, 'like a dog returning to his own vomit.'

'The dog has a lot of soldiers,' remarked Akmon dryly.

I wondered what was going through his mind as the enemy began to deploy before the walls of his city, immediately in front of the gates, albeit beyond the range of our slingers and archers. There was Atrax and those lords who had defected to him. The majority were horse archers, the others being mounted spearmen with round shields bearing a dragon insignia. I estimated their combined total to be four thousand, perhaps less.

The Pontic foot archers and slingers numbered around a thousand in total, but I grew concerned when I saw what appeared to be an understrength Roman legion marching into view. Akmon and Joro shot me concerned looks but Lucius made an attempt to calm our fears.

'They are called Romanised foot soldiers, and are modelled on Roman legionaries. Atrax must be high in the esteem of King Polemon for him to send his best foot soldiers south with him.'

They marched like legionaries and seemed similarly equipped, with large oblong shields that protected the owner from the shoulders to the knees, helmets with yellow crests and each man carrying two javelins. When they halted in their cohorts the only consolation from our point of view was that they numbered only around two and half thousand men – half a legion.

The largest enemy contingent presented a sorry sight: a mass of men wearing no helmets, carrying wicker shields and armed with axes and spears, a few wearing mail and leather armour. They stood in groups with no semblance of discipline or organisation.

'Hill men from somewhere,' opined Lucius. 'Poor quality soldiers whose only advantage is their number.'

There were thousands of them and they formed at least a third of Atrax's army, which gave me some hope we would be able to hold out until my army arrived. In my experience hill men were good for slaughtering civilians, little else. That said, if they managed to get inside Irbil...

'Rider approaching.'

A horseman had left Atrax and his senior officers to canter towards the gates we stood above. He carried his right arm aloft to indicate he carried no weapons.

'Stand down,' ordered Joro as the archers flanking us nocked arrows in their bowstrings.

The horseman slowed his horse before walking it up to the bridge across the ditch; aware many eyes and not a few bows were trained on him.

'King Atrax sends his greetings,' he shouted.

'King Atrax?' muttered Joro.

'The dog has ideas above his station,' sneered Gallia.

'In an effort to spare unnecessary bloodshed,' shouted the horsemen, 'his highness proposes a meeting between himself, King Akmon and King Pacorus.'

I was surprised I was mentioned. As far as I knew Atrax did not even know I was in Irbil. I looked at Gallia.

'The traitor Cookes keeps his master well informed, Pacorus.'

177

'Let me put an arrow in him, majesty,' said Pogon, whose flustered demeanour had miraculously vanished, to be replaced by a more serious and calculating manner.

'No,' replied Akmon, 'it is considered bad manners to kill those under a flag of truce. What would you advise, lord?'

He and his wife looked at me expectantly.

'Agree to meet him, anything that wastes time. If you refuse, he will launch an assault.'

'He will launch an assault anyway,' warned Joro, 'after killing you two first. I know Atrax. He has a malicious and resentful nature.'

'We will take the usual precautions,' I assured him, 'to ensure we are not murdered. Besides, I'll warrant Atrax is more interested in lecturing us than killing us.'

Akmon agreed, calling down the horseman.

'Inform your lord we will meet him.'

It took three hours to arrange the formalities of the meeting, which meant it was midday when we rode through the northern gates to the tent that had been pitched half a mile away, the enemy army having quit the field to establish a camp. The latter was a familiar affair, a great square around which was dug a ditch and rampart, wooden stakes topping the latter. Clearly the commander of the Pontic legion was copying his Roman overlords in every respect.

We rode to the meeting with an escort of six cataphracts, one of whom carried Akmon's dragon banner. It was unfortunate that a member of Atrax's guard carried an almost identical standard. It had been agreed that Joro would also accompany me and Akmon, the veteran general saying nothing when he spotted the standard of the son of his former king. But the worry lines on his face appeared to have doubled when we arrived at the tent, a large rectangular structure that had been pitched halfway between the city gates and the rapidly forming enemy camp.

The sun was beating down and we were all sweating profusely when we entered the tent from the southern side, the flaps tied open to allow what little breeze there was to enter the interior that was just as hot as the temperature outside. Cataphracts removed their helmets and shouted at slaves rushing round to fetch water for themselves and their horses, sliding off their saddles and resting their lances on the ground. Atrax's escort, visible beyond the open opposite entrance to the tent, were also sating their thirst. Inside the tent five couches had been placed on the red carpets that covered the grass, a shaven-headed slave bowing and inviting us to take the weight off our feet. We were glad to do so, as was Atrax and who I assumed was the commander of his army. My eyes, adjusting to the interior of the tent, did not recognise him at first. But when I had removed my helmet and accepted the offer of a rhyton of wine, I nearly choked when the thickset individual in a muscled cuirass made of hammered bronze and embossed with silver smiled at me.

'Titus Tullus,' I said in disbelief.

'Good to see you again, King Pacorus.'

'By what strange quirk of fate do you find yourself here?'

He snapped his fingers to bring a slave bearing a tray holding a chalice of wine.

'We all have to learn a living, lord. After the expedition to Uruk my service was up with Rome, so I had to search around for new employment. To cut a long story short, I found it with King Polemon of Pontus.'

'We are not here to discuss your life history, general,' snapped Atrax.

The prince was certainly a lot healthier than the last time I had seen him. Then he had been pale, on a litter and close to death. Lucius Varsas had escorted him and his sisters to Hatra where he was expected to expire. But here he was, attired in a silver muscled cuirass, blue silk tunic and red leather boots. He resembled his father with his slim figure, handsome face and height. I prayed he did not resemble him in personality.

He looked directly at Akmon. 'Well, here we are. I will make this short. You have one day to leave my city and kingdom.'

Akmon sipped at his wine. 'Your kingdom? I was created King of Media by King of Kings Phraates himself, following your father's decision to support the traitor Tiridates. That makes *you* a traitor, *Prince* Atrax.'

Atrax did not rise to the bait but rather removed a roll of papyrus from inside his cuirass. He held

it out and a slave took it, handing it to Akmon.

'You recognise the seal, the handwriting?' said Atrax. 'You would agree the wording is hardly hostile. I say again, you have one day to leave *my* city.'

Akmon said nothing as he read the letter, though his shoulders slumped as he did so, and all the time the eyes of a smirking Atrax flitted between him and me.

'Allow King Pacorus to read it,' gloated Atrax, 'for he too now stands on the wrong side of history.'

Akmon passed me the missive. I instantly recognised Phraates' handwriting and saw the seal of a bull's head – the seal of Babylon, the city of the high king's birth. My heart sank when I digested its contents. It began with the words 'My dear Prince Atrax' and stated that 'who wears the crown of Media is an internal affair of that

180

kingdom, which the high king has little interest in, as long as whoever rules Media remains loyal to the legitimate high king of the Parthian Empire'. I waved the letter in the air to indicate to the slave I had finished with it. He took it and returned it to its owner. In that moment, I could have cheerfully throttled Phraates for his betrayal of Akmon.

But why?

'This changes nothing,' said Akmon. 'You may have an army of mercenaries at your back but I still hold the city.'

'With what?' asked Atrax. 'A paltry garrison reinforced by two hundred soldiers from Dura, of which half are women? You have seen my army. Even with your new wooden wall, you will not be able to prevent my soldiers from breaching it. Do you really want to condemn the citizens of Media to death for the sake of your vanity?'

'I see the traitor Cookes has kept you fully abreast of developments,' I said to Atrax.

'He is loyal to the rightful King of Media,' replied Atrax, 'the son of Darius, grandson of Atrax and great grandson of Farhad. I wonder, King Pacorus, what the last two would have made of your siding with a foreign usurper.'

'Unlike your father,' I told him, 'they did not drag Media into catastrophic wars, which bled the kingdom white. King Akmon and his queen have embarked on a programme to rebuild the kingdom that was wrecked by the intrigues of your father and Queen Aliyeh, my sister. I see no reason to interrupt that programme.'

Atrax regarded me with contempt.

'Is it not curious that in every misfortune Media has been subjected to, the spectre of King Pacorus is always present. My grandmother was always carping on about how it was a black day for

Parthia when you returned. I always thought she was eaten away by bitterness that distorted her mind. But I now realise she was right.'

'She flattered me,' I said dryly, causing Tullus to smirk. A reproaching glance from Atrax wiped it off his face.

'You murdered my uncle,' spat Atrax, 'and brought about the destruction of my family.'

'I think your father and my sister achieved that all by themselves,' I replied.

I thought he was going to explode in anger, which would have been entirely predictable. But instead he gave an unconcerned shrug.

'I can see that my attempt to avoid bloodshed has failed. So be it.'

He stood and tipped his head to Joro, ignoring Akmon and me.

'Know that when I unsheathe my sword there will be no mercy. No mercy for you and no mercy for those in Irbil.'

He stood, turned and marched from the tent. Joro was appalled by his lack of manners. Akmon appeared unsurprised. He had obviously been well briefed by his general about Prince Atrax. I picked up my helmet and rose from the couch, Tullus accosting me as I followed Joro and Akmon back to our horses.

'He means what he says about butchering everyone inside Irbil, majesty.'

'I have no doubt. It saddens me to see you in the service of such a man.'

He shrugged. 'I was a soldier and the idea of being a farmer or merchant in some small provincial town does not appeal. Unlike like you, sir, I do not have my own kingdom to keep me amused.'

'So, you keep yourself amused killing people?'

Another shrug. 'It's what I do. I'm good at it. And King Polemon is paying me well.'

'Not Atrax?' I probed.

'He hasn't got a pot to piss in, but he is a useful idiot in a greater scheme.'

'Greater scheme?'

Tullus finished his wine and tossed the chalice to a slave.

'Your nephew has managed to make enemies of Rome, Pontus and Armenia, majesty,' he said, 'and whereas Octavian has no desire to wage war on Parthia, he is more than willing to see Gordyene humbled. The army you saw arrayed before the walls earlier has been paid for by Rome, not Pontus. And King Artaxias of Armenia was quite happy for it to march through his kingdom if it meant replacing the current King of Media with one more hostile to Gordyene.'

'You may be interested to know that as we speak here, the King of Gordyene is marching at the head of his army into Armenia.'

He replaced his helmet, which sported a magnificent yellow crest.

'Even his own high king has grown tired of him, it would seem. Someone should try to make him see sense.'

'Someone already has,' I sighed.

He suddenly grabbed my arm.

'Leave Irbil tonight, majesty, you and your wife. It was an honour fighting beside you both at Ctesiphon and I have no desire to fight against you now. But come the morning, I will have no choice but try my utmost to breach the city walls and storm Irbil. You understand, lord?'

I rested a hand on top of his.

'From one soldier to another, I would not expect anything less.'

He knew I would not leave the city and neither would Gallia and in that moment, I thought I detected sadness in his cold, black eyes, and if not sorrow then regret. The veteran of Pharsalus, Philippi, Phraaspa and Ctesiphon let go of my arm and nodded.

'Until tomorrow, then.'

'Until tomorrow, general.'

He looked me up and down.

'You look well, sir. Very well. A trip to the hot springs, perhaps?'

'Hot springs?'

'To restore the mind and body. Wherever you have been, it has done you the world of good. You look twenty years younger.'

His eyes rested on my gleaming armour cuirass.

'The armourers of Dura must be highly skilled to produce such a piece.'

'Actually, it was a gift,' I said.

'Nice gift. It would be a great shame to get it damaged, sir.'

He stepped back, raised his right arm in salute, turned on his heels and marched from the tent.

We rode back to the city in silence, the sun still high in the sky, sweat dripping from our faces. The days were long, which would mean hot and prolonged fighting when the enemy attacked. I looked left and right. There were as yet no siege lines, no archers and slingers shooting at defenders on the walls, and indeed no sign of the enemy at all, Tullus having withdrawn them into camp, hill men and all. It was deliberate ploy to invite Akmon to flee the city via the southern, eastern or western entrances. And go where? To Gordyene, whose ruler had called his wife a whore? Ctesiphon, whose high king had essentially abandoned him? His only recourse would be to flee back to Palmyra and live the life of a wandering, landless prince. The truth was, if he chose to do so, I would not blame him for such an action would save many lives.

In the citadel he declared his intention to stay and fight, Lusin standing beside him as he did so. I informed Lucius the enemy forces were commanded by a Roman veteran, Gallia seething when I revealed his name.

'I will take great delight in putting an arrow through his heart,' she threatened.

'In my experience, such as it is, majesty,' said Joro, 'when he and his superior, Quintus Dellius, were allies of King Darius, I found him a capable officer, if a little rough around the edges.'

'Judging by the encampment the enemy has created,' said Lucius, 'I believe the enemy might be more disciplined than we had hoped for.'

'What does that mean?' asked Lusin, sitting beside her husband in the throne room, a huge dragon banner hanging on the wall behind them.

'It means the coming battle will be more difficult than we anticipated, majesty,' said Joro.

'I suggest we take up our allotted positions tonight,' I said.

Pogon was dismayed by the idea. 'Parthians do not fight at night, majesty.'

'No, but Romans do,' I told him, 'and if I were Titus Tullus I would be thinking the same as you do. A night assault against our thinly held wall might just succeed.'

185

'I agree with King Pacorus,' said Akmon, 'we will man the walls immediately.'

Lucius' plan had divided our forces into four self-contained units, each one allotted to one of the gates in the perimeter wall. All units were equal in number, with the two hundred men of the palace guard forming a small reserve. But we were spread thinly, and I worried we would be overwhelmed in the first assault, though I kept my apprehension to myself.

I went with Gallia to the western gates, torches on the walls and towers illuminating the defences and those manning them. I found Klietas standing on the battlements above the gates, peering at the distant glow of the enemy camp to the north. Amazons, Daughters of Dura and legionaries slept on the bone-dry ground at the foot of the sloping embankment on the city-side of the wall, sentries pacing the ramparts above and keeping watch for any movement beyond the ditch. As usual, Bullus stalked the area like a wolf looking for prey. I told him of my meeting earlier with Atrax and Titus Tullus, who we had fought alongside at the Tigris and Ctesiphon.

'So the enemy aren't all an ill-disciplined rabble?' he grunted.

'No.'

'That will make the coming battle interesting, majesty.' He looked up at Klietas on the city wall. 'He should get some sleep. He will need it.'

'So should you, Bullus.'

'I will get a few winks, majesty, have no fear. What about you?'

'What about me?'

'Well, meaning no disrespect, but at your age.'

'I will get some rest as soon as I speak to Klietas.'

186

He saluted and marched off, tapping his cane against his thigh. In truth, though, I felt alert and the last thing on my mind was sleep. It was odd but I thirsted for the fighting to begin, to hear the sounds of battle and test my mettle against the enemy. I had not felt as eager for combat in years. I paced up the earth bank to stand beside Klietas, the youth flashing me a smile.

'We fight tomorrow, highborn?'

'We do indeed, which is why you should get some sleep.'

'I do not want to miss anything, highborn.'

I laughed. His innocent naivety was most endearing.

'I will keep watch. I promise you will be woken before the battle begins. Go on.'

He scurried off to sleep among the other civilian slingers camped either side of the gates. I stood and peered into the darkness before turning my head to better hear. I heard crickets and the occasional bark of a fox but no trace of human activity. I felt disappointed; it had been long time since I had shot a bow at night, trying to hit a target by sound rather than sight.

'Eager for battle?'

Gallia was beside me, bow in hand, quiver slung over her shoulder.

'How do you feel?'

She grinned. 'I can hear the sound of every creature and the breathing of all those sleeping below. I have never experienced such sensations. You?'

'The same. I yearn for battle, like a drunk craving wine or beer. But I do not need sleep.'

'Me neither. I wonder how long it will last?'

I breathed in the warm night air. 'Only the gods know that.'

'Do you think they will aid us?'

'A pair of fire-breathing dragons would be nice.'

'Or a demon, like the one Claudia summoned at Sigal.'

I shuddered when I remembered the price Sakastan had paid for such help.

'The gods give nothing for free.'

She caressed the armour of her cuirass.

'What price will we have to pay, I wonder?'

Chapter 9

'Blast like the wind, scan the circumference of the earth.'

The dawn came soon enough, the sun an angry red ball rising in the east to herald the spilling of blood. Despite my eagerness for the clash, I managed to grab a couple of hours' sleep, Gallia slumbering beside me. I woke to the cry of a trumpet being sounded to rouse those earmarked to defend the western gates. Cooks prepared a breakfast of cured meat, cheese, porridge and bread, all washed down with water. To us it was basic fare, to Klietas a veritable feast. He gobbled down the food heaped on his wooden plate, sitting huddled over his breakfast and casting his gaze left and right to ensure no one was close enough to steal it. I sat next to him, our backs against the wall, picking at my food. He gave a loud belch.

'Apologies, highborn.'

'You will get indigestion, eating so fast.'

He finished his food and gulped down some water, his eyes fixed on my full plate.

I ate some cheese and a strip of cured meat, but I had other things on my mind aside from food. I saw his eager eyes. I handed him my plate.

'Here, don't bolt it down.'

No sooner had I finished my sentence than his right hand went to work shovelling food into his mouth, his jaws working overtime to consume the fare. He finished, belched again and handed me back my plate.

'Thank you, highborn.'

He emptied his cup of water. 'Now I am ready to fight.'

189

As if on cue, the sound of drums broke the morning silence, a low rumble indicating the drummers were some way off. The enemy was leaving camp.

'On your feet.'

Bullus' booming voice filled our ears and as one those on the ramparts stood and tested their bowstrings. Bullus' legionaries walked up the earth bank and took up position on the wall. Empty barrels around three feet in height had been placed against the inside of the wall to allow each legionary to rest his shield on top of one, thus extending the height of the wall and crucially creating gaps through which the Amazons could shoot. This would provide a modicum of safety for archers shooting down at an enemy that would be shooting back arrows and slingshots. The Daughters of Dura's task was to replenish ammunition stocks, assist the wounded and act as runners to liaise with the other sectors of the wall. They would fight only as a last resort.

Bullus called all the civilian archers and slingers together and assembled them at the gates, the sound of drums filling the air. While Gallia conferred with Zenobia, I walked down the earth bank to address them, their faces betraying nervousness. Many were biting their lips and looking around anxiously. Bullus shook his head and began tapping his cane against his thigh – always a bad sign.

'The enemy will soon be testing us,' I began as I stood before them all. 'I realise none of you are soldiers, so I will give you some simple advice. Obey the commands you are given. They are intended to save your lives. Do not stand on the wall when the enemy attacks; peek over it. Make yourself as small a target as possible. When you take a shot, afterwards immediately take cover behind the wall. That goes for those among you who are slingers and who will be manning the towers. Any questions?'

There were none.

'Then may the gods keep you safe.'

'Right, then,' hollered Bullus, 'to your positions. Collect your helmets first.'

The royal armoury had issued spearmen's helmets to all those who had volunteered to fight on the walls, and under the watchful eye of an armourer slaves handed them out from the back of a cart to the volunteers. The headgear would reduce casualties, *if* the wearers remembered to peek over the wall and not stand to expose their torsos and heads.

The majority of the slingers were deployed in the towers because a skilled slinger had a greater range than an archer. And that range would be increased when shooting from a more elevated position. The stones they would be shooting were already piled on the fighting platforms of the towers, four slingers assigned to each tower. The rest would be fighting alongside the civilian archers either side of the gates and on the flanks of the Amazons. I expected casualties among the civilians to be high and I did not want them panicking and bleeding among my disciplined troops. It was a harsh but correct decision.

I saw Klietas with an over-sized helmet on his head and pointed at him.

'You are with me.'

He hurried over, the helmet falling off his head on the ground. He picked it up and joined me as I walked up the earth embankment, the sound of drums now quite pronounced. When we reached the battlements, the enemy was coming into view.

'Everyone down,' commanded Bullus.

Amazons, legionaries, Daughters of Dura and civilians crouched down to make themselves invisible to those beyond the walls. I grabbed Klietas' tunic and yanked him down.

'We don't want to spoil the surprise, do we?'

'No, highborn.'

I glanced up at the two nearest towers and saw no signs of life. So far, so good. I peeked over the wall and saw skirmisher horsemen approaching, behind them horse archers and mounted spearman. Either side of them marched a small number of foot archers and slingers.

'Keep down,' bellowed Bullus, walking up and down the midpoint of the embankment so the enemy would not spot him.

I crouched down and winked at Klietas, who was fiddling with his sling, a simple weapon consisting of a hide pouch through which were threaded two sinew cords. He stopped when a new sound joined the thumping of the kettledrums: the hollering, whooping and shouts of hill men. Once more I peeked over the wall and saw upwards of three or four hundred barbarians walking towards the wall, shields and axes held high as they taunted us to show ourselves. The horse and foot archers had halted around two hundred paces from the ditch to nock arrows.

'Arrows!' I called.

Immediately, legionaries raised their shields above their heads, the long edge flush to the wall to allow Amazons to take shelter beneath them. The Daughters of Dura ran down the embankment to take shelter in the buildings that had been commandeered for stables, arrows being unable to penetrate their tiled roofs. I grabbed one of the spare shields arranged by Bullus and hoisted it above my head, ensuring its long edge was against the wooden wall behind me. I pulled Klietas to me.

'Arrows cannot penetrate the wall, highborn.'

'No, but they can shoot over it.'

And so they did, arrows shot at a high trajectory falling on the battlements and immediately behind. The enemy loosed three volleys to the accompaniment of the hill men's taunts and whistling, the missiles thudding into shields, wood, earth and a few hapless individuals who were in the wrong place at the wrong time. Piercing screams unnerved Klietas as he tried to push himself further into the wooden wall at his back, an arrow striking the planks a couple of paces from his feet.

'Stay still,' I commanded, above us two loud thuds as arrows struck the shield we were sheltering beneath.

To our right a man, a civilian, still wearing his helmet, tumbled down the embankment, two arrows lodged in his back. The taunts of the hill men grew louder, though they flung their insults and curses at us in a language none of us understood, and then I heard horn blasts and a great cheer went up.

They were rushing the gates.

'Shooting positions,' I shouted, hoisting the shield on to the top of the wall to get a clear view of proceedings. To see the hill men charging towards the gates.

Around me legionaries were positioning shields on top of barrels to create arrow slits, through which the Amazons began shooting at the enemy. Sharp thwacks echoed all around as Gallia's warriors loosed arrows at the rapidly forming column of hill men heading for the bridge across the moat. On the towers slingers began shooting with overhand throws, their missiles invisible in flight when they left their pouches. The civilian archers added their missiles to the fray, shooting at a far slower rate than the Amazons.

I discarded the shield, crouched down, picked up my bow and took an arrow from the quiver on the planks, nocking it and standing to search for a target. Hill men were now falling, raising their wicker shields in a forlorn attempt to protect themselves from the dozens of arrows being shot at them. But I was unconcerned about them. They would not be able to batter down the gates and I put down their wild assault to indiscipline. Far more important were the enemy's arches and slingers, who were still shooting at us. But they were stationary in an exposed position and easy meat for skilled archers. I smiled when I heard Gallia's voice.

'Pick off the archers and slingers.'

Instantly the shooting of the Amazons was directed at the enemy's missile troops, her bodyguard shooting up to seven arrows a minute against the line of enemy archers and slingers. Which soon buckled under the deluge of nearly a thousand arrows in just over a minute. The first to turn tail and withdraw out of range were the traitorous Medians who had sided with Atrax, the horse archers and mounted spearmen abandoning their Pontic allies. The latter followed them, but not before at least two dozen had been killed where they stood, their bodies struck by many arrows.

Beside me Klietas hurled a stone at the fleeing enemy, whooping with joy as he placed another missile in the pouch of his sling and launched it with an overhand throw.

I heard a chopping sound and realised with horror that the hill men had reached the gates and were hacking at them with their axes.

'Javelins,' I called.

Bullus blew his whistle to reorganise his men, who stepped back from the wall to retrieve their javelins lying on the arrow-peppered embankment. The hundred legionaries shouldered their javelins, ran to the wall and threw them at the hill men clustered on the bridge. The civilians in the towers and on the walls shouted in triumph as ear-piercing screams came from below when a hundred javelins pierced flesh and shattered bones.

'Find your targets,' shouted Gallia.

Seconds after the javelin storm came a hail of arrows directed at the hill men from the walls, the Amazons taking careful aim to ensure every arrow struck flesh. The chopping ceased abruptly as the wild men from Pontus ran for their lives, scrambling over their dead and wounded comrades to flee back across the bridge and away from the walls. Klietas took aim and loosed his missile, the stone striking a man in the back and knocking him to the ground. One or more bones broken, perhaps even his spine, the hill man tried to get up but failed before being trampled on by his panicking comrades.

'I hit him, highborn,' shouted Klietas, 'did you see?'

'Well done, Klietas, that only leaves another fourteen thousand or so.'

'Stop that shooting, you bastards,' Bullus was screaming at the civilians still launching arrows and slingshots at the enemy, now well out of range.

Victory is a heady brew. Men who had previously questioned their sanity for volunteering for service on the walls now believed themselves to be invincible, invulnerable and able to defeat anything the enemy threw at them. Flush with victory, they shouted their experiences to those they had fought besides, embellishing their deeds as they did so. They would feast off this day's battle for years. If they survived the siege to tell the tale.

I ordered my horse to be brought from the stables, a gleeful Daughter of Dura handing me Horns' reins as Bullus had the gates opened and the dead hill men collected and dumped on the ground on the other side of the ditch where they would rot in the sun and remind the enemy what awaited him if he ventured too near the walls again.

I rode with Gallia from the gates in the company of half a dozen Amazons, our bows at the ready in case any enemy horsemen appeared. But the ground to the west of the city was now empty save for the dead and the dying, the latter either crawling in a pitiful fashion or lying still and gasping for air. I saw one hill man, the back of his tunic stained with blood, grabbing at the earth with his hands as he attempted to flee from us, his legs quite useless. I wondered if he was the individual Klietas had struck with his stone. I slipped my bow back in its leather case fixed to my saddle and jumped down from Horns.

'What are you doing?' asked Gallia.

I drew my dagger, straddled the hill man and with a swift motion drew the blade across his neck, severing his windpipe. He gasped for a few seconds before falling silent. I wiped the blade on the grass and slipped it back in its sheath, returning to Horns and vaulting into his saddle.

'Going soft?' Her tone was mocking.

'I take no pleasure in suffering,' I told her.

We trotted on, seeing no sign of the enemy who I assumed had withdrawn back into camp.

'Today was just a probe of our defences,' said Gallia, looking back at the city wall. 'Tomorrow will be different.'

That night we rode to the citadel where Akmon, Pogon and Lucius told a similar story: the enemy had only tested their resolve and defences. Casualties had been minimal and passing the test of combat had fortified morale tremendously, especially among the civilian volunteers. We sat at one table in the palace's banqueting hall where we tucked into a fare of a single meat dish – chicken – and parsimonious quantities of bread, cheese and fruit. Lusin had ordered the royal kitchens to be abstemious until the siege ended, to the approval of Joro and the unhappiness of Pogon. Parmenion, eager to display his piety and determination, confined himself to bread and water only.

'Today was a good start,' said Joro, raising his chalice to Akmon, 'and if we can hold the perimeter wall, I am sure we can prevail until King Pacorus' army arrives.'

'I have sent a courier pigeon to Vanadzor,' said Akmon, 'requesting aid.'

Lucius looked surprised and Joro said nothing.

'Alas, lord king,' I said, 'even if your father had a mind to aid you, he and his army will be campaigning in Armenia by now, two hundred miles away from Irbil.'

Akmon stared at his chalice.

'The high king having abandoned us, I have little choice. Media needs allies.'

'I fear it is not so much a case of Phraates abandoning you,' I said, 'but rather his desire to rein in your father.'

'I do not understand,' said Lusin.

'It is all part of a great game played out between Parthia and Rome,' I told her. 'Octavian has Phraates' son, the high king wants him back and, subject to the Roman eagles being returned to him, Octavian will return the infant to Ctesiphon.

'Octavian desires peace with the Parthian Empire, but he cannot appear weak to his own people or indeed foreign powers. He therefore cannot allow the client kingdom of Pontus to be raided with impunity by the allies of Gordyene.'

'But what has that to do with us?' asked Lusin in exasperation.

'Media has become the sacrificial lamb in the great game,' I answered. 'Phraates would never challenge Gordyene directly, but if Atrax triumphs then Spartacus will be faced with hostile kingdoms to the north and south, and Phraates will also not support Gordyene if Octavian launches a campaign against Spartacus.'

'That is a lot of "ifs", majesty,' opined Joro. 'The high king, when he learns of your presence here, will realise Dura fully supports King Akmon.'

I nodded. 'Indeed, and I doubt he wants to see Atrax, the son of Darius and grandson of Aliyeh, two individuals who did so much to threaten his rule, triumph. But neither does he want Gordyene to become too powerful.'

'It is all very confusing,' said Lusin.

'When we defeat Atrax, majesty,' Joro reassured her, 'things will become much simpler.'

'With the help of the gods, Irbil will be safe, rest assured,' stated Parmenion, nibbling a piece of crust.

I looked at Gallia who rolled her eyes. Like many priests, he had an aloof nature, regarding the affairs of men as secondary to service to the gods. Of all those besieged in Irbil, he was probably the safest. He had been a priest and then a high priest during the reigns of King Atrax and King Darius and probably believed the latter's son would never violate Irbil's temples and those who served in them. Of course, he reckoned without the influence of Titus Tullus and the soldiers of Pontus, who worshipped different gods and cared little for Parthia's deities or the temples built to honour them.

'Perhaps you would visit the walls tomorrow, high priest,' I suggested, 'to fortify the spirits of those defending the city.'

He stopped his nibbling. 'My first duty is to attend to the Sun God, King Pacorus, to pray and offer sacrifices so that the city will be safe.'

'Your priests, then,' I proposed.

His brow furrowed. 'Their days are fully occupied, majesty, though all those of noble blood are welcome to join them in the Sun God's temple.'

'They too will be occupied tomorrow,' I said.

Pogon emptied his chalice. 'The enemy will be stronger tomorrow.'

'How so?' demanded Joro.

'Lord Soter will be joining Prince Atrax after his desertion of the king, he and his retainers. His estates are but a day's ride from the city and by now he will have rallied his horsemen.'

'We do not know that, Lord Pogon,' said Akmon.

The governor was now drunk, his inebriation adding to his bitterness.

'We do. Why else did he leave the city with his family? You should seize his house in the citadel, majesty, and kill his slaves as an example.'

'A wise move,' agreed Parmenion.

'Why should innocent people die just because the man they work for is a traitor?' snapped Gallia.

Parmenion gave her a condescending smile.

'I realise the attitude to slaves and slavery is different in Dura from other kingdoms in the empire, majesty, but slaves are the property of their owners. If those owners prove disloyal to the crown, then their property can be seized. And of course, their slaves are judged to be guilty of their owner's crimes.'

'So if one of your priests molests a young girl,' seethed Gallia, 'does that mean you will hang alongside him?'

Everyone stopped eating and drinking and stared at her, Pogon with an open mouth and Joro's blue eyes wide in astonishment. Lusin's jaw dropped and Akmon looked distinctly uncomfortable.

'It is late,' I said, rising and bowing my head to Akmon, 'and I need my bed to prepare for tomorrow. Thank you for your hospitality, lord king.'

Gallia joined me, smiling at the king and queen and giving Parmenion a contemptuous sneer. Aside from Akmon and Lusin, everyone stood as we walked from the hall, Gallia beaming from ear to ear at putting the high priest in his place.

Chapter 10

'Burn like fire, scorch like flame.'

Two minutes after we had retired to our bedroom there was a knock at the door. I ordered whoever it was to enter and was stunned to see the boy who had taken us to the camp of the high ones standing before us, tray in hand and on it what appeared to be two glowing silver chalices.

'A gift for the King and Queen of Dura,' he said, walking over to us.

Gallia looked at me and then him. 'A gift from whom?'

'It is bad manners to enquire as to who has gifted you a treasure.'

'Who are you?' she demanded.

'Who are you?' he retorted angrily. 'You who insult the priests of my masters while the enemy creeps up on this city?'

I grew alarmed. 'What?'

His eyes glinted with evil relish. 'The enemy has stolen a march on you, King Pacorus. No sleep for you tonight. Drink. You will need it.'

I took one of the chalices and sipped at the liquid. It was the same intoxicating, ethereal drink we had been served in the camp of the immortals and I gulped it down greedily, a warm, invigorating sensation racing through my torso and limbs. Gallia also drank rapaciously, her eyes a vivid blue after she had finished.

'Thank you,' I said.

'Better hurry,' he grinned, 'before it is too late.'

I did as he advised, pulling on my armoured cuirass and strapping on my sword belt, Gallia doing the same. In our haste we forgot about the boy, buckling our belts and pulling on our boots. But when we looked up there was no one in the doorway. He had vanished. We headed for the throne room where guards stood sentry night and day to protect the great dragon banner hanging on the wall.

'Sound the alarm,' I shouted at them when we burst into the chamber.

They looked at each other.

'Now!' I screamed.

The silence of the palace was broken as the alarm was raised and a bleary-eyed Akmon and Lusin came into the chamber moments later, followed by a half-dressed Pogon and an irate Joro. Lucius Varsas alone among us looked as though he was about to take a morning stroll.

'What is the meaning of this?' demanded Joro.

'The enemy is attacking the walls,' I told him, 'we must go to the gates immediately.'

Gallia turned and marched towards the doors.

'I would advise you all to get to your positions as soon as possible,' I said, hurrying after my wife, 'that is an order, Lucius.'

He followed us, leaving the Medians totally befuddled. But Akmon, perhaps sensing that the gods had visited his palace, commanded his governor and general to hasten to their positions, calling for his armour and sword as we left the chamber. We went straight to the stables to fetch our horses, saddling them ourselves as the equine night watchman apologised profusely for the lack of stable hands and farriers present. I told him he was not at fault but warned him that his king and General Joro would soon be with him, and he

202

had better rouse whoever he could to prepare their horses and those of their bodyguards.

The four Amazons who had escorted us to the citadel were all young and eager, but at this ungodly hour even they were sluggish and irritable, but managed to saddle their horses well enough, before following us with their mounts into the courtyard where the palace guard was manning the walls. I vaulted into Horns' saddle.

'Open the gates,' I shouted, the duty officer at the closed entrance ordering his men to remove the thick wooden beam slotted horizontally into iron brackets across the inside of the gates. When it had been removed and the gates opened we trotted from the courtyard to head towards the gates at the entrance to the citadel itself. Once the duty officer had equipped us with lighted torches to enable us to negotiate our way through the city below, we rode down the ramp through the empty streets. We were fortunate in that Irbil's layout – essentially buildings packed tightly together round the citadel – meant we did not have to ride far to reach the perimeter. Akmon had imposed a night curfew so our ride was uninterrupted through the city, sliding off our horses at the western gates only ten minutes or so after leaving the citadel.

Torches illuminated the walls and towers where sentries peered out into the blackness, searching for any movement. Bullus and his centurions, most of the volunteers and Amazons were sleeping, leaving Zenobia in charge of the skeleton force on guard duty. She came to us and saluted, surprised to see her king and queen.

'Sound the alarm,' Gallia told her, seconds later a scream piercing the still of the night.

One of Bullus' men was struck by an arrow, the missile piercing the soldier's neck. I rushed to the battlements as he collapsed to the ground.

'Have a care!' I shouted as the air was suddenly filled with hisses and cracks as arrows and slingshots were directed against the walls and towers.

He was dead before I reached him, blood gushing from the wound and his eyes vacant. Multiple trumpet blasts woke men and women from their slumbers, joined by Bullus' whistle as he called his soldiers together. The torches on the walls provided perfect illumination for enemy archers and slingers, their missiles hissing over my head like angry hornets.

'To the walls,' shouted Bullus, leading his men up the embankment to join the other legionaries on the ramparts, now crouching low to avoid the deadly rain of arrows and stones being directed at them. The centurion came to my side.

'Thought you were in the palace, majesty.'

'A friend warned us of a night attack,' I told him.

'Shields,' he called, to our left and right legionaries propping their shields on top of the barrels to create vision slits in between.

I peeked above the wall to try to see what was happening beyond the ditch, to receive a bang to the head when a stone hit the top of my helmet, knocking out a goose feather.

'Are you hurt, majesty?'

I shook my head. 'I'm fine. We need to fire the bridge.'

'What's that?'

He craned his head to try to hear something above the din of volunteers panicking below and the hisses and cracks of enemy bows and missiles. Then I heard it: a rumbling noise accompanied by groaning sounds.

A battering ram!

I scrambled back down the embankment, passing Amazons going the other way, nearly tripping over myself when there was a loud crack at the gates. The enemy ram had been wheeled across the still-intact bridge to reach the gates. Gallia ran to me, bow in hand, staring past me as the ram was launched for a second time at the gates, which shuddered under the impact.

'We need to fire the bridge,' I told her, 'if the enemy breaks down the gates, Tullus will commit his half-legion and the city will fall.'

The brushwood beneath the bridge had been doused with pitch and more of the sticky black substance had been stored in a warehouse a short distance from the gates. Gallia called Zenobia to her and told her to select a dozen Amazons and instruct them to prepare fire arrows.

'And douse those torches,' I called up to Bullus on the battlements, 'they are markers for enemy archers and slingers.'

My words were ill conceived because the civilian archers and slingers, eager to once more battle the enemy after their 'victory' the day before, scrambled up the embankment to extinguish the torches in the towers and along the wall. But in doing so they exposed themselves to the enemy, especially the ones scrambling up ladders to get into the towers. A succession of screams filled the breaking dawn as men were hit and toppled from their exposed positions, some falling on the stakes on the other side of the wall. Out of the corner of my eye I saw Klietas, sling in hand, scrambling up the embankment.

'Klietas, come here,' I called.

He stopped, turned, gave me a grin and hastened over. The half-light of dawn was upon us now, making anyone showing themselves on the walls even more vulnerable. Bullus had his men under tight control but the civilian volunteers were still being reckless, showing themselves above the wall to take shots at the enemy. But they were farmers playing at soldiers whereas those on the other side were the real thing, and soon the enemy had reaped a rich harvest of dead and wounded as our volunteer slingers and archers, despite Bullus nearly bursting his lungs to implore them to keep their heads down, were picked off with relative ease. The rest, around a hundred or so, lost heart and took cover by crouching behind the wall.

Another crash against the gates, which creaked under the strain, the crossbeam in brackets holding them shut splintering. The enemy's missiles were fewer now as all the defenders were crouching behind the wall. Then they stopped altogether, and I knew we had but minutes to fire the bridge before the enemy broke through. Another crash and the gates shook, the beam splintered some more and the enemy sensed victory.

Under the instruction of Gallia, Daughters of Dura worked furiously to wrap cloth around arrows near the head and tie them with leather cord. Then they were dipped in a small barrel of pitch and handed back to us in bundles. I ordered legionaries to leave their positions on the wall to manhandle two burning braziers to the battlements, I, Gallia and the twelve Amazons, all of us clutching fire arrows, followed them. We crouched low to get into position either side of the gates below, so we could shoot down at the brushwood packed under the wooden beams of the bridge.

206

The legionaries placed their shields on top of the barrels, we lit the rags tied to our arrows and nocked them in our bowstrings.

'Now,' I called.

As one we stood, took aim through the gaps between the shields and shot at the bridge – fourteen flaming arrows hurtling through the air. I heard a groan and saw an Amazon fall backwards, hit by an arrow. Gallia ran over to her, but the missile had struck her below the rim of her helmet to penetrate her eye socket, killing her instantly.

The appearance of the row of shields above the wall prompted the enemy archers and slingers to recommence their shooting, and so the air was again thick with arrows and stones when we took our second shot, another two Amazons being killed, one being struck by an arrow and the other by two slingshots. Another crash. Below us the gates were prised open. The enemy ram – a tree trunk secured to a four-wheeled cart by ropes and propelled forward by hill men gripping the sides and rear and pulled back by other barbarians holding ropes fixed to it – was hauled back preparatory to another push at the gates. But alongside the cheers, grunts and curses of the Pontic hill men was a roaring sound as the brushwood burst into flame.

'Bullus, off the wall. To me,' I called, the centurion blowing his whistle.

Gallia also called the Amazons to her, deploying them on the embankment either side of the inside of the gates, arrows nocked in bowstrings. Bullus formed up his men in close order around twenty paces from the gates, eight ranks deep and ten men in each rank, javelins shouldered.

Most of the civilian volunteers had fled, their courage having deserted them after seeing their friends wounded and killed by enemy arrows and stones. In truth, I could not condemn them. When the enemy broke through they would be next to useless and might get in our way. I called over one of the Daughters of Dura while we waited for the gates to give way.

'Get a horse and ride to the palace. Tell the commander of the palace guard the western gates are in danger and tell him King Pacorus requests his aid. You understand?'

She nodded.

'Then go.'

She ran off to the stables, the ram being hurled forward again to fracture the beam and force the gates open to create a gap around a foot wide.

'They will be through after the next blow,' I shouted, 'pick your targets carefully.'

Next to the Amazons stood the Daughters of Dura, bows in hand ready to kill like their older mistresses. I nodded to Gallia on the opposite embankment. She nodded back. There was a great roar as the ram was hurled forward again, the beam snapped in two, the gates were forced open and the enemy were upon us.

Straight into a blizzard of arrows.

The first hill men through the gap in the gates were felled instantly when over ninety Amazons and fifty female squires loosed a volley, seconds later shooting another that cut down at least two-dozen men. Out of the corner of my eye I saw thick black smoke billowing into the morning sky, confirmation that all the brushwood was aflame and was roasting the bridge. I nocked a third arrow and shot it, repeating to shoot a fourth, fifth and sixth missile. And still

208

the enemy kept coming. The ram had been withdrawn and the gates forced open to allow the hundreds of men waiting beyond the ditch to flood into the city. Then I saw flames lapping around the edge of the bridge but as yet the structure still held.

And then a mass of hill men surged forward.

They tripped, staggered and clambered over their dead and dying comrades that had been pierced by arrows, slowing their advance but not halting it. I shot arrow after arrow into the seething, stinking mass of barbarians intent on seizing Akmon's city, teenage girls, gripped with fear now the enemy was within touching distance and battle was no longer a fanciful notion, either froze and were unable to shoot, or shot wildly without aiming. In contrast battle-hardened Amazons maintained a steady rate of shooting, loosing up to seven arrows a minute – over six hundred arrows in total – at the hill men. But suddenly the volleys withered and died – our quivers were empty.

Two things saved us.

Thus far Centurion Bullus had held his men in check. But as soon as our volleys stopped he led them forward in a charge, his men screaming curses as they ran forward, the front ranks hurling their javelins before drawing their swords. The javelin storm reaped a cruel harvest, the missiles piercing unarmoured bodies and heads to penetrate flesh and bone before their thin metal shafts bent as they were designed to do. Bullus' men then smashed into the disorganised enemy, stabbing with their swords above and below shields held tight to their bodies, creating an effect like a giant saw that ground its way into the hill men. There was a frenzy of rasping sounds as *gladius* points stabbed torsos, necks, faces and cut arms and legs. The hill men hacked at Bullus' men with their wicked war axes, but invariably their only option was to use an overhand swinging motion to chop down on their tightly packed opponents. But the legionaries were wearing helmets with large cheek and neck guards and their bodies were protected by mail armour, reducing the effectiveness of the axes. Conversely, the heads and bodies of the hill men were unprotected, and they suffered accordingly.

Bullus' charge had halted the enemy charge, but only temporarily. More and more were pushing through the open gates and it was only a matter of time before sheer weight of numbers overwhelmed the less than one hundred legionaries. But then the enemy began to shuffle backwards, urged to do so by frantic horns calls beyond the ditch. The bridge was now wreathed in smoke and flames, red tongues showing between the boards. The hill men, assaulted first by an arrow storm and then battered by Bullus' charge, needed no second prompting and soon those still able were running back across the bridge.

I ran down the embankment, Gallia coming to me. The Amazons and their squires began to cheer and mock the enemy. There was a loud roar and the whole bridge was suddenly engulfed in flames, men falling through its boards as it disintegrated in a loud crash. Hideous screams came from the bottom of the ditch where men were being roasted alive, several of the female squires bursting into tears as the sounds tipped their nerves over the edge. For myself I hugged Gallia and grinned like an idiot.

'That was a close call,' I smiled. 'Are you hurt?'

There was not a scratch on her and her armour looked as though it had just been polished.

'Arrows!'

An eagle-eyed Amazon, peering through the gates and the smoke beyond, had spotted a line of enemy archers drawing back their bowstrings.

'Take cover,' I shouted, pulling Gallia towards the stables where our horses were billeted.

The arrows were shot in a high trajectory, so they would land around the gates and just beyond them. Bullus' men adopted a *testudo* formation to defeat the enemy missiles but those of us who had no shields to huddle under were more vulnerable. Despite our age, Gallia and I reached the stables before the arrows landed, panting and doubling over when we entered the tile-roofed stables. But at least a dozen others were not so lucky, three Amazons and nine of their squires being killed outright as dozens of arrows thudded into the embankment, battlements and area immediately behind.

From the safety of the stables I saw another Amazon near the open gates stagger and collapse, clutching at her neck. It was Haya, the orphan girl who had recently joined Gallia's band. Without thinking I sprinted from the stables towards her, arrows thudding into the ground as I zigzagged towards the gates, throwing myself on the ground beside her. Blood was oozing from an arrow wound to the neck, the shaft protruding from her flesh just below her helmet's cheekguard. She had been desperately unlucky, and my first thought was the wound was fatal.

'Shields,' I called, pressing my hand to the wound in a vain attempt to staunch the flow of blood.

Bullus and a detachment of his men in *testudo* formation shuffled over, their progress agonisingly slow as they covered the ground without breaking formation, arrows slamming into their shields; others glancing off. When they reached the gates they broke apart, Bullus knelt beside me, took one look at Haya and shook his head.

'You are wasting your time, majesty, she's a dead woman.'

Haya, unable to speak, looked at me with pleading eyes, a tear falling from the corner of her eye. If she was going to die she would not do so alone and abandoned.

'Pick her up,' I commanded.

He shrugged, did as he was told and the *testudo* reformed, its shape slightly out of kilter to accommodate the dying Haya and me.

We got her back to the stables where horses were being saddled.

'What's going on?' I asked.

'The courier you sent earlier to request reinforcements,' said Gallia, 'has returned. No reinforcements are coming. The palace guard is fighting at the northern entrance to the city where the enemy has taken possession of the gates.'

She knelt beside the ashen-faced Haya and cradled her in her arms, yanking out the arrow in one swift motion and stuffing a bandage in the wound. But it was too late. Haya gave her a wan smile before leaving this life, my wife closing her eyes and holding the girl tight to her.

'Let me see the wound, warrior queen.'

An Amazon was kneeling on the other side of Haya, encased in mail armour and helmet, her hand already on the bloody bandage.

Gallia opened her eyes and they filled with tears, but not of sorrow but of joy. I stared at the Amazon, my eyes involuntarily drawn to the chest area where her breasts were threatening to break the links of her mail armour. I saw lustrous dark brown hair tumbling beneath her helmet and a hand with perfectly manicured nails take away the bandage and press on the bloody hole. Gallia did not take her eyes off the woman whose voice was authoritative yet at the same time calming.

'Open your eyes, Haya.'

The commotion around us receded into the distance and suddenly we were but three individuals seemingly apart from everyone around us, and ignored, as though we had become invisible. Haya's eyes opened wide and she gave a loud gasp, Gallia beaming with delight and planting a kiss on each of her cheeks. The Amazon took away her hand.

'It cannot be,' I heard myself saying.

There was no wound on Haya's neck, just a slight scar where the arrow had penetrated. Gallia assisted the young woman to her feet, Haya looking quizzically at her when she hugged her tight, as did I. I had seen a miracle before my eyes and went to thank the goddess who had performed it, only to discover she had disappeared.

'What do you remember?' I asked Haya.

'A pain in my neck and you coming to my aid, majesty. After that, nothing.'

'Get your horse, we are leaving,' Gallia told her.

Haya saluted and paced away. Gallia turned to me.

'If the enemy has the northern gates then it is only a matter of time before Atrax sends his troops into the city. Our only alternative is to withdraw to the citadel.'

She was right, but it was a bitter blow after throwing back the enemy at the western gates. Bullus came over to receive orders.

'We fall back to the citadel immediately,' I told him, 'the enemy has taken possession of the northern gates into the city. We will cover your withdrawal.'

213

'Yes, majesty,' he saluted and went back to his men waiting down the street, beyond the range of the enemy's arrows that had ceased falling from the sky.

Wounded Amazons and Daughters of Dura were loaded on carts and left the stables area, followed by those able to ride leading the horses of the wounded and dead. It left a bitter taste in the mouth to abandon our fallen, but we simply did not have the time to collect the bodies and cremate them. We mounted our horses in the stables and rode them out of the rear entrances to head east into the city, heading for the citadel. It was curious how bad news spread like wildfire through a civilian population because already families were leaving their homes to seek refuge in the only place that offered safety from the enemy: the citadel.

I stayed with Gallia until the stables were empty, then cantered after the rear of the column away from the gates, glancing back at the scene of carnage one last time. To see Klietas standing in the middle of the street near the gates.

'I will catch you up,' I said to Gallia, pulling up Horns before turning him and directing him back towards the gates.

He gave me a boyish grin when I pulled up Horns in front of him, pointing at the open gates.

'The enemy has gone, highborn, we have beaten them.'

For a couple of seconds I peered through the gates and hazy brown smoke to see that the land beyond the ditch did indeed appear to be devoid of the foe. I extended my arm to him.

'Up you come, we are leaving.'

But he was looking past me, reaching into the hide bag tied to his belt to retrieve a stone, without looking placing it in the pouch of his sling.

'The enemy, highborn.'

I saw with disbelief a file of soldiers running along the wall from the north, another file following some distance behind. The reason the enemy had withdrawn from the western gates was to reinforce their breach of the city wall to the north. Now Atrax's men were taking possession of the other entrances into the city. Klietas began to swing his sling.

'No, there are too many of them, get up here.'

'Stand still!'

I swung in the saddle and saw another group of enemy soldiers approaching from a side street, which ran parallel to the wall to my right. I jumped down from Horns, grabbed Klietas, shoved him into the saddle and handed him the reins.

'Don't let go.'

I slapped Horns hard on the rump, inducing him to bolt away down the street to hopefully catch up with Gallia and her Amazons. Horns was galloping and soon out of reach of the enemy soldiers now circling me menacingly. I drew my *spatha* but their commander, a yellow transverse crest atop his helmet in the Roman style, slipped his sword back into its scabbard and shook his head.

'Put away your sword, majesty, we have no wish to kill the King of Dura.'

215

Chapter 11

'Go out everywhere and spare no one.'

I was not the only captive forced-marched out of the city to the enemy camp positioned north of Irbil. Dozens of men, women and children, heads hung low, trudged alongside me. They had probably been too slow to vacate their dwellings when the enemy had burst into the city, though I wondered how the foe had entered the city at all if all the bridges had been burnt. I looked behind me at the northern gates and saw no smoke. As if reading my thoughts, the centurion who had demanded my surrender spoke.

'The bridge never caught fire, majesty, which allowed us to seize the gates, though we lost many men doing so.'

I looked at the soldiers guarding the line of captives, all of them Pontic legionaries with yellow crests atop their helmets, wearing mail armour and carrying shields sporting a double-headed eagle motif.

'You mean you lost many hill men. I doubt General Tullus wasted his best troops attacking the walls.'

'Keep them moving,' the centurion shouted to his men, choosing to ignore my caustic remark.

The civilian captives were herded into a compound outside the camp housing Atrax's army, guards ignoring their pleas for water as they wilted under a fierce Mesopotamian sun. I was escorted inside the camp, which was very familiar as the army of Dura used the same layout for its marching camps. The earth rampart and ditch surrounding it formed a rectangle with rounded corners, within which were neat rows of tents, stables, workshops and kitchens. In

216

the centre of the camp stood the general's tent, larger and more luxurious than the eight-man tents in which the legionaries slept. It almost felt like home. Almost.

The centurion who had captured me had relieved me of my armoured cuirass, helmet, sword and dagger, which he carried into the tent ringed by sentries, two of his men flanking me with swords drawn escorting me into the presence of the tent's resident.

Atrax was seated in a high-backed wooden chair positioned on a dais covered by a purple carpet. Flanking him were Titus Tullus and a tall man with wild hair and even wilder eyes who glared at me. Atrax smiled when the soldiers with drawn swords forced me down on my knees with their shields.

'King Pacorus, this is a pleasant surprise,' his tone was mocking.

'I wish I could say the same,' I replied.

One of the soldiers kicked me in the back, sending me sprawling on the carpet.

'I have played out this scene in my mind many times,' he said with relish. 'How I would exact vengeance on you for all the misfortunes you have visited upon my family.'

'You are too kind,' I said, coughing when a boot was kicked into my side.

'You always did have something clever to say, slave king,' remarked Atrax, 'but now the tables are turned. For too long you have stuck your nose into matters that do not concern you. Finally, you have over-reached yourself.'

'Kill him,' demanded the man with wild hair, his words a form of bastardised Greek.

I slowly rose to my feet, looking behind me at the two soldiers and expecting another blow. None came and the centurion who held my armour and sword looked embarrassed by their behaviour.

'This is Lord Laodice, one of King Polemon's most loyal subjects who holds great sway among the hill tribes of Pontus.'

'Tell me, Atrax,' I said in Greek, 'for a man who is a supporter of Parthian purity, how is it that the bulk of your army is made up of foreigners who have invaded Parthia, people you would normally regard as mongrels?'

Titus Tullus chuckled, earning him a castigating stare from Atrax. But Laodice was confused.

'What is Parthian purity?'

'A belief that only pure-blood Parthians who can trace their lineage back generations should inhabit the Parthian Empire,' I explained. 'All other races are considered inferior to Parthians and should be treated accordingly. But you have just seen it in action, have you not?'

He scratched his feral mane. 'What do you mean?'

I jerked a thumb behind me. 'Go and count all the bodies of your men outside the city walls, then count the number of dead Medians and indeed the casualties among those who wear yellow crests.'

I nodded at Atrax. 'He is quite happy to see you and your men butchered to place him on Media's throne.'

'Silence,' snapped Atrax. 'My Pontic soldiers are valued allies and friends and will be richly rewarded *when* I take my rightful place as Media's ruler.'

'The citadel is strong, and you have no siege engines,' I told him.

Atrax leaned back in his chair and licked his lips. Titus Tullus looked bored by it all and the lord of the hill men appeared confused, probably still trying to work out in his head how many men he had lost in the fight for the walls.

'But I do have you, King Pacorus,' said Atrax with relish, 'truly a gift from the gods.'

'If you are going to make an example of me, then at least release the hostages roasting in that pen outside your camp.'

A slave brought in a silver tray holding silver rhytons and served Atrax, Tullus and Laodice. The latter grabbed his drinking vessel and drank greedily, much to the disgust of Atrax.

'What about King Pacorus?' asked Tullus.

'What about him?' sneered Atrax.

'Well,' said the Roman, 'I believe you owe him a debt of gratitude.'

'Me?'

'When King Spartacus had captured Irbil in the aftermath of you father's death, he wanted to haul you and your sisters back to his capital, or so I heard.' He tipped his head at me. 'King Pacorus was the one who insisted you and your sisters be escorted to Hatra where you made a full recovery, and....'

'Yes, yes, yes,' snapped Atrax. 'Bring drink for our guest.'

'And a chair,' added Tullus.

The wine was delicious, but then Atrax and his family had always indulged themselves when it came to high living. It was their love of everything grand that had led to Aliyeh's machinations to make Media the first kingdom of the empire, ultimately resulting in its near ruin.

219

Atrax leaned forward. 'Tell me, why are you so concerned about the welfare of commoners, people who are beneath the consideration of kings and princes? Is it because you were once a slave and fought in a slave army? After all, a lion does not consider the lot of lambs.'

His tone was mocking and for a moment I thought he was the reincarnation of my sister. He clicked his fingers and the centurion holding my armour and weapons came forward, bowing and handing Atrax my sword when the prince pointed at it. Atrax slowly pulled it from its scabbard and examined the straight blade.

'So, slave king, this is the fabled sword gifted you by another slave king.'

'He was not a king,' I corrected him.

'No, indeed,' mocked Atrax, 'he was a thief and a murderer, just like his son who pollutes the north of the empire. General Tullus has fully acquainted me with the depredations of the slave leader, along with your own part in ravaging Italy.'

I roared with laughter. 'You honour me, general. But I fear time has embellished my small part in the war we fought against the might of Rome.'

'You are wrong, majesty,' he said, 'for in southern Italy mothers still frighten their children with threats that "the Parthian" will come for them in the night if they do not behave.'

I was immensely flattered. Even after all these years I was still remembered in Italy, albeit as a demon of the night. Still, it was a testament of sorts to the achievements of the horsemen I had led, and their commanders. The images of Nergal, Praxima and Burebista appeared in my mind. It was a happy memory.

Atrax stroked the blade. 'I wonder how many innocent lives have been ended by this weapon.'

'None.'

He raised an eyebrow at me. 'None? In all the years of your campaigning you have never cut down an innocent? I find that difficult to believe, King Pacorus.'

'I may have inadvertently killed an innocent,' I said, 'but unlike you I have never consciously murdered the guiltless. On the battlefield I have tried to kill the enemy, for that is the duty of every soldier. But I have never ordered the murder of prisoners or the sack of cities.'

'Liar!'

He spat the accusation at me, causing Laodice and Tullus to flinch. He pointed my sword at me.

'How selective is your memory, slave king. You murdered my uncle, Prince Alexander, at Estakhr having first killed General Spada and his officers under a flag of truce. Do you deny these things?'

The past came back to haunt me, though in truth I had not been responsible for those deaths. During the campaign to avenge the rape of my daughter Claudia and the murder of her betrothed Valak, both at the hands of the loathsome Alexander, I had marched Dura's army into Persis. An able Persian named Spada had outmanoeuvred us and so Gallia had lured him and his officers to a parley where Dura's lords had murdered them. It was a dishonourable act, one that I bitterly regretted. But I did not regret the death of Alexander, who fell from his horse after being rescued by an army led by Phraates himself, breaking his neck. Before I had time to answer, Atrax was jabbing my *spatha* at me.

'I have a mind to melt this down and pour the molten metal down your throat for the crimes you have committed against my family.'

'An excellent idea, lord,' grinned Laodice.

Atrax slipped my sword back in its scabbard and held out an arm so the centurion could hand him my gleaming cuirass. His eyes lit up when he examined the burnished metal plates and stroked them.

'A fine piece of armour,' said Atrax, 'the smiths of Dura have excelled themselves.'

'It was not made at Dura,' I informed him.

'Then where?'

'It was a gift from the gods,' I answered.

Atrax's top lip lifted to create a sneer. 'You dare mock the gods?'

'I have never mocked the gods or taken their name in vain, *prince.*'

The last word made him angry and he jumped from his make-believe throne.

'You might die, today, slave king, but first you will assist me in reclaiming my rightful position as King of Media.'

'I will not,' I insisted.

But I was bundled outside Atrax's large tent where a rope was put around my neck and held by the centurion I had surrendered to until Atrax appeared wearing my armoured cuirass. A slave brought his horse, he vaulted into the saddle and the centurion handed him the rope, which he used to lead me behind him like a dog.

'Is that necessary?' queried Titus Tullus, embarrassed that I was being treated like a slave.

222

'Quite necessary, general,' came the terse reply.

The horses of Tullus and Laodice were brought so they could ride beside Atrax, who took pleasure in parading me around the camp, soldiers jeering and mocking me as he did so. The rope was actually a noose that tightened around my neck when Atrax gave it a jerk or I failed to keep up with the pace of his horse, which he found endlessly amusing. Eventually he led me out of camp back towards the city. It was mid-afternoon now and the heat was intense. Sweat poured into my eyes and I squinted in the bright light.

Atrax's guard was provided by a party of horse archers, all wearing blue tunics and grey leggings and one of their number carrying a black banner bearing a white dragon motif. Tullus' soldiers manned the northern gates into the city and patrolled the walls, more lining the street I trudged down leading to the citadel. The former Roman tribune had his men under control because I spotted no burning buildings, though the street was littered with smashed pottery, overturned carts and the personal belongings of those who had fled from their homes.

'No cheering crowds, Atrax,' I shouted, 'not the homecoming you expected, is it?'

He gave the rope a yank, causing me to tumble forward flat on my face. The horse archers behind me laughed as I tried to stand, stumbling when Atrax dug his heels into the flanks of his horse to make it break into a trot. My reward for my utterance was a grazed elbow and a mouthful of dirt. I thanked the gods the kings of Media had not paved the roads of their capital.

Eventually we reached the citadel, Tullus riding forward to inspect his men deployed around the great circular stone mound. I saw the sun glinting off helmets on the battlements above, our arrival prompting an archer to take a shot at us, the missile falling harmlessly short. There was a strip of cleared land around the perimeter of the mound to allow archers and slingers to have an uninterrupted field of view to take shots against enemy soldiers, but only if the enemy ventured too close to the mound. When we reached the stone ramp leading to the citadel's gates, Atrax called forward one of his horse archers and sent him up it. But before he cantered up the ramp he untied his bowstring and held the disarmed bow aloft to signal his desire to talk.

The horseman rode up the ramp, the door in one of the thick, iron-reinforced gates opened and a soldier stepped out. A tall individual followed him with a huge blue crest atop his helmet, Joro I assumed. Above the gates archers trained their bows on Atrax's man, who had now dismounted and stood conversing with the general. I took it for granted they were not debating the terms of my release and so was curious as to what Atrax wanted. The herald stepped back from Joro, saluted, gained his saddle and rode back down the ramp. When he reached Atrax he bowed his head and they exchanged a few words. Atrax nodded and turned to me.

'Come, King Pacorus, let us see if the usurper Akmon is a reasonable man.'

He tugged on the rope to force me forward, walking his horse around twenty paces or so towards the foot of the ramp. The walls above were suddenly full of individuals peering down at us. To our left the sun was beginning its descent into the west, though it was still very hot and there was no wind. My tunic and leggings were dirty, drenched in sweat and my mouth felt dry and about twice its usual size.

Atrax looked up at those on the walls over one hundred feet above us and spread his arms.

'Behold your king, your true king. I am Atrax, son of Darius, grandson of the king I was named after and great grandson of Farhad. The blood that flows through my veins is pure Median and I can trace my lineage back through history to the time of Arsaces, the first ruler of the Parthian Empire.'

Silence greeted his words, which was hardly surprising as everyone knew Atrax's heritage. But he was just warming up.

'One land, one king. One kingdom, one legitimate ruler. King of Kings Phraates has agreed that the affairs of Media are to be resolved by the parties involved in that kingdom, so I say to you now, Akmon, go back to Gordyene where you were born. Go back to your father's kingdom with your Armenian wife.

'You may feel tempted to defy me, Akmon, especially as you have possession of the citadel. Two things you should know.'

He yanked on the rope to drag me forward.

'I have King Pacorus and will not hesitate to have him executed before your eyes unless you agree to leave the citadel immediately.'

He tossed the rope to the Pontic centurion and held out his right hand. Another legionary rushed forward holding a bucket, which he held up to Atrax. The latter reached into it and pulled out a severed head.

'I know you believe the army of Dura is on its way to rescue you,' shouted Atrax to those on the walls, 'but in fact no message reached Dura.'

He held the bloated, purple head by its long hair, which was plaited in the style of the Amazons.

225

'This woman, this harridan, one of Queen Gallia's infamous female assassins, was intercepted before she crossed the Tigris. No army is coming, Akmon. You have no friends, no allies and no hope.

'But I am merciful and will allow you and your deluded supporters to leave Irbil, never to return. You have until the morning to decide. Failure to agree to my terms will result in King Pacorus being crucified before your eyes. Until tomorrow, then.'

He tossed the head on the ground, turned his horse and walked it away from the ramp, those on the walls remaining silent as they observed me being led away by the centurion.

'I have arranged some entertainment for you, King Pacorus,' said Atrax mockingly as he urged his horse to pick up speed, Tullus and Laodice accompanying him as he rode back to his camp.

The centurion watched him go, contempt etched on his face, four of his men flanking me to ensure I did nothing untoward.

'If you give your word you will not to try to escape, I will remove the noose around your neck, lord.'

'I give you my word.'

Despite having had no sleep since the night before and little food or drink, and bearing in mind my age, I felt remarkably alert, though achingly thirsting.

'Some water if you would spare any?' I asked.

He nodded, uncorked the water bottle hanging from his belt and handed it to me. I tried to remember the words I spoke to my own soldiers during a lull in battle.

'Don't gulp, take small sips. If you gorge yourself, you will get cramps and use up all the contents at once.'

It was easier said than done and I drank greedily. It took an iron will not to hand it back empty. The centurion replaced the cork in the water bottle and led us back to camp, the sound of high-pitched screams stopping me in my tracks.

The centurion turned to me.

'Please remember your pledge, lord.'

We turned the corner to see a vision of horror I had not thought possible in a Parthian city. The men, women and children who had been captured earlier were being nailed to crosses laid flat on the street I had walked down, prior to them being raised up and the crosses fixed in place by holes dug in the dirt. Women squealed in pain as long, triangular-shaped nails were hammered into their wrists, writhing on the cross in a futile attempt to free themselves. But their arms were also held in place by ropes to ensure when they were hoisted up, the weight of their bodies would not cause their impaled wrists to be pulled apart. The ropes were not tied too tightly so the weight of the body pulling down on the arms would make breathing difficult.

Soldiers were also hammering nails through feet into the upright part of crosses, so that victims' knees were bent at approximately forty-five degrees. Once fixed into position the victim faced an agonising death. The legs gave out first, transferring weight to the arms, resulting in dragging the shoulders from their sockets. The elbows and wrists would follow a short time later. Consequently, breathing became difficult, eventually leading to suffocation. It was a degrading, disgusting way to die and I could not believe Atrax was inflicting it on his own people.

I walked through the corridor of death with my head down, ashamed to be Parthian and even more ashamed to be unable to do anything. How I loathed Atrax in that moment and fumed with myself that I had allowed him to leave Irbil when Spartacus had wanted to take him to Vanadzor, there to be probably executed or left to rot away in a cell.

A cross a few paces away collapsed on the ground, the poor wretch nailed to it groaning in pain as the shock shot through her already broken and lacerated body. In their rush to erect the crosses on each side of the street, Tullus' men had failed to make the holes to hold them deep enough or had failed to pack enough earth around them once in place. As a result, heavy wooden crosses with people nailed to them began to keel over, adding farce to the scene of horror. The screams and pleas for mercy tormented my mind as I was escorted out of the city back to the camp of the individual I wanted to kill most in the world.

Chapter 12

'Let a mountain collapse when you present your fierce arms.'

Notwithstanding the animosity Atrax felt towards me, he did not confine me to the now empty pen outside the camp but gave me my own tent for what I assumed would be my last night on earth. A simple circular affair with a cot, oil lamp, small desk and a chair, I could at least stand inside it and there was a carpet on the ground, albeit a trifle threadbare. I was served food, wine and given clean bedding, plus papyrus and a pen to write anything by way of last words to my wife. It was all rather civilised and as I sat at the table finishing off a slice of cheese, I reflected on whether I had any regrets. The deaths of Nergal, Praxima and Silaces still weighed heavily on my mind, but that was because they were recent and as I grew older I felt the loss of friends more keenly. I had been distraught over the deaths of Spartacus and Claudia in the Silarus Valley all those years ago, but my depression had soon passed. As a soldier, I knew that my trade often commanded a high price in blood and it was churlish to dote too long on the loss of those who had shared my profession. I could think of only one regret: that I had not seen my only grandchild, Peroz.

I stared at the blank piece of papyrus on the table. There was no need to pen anything to Gallia. She was my first, my only true love. I did not need to write a letter to inform her of what she already knew. I smiled. A letter to Phraates condemning him for his duplicity, on the other hand…

'Make way for the king.'

I rolled my eyes when one of the guards keeping watch outside my tent opened the flap and Atrax walked in, Laodice and two of Tullus' legionaries with him. I did not get up, which made him hesitate for a few seconds. He was not used to such open displays of disrespect. He saw the blank sheet of papyrus.

'Lost for words, King Pacorus? It's quite straightforward. Write a letter to Akmon begging for your life. I am sure it will sway him to surrender to me.'

He was not wearing my armour, only a lustrous blue silk tunic, white silk leggings and soft red leather shoes. At his hip was the sword of Media's kings with a dragon's head pommel. I pointed at it.

'Your grandfather would never have used that sword against his own people.'

He chuckled. 'I do not concern myself with the people, King Pacorus, I rule them. That is what kings do, or should do.'

'And that is what King Akmon is doing,' I replied, 'and making a decent fist of it, by all accounts. As for pleading for my life, I am too old to start begging.'

'You will change your mind when they start hammering nails into your flesh,' smiled Laodice, who looked as though he had been dragged behind a horse for a few miles, in stark contrast to the expensive clothes and well-groomed appearance of Atrax.

I ignored the wild man from Pontus.

'Tell me, Atrax, when you have killed me and Akmon still holds the citadel, what will you do?'

'Besiege him until he surrenders, of course,' he replied. 'Like an idiot, Akmon has given sanctuary to hundreds of Irbil's citizens. They will soon consume all his food supplies, forcing him to surrender.'

'After which you will murder him,' I said, 'because your actions today showed you are above all a murderer. Your grandfather would have been so disappointed.'

I thought he was going to erupt but he managed to keep his rage in check.

'You seem to forget one thing, King Pacorus.'

'Please enlighten me.'

'I have the support of King of Kings Phraates, King Polemon of Pontus and King Artaxias of Armenia, to say nothing of the encouragement of Octavian, the Roman leader.'

I poured myself some wine and held up the cup to him.

'Excellent wine. And you are right in what you say.'

He looked down his nose at me in triumph.

'Up to a point,' I continued. 'You are in fact no more than a mere foot soldier in a grand game of strategy being played out between Parthia and Rome. Your father and grandmother, though chiefly the latter, conspired with Mark Antony and then Tiridates to bring down Phraates. That being the case, I doubt if Phraates gives a fig for your claim to the throne of Media. He is more interested in clipping the wings of King Spartacus, which he will do if you depose Akmon.'

'The letter of support from Phraates confirms he despises King Spartacus,' gloated Atrax.

'I doubt that. Why would he despise a man who has come to his rescue on numerous occasions, whose army acts as the northern shield of the empire? No, he merely wishes to remind King Spartacus that he is high king and the ruler of Gordyene is his servant, not the other way around.'

I took another sip of wine, rather enjoying explaining things to Atrax.

'Your army may have been raised in Pontus but it was paid for by Octavian, who wishes to send a message to Phraates that Rome will not tolerate one of its client kingdoms being raided by the Sarmatian allies of King Spartacus. You merely happened to be in the right place at the right time and fitted in with Octavian's plans perfectly.'

'You babble like an old woman,' sneered Laodice, ordering wine to be brought for himself and Atrax.

'I assume King Polemon wants his soldiers back after you have captured Irbil?' I asked Atrax.

He turned his head away, saying nothing.

'I will take that as a yes,' I smiled.

'That will leave you with what?' I continued. 'Three thousand men, perhaps more? Not many to fight the combined forces of Gordyene, Hatra and Dura.'

'Who are these people, lord?' asked Laodice, revealing his ignorance concerning Parthia.

I pointed at him. 'You at least can return home to your hovels in the mountains, but for you, Prince Atrax, there will be no place to hide when the wrath of Dura, Hatra and Gordyene is turned on you. Do you think King Spartacus, a man not given to forgiveness, will show you mercy after killing his son? Do you think my daughter Claudia, a Scythian Sister who is now the chief adviser to Phraates, will rest until she has avenged the deaths of her parents? And do you believe King Gafarn will not unleash his army against Media when he learns you had his brother crucified?'

I laughed in his face. 'You have been well and truly manipulated, Atrax. You are a deluded fool who has conspired to bring about his own doom.'

He struck me hard across the face with the back of his hand, pain shooting through my cheek, though the blow was not forceful enough to unseat me.

'You will die tomorrow,' was his terse departing comment, he and the others turning to leave me alone with my bruised cheek.

I actually managed to grab a few hours' sleep before trumpets sounded to announce the beginning of a new day for the mercenary army of Prince Atrax. A slave, his eyes cast down to avoid my own, arrived with water, soap and a towel to allow me to wash and shave, another bringing a fresh tunic. This was followed by breakfast, which was a frugal affair of figs and water. I heard the familiar sounds of centurions barking orders, soldiers grumbling and smelled the reassuring aroma of horses. I could have been in the camp of my own army but instead my hosts were foes and after I had been allowed a few moments after eating breakfast, Titus Tullus arrived at my tent with a century of men.

'No rope, general?'

He presented a splendid sight in his muscled cuirass and burnished helmet sporting a huge yellow crest.

'No, majesty. Bearing in mind the service I undertook for you recently, I would request you to reconsider and ask Akmon to leave the citadel. A fine soldier and commander such as yourself should not end his days nailed to a cross.'

I walked from the tent into the bright sunlight, closed my eyes and inhaled deeply.

'Come, general, let us take the morning air.'

A centurion held the reins of his horse as he walked beside me, the century of legionaries marching in step behind us.

'I hope you live to enjoy what I assume to be the handsome amount you are being paid by Octavian, general.'

'Don't you worry about me, majesty, I'm doing just fine.'

'I would advise parting company with Atrax as soon as possible. He will suffer a bad end, like others of his family.'

'He's an uncouth little bastard, I agree. But I have been paid a princely sum for this job and I always honour a contract, majesty. Once Atrax is sitting on his throne, I and the soldiers of King Polemon will be off.'

We left the camp and headed towards the city's northern gates, now flying a dragon banner, though it hung limp in the still air. He looked around at the lush landscape, islands of green orchards and vineyards in a sea of bronze ripening crops, probably never to be harvested.

'When I first came to Parthia with Mark Antony and another hundred thousand Romans, I thought it was an uncivilised land filled with barbarians. We were unceremoniously chased out of Parthia after failing to take Phraaspa, you yourself commanding the army that did so. I returned with Mark Antony when the *triumvir* made an alliance with Media, though it is more accurate to say it was your sister who pulled the strings of that little arrangement.

'Have to admit by that time Parthia had grown on me, strange to say, not least because it stands on an equal footing with Rome. No other power has ever achieved that.'

He fell silent when we reached the street lined with the crucified civilians, all of them now mercifully dead, their torments at and end, or at least I could see none moving. The birds that always

234

came to feast on living and dead flesh scattered on our arrival, the big black ravens with cruel beaks ideally suited to ripping at flesh landing on the roofs of buildings a short distance away. They would return at the first opportunity for such a lavish banquet was too tempting to resist. I refrained from staring at eye sockets pecked clean, distended purple tongues and smashed bones protruding from flesh. It was a scene of horror and I cursed Atrax for creating it.

We arrived at my designated execution site: the open space near the foot of the ramp cut in the southern side of the stone mound on which the citadel stood. Above us a sea of faces stared down from the walls at the scene below, above them the sun shining in a clear blue sky. On the ground, a safe distance from the base of the mound to ensure he was not struck by arrows shot from the citadel, was Atrax. He was surrounded by a coterie of Median lords and Laodice and flanked by at least fifty horse archers. He sat on his horse gleefully watching me walk towards the cross laid on the ground. Behind him a century of Pontic legionaries stood in open order and were joined by the century that had acted as my escort, leaving me along with Tullus and three of his men, one holding a hammer and a bag of nails. The other two carried rope to fasten my arms to the crossbeam once my wrists had been nailed to the wood.

'General Tullus,' called Atrax, 'your place is beside me.'

The Roman was going to say something but merely nodded to me, turned and walked over to his new lord, a slave holding the general's horse. As he gained the saddle Atrax nudged his horse with his knees, which walked forward to within ten paces of where I stood.

'Your time has come, slave king,' he said. 'You friends have abandoned you and now justice will be served on you for the many crimes you have committed against my family and Media. Proceed.'

He turned his horse to retake his place among his traitorous lords and mercenary allies, half a dozen trumpeters among the horse archers sounding a fanfare to herald the commencement of my punishment. The soldier holding the hammer gave me an evil leer and licked his lips, relishing the prospect of inflicting pain and torment on another person.

Before collapsing into my arms.

His two companions stood with mouths open, staring in disbelief at the arrow lodged in his back, before grimacing in pain when arrows struck them. They collapsed on the ground as more arrows hissed through the air to cut down horse archers on either side of Atrax. I threw the dead soldier aside and instinctively threw myself on the ground, looking up to see a line of archers nocking arrows and shooting them at the horsemen, or rather their horses. Who in the name of the gods were they? I saw perhaps thirty or forty, but though their arrows had wreaked havoc among the enemy horse archers, two hundred Pontic legionaries were now deploying to swat them away like flies. Only to halt as they and the horsemen with Atrax were blinded by a blaze of bright light.

It was as if a hundred suns had suddenly appeared above. The effect was to shine dazzling light into the faces of the two hundred foots soldiers, as well as cause further mayhem among the horsemen around Atrax. Wounded horses bolted hither and thither, their riders more concerned with trying to control their beasts than engaging the line of phantom archers that had wrecked their prince's execution of the King of Dura. The latter was completely forgotten in the excitement.

The archers suddenly rushed forward to flank me.

'Stay down, majesty, are you hurt?'

'No.'

The archer reached into his quiver and shot an arrow, his comrades flanking him doing the same to shower the enemy with missiles and scatter the horsemen. The Pontic legionaries had halted in some disorder, centurions trying to restore ranks as they and their men were dazzled from above. I saw the commander of my rescue party smile to himself and then heard whistles and shouts, all coming from above. Still lying on the ground to avoid any arrows shot in my direction, I looked behind to see Titus Tullus grabbing the reins of Atrax's horse to lead him away, those of his horse archers still in the saddle also wheeling about.

'Kill Atrax!' I shouted.

Those around me directed their arrows at the fleeing prince but he was no fool and crouched low in the saddle to make himself a smaller target, and in any case his horse archers shielded him, at least three being hit and knocked from their saddles by arrows. The two centuries of Pontic legionaries had stopped advancing to turn left to follow the horsemen, marching in quick time to flee the area. I jumped up when I saw soldiers pouring from the gates of the citadel and race down the ramp.

I punched the air when I recognised Akmon's palace guard flooding down the ramp, behind them Bullus and his century of Durans. Behind them rode Akmon, his cataphracts and horse archers, and Gallia's Amazons. It suddenly became dimmer, or at least not as glaringly bright, and I looked up to see the hundred suns had disappeared. The archers around me were still shooting, their arrows striking the locked shields of the Pontic soldiers who executed a splendid forced withdrawal while being shot at.

Atrax had disappeared down the street lined with crucified civilians but Akmon's horsemen were prevented from pursuing them by the appearance of more Pontic legionaries who had been deployed in the streets and buildings around the citadel but had been alerted by the commotion around the ramp. Their commander having deserted them along with their prince, they were unsure what action to take but the officers in charge instantly recognised the uniforms of their enemies and decided to block the street leading to the northern gates, the only route into and out of the city.

Akmon, fully encased in scale armour like the rest of his cataphracts, came to me and raised a hand.

'It is good to see you well, lord, if you will forgive me I have pressing matters to attend to.'

He led his riders away from the line of Pontic soldiers now barring the entrance to the street of death and presenting a compact line of locked shields that bristled with javelins held at an angle of forty-five degrees to deter horsemen. I looked behind me to see Zenobia following Akmon's cataphracts and horse archers with the Amazons, wondering what was going on. A female voice answered my question.

'Akmon knows his city better than the enemy. He will try to sweep around them using backstreets and attack them from behind.'

I spun to see a beaming Gallia leap from her horse and throw herself into my arms, removing her helmet to kiss me long and hard on the lips.

'You did not think I would abandon you to die a Roman death, did you?'

I laughed. 'You certainly gave Atrax a shock.'

'I will give him more than that when I catch up with him.'

Bullus and the commander of the palace guard were marshalling their men into a wedge formation, or a *cuneus* as the Romans termed it, prior to smashing through the line of Pontic soldiers, who must have numbered around three hundred or so. Around fifty or so of Akmon's horse archers were readying themselves to provide missile support for the attack when it was launched.

Gallia put a finger and thumb into her mouth and whistled. Moments later a grinning Klietas appeared with Horns in tow.

'Your horse, highborn.'

Strange to say emotion welled up inside me when I saw Horns, tears coming to my eyes at the sight of his familiar face. I stroked his neck and head and he nickered in response, nudging his nose into me.

'Your battle against the enemy will be told for generations, highborn,' the slinger grinned.

I took Horns' reins. 'What battle?'

'Apparently, you fought a hundred or more enemy soldiers to allow Klietas to escape, or so he told us,' said Gallia, 'you are truly a modern-day Achilles, Pacorus.'

I thought of how meekly I had surrendered to the enemy centurion at the western gates.

'More like Achilles and Hector rolled into one.' I vaulted into the saddle. 'Time to concentrate on the here and now.'

There were actually two wedges, one smaller with Centurion Bullus at the tip, the other, larger one composed of Akmon's palace guard, each poised to smash through the line of Pontic soldiers. The latter had a strong position, their flanks secured against mud-brick houses that marked the end of the street where the civilians had been crucified. But they had no missile troops to support them and so the horse archers, plus civilian slingers and archers, gathered on the flanks of our two wedges were able to shoot arrows and stones at the line of enemy shields with impunity.

Klietas reached into his bag, pulled out a stone and placed it in the pouch of his sling.

'Aim for where our soldiers will strike the enemy line,' I told him.

He looked at me as though I was speaking a foreign language. He was just a boy and had no knowledge of tactics.

'Do your best,' I said.

The professional Median horse archers were already shooting at the spot that would be struck when their palace guard attacked the Pontic legionaries. The latter's shields were able to stop a three-winged bronze arrowhead easily enough, but such was the volume of arrows being shot at a specific point that the enemy line was buckling. It was a similar story on their right flank where the civilian slingers and archers were supporting the compact wedge of Durans. Their rate of shooting and accuracy was poor compared to the Medians but the weight of slingshots and arrows being launched against the enemy line was not unsubstantial.

Gallia clenched her first when trumpets sounded to announce the attack of the palace guard, followed seconds later by the war cries of the Durans as they too charged. Bullus' men had javelins that the first two ranks hurled before racing forward with their shields held nearly horizontally to smash into the battered and bleeding front rank of enemy soldiers. I held my breath as there were two loud cracks when the attackers hit the Pontic legionaries, followed by frenzied clicking sounds as the Durans went to work with their short swords and the palace guard battered the enemy with their maces.

I rode up and down the line of archers and slingers, who had stopped their activities to marvel at the sights and sounds of two groups of heavily armed and armoured men locked in deadly combat a few paces away.

'Continue shooting,' I shouted, 'aim for the enemy soldiers you can still see in front of you.'

In truth, there was not too much to shoot at. The street was only twenty paces wide so when the two wedges attacked the Pontic line, our own men soon obscured the line of enemy soldiers. I saw javelins arch into the air to land in the rear ranks of the enemy, the Pontic legionaries launching their own javelins that landed among the Durans and palace guard. Above the din of metal striking metal I heard screams, yelps and shrieks as sword points and maces cut flesh and smashed bones.

I felt my heart thumping in my chest as the excitement of battle, a mixture of fear, exhilaration and feral rage, took hold of me. I shouted my encouragement, though soldiers locked in mortal combat would not have heard, but I gave a shout of triumph when the century of Durans began chanting the battle cry I had heard so many times when we had been on the brink of victory – 'Dura, Dura' – and knew Bullus had broken the enemy line.

And then suddenly there were no enemy soldiers, only fleeing men abandoning their shields as they turned tail and ran. Straight into

Akmon's cataphracts. Not all the Pontic legionaries died on that street; many fled into alleyways and side streets in their desperation to escape the maces and swords to their front and the armour-clad horsemen and female horse archers in their rear. Akmon's horse archers trotted through the heaps of dead soldiers and avoided the wounded that crawled away from the scene of the brief but brutal carnage. They rode to join their king who ordered them to scour the side streets for the enemy.

'Get back to the citadel,' I told Klietas, he and the other civilian slingers and archers milling around, unsure what to do now the brief bloodletting had finished.

Zenobia returned with the Amazons, removing her helmet and bowing her head when she drew alongside us.

'It is good to see you, majesty.'

'Even better to see you, Zenobia. The enemy is routed?'

'Yes, majesty.'

'All that remains is to seize the northern gates and destroy the bridge over the ditch.'

Zenobia gave Gallia a glance.

'That has been taken care of, Pacorus.'

Gallia pointed to the north where black smoke was billowing into the sky.

'Lucius Varsas with a small party of horse archers left the citadel just after the foot and horse led by myself and Akmon. His orders were to capture the northern gates and fire the bridge. As you can see, he has succeeded.'

'So, we are back to where we started before the siege began,' I said, 'though Atrax has my helmet, armour and sword.'

Gallia looked pained. 'I'm sorry, but at least you are still alive to regret losing them.'

'If I ever encounter Atrax again, I will kill him,' I promised.

Chapter 13

'Wherever you go, spread terror. Have no equal.'

Lucius returned from the northern gates after his successful mission to destroy the bridge in front of them. Governor Pogon had remained in the citadel to guard Lusin from the thousands of civilians packed tightly into the stronghold, his spearmen manning the walls and gates of the palace in case the great army of bedraggled souls tried to batter down its gates. He need not have bothered. When I made my way into the citadel in the aftermath of Atrax's inglorious retreat, I found its alleys, paths and streets jammed with old men and women, young women and girls, mothers clutching infants, men shielding their families and wailing orphans. They all had listless, frightened expressions and even the hardest hearts would have taken pity on them.

'They must be ejected from the citadel at once.'

The candles on stands around the table at which we sat cast everyone in a pale-yellow light. Tired, drawn faces stared at the high priest, who along with Gallia looked remarkably fresh and calm. He sipped at a silver chalice holding wine, frowning that his suggestion appeared to fall on deaf ears.

'Impossible,' snapped Akmon, 'to do so would abandon them to certain death.'

'May I remind your majesty,' said Parmenion slowly and deliberately, 'that the citadel is reserved for Media's royal family, its nobles and the servants of Shamash. By bringing the common folk into its confines, we risk insulting the Sun God.'

'How so?' I demanded to know.

'The temple is the abode of the Sun God, majesty,' he informed me, 'and he requires offerings daily to appease him.'

'I know this,' I told him.

He took another sip of wine. 'If we displease the Sun God, he will abandon us, the more so since Prince Atrax was blessed in the temple in the citadel when an infant.'

'The same Atrax who crucified some of my people,' growled Akmon.

'He is, of course, a rebel, majesty,' smiled Parmenion. 'But that does not change the fact that the Sun God's temple is in peril.'

'In what way?' asked Lusin.

'Four meals are served to the Sun God Each day, majesty,' Parmenion told her.

'I know that,' she snapped at him. 'I may have been born an Armenian, but I am fully acquainted with the care and treatment of the immortals.'

Parmenion put his chalice down on the table and held up his hands.

'I meant no offence, majesty, but my point is that the meals served to Shamash every day may provoke envy among the commoners given sanctuary in the citadel.'

He was referring to the main meal and a second meal served to the Sun God in the morning and another main meal and second one served to Him again in the afternoon. I was not acquainted with the specific dietary requirements of the Sun God but knew that in general the gods were served a variety of drink and food daily. The quantities could be prodigious, comprising casks of wine, milk and beer, dozens of loaves of bread, bushels of dates and the meat of rams, bulls, bullocks, lambs, birds and ducks. It was a common custom to not let the offerings rot but distribute them among the temple's priests and officials and their families. In this way the servants of the gods lived like kings, though the more unscrupulous among them were not averse to selling their portions in the markets.

'Then instead of eating them yourself, why don't you give them to the refugees in the citadel?' said Gallia. 'They are, after all, servants of Shamash, are they not?'

'That is not our custom, majesty,' he replied icily. 'Besides, with the city and countryside denied to us, the daily offerings will greatly diminish, risking the ire of the Sun God.'

'He will forgive us,' I said absently.

They all looked at me, Parmenion fuming that I, a mere mortal, dared speak on behalf of the Sun God.

'If we defeat Atrax then Shamash will forgive us, I meant to say,' I said hurriedly.

'That is a remote prospect, majesty,' stated a glum-faced Pogon, dark rings around his eyes. 'The first thing Atrax's soldiers did when they took possession of the city was to empty the granaries, which means we are dependent on the royal granaries in the citadel.'

He cast a glance at Parmenion. 'Plus the temple granaries.'

'How long will our supplies last?' asked an exhausted Joro.

'Seven days,' replied Pogon, 'after that we will have to slaughter the camels and then the horses, though their flesh will only give us a few more days' respite.'

'And alas the army of Dura will not be coming,' said Akmon, 'we all saw the severed head of the Amazon despatched to Dura to bring General Chrestus and his army here.'

Shoulders slumped and Pogon held his head in hands. Akmon looked at Lusin who reached over to grip his arm.

'We will need the horses to break out from the city,' I said.

'Impossible,' insisted Akmon, 'if I flee then my credibility collapses and Atrax will take Irbil and the whole of Media. I have little doubt that Lord Soter is rallying his retainers to join with the rebels even as we speak. If I desert Irbil I will have no army with which to retake the city.'

'No,' he said firmly, 'I will stay here and die here if necessary.'

'*We* will stay here,' added Lusin.

It was a touching scene but did nothing to alleviate the predicament we found ourselves in. I looked at Lucius.

'How many soldiers can we muster?'

'Around seven hundred, majesty, discounting the squires and civilians that were enlisted as archers and slingers.'

'Another five hundred at most,' said Joro, pouring himself more wine.

'It is highly unlikely such a force would be able to effect a breakout,' opined Lucius, 'unless the foot soldiers were sacrificed to allow the horsemen to escape.'

It was a logical assessment, but one greeted with looks of horror from the king, queen and the Medians present.

'I will not sanction such a dishonourable course of action,' said Akmon.

'Is this how war is waged in Dura?' growled Joro.

Lucius stood his ground. 'General, at Dura we are taught to win wars, using whatever tactics will achieve that end.'

'There is no victory in an inglorious flight,' sneered Parmenion.

'No indeed,' I said, 'but he who fights and runs away, lives to fight another day.'

I pointed at Akmon. 'Your life is more important than any sitting here at this table or in this citadel, much as you might like to argue otherwise. As long as you live, Atrax will not be able to rest easy. If you die, it is all over.'

'If there is to be a breakout, it should be launched sooner rather than later,' advised Lucius.

No one bothered to reply, all eyes focused on Akmon. I could have cut the tension in the air with a knife. The king was young, yet to reach his mid-twenties, his wife even younger, and perhaps it was unfair that he found himself in such a perilous situation. But the gods care little for fairness and I wondered if Gallia and I had been lured here to satisfy their callous natures.

'I will not flee,' said Akmon, 'my decision is final. If you wish to leave Irbil, King Pacorus, you should follow the advice of your quartermaster general.'

'We are staying,' said Gallia without bothering to consult me.

'We had all better get some rest, then,' I suggested.

On the way out, I cornered Lucius to thank him for devising the plan to rescue me, Gallia informing me I had him to thank for my salvation.

'It was quite simple, majesty,' he told me. 'I remembered an incident during the Servile War.'

'The what?'

He blushed. 'Apologies, majesty, but in Rome the war against Spartacus is called the Servile War. Well, I remembered Spartacus being trapped on Mount Vesuvius by a large force of Romans soldiers. He solved that problem by making ropes from the many vines that grew on the slopes of Vesuvius, which allowed his men to abseil down a sheer rock face to attack the Roman troops from the rear.'

'I remember Claudia telling me that story,' exclaimed Gallia. Lucius appeared confused.

'Not my daughter,' I said, 'Claudia was the wife of Spartacus whom we named our first child after.'

'Using mirrors to reflect sunlight,' he continued, 'was copied from the tactic your own father used in the battle where you captured the eagle that resides in the Great Temple at Hatra, majesty.'

I slapped him on the shoulder. 'You have a better memory than me, Lucius.'

We parted company with him at the entrance to the royal quarters where Gallia and I had been allotted a bedroom, two of Pogon's spearmen snapping to attention and opening the door to allow us to enter. Normally the palace guard would be guarding the residence of the king and queen, but after their exertions earlier Joro had allowed them all a night's rest before the fighting that everyone expected on the morrow.

Gallia linked her arm in mine. 'You are getting too old to be playing hero.'

'I have grown rather fond of Klietas. If we get out of Irbil alive and not in chains, I'm going to take him back to Dura.'

'What use will an illiterate village orphan be? What will he do?'

'He can join the Daughters of Dura,' I quipped. 'He's an orphan, so he qualifies for your teenage assassins.'

She poked me in the ribs. 'In case you had not noticed, he is a boy.'

'In that case I will establish my own body of waifs and strays. It will give me something to do.'

'What will you call it?' she asked.

I thought for a moment. 'How about, the Orphans of the Exiles?'

We laughed, and I held her close. It was good to be back by her side, even though we both stood on the edge of calamity. We turned the corner and our smiles disappeared. Leaning against the wall painted with a fresco of a lion hunt was a man with white hair, pale skin and wearing a silver scale-armour cuirass exactly the same as the one owned by Gallia and me, though Atrax now wore mine. Girra turned to us.

'I have returned some items that belong to you, King Pacorus. Sacrificing yourself for the boy was unexpected. Ishtar was delighted.'

He opened the door and walked inside.

'Come.'

Feeling like small children we did as we were told, my eyes immediately alighting on the sword, helmet and armour lying on the bed. Without thinking I rushed over to them, pulled the *spatha* from its scabbard and examined it closely.

'It is not a copy,' said Girra, 'though in truth a better example could have been made if Atrax had made good on his promise to melt it down.'

'Will you and the others assist us, lord?' asked Gallia.

Girra pointed at my armour and sword. 'I have helped you, warrior queen. But you must use your own wits to defeat Atrax, as well as paying heed to the story of the seven sons. Do you regret not calling on King Gafarn for assistance, King Pacorus?'

'No,' I said firmly, 'I have lost too many of those close to me already.'

He looked at us kindly. 'So be it. I bid you goodnight.'

He turned and marched from the room, closing the door quietly behind him. I slid my sword back in its scabbard, grateful beyond words it and the helmet gifted to me by Castus all those years ago were back in my possession. I went to bed a happy man with Gallia in my arms and an inkling the gods just might be on our side.

The next morning the enemy attacked once again.

Atrax might have been a preening young fool but his general knew what he was doing. Titus Tullus had over twenty years' experience in one of the best armies in the world and he used his knowledge to good effect. After a hasty and meagre breakfast of bread, cheese and yoghurt, we rode down into the now-deserted city to the walls, which had been manned by a small force of Pogon's spearmen. Once more the garrison and its Duran allies were split into four groups, each one again assigned to a specific section of the perimeter wall.

This time our numbers had been reduced by casualties and desertions, though to be fair the majority of the civilian archers and slingers once again reported for duty. But our supplies of arrows were low, and we could only allocate the civilian archers one quiver each. They seemed happy enough: the western gates were locked shut and the bridge over the ditch was gone. Believing the enemy could not breach the walls, their morale was high, though only because they did not know no relief was coming.

I stood on the wall with Zenobia, Gallia, Bullus and Klietas, the latter counting the number of stones in his bag, in between casting glances at the enemy marshalling beyond the ditch. Bullus had a bandage on his right arm and his helmet's crest had been destroyed in the previous day's fighting.

'They will hit us hard today,' he warned.

Accompanied by the racket of kettledrums and the abuse of thousands of hill men, the first assault was a highly coordinated affair, far removed from the earlier tactics of Laodice's wild hordes. Once more I deployed the civilian slingers and archers in the towers spaced along the wall either side of the gates, both to get them out of the way of the Amazons and legionaries who were trained to work together, and to increase the effectiveness of their slingshots and arrows, as they would be shooting down on the enemy.

That was my first mistake.

Whereas before we were shooting at hill men carrying wicker shields and wearing no armour, this time we faced the locked shields of Pontic legionaries, behind which were foot archers aiming at those in the towers. Once more Bullus arranged his legionaries so their shields became an extension of the wall, through which the Amazons could shoot at the enemy. But the enemy they were shooting at were slingers whose weapons had a longer range than the compound bows used by Zenobia's warriors. And whereas their arrows fell short, the lead shots of the Pontic slingers were deadly even at ranges of up to four hundred paces and beyond.

I heard a thud and saw an Amazon collapse a few paces away, a lead shot having pierced her eye socket to enter her brain. Gallia ran over to her but there was nothing anyone could do.

'Cease shooting,' she called.

As one her women took cover behind the wall, slingshots slamming into shields and going over our heads to land harmlessly among the buildings near the ramparts. Screams were coming from the towers as the enemy picked off the civilians, who always stood and watched where their missiles fell instead of making themselves a smaller target after they had taken their shot. Soon the towers were filled with dead and wounded men, those who had not been hit by the deluge of enemy arrows shot at them deciding to flee the raised fighting platforms. But to do so required them descending ladders that were exposed to the elements, and the enemy. As a result, more civilians were killed trying to escape the towers that had become nothing more than raised death traps.

I did not blame them. What were they but farmers and the like who had performed as well as expected against professional soldiers? And the Pontic legionaries were above all professionals. After clearing the towers there was a brief lull in the battle as Atrax's slingers and archers ceased shooting and the Amazons and Bullus' men continued to take shelter behind the wall. I peeked over the latter to take stock of the situation. I saw around five hundred Pontic legionaries deployed in two lines, the foot archers behind them and between them a line of slingers. Behind them all was a mass of hill men. I could not see any horsemen or a dragon banner and assumed Atrax was somewhere else, most likely at the northern gates where another dragon banner would be flying.

Klietas beside me looked over the wall.

'What now, highborn?'

I pushed his head down as a lead shot ricocheted off the top of the wall a couple of feet away.

'Now they will make a lot of noise, but they have no way of crossing the ditch and scaling the walls,' I told him.

That was my second mistake.

I had forgotten Media was littered with orchards and vineyards and Atrax had been diligent on his march, harvesting the ample amount of wood to construct the means to cross the ditch and scaling ladders for his soldiers to climb the wall. I watched with horror as dozens of hill men rushed forward under the cover of the archers and slingers, groups holding what looked like long wooden trestles and others shouldering scaling ladders. I looked at Gallia, who nocked an arrow in her bowstring.

'To your positions,' she called.

I too nocked an arrow and shot it at one of four men holding a trestle they intended to throw across the ditch, hitting him in the stomach, causing him to pitch forward on the ground. The others stopped, allowing me to string another arrow and shoot a second hill man, prompting the others to drop the trestle and flee.

The Amazons were shooting at a rapid rate, ignoring the hail of missiles being shot at them by the enemy, the raised shields of Bullus' men providing some protection. An arrow glanced off the shield being held by the centurion, fortunately deflecting upwards away from me. Bullus growled with fury when two or more lead shots struck his shield, to lodge in the wood. But Duran shields were well made and even though the shots penetrated the hide and splintered the wood behind, they did not break through.

The air was filled with cracks and thwacks as the Amazons cut down dozens of hill men, shooting a combined total of over six hundred arrows a minute. To our front the ground beyond the ditch was littered with dead and dying men and for a moment I thought we might repulse the enemy's attack. But we were less than a hundred archers manning a small section of the wall, and to our left and right, on the edges of Lucius' field defences, other groups of hill men had reached the ditch and were crossing it on their rickety, makeshift bridges.

'Sound withdrawal,' I commanded Bullus.

For a split-second I saw surprise in his eyes, but he turned to the signaller crouching nearby and issued the order.

The trumpet sounded and immediately the Amazons ceased shooting and crouched low behind the wall, the legionaries doing likewise. Gallia was incensed but I had no time to explain.

'Reform at the bottom of the embankment,' I told Bullus.

His men and the Amazons scrambled down the earth bank to form up near the temporary stables. I grabbed Klietas and threw him down the embankment, following him with Gallia at my side.

'What are you doing?' she cried.

'We are about to be outflanked,' I said, reaching level ground and pointing to further along the wall where bareheaded hill men were swarming onto the ramparts after climbing their ladders.

'Get your men back to the citadel,' I ordered Bullus, 'we will cover you.'

'The Amazons will mount up,' I shouted.

Zenobia glanced at Gallia who nodded, her commander shouting at her women to move. I ordered Klietas to fall back with the legionaries, Bullus grabbing his tunic and hauling him away as his men commenced a forced march back to the citadel.

I ran to the stables to saddle Horns and join Gallia and her Amazons, who were forming up near the gates, bows in hand but now running desperately low on ammunition. I rode Horns from the stables and saw hill men running along the walls towards the gates.

'Move,' I commanded.

Gallia stayed with me as two files of Amazons trotted away as more enemy hill men came from the right and left and began running down the embankment, intent on getting to grips with us. Gallia shot an arrow to hit a bare-chested man in the mid-rift and I loosed an arrow at a wild axe man screaming at the top of his voice as he hurtled towards me, the missile hitting him in the chest to cause him to crumple in a heap on the ground. We turned our horses and galloped away from the gates to follow the Amazons.

The hill men at first concentrated on celebrating their capture of the gates rather than launching a pursuit. I slowed Horns and Gallia halted her own horse to observe the mass of barbarians at the entrance, all whooping and cheering deliriously. I pulled an arrow from my quiver and nocking it in the bowstring. We were about two hundred paces from the gates, but I had a clear view of the crowd of hill men that was growing in size by the minute. I raised my bow and let the sinew cord slip through my fingers, watching the arrow arch upwards as it flew through the air to land among the enemy. My gesture did nothing to interrupt the celebrations and I considered shooting another arrow.

'You should save your ammunition,' Gallia told me, 'we do not know what has happened at the other gates.'

Her words were prophetic because when we reached the ramp leading to the citadel we found a scene of chaos. The assault on the western gates had obviously been delayed for some reason, because whereas Bullus and his Durans and Zenobia and her Amazons had the time to conduct a disciplined withdrawal, the retreats from the other city entrances had been more desperate.

The palace guard, arrayed in a semi-circle around the base of the ramp, was endeavouring to hold back what looked like hundreds of hill men who were flooding from every side street. On the ramp itself, Akmon's dismounted horse archers were shooting at the barbarians, their arrows seemingly making little impact on the swelling numbers of Laodice's heathens. And we were all bystanders to the drama, unnoticed by friend and foe alike. But it would not last for long. I rode over to Bullus.

'Reinforce the palace guard at the foot of the ramp. The Amazons will provide support behind your wedge.'

Once more the grizzled centurion placed himself at the tip of a wedge of legionaries and led the charge into the maelstrom, he and his men with their shields tucked tight to their bodies, stabbing and jabbing their swords into enemy torsos, legs and necks as they sawed their way forward. Behind them, their horses at walking pace, came the Amazons, shooting their bows only when they were certain to strike a foe. Gallia organised half of them to concentrate on what was going on behind, for as soon as Bullus and his men attacked, the enemy became aware of our presence.

I stayed with the rear rank of the Amazons, turning Horns frequently to get a clearer indication of what was happening. Of my two quivers one was empty and the other contained around a dozen arrows.

Enemy soldiers armed with axes tried to get close to the horses to slash at their legs and bellies. One or two succeeded, inflicting horrendous wounds on the mounts of Amazons, both horse and rider collapsing before being surrounded and hacked to pieces by blood-crazed barbarians. I shot one, two, three hill men in quick succession, Gallia coming to my side to shoot more arrows at men with bloodlust in their eyes closing in on us. There was a trumpet blast and Zenobia turned all the Amazons towards guarding the rear of Bullus' wedge. I heard a succession of wicked hisses and saw at least a score of enemy soldiers fall, then more when a second volley was unleashed at them.

'Let them through.'

I turned to see the ragged semi-circle of palace guard part to allow Bullus and the Amazons through. I gave Gallia a smile of huge relief and she grinned back. I heard a shout and saw with horror a half-naked hill man rush at her with axe gripped with both hands. He screamed in rage and used all his strength to swing it sideways at her belly, my mouth dropping open as the curved blade struck her body.

To shatter like a clay pot dropped on a stone floor.

He stared in disbelief, gaping up at Gallia who drew her sword and slashed it across his neck, sending a spurt of blood into the air. She turned her mare to follow the Amazons, now almost devoid of arrows, cantering through the now closing gap, their queen ordering them up the ramp and into the citadel. I rode Horns forward and the palace guard closed the gap, a horde of hill men rushing forward to attempt to hack their way through the locked shields with their axes.

I saw a banner appear and recognised the figures of Akmon and Joro on their horses, around them cataphracts and squires hacking left and right to force a way through the throng of hill men. The archers behind me on the ramp saw them too and began directing their arrows towards the barbarians trying to kill their king.

'Get off your horse,' I heard someone shout, prompting me to slide off Horns' back.

Gallia did the same so as not to impede the archers' view. Arrows hissed over our heads as the banner inched its way towards the semi-circle of soldiers, now extended outwards by the addition of Bullus and his men. The palace guard and Durans were holding their defensive formation, assisted by the growing pile of enemy dead in front of them, over which the hill men had to clamber to give battle them.

I could see Akmon's face now, contorted with concentration while hacking at men with his sword as he moved forward. I could also see foot soldiers and even civilian archers and slingers in the gaps between his and Joro's horse and those of the cataphracts. The mounted soldiers were shielding those on foot, thus sacrificing their mobility and speed. But Akmon was rewarded by bringing the bulk of his men back to the citadel, his palace guard opening ranks a second time to allow him and those with him through. He raised his sword in salute when he saw me and Gallia, utter relief etched on his face. I bowed my head at him in salute at his achievement.

'You must withdraw to the citadel,' said Joro in a no-nonsense fashion, 'as should you, majesties.'

'Where is Governor Pogon?' asked Akmon.

No one knew, and I feared he was dead, for only enemy soldiers were coming from the streets that led to the southern gates. Akmon shook his head.

'And your own man, Lucius Varsas, King Pacorus?'

An arrow felled one of the archers standing on the ramp.

'He is in the citadel, majesty,' the commander of his palace guard told him, 'as you should be, high one.'

Joro unceremoniously grabbed his king's reins and led him up the ramp, his cataphracts following. The spearmen and civilians had not stopped to gossip but were already inside the citadel and I decided it was time to follow them. Arrows were flying overhead and around us, signalling the enemy's archers had been brought into the city. It was only a matter of time before the Pontic legionaries would be upon us.

The palace guard conducted a magnificent withdrawal up the ramp, maintaining their *testudo*-like formation as they inched upwards towards the open gates into the citadel. The air was now thick with arrows and slingshots, the latter making loud thuds as they hit shields. Suddenly a guard would collapse as either an arrow or lead shot found its way between two shields or went through the narrow gap between those shields held vertically around the edges of the formation and those held horizontally to form a roof of hide and wood. Momentarily a gaping hole was created, into which one or more missiles would be shot. But the space would be closed, and the wounded man hauled inside the *testudo*, or abandoned if he was dead. But halfway up the ramp the *testudo* was stopped in its tracks by the sheer volume of missiles being directed at it, hundreds of archers and slingers shooting at it. This allowed the hill men to surge up the ramp to launch a frenzied attack on the rear of the palace guard. I stood with Bullus at the gates, his men forming a reserve just inside the citadel, and shook my head.

'It is like watching a deer being dragged down by a pack of hyenas.'

And then it started to rain clay.

There were hundreds of hill men in a huge press around the bottom of the ramp and more in a great mass on its lower half, and all were suddenly assaulted with clay pots.

'What in the name of all that's holy is that?' exclaimed Bullus.

I later learned it was called 'dragon fire' and had been invented in the armouries at Vanadzor. Akmon had brought the recipe south with him, though had never intended for it to be a part of Irbil's arsenal. But he had reckoned without the inquiring mind of Lucius Varsas, who when the king had mentioned the toxic substance to my quartermaster general, had proposed creating an amount to offset the numerical superiority of the enemy.

A mixture of quicklime, bitumen, sulphur, naphtha and resin, 'dragon fire' was a highly inflammable, sticky liquid that burnt for a long time and stuck to what it landed on. Bullus was wearing a malicious grin when the small pots began smashing among the press of hill men, flames spreading in all directions as the burning liquid attached itself to skin, clothes, shields and weapons. From the walls above pots were tossed into the seething mass of hill man, erupting in flames when they impacted on the ground or hit the heads of victims. Hideous screams pierced the air and I was horrified to see men burning like torches running around like demented animals, clawing at their bodies in a futile attempt to remove the burning liquid that was peeling away the layers of skin on their bodies.

They scattered in all directions in a vain attempt to escape the torment being inflicted on them: down the ramp, spilling over the sides of the ramp, and careering into the slingers and archers shooting at the immobile palace guard. The missile troops forgot the latter as they fled from the grotesque human torches running at them. The deluge of arrows and slingshots abruptly ceased, allowing the palace guard to abandon its *testudo* to reach the sanctuary of the citadel. When the last soldiers of the palace guard had hastened through the gates, they were slammed shut and barricaded, the nauseating smell of burning human flesh hanging in the hot air, causing many to retch.

We had survived but were once again besieged in the citadel.

Chapter 14

'Slay whatever lives.'

'I must say the enemy tactics were both innovative and daring,' remarked Lucius, the only one among us who could see anything positive in our current situation.

'Daring, innovative?' Joro spat the words at him like a soldier hurling javelins. 'We have lost nearly two hundred men today; the palace guard has been reduced by nearly a quarter and our ammunition supplies are almost non-existent.'

'And Governor Pogon is dead,' said Akmon softly.

Lucius nodded. 'But we still retain the citadel, which has its own water supply, the enemy has no siege engines and no hope of scaling its walls.'

Joro clapped his hands together. 'Excellent, we will only starve to death instead of dying of thirst.'

Parmenion, the only one among us not looking the worse for wear following the morning's exertions, held out his chalice for it to be refilled by a slave. The palace was unbearably warm in the late-afternoon sun, the air still and tinged with the mere hint of the dreadful fragrance of burnt human flesh. As a result, we had gathered in the calm of the gazebo in the centre of the royal garden, the sound of bubbling fountains only partially masking the drums being beaten around the citadel. The slaves were nervous, the one holding the wine jug staring up at the sky as the enemy's drums sounded constantly.

'My chalice,' snapped Parmenion.

The slave panicked and tripped, spilling wine over the high priest's pristine white robe. Gallia laughed but Parmenion jumped up and struck the slave across the face.

'You will be flogged for your insolence.'

'It was a mistake,' I said.

The priest turned on me.

'I insist he is flogged, majesty,' Parmenion said to Akmon, ignoring me.

The frightened slave, a boy no older than sixteen, stood quaking holding the wine jug. Akmon beckoned over another slave, older than the boy, and told him to take him away, and to bring a towel and warm water for the high priest.

'We have more important things to worry about than a clumsy slave,' said Akmon.

'The situation is hopeless,' said Parmenion in anger, 'any fool can see that Atrax will win. At least let me meet with him to evacuate the civilians from the citadel.'

'An excellent idea,' enthused Lucius. 'It will make our food supplies last longer.'

'How will that help us?' asked Joro, holding out his own chalice for it to be refilled.

'King Gafarn at Hatra will be aware by now that his brother has seemingly vanished from the face of the earth,' explained Lucius, 'and will be sending out scouts to search for him. He will also be liaising with Governor Kuris at Vanadzor by courier. It is only a matter of time before Hatra turns its eyes towards Media.'

Two female slaves hurried from the palace with towels and water to attend to Parmenion, who regarded my quartermaster general coolly as they wiped his robe.

263

'Will you allow me to speak to Prince Atrax, majesty?' the high priest asked Akmon. 'He was born and raised in Irbil and will not wish to see its people suffer.'

Gallia scoffed at such a notion.

'Having already crucified some, I doubt Atrax has thought once about the people. All he is interested in is becoming king of Media and he will do anything to achieve that aim, including walking on the corpses of every man, woman and child in Irbil.'

'You should not meet with him,' I advised, 'he is consumed with hate and loathing.'

'I have known the prince for almost his entire life, majesty,' he told me, 'and besides, he would not dare inflict harm on a servant of the Sun God.'

I looked at Gallia who rolled her eyes, but Akmon had a purposeful look on his face and I could see the words of his high priest had influenced him.

'I have no desire to see the thousands of innocents packed into the citadel suffer unnecessarily,' the king declared. 'You have my permission to meet with Prince Atrax, High Priest Parmenion, though you must stress to him that you do so only to save this city's civilians from further suffering, nothing more.'

Parmenion rose slowly and bowed deeply, waving the slaves away. 'It shall be as you desire, majesty. Now if you will excuse me, I will go to the temple to ask the Sun God to bless my mission.'

'You will meet Atrax in the morning,' Akmon told him, 'we do not want to give the impression we are desperate.'

Once more Parmenion bowed to him before taking his leave. Following his cue, Akmon and Lusin rose from their couches, occasioning the rest of us to do likewise. Akmon smiled at us but

Lusin, pale and looking desperately tired, said nothing and avoided our eyes. It was obvious she was at the end of her tether and I wondered how long Akmon would be able to maintain the façade of kingship, only recently bestowed upon him. He was a foreigner in a foreign land and lacked the authority that came with being a descendent of an ancient Median family, unlike Atrax who could claim to be descended from Media's long line of kings.

I said as much to Gallia as we walked back to our bedroom, my limbs suddenly aching and tiredness sweeping over me. It had been a long day and I needed to lie down to regain my strength, notwithstanding the mythical beverage we had been served that infused our bodies and minds with vitality. We were, after all, mere mortals and not gods.

'That priest is a fool,' she said, 'an arrogant, high-minded fool who knows nothing.'

'But a useful fool,' I said.

'In what way?'

We turned a corner to enter the corridor leading to our bedroom, a guard posted outside the room opening the door and snapping to attention as we entered.

'Parmenion will give us time,' I answered, the guard closing the door behind us. 'I'm sure he and Atrax will have lots to talk about as they reminisce about the past. It will probably buy us another day.'

'Atrax will kill him.'

I nearly jumped out of my skin when I saw the stocky individual in a long robe leaning against the wall, beside him a male lion baring its canines at us. In Erra's right hand he held a mace topped by a double lion's head; in his belt was tucked a scimitar. He patted the lion on the head.

'Hush, now.'

He turned his face to me. 'But you know that, don't you?'

I looked at the door. Erra appeared disappointed.

'If I wished you both harm, you would be dead already.'

'Then what do you want?' I demanded, eager to get some rest.

Erra smiled. 'How arrogant you have become, King Pacorus, and so ungrateful. Your beloved wife would be dead by now if it had not been for the armour gifted to her by Girra.'

He shook his head and tut-tutted. I swallowed my pride.

'I meant to give no offence.'

'As to what I want,' said Erra cheerily, 'I wished to convey my congratulations. Your presence has stiffened young King Akmon's resolve and your Roman has proved most entertaining. It was delightful to witness the incineration of the Pontic barbarians. Very clever.'

'You inform us of the danger to High Priest Parmenion so that we may save him?' enquired Gallia without enthusiasm.

Erra laughed. 'Even though you are a foreigner, Queen Gallia, I have to tell you that of all the queens in Parthia, you are esteemed first among equals. As to saving Parmenion, I present you both with a dilemma.

'If you prevent Parmenion from meeting with Atrax, then you will save his life. But if you do nothing and the high priest dies, then Lord Shamash will damn Atrax, for it is death to murder one of his high priests in cold blood. The choice is yours. Come.'

The lion rose from the floor and followed its master as he opened the door and casually walked into the corridor, closing the door behind him. I looked at Gallia and she stared back. She was going to speak but I rushed over to the door and opened it. The guard turned to face me, hand on the hilt of his sword.

'Is everything as it should be, majesty?'

I looked up and down the corridor.

'Have you seen anything amiss?' I asked him.

He gave me a quizzical look. 'No, majesty.'

I re-entered the bedroom.

'Is this a dream?'

She removed her cuirass and stretched her tired limbs. 'If it is, it is very lifelike.'

I too removed my armour, which was as light as a feather, and tossed it on the couch near the double bed.

'So, what do we do about Parmenion?'

Gallia sat on the bed and began to remove her boots.

'We do nothing. As I said, he is a fool and the world will not miss one less fool. Let him go to his prince and receive his reward. But if Shamash abandons Atrax, then we are saved, and so is Akmon's reign. And that is what we came for, to save his arse.'

She was right, we had come to Irbil to assist Akmon. But I slept uneasily that night thinking about what would happen when Parmenion met with Atrax. Did the high priest deserve to die and would I stand by and watch him unwittingly go to his death?

Atrax, who had agreed to meet Parmenion following the despatch of an envoy at dawn, had made no effort to clear away the bodies of those slain fighting and burnt alive when Parmenion walked from the citadel in the early morning sunlight the next day. In honour of his mission, Akmon had commanded Joro to array the palace guard either side of the road that led to the gates, or at least those still able to shoulder weapons and armour. Out of courtesy I had ordered Bullus to draw up what was left of his century beside the palace guard, eighty Durans standing crisply to attention as the high priest walked past them. Beside him was Akmon, resplendent in a gleaming dragon-skin armour cuirass, Lusin beside him attired in a beautiful blue dress and both wearing gold crowns. I walked beside Gallia behind the trio, behind us four white-robed priests from the Temple of Shamash who would accompany Parmenion. One carried a white sunshade to protect their high priest from the heat, though it was pleasantly warm as opposed to the scorching heat that would come later.

As we walked towards the gates, the door cut into one of them opened to allow the priests to exit, I began fidgeting with the hilt of my sword, turning over in my mind whether I should warn Parmenion he was in grave danger. I was about to speak when Gallia grabbed my arm. I looked at her and she shook her head.

'It is fate,' she said softly.

The commander of the palace guard went to step beyond the open door but Parmenion stopped him.

'I am under the protection of Shamash, there is no need for armed guards.'

With all the authority and conviction of his position, he stepped onto the ramp and disappeared, his priests following. We left the gates to walk up the stone steps beside the guardroom leading to the battlements, spearmen and archers snapping to attention as we passed them. The ramparts gave a magnificent view of Irbil below and the lush green plain surrounding the city beyond. In the far distance could be seen the Zagros Mountains, but all eyes were fixed on the small group making its way slowly down the ramp. They gingerly dodged the results of Lucius' handiwork to arrive at the foot of the ramp, a lone horseman trotting forward from one of the streets leading from the citadel to the perimeter wall. He halted his mount and gestured to the high priest, then turned his horse to head back to the street. I could see groups of soldiers – Pontic legionaries, most likely – in the side streets conducting patrols, but there was no sign of Atrax. Then Parmenion and his priests disappeared into one of the buildings halfway down the street, a shop probably, though it was difficult to identify precisely from a distance.

'It is very quiet,' said Lusin, looking around at the death and destruction visited on the city where she was queen.

'Better that than the din of battle, lady,' I said. 'Anything that buys us time is to be welcomed.'

I turned to Akmon. 'If Parmenion secures safe passage for the civilians in the citadel, will you let them leave?'

'Of course, why would I not?'

'Because they will see Atrax as their saviour when they walk out of this place and return to their homes, especially if he fills their bellies.'

His brow creased. 'There is no alternative. If they stay in the citadel, our food supplies will run out very quickly. With our numbers reduced to just the garrison and your soldiers, King Pacorus, we stand a chance of holding out until help comes.'

I caught Joro's eye and his expression told me what I was thinking. No immediate help was coming and even if Hatra was roused to action, initially it would only be a token force to investigate what had happened to Dura's rulers.

'Quite right,' I said to Akmon.

'There's Parmenion.'

269

We all turned to look in the direction Lusin was pointing. To see a small group of white-robed figures emerge from the building they had entered just a few minutes before. I was relieved to see five individuals.

'Atrax hasn't murdered them,' said Gallia, 'that is something, at least.'

'Perhaps the gods do not know everything, after all,' I remarked, absentmindedly.

Lusin gave me a confused look. 'Lord?'

'Nothing,' I smiled, 'just an old man thinking out loud.'

I had to admit I was astounded when Parmenion returned to inform us Atrax had agreed that those civilians that desired to leave the citadel could return to their homes. He further promised to provide them with food and even allow those farmers who had become refugees after fleeing their villages, to return to their homes to gather in the harvest.

'Not so generous, then,' I remarked, 'Atrax will send the farmers back to their villages to harvest the crops ripening in the fields, after which he will take those crops to feed the city.'

Akmon, his spirits having been revived by Parmenion's embassy, leaned back on his throne and frowned at me.

'That is the nature of commerce, lord, the farmers harvest their crops, which are sold in the city.'

'Except there will be no exchange of money,' I cautioned, 'which makes it theft.'

Parmenion cleared his throat. 'King Pacorus, your enthusiasm regarding the welfare of farmers is to be commended. However, having met with King, er Prince Atrax, I can state unequivocally he will abide by his words. He has only the interests of Media at heart.'

'If that was the case, he would have stayed in Pontus or Armenia, or wherever he was skulking, rather than march an army into this kingdom,' remarked Gallia caustically.

'When can the civilians return to their homes?' asked Akmon in haste, eager to avoid a clash between my wife and the high priest.

'This afternoon, majesty,' said Parmenion. 'I will go to the temple to give thanks to Shamash for bringing about this miracle.'

'It might be wise to remove the bodies on and around the ramp,' advised Joro, 'we don't want to cause a panic.'

'And put them where?' I asked.

'Perhaps Atrax can arrange their cremation,' offered Gallia, 'seeing as he is in a generous mood.'

'I will go out of the citadel once more to ask if he can arrange for the removal and disposal of the dead,' said Parmenion.

Akmon nodded his assent. Parmenion bowed his head to the king, turned and marched from the throne room, Gallia curling her lip at him as he did so, a gesture that made Lusin laugh. I grinned. It was good to see some colour back in the queen's cheeks, her lovely face wearing a smile.

Many of the civilians were also smiling as they made their way to the citadel's gates, mothers holding the hands of their young children and elderly couples arm-in-arm and chatting excitedly now their ordeal was over. Many men, whom I assumed had volunteered to be archers or slingers but who had fled from the reality of combat, cast down their heads when they passed through the open gates of the citadel, ashamed their courage had faltered. Klietas stood beside me, smiling like a fool and nodding his head as hundreds of civilians made their way down the ramp, which Atrax had cleared of corpses. I

271

had offered him sanctuary in Dura and he had accepted, though whether we would get out of Irbil alive remained to be seen.

'It is not too late to go with them,' I told him.

His head stopped nodding. 'No, highborn, I will go to the rich city of Dura and find myself a princess to marry.'

'Princesses usually marry a prince, Klietas.'

'When I kill Prince Atrax, then King Akmon will make me a prince,' he said with conviction.

I had to admit I found his simplistic notion of the world and everything it in endearing. That and his unshakeable belief he would survive the predicament he found himself in.

Klietas smiled at Parmenion who passed us with a coterie of priests, the high priest ignoring him and giving me a triumphant smile. As a servant of Shamash his overriding loyalty was to the Sun God; everything else came second, including allegiance to the man who currently occupied Media's throne. As he joined the throng of civilians moving down the ramp, I wondered what, aside from the agreement concerning the non-combatants, had passed between him and Atrax during their meeting.

Pontic legionaries could be seen across the ends of some of the streets, leaving the main one through from the citadel to the western gates into the city open, to presumably channel the civilians down that route. I did not give this a second thought until I heard Gallia's voice coming from the top of the steps inside the gates.

'Pacorus, you should see this.'

I walked from the ramp and ascended the stone steps, a sense of unease enveloping me as I stepped onto the battlements where a row of concerned faces was staring at the thousands of civilians milling around the base of the ramp, hundreds of others on the ramp itself. Pontic legionaries were preventing them from entering streets, the only avenue open being the one leading to the western gates. But that was now filled with a throng moving towards the citadel.

'Get them back inside,' I said, 'get them all back inside.'

Joro gave the order, which was instantly relayed to the commander of the palace guard at the gates. He chose the only course open to him: to use his signallers to sound recall. But the trumpets sounding at the top of the ramp merely spread panic among those civilians on the slope.

Greater panic ensued when the hill men pounced upon the civilians. We could only stand and watch the unfolding horror, the barbarians from Pontus using their axes and shields to go among the now panicking and screaming civilians to separate them into groups.

'What are they doing?' asked a distraught Lusin.

Horrible screams reached our ears as innocents were cut down.

'They are killing them!'

Lusin was beside herself, Akmon placing an arm around her shoulders.

'Not all,' said Gallia bitterly.

Groups of civilians were being bundled down the street that led to the western gates. It was difficult to identify what exactly was going on, but Gallia was quick to offer her opinion.

'They are seizing the women and the young for slaves and killing the rest.'

The commander of the palace guard was beside Joro.

'Do you want me to launch an attack, lord?'

'We have been well and truly duped,' Joro told him. 'Use your men to get as many civilians back inside the citadel as possible.'

Young women, girls, babies and teenage boys were highly prized as captives because they would fetch a good price in slave markets. Women who could bear children were particularly valuable because they could be bred to produce future slaves. Conversely, the old and crippled were worthless as far as slave traders were concerned. So the hill men were slaughtering them, chopping them down mercilessly with their axes. They were also killing any men they came across because able-bodied males were often more trouble than they were worth on their way to the slave markets.

Those still on the ramp when the hill men attacked were the lucky ones, though a few tumbled off its edge to fall on the hard ground below when the panic started. But those on the ramp were in the minority and soon the area around its base was once again littered with bodies, with hundreds of hill men bundling thousands of screaming and weeping civilians away from the citadel.

And all we could do was watch helplessly as the full extent of Atrax's treachery was revealed. Lusin had buried her head in her hands and was weeping, Akmon was bereft of hope and Joro's jaw was locked rigid in anger. This was a black day for Media indeed.

The commander of the palace guard performed a minor miracle in getting hundreds of people back into the citadel, sending his men down the ramp in single file to form up at the bottom to do battle with the hill men. Bullus and his legionaries followed and for a while the Pontic barbarians had their wings clipped. But Titus Tullus, mounted on a horse with his officers around him, sent detachments into the crowd to search out and destroy the rescue force. Bullus and his counterpart were too experienced as commanders to allow their men to be cut off and butchered, and so they rescued as many civilians as was possible before conducting a skilled withdrawal. The gates were slammed shut and the wails and weeping of civilians filled the citadel. Below, the hill men and their captives disappeared to leave a carpet of dead.

Titus Tullus and his legionaries were still present, though, and they began banging the shafts of their javelins against the insides of their shields to create an annoying racket, added to which were kettledrums from a mounted party that suddenly appeared, among them Atrax in a shining armour cuirass. He held a spear in his right hand, which he used to jab a tall, white-robed individual in the back with the point – Parmenion.

'Oh, no, please.'

I heard Lusin's faint voice, but my eyes were fixed on the scene being played out below, the outcome of which I did not doubt.

'He would not dare,' said Akmon.

The other four priests that had accompanied Parmenion were also pushed in front of the mounted party, their heads cast down, though the high priest himself was not cowered by the prospect of imminent death. He turned his head to stare at Atrax, gesticulating with his arms and I assume spitting words at the venomous son of Darius. We could not discern what he was saying but I heard the gasps from those on the walls when Atrax thrust the spear into Parmenion's back. The high priest's body stiffened for a few seconds before crumbling to the ground.

'Murderer!' shouted Akmon, prompting others on the ramparts to hurl curses and threats at Atrax.

Parmenion writhed on the ground as he died a slow and painful death. Archers shot down the other four priests, each one being hit by one or more arrows. At least their ends were quick. Atrax sat on his horse staring up at us as his former high priest crawled forlornly towards the ramp, a large stain appearing on the back of his robe where the point of the spear had been plunged into his body. Then his movements stopped, as did the threats coming from the battlements.

'You will die a slow and painful death, that I promise,' I said to myself.

'It is over,' announced Joro, 'take the queen back to the palace, majesty.'

'Yes, yes, of course,' said a shaken Akmon, ushering his wife away from the scene of carnage below.

'Klietas,' I called, 'get your scrawny arse up here.'

Wearing his permanent grin, he came sprinting up the steps, nearly crashing into the king and queen and receiving a cuff round the ears from Joro as his reward. Undeterred, the boy ran to my side, his grin disappearing when he saw the extent of the carnage below. I pointed at Atrax in front of the group of horsemen.

'You see that rider in the middle, holding a spear and wearing shiny armour?'

'Not as shiny as yours, highborn.'

'Concentrate,' I snapped. 'You see him?'

'Yes, highborn.'

'Think you can hit him from here?'

He squinted at Atrax below, around two hundred paces from the bottom of the ramp. It was a long shot from a height of one hundred and twenty feet above the ground, but I had to do something.

'Yes, highborn.'

'Then do so.'

He took a stone from his bag, pulled the sling from his belt and placed the shot in its pouch. I stepped away from him as he began spinning the pouch above his head in a circular motion. Gallia was giving him a sceptical look as Klietas concentrated on the target, Atrax suddenly turning his horse to head away from the arena of death he had created. Klietas took his shot and I burst out laughing when the stone hit the rump of Atrax's horse, sending it bolting down the street where the crosses had been planted and the hill men had carted off their new slaves.

It was a minor victory on a black day.

Chapter 15

There was no weeping or wailing in the citadel that night. Among those civilians that had got back into the walled sanctuary to avoid the axes or bondage of the hill men, utter demoralisation provoked blank faces and exhausted bodies. Survivors slumped in doorways, families huddled in alleys and couples held each other tightly on the sides of streets and sobbed quietly. Only the children accepted the food that Lusin had distributed among them from the palace stores, consuming the simple fare of bread, cheese and fruit rapaciously – their first meal of the day.

There was no feast in the palace that night, the king and queen retiring to their private quarters after Akmon informed us there would be a council of war the next morning. I sat with Gallia in our bedroom, the shutters leading to the balcony open to give us beautiful views of the reds and purples of the sunset.

'It would appear we will be eating camel meat from now on.'

'Followed by horse,' said Gallia.

No doubt Lucius would agree that slaughtering the beasts made sense now we were under close siege, but for a Parthian the idea of killing and eating one's horse was not only stomach-churning, it was close to sacrilege.

'There must be another way,' I said forlornly.

She stretched out her long legs.

'I am open to any suggestions.'

'Our disappearance must have been noticed by now.'

She smiled. 'Why should anyone think we have disappeared? For all Gafarn and Diana know, we have ridden to Ctesiphon or

Babylon, or even Elymais to see your namesake and the infant child of Silaces.'

I too smiled when I thought of our old friend.

'He was deliriously happy with Cia, you know. He told me so at Dura. I'm pleased he has a son to continue his line.'

Gallia's face hardened. 'We need to make sure he ascends to Elymais' throne and not become a victim of Phraates' duplicity.'

'Agreed, when we get back to Dura we will think about a plan to clip the talons of our scheming high king.'

'To say nothing of ungrateful,' she added. 'To think, we saved his arse, and this is how he repays us.'

I raised my eyebrows.

'What?' she asked.

'I don't like to split hairs, but your scheming with Diana and Rasha was to exact revenge on Tiridates, was it not?'

She nodded.

'And I seem to recall you telling me you cared nothing about whether Phraates kept his throne or indeed his head.'

'So?'

'So, such disregard for the high king can hardly be placed in the category of saving his hide. It was more a by-product of your scheme.'

'He's a liar and a rogue,' she insisted.

'Perhaps we could ask Claudia to poison him.'

Our eyes met, and we burst out laughing. Dark humour seemed entirely appropriate in the dire situation we found ourselves in.

The mood in the palace had not changed the next morning. Akmon, tired and pale, sat beside his wan queen at the council meeting convened in the office to the rear of the throne room. Or at least it should have been, for we were just about to take our seats when the duty officer of the palace guard rushed in and bowed to his king.

'The enemy has gone, majesty.'

Akmon stared at him, not realising the gravity of what he had announced.

'Gone?' said Joro. 'Are you certain?'

'Quite certain, lord,' the officer told him.

Akmon grabbed Lusin's arm. 'We will see for ourselves.'

It was amazing how a rumour could transform people. Strictly speaking, only the officer should have known the news that the enemy had apparently disappeared. But there were soldiers on the walls and they would have gossiped to their comrades and they in turn would have informed others, with the proviso 'do not tell anyone'. In no time at all the rumour would have spread like wildfire throughout the citadel. This was confirmed when we had hurriedly saddled our horses to ride from the palace to the citadel's ramparts, exhausted people rising to their feet to cheer and applaud Akmon and Lusin. This in turn delighted them, especially Lusin, a broad grin spreading across her pale face.

At the gates we left our horses to once again climb the stone stairway, a spring in everyone's step. The sun was climbing into a cloudless sky to herald another beautiful late summer's day, though the unimpeded view afforded us when we reached the battlements also reminded us of the horror that had taken place the day before. Bodies lay strewn over the ground on and around the ramp and the citadel, the ghastly sight of ravens picking at dozens of corpses. For them it was a veritable feast; for us, a stomach-churning spectacle.

Lusin's smile disappeared but as we scanned the streets, the buildings and the perimeter wall, the enemy having replaced at least two of the destroyed bridges across the ditch to give access to Irbil, we could see no signs of life. I switched my gaze to the enemy camp a mile north of the city and could see nothing: no horsemen, no carts, no individuals, nothing.

The duty officer pointed to the west.

'Horsemen, majesty.'

We peered towards where he was indicating, everyone straining to identify the small black shapes riding down what had been the street of crosses and more recently the avenue along which the hill men had dragged off Irbil's women and children into captivity. No one said anything as the riders – six in number – cantered down the street, the horseman at the head of the column halting to order two of his men to ride into a side street. A second group of riders appeared behind them, these too attired in dark robes. They cantered up to the halted first group and were also diverted into side streets.

'They appear to be carrying out a reconnaissance of the city,' said Bullus, the burly centurion frowning at Klietas who had suddenly appeared behind me.

'Do you wish me to kill them when they get close, highborn?' he asked.

Bullus clipped him round the ear and Joro's blue eyes bored into him, but the teenager ignored them to reach into his bag to retrieve a stone shot.

'Not yet, Klietas,' I said.

After perhaps ten minutes the riders despatched into side streets returned to their commander, after which the whole group trotted on, towards the citadel.

'Archers,' called the duty officer.

On our flanks bowmen nocked arrows in their bowstrings. But the horsemen were still out of range and so there was no need for haste. Only if they rode to the ramp itself or the base of the mound would they shoot at the riders. But the latter once again scattered into other streets as they reconnoitred the city north and south of the citadel.

'Perhaps they are bandits looking for loot,' suggested Lusin.

'Not bandits, lady,' I said, 'because bandits would not be so thorough in their reconnaissance.'

'Then who are they?' asked Gallia.

No one had an answer to her question, so we just stood and stared, watching black-clad horsemen disappear before reappearing in a different place. They were slowly getting nearer to the citadel, though it would take a while yet. The archers either side of us relaxed and Klietas placed the stone back in his pouch. Eventually, one rider walked his horse from a side street and halted it on the edge of the open space between the buildings and the foot of the mound on which the citadel stood. He was out of arrow range and even a slinger would have difficulty hitting him. He was looking left and right, also glancing up at those of us standing on the ramparts. He waited until more of his men arrived before urging his horse forward.

'It's Talib.'

I heard Minu's voice and squinted at the black-robed figure on the horse.

'It's Talib,' she said again, 'praise the gods.'

282

'It is,' cried Gallia.

'Who's Talib?' asked Lusin.

I ran across and kissed her on the cheek.

'My chief scout.'

I bounded down the steps, Gallia, Zenobia, Minu and Klietas following.

'Open the gates,' I called, 'open the gates.'

When I reached the gates, I ordered the soldiers to open the door cut in one of the gates as I did not wish to wait until they had removed the heavy wooden beam slotted in iron brackets that spanned the rear of both gates. The door was opened, and I stepped on to the ramp and ran down the concourse, the others following.

I began waving my arms. 'Talib, Talib.'

It was perhaps rather undignified for a king of the Parthian Empire to behave in such a way, and was undoubtedly the first time it had happened in Media. But I was so delighted to see my chief scout I cared not. He saw me and urged his horse towards me, the beast moving nervously as it negotiated a route through a carpet of corpses. When I reached him, he jumped down from his horse and bowed his head. I gripped his shoulders with my hands.

'You are a sight for sore eyes. By what sorcery are you here in Irbil?'

Slightly discomfited by my gesture of familiarity, he shifted uncomfortably on his feet. I released my grip on his shoulders to put him at ease.

'No sorcery, majesty, I am with the army. General Chrestus is less than a day's march from the city.'

He looked around at the dead. 'What is left of it. Prince Atrax has fled north.'

'You know about Atrax?'

He nodded. 'At the Tigris we were met by Lord Soter and his forces. He acquainted us fully on the recent events in Media.'

I was elated. So Soter had proved himself a loyal lord of Akmon after all. This was wonderful news indeed. Gallia, Zenobia and Minu arrived, the latter throwing herself into Talib's arms and the two embracing warmly. Talib stroked her hair and she kissed him fully on the lips. I looked at Gallia who was as surprised as I was. The two parted and looked at us sheepishly. Gallia laughed and embraced the deputy commander of the Amazons.

'I had no idea.'

'We thought you would disapprove, majesty,' said Minu, glancing at Zenobia who flashed a reassuring grin.

I slapped Talib on the arm. 'You should always seize the chance of happiness, Talib. Let us go and give King Akmon some good news.'

Talib, leading his horse, walked beside Minu, both oblivious to the grisly scene around them as they talked to each other in hushed tones. With hindsight, it made perfect sense. They were both unmarried, attractive and had spent much time in each other's company when the army marched or engaged in manoeuvres.

'Looks like we will be attending a wedding soon,' I grinned, nodding at the couple in front of us.

'*We?*' said Gallia. 'What makes you think you will get an invite?'

'Well, I am responsible for bringing Talib to Dura,' I replied smugly.

'You are also responsible for saving Atrax's life and look how that turned out.'

'Sometimes, you can be very cutting with your remarks.'

Akmon welcomed Talib to his palace after we had entered the citadel, unsure of what to make of the short, slim individual with a sharp beard dressed in black robes who stood before him in the throne room. Like most Agraci and indeed many Parthians, he wore black eye make-up made from antimony powder sourced from a black stone, which was ground to dust and diluted with olive oil. Regarded by the Egyptians as attractive and pleasing to the gods, they and we wore the black eye make-up to repel flies that carried diseases and as a defence against the glare of the sun.

'This is my chief scout, Talib, majesty,' I informed Akmon, 'who rides ahead of Dura's army.'

There was a chorus of excited and approving grunts from the officers present, as well as the priests, now few in number, from the Temple of Shamash.

'You are most welcome, Lord Talib,' smiled Akmon.

'I am not a lord, majesty,' Talib corrected him, 'just a scout in the service of the King of Dura.'

'Well you are welcome anyway.'

'Tell the king who accompanies the army, Talib,' I said.

'Lord Soter and his forces joined with the army of Dura at the Tigris, majesty,' reported Talib, 'and it was Lord Soter who notified Dura of the situation in Irbil.'

The news was greeted with smiles and nods. Akmon closed his eyes and gave thanks to the god he worshipped, the Horseman I assumed.

'How many men?' asked Joro, professional to the last.

'Two thousand horsemen, lord,' Talib told him.

'And the army of Dura?' queried Akmon.

'Ten thousand foot soldiers and the same number of horsemen, majesty.'

I was surprised. With the army's professional horse archers and the cataphracts absent in the east, to raise such a number must have denuded my kingdom of all its lords and their retainers. As if anticipating my query, Talib provided further information.

'Kalet leads five thousand horsemen, majesty, and the rest are commanded by Lord Orobaz.'

'Who?'

'A rich lord from the Kingdom of Hatra, majesty. The commander of the army sent an urgent request to your brother, King Gafarn,' said Talib, 'to send horse archers to rendezvous with the army.'

Gallia raised an eyebrow. 'General Chrestus has grown bold in our absence.'

'It was not the general who sent the request, majesty,' explained Talib, 'but the army's commander.'

I looked at Gallia in confusion. 'And who is that?'

'Princess Eszter, majesty.'

I was not amused. 'What?'

'As soon as news reached Dura of your predicament, majesty, the princess was most diligent in mustering the lords and liaising with Hatra, as well as sending instructions to Lord Soter concerning when and where to meet the army.'

Joro emitted a gruff chuckle. 'That must have come as a shock to him, a woman telling him what to do. Dura is different from Media.'

'Very different,' snapped Gallia, 'and to the benefit of Media, I think.'

Joro, ever the stickler for court rules, bowed his head to her.

'Both I and Media are most grateful for your daughter's diligence, majesty.'

The news of our relief spread throughout the citadel, people flocking to the Temple of Shamash to give thanks for their delivery. In a generous gesture, Lusin ordered food to be distributed to civilians before they returned to their homes. Fortunately, Media's homes, businesses, temples and warehouses were still intact. Normally when a city was stormed, its inhabitants were usually slaughtered or enslaved and the buildings were put to the torch after they had been plundered. As Atrax intended to rule after Akmon had been deposed, he had not embarked on a rampage of destruction. That was a blessing, at least.

The first task was a grisly one and involved heaping the now bloated and gaseous corpses on carts to transport them outside the city for cremation. I sent Talib back to the army with orders for my daughter and Chrestus to hasten to Irbil and take possession of the campsite of Atrax's army. Its ditch and earth palisade were still extant and would save the Durans and Exiles time and energy. Talib's scouts rode with their leader back to the army, though others had been sent north to trail Atrax and his army. I too would be following the fleeing prince at the head of my army. But first I intended to greet Chrestus and my daughter.

Akmon and Lusin accompanied us on our short ride, Media's dragon banner flying beside Dura's griffin behind us and the Amazons and Joro's surviving cataphracts providing an escort. The first troops we encountered were some of Dura's horse archers, attired in dark robes and riding nimble horses capable of great speed and endurance. They recognised the griffin banner and galloped towards us, pulling up their mounts sharply and bowing their heads.

'Greetings, lord,' said their olive-skinned commander, his teeth white and his eyes keen and dark brown.

He was bare headed but most of his men were wearing *shemaghs*, the headdress favoured by the Agraci. All carried bows and at least two full quivers of arrows, every man also armed with a curved sword and dagger hanging from his hip.

'How far away is the army?' I asked.

'Less than five miles, lord.'

We left them to their vanguard duties and carried on, passing deserted farms and riding through a village that was also devoid of life. Akmon said nothing as we trotted past the mud-brick huts with reed roofs, but I saw the pained expression in his eyes. Media had already suffered because of his father's invasions of the kingdom, and now it had endured a further setback at the hands of Atrax, though the real culprit was Phraates. All to make a point to the King of Gordyene. At that moment, I deeply regretted fighting to put the son of Orodes back on the high throne.

'It is Eszter,' said Gallia, breaking the silence.

A mile south of the village, the dirt track we were riding on cutting through fields filled with ripe golden barley that swayed in the gentle breeze, we ran into our youngest daughter at the head of a large party of horsemen. She was dressed in mail armour, open-faced helmet and had a sword strapped to her waist. Her bow was in a leather case fixed to the right side of her saddle and two quivers hung on its left side. On her right side rode her husband Dalir, also wearing mail. Next to him rode his father Kalet who wore no armour and resembled an Agraci warrior in his dark robes. On Eszter's other side was Lord Soter, the sun glinting off the burnished scales of his scale-armour cuirass and his helmet adorned with a blue plume. To his left was a man I had not seen before but who must have been Lord Orobaz judging by the expensive scale armour that covered his torso, shoulders and thighs. He too wore an open-faced helmet, though a white plume adorned it. Eszter held up her hand to halt the column she led before giving us a mischievous smile.

'Greetings, father and mother, I hope we are not too late.'

'Too late for what?' I asked.

'To fight Atrax, of course,' came the impious reply.

'Atrax has fled,' I told her.

'We are most pleased to see you, princess,' said Akmon, halting his horse in front of hers, 'I, my wife and Media are in your debt.'

'We are all in Lord Soter's debt,' I said, 'for without his foresight we would not be at this happy reunion.'

'My sincere thanks, lord,' said Akmon.

The Median noble, his expression haughty and severe, bowed his head to Akmon.

'Media has a king and does not need another. What it needs is peace, so it may be rebuilt to once again become the first kingdom of the empire. I took an oath of loyalty to you, sire, that neither my sons nor I will break. And we will not tolerate foreigners invading Media and turning it into their plaything.'

'We will build a new Media, that I promise,' pledged Akmon.

'This is Lord Orobaz, majesty,' Eszter said to Akmon, 'who has brought five thousand Hatrans to fight by your side.'

Orobaz, tall in the saddle, slender, with broad shoulders, bowed his head to the King of Media. I estimated him to be in his fifties, though I could see no hint of grey in his beard. His eyes were green, and they conveyed a man of intelligence and breeding.

'It is an honour to serve you, majesty,' said Orobaz, 'you who are the son of King Spartacus, who in turn is the son of King Gafarn of Hatra and the brother of King Pacorus. Hatra and Media are thus linked to each other by blood ties. My king's only regret is that he himself could not be here.'

'And how is my brother?' I asked.

'Healing, majesty,' Orobaz told me, 'though the queen informed me his patience is somewhat frayed.'

'You look like you've been on holiday, lord, as opposed to being under siege. And who did you steal that armour from?'

Kalet could always be relied upon to lower the tone of the conversation and both Soter and Orobaz shifted uneasily in their saddles.

'Perhaps we should ride back to the city,' suggested Joro, ignoring my chief lord.

'Excellent idea,' agreed Akmon, turning his horse to commence the journey back to Irbil.

'I will ride ahead to speak with Chrestus,' I said, pointing at Eszter, 'and you will be coming with me.'

Gallia joined us as we cantered south to link up with Chrestus, encountering more of Dura's lords and their horsemen as we approached the army. Kalet and Dalir also accompanied us, the former pestering me with questions about my cuirass and the one worn by Gallia.

'Where did you get them from?'

'They were gifts.'

'Can I get one?'

'I think that is very unlikely.'

'Have you lost your Roman armour?'

'No.'

'So you have two suits of armour and I don't have one.'

I sighed. 'You remember the two hundred horses I paid you so Eszter and your son could get married?'

He appeared to wrack his brains. 'Vaguely.'

'Then sell some to buy yourself some armour.'

He cast his eyes on the fields of golden crops we rode by, interspersed with vineyards and orchards heaving with fruit.

'Rich country this. Soter tells me there is so much water anything can be grown here.'

'Indeed.'

'Lots of livestock, too.'

I knew where this was heading.

'What a shame you are forbidden from plundering Media, Kalet. It must be hard for an old raider like you to see such bounty and be unable to steal it away.'

He went into a sullen silence, mumbling under his breath. He was wealthy in his own right, owning many horses, goats and camels, as well as having lordship over hundreds of people. In his youth he had fought the Agraci, raided Roman Syria and even ventured south into the lands of the Bedouin. But now there was peace with the Agraci and Rome and only the Bedouin provided sport for my desert lords.

'How are you finding married life, Dalir?' asked Gallia.

His name meant 'brave' and he had proved it was an appropriate moniker during the campaign against Tiridates. In looks he resembled a younger version of his father, with wild hair and beard, and just as forthright.

'I hope to put a baby in her belly soon, majesty, to give you another grandson.'

I winced at his coarseness, but Gallia took it in her stride.

'I remember when I first became aware I was pregnant with Claudia. I was on campaign at the time, fighting a king called Porus. Perhaps the fact you and Eszter are on campaign is a good omen.'

I laughed. 'I remember you fainting in our tent after the battle. Alcaeus berated me for taking a pregnant woman on campaign. Is he with the army?'

'He is,' said Eszter, 'and is as free with his comments as ever. Greece must be a terrible place to live if they are all as sharped-tongued as Alcaeus and Scelias.'

'Greece is a terrible place to live because it is a Roman province,' said Gallia.

It was good to see the army again, reassuring to see the long lines of legionaries in mail armour, helmets and white tunics marching six abreast in perfect step. I rode to the command group where Chrestus and his senior officers were located, together with Alcaeus, who used to walk with his medical orderlies but now sat in a saddle out of consideration for his age. Chrestus, attired in mail armour and a helmet sporting a magnificent white crest, saluted stiffly when we drew alongside him. Now a veteran commander in his forties, he rarely smiled and his black eyes conveyed menace and determination. They now rested on my shining armour.

'It is good to see you, majesties, you look well.'

'Very well,' added Alcaeus, 'I thought you had been under siege and fighting for your lives, but you both look remarkably healthy and invigorated.'

'Clean living and a healthy mind will do that, Alcaeus,' I said. 'Is everything well, Chrestus?'

His eyes portrayed no emotion, though I did notice he tightened the grip on his reins.

'All is well, majesty.'

'Ever the calm professional, Chrestus,' said Alcaeus, 'though the mask did slip a little when Princess Eszter announced she would be commanding the army.'

'She is *joint* commander,' emphasised Chrestus.

'Try telling her that,' smiled Alcaeus. 'I must say she has done a commendable job getting all the disparate elements assembled so quickly and getting them to Media in a short time. Perhaps you should make her Chrestus' deputy, Pacorus.'

Chrestus' knuckles went white as he throttled the reins with his hand.

'It would be an honour,' beamed Eszter behind us.

'Well, let's see,' I said. 'How many campaigns have you taken part in, Eszter?'

'Two, including this one.'

'And have you ever commanded soldiers in battle or in a siege?'

'No, but…'

I held up a hand. 'Now, General Chrestus has commanded Dura's army for over twenty years, and before that was a soldier in the Exiles for…'

I looked at Chrestus.

293

'Ten years, majesty.'

'I therefore think Alcaeus' idea has merit,' I told my daughter.

'You do!' she exclaimed.

'And once you have served for thirty years in the army, then you will be made its deputy commander.'

Chrestus' hard visage briefly wore a smile, though when I turned to look at Eszter she had a scowl that could curdle milk at a hundred paces.

'But you have done well, daughter, and King Akmon owes you his life.'

'As do we,' said Gallia.

Eszter's scowl disappeared, to be replaced with a smile when I announced we would be hunting down and destroying Atrax and his army.

'Not tempted to save his life a second time, then?' asked Alcaeus mischievously.

'No.'

The army made use of the extant earth ramparts that had been created by Atrax, or rather his general Titus Tullus. As I walked through the camp with Chrestus as the sun was beginning to dip in the western sky after a gloriously warm day, I mentioned that the bulk of the prince's army was made up of soldiers from Pontus.

'That is a great shame, majesty, but is the consequence of Pontus being a client kingdom of Rome. That is the reason I left all those years ago.'

He had been a threadbare, bare-footed sixteen-year-old when he had arrived at Dura, or so Domitus had informed me. Just one among thousands who had travelled from their homelands to take service in the army of Dura. And they still arrived, mostly runaway slaves who desired a life worth living as opposed to a living death in bondage. Cruel tongues ridiculed Dura for being a slave kingdom with a slave army and a slave king, but Dura's army had never been bested on the battlefield thanks to men like Chrestus and thousands of others who had preferred to die on their feet rather than live on their knees.

'How large is the enemy army, majesty?'

'Around fifteen thousand men, give or take. The best are the legionaries, essentially copies of their Roman counterparts, but they number only three thousand at most. Around a third of Atrax's army comprises poorly armed hill men, so we can discount them.'

Chrestus' eyes scanned the rows of tents taking shape around us, all neatly laid out in blocks that duplicated the layout of the legionary camp that was a permanent feature a short distance from Dura's walls. The first tents to be pitched, even before my own, were those housing the army's most sacred symbols – the golden griffin of the Durans and the silver lion of the Exiles. I walked with Chrestus to pay them a visit, as usual each tent ringed by legionaries and a centurion assigned to each guard section.

'Drop him,' I suddenly heard, turning to see one of the legionaries shouldering his javelin.

I looked around and saw Klietas bounding towards us. He waved and smiled at me.

'Stand down,' I commanded.

The legionary relaxed and rested the end on his javelin on the ground, the centurion who had given the order to spear Klietas curling his lip at the youth who stopped before me, panting after running in the heat.

'Highborn.'

Chrestus placed a hand on the hilt of his *gladius*.

'This is Klietas, Chrestus, who took an active part in defending Irbil during the recent siege.'

Chrestus looked the boy up and down.

'Things must have been desperate indeed, majesty.'

'How did you get past the guards?'

He suddenly remembered something and pulled out a folded piece of papyrus.

'The queen gave me this for you, highborn.'

I took the note and read the words. It was an invitation for me, Gallia and Eszter to attend a feast in the palace in celebration of Irbil's deliverance.

'Tell the queen we will be delighted to attend,' I said.

'Yes, highborn,' said Klietas, stepping past me to enter the tent holding the gold griffin. To be stopped in his tracks by Chrestus who grabbed his tunic.

'Get back to your queen, boy, unless you want a flogging.'

Crestfallen and looking to me for support, in vain, he shrugged and trooped away, shoulders slumped.

'You should come, too,' I told Chrestus, 'you and Lucius can talk about dragon fire, which he used against the enemy.'

'Yes, majesty,' he said without enthusiasm.

The citadel and the ground around it had undergone a transformation since I had left Irbil that morning. The dead bodies on and around the mound had been removed, the refugees had gone back to their homes and order and calm had been restored to the residence of Media's royalty and nobility. I smiled when I saw slaves and soldiers on their knees using scrubbing brushes to clean pavements and doorways that civilians had used as makeshift latrines, the odour from their bodily functions still lingering in the still air.

The air and indeed the company were far more agreeable in the palace that evening, the babble of conversation in the banqueting hall lively and optimistic. As it was a formal occasion, all the women wore dresses and jewellery, Lusin's head adorned with a gold crown. Gallia and Eszter, though queen and princess respectively, had no crowns to wear but diamond tiaras loaned to them by Lusin graced their heads. Eszter's mop of unruly hair was kept in place by silver hair clips, her fingers were adorned with silver rings and around her neck was an emerald necklace. She sat between Dalir and Kalet, both attired in black flowing robes and looking very much like desert warriors. But at least Kalet had put a comb through his hair and had trimmed his beard, or at least a slave had.

Notwithstanding the siege and privations endured by the general populace, the fare being served to us was varied and appetising. The only indication that the palace kitchens had any shortages was the serving of only two meat dishes – chicken and mutton – as opposed to the usual five or six. But there was no shortage of onions, garlic, radishes, beetroot and olives, and the meal also included an abundance of apples, pomegranates, grapes, figs, apricots, melon, raisins and pears. Everything was washed down by generous quantities of wine and beer, Kalet being restrained by Eszter who ordered slaves away before they had an opportunity to refill her father-in-law's gold rhyton too often.

Dura's senior officers greatly outnumbered the lords and ladies of Media, and even Lord Orobaz's fellow Hatran nobles appeared numerous in comparison to Joro and his family and Lord Soter and those nobles who had rallied to his banner. Everyone knew, though no one commented on the fact, that many Median lords and their retinues were still with Atrax, which provided the prince with a high degree of legitimacy regarding his claim to Media's crown. He and they had to be dealt with, and swiftly.

The chatter died as I slowly rose from my seat and raised my rhyton to Akmon.

'I would like to propose a toast to the King of Media in recognition of his courage and fortitude during the recent assault on his city by the renegade Atrax.'

As one everyone stood and toasted Akmon, the young king slightly embarrassed but grateful for the show of support. I continued standing after the other guests had retaken their seats.

'Lord king, tomorrow I propose to march my army north in pursuit of Atrax,' I did not give him a title for his base actions were not worthy of nobility. 'My aim is to both destroy his army and either kill him on the battlefield or serve summary justice on him when he is in my custody.'

Dura's lords and officers rapped their knuckles on the table tops to indicate their support. Those from Hatra and Media nodded in agreement.

'I invite you, lord, to accompany me to rid Media and Parthia of this rebel and his band of foreign mercenaries.'

Akmon rose and toasted me. 'It would be an honour, lord king. My one desire is to see Media and its people enjoy peace and prosperity, free from foreign invasions so it can become once more the premier kingdom in the Parthian Empire.'

Warm applause greeted his words along with not a few cheers. I smiled, sat and took a large sip of wine. Atrax had sowed a wind and now he was about to reap a whirlwind.

Chapter 16

Ideally, it would have been better for Akmon to stay in Irbil to supervise the rebuilding of the city defences, the feeding of the population and the not-inconsiderable task of organising the harvesting of crops standing ripe in the fields around the city. But honour demanded he lead the army that struck camp at dawn and headed northeast. The Median component in the composite force was smaller than the other elements, but symbolically the presence of the King of Media was a powerful statement of Akmon's right to the throne. He had repulsed an assault on his capital and now all that remained was to hunt down Atrax and kill him.

Lusin stayed in Irbil with what was left of the city garrison, the palace guard and the seventy survivors of the century under the command of Bullus that had left Dura weeks ago. I decided the battered and courageous centurion should stay in the city to supplement the garrison and give him and his men a period of deserved rest. I also left Lucius in Irbil, both to supervise the repair of the city walls and organise the gathering of the harvest. He would also provide advice for the queen, who bereft of her husband, plus Joro who was on campaign and Parmenion and Pogon, both dead, might find ruling Irbil a daunting task. Lucius would provide a steadying influence while her husband was away. Those civilians who had volunteered their services as archers or slingers returned to being farmers, though one slinger remained with the army.

I found Klietas an aged mare to ride so he could accompany me during the march north. I appointed him my squire and informed him from now on he would clean my armour, helmet and boots, as well as care for his own horse. He was delighted, especially when I informed him he would ride with me and Gallia during the march, that and being issued with leggings, boots and a clean white tunic from Dura's stores. He sat awkward in the saddle and looked out of place among the party of royalty and nobility that left Irbil to catch up with the army after Akmon had said farewell to his queen, a tearful, touching scene that made me loathe Atrax even more for bringing it about. But, the gods willing, Akmon would be back with his wife soon enough after what I anticipated would be a mere mopping-up exercise.

Earlier, before we had left the citadel, I sent a message to Kalet to attend me in the royal garden. It was early, and the garden was cool, the sun yet to peek above the palace walls to shine into the well-kept oasis of greenery and running water where one could forget the travails of the world. I was delighted to discover Kalet was not suffering from a hangover, Eszter's determination he should not become a drunken boor having succeeded. As a result, he looked remarkably fresh and alert and I was surprised to see he had trimmed his hair and beard. He saw my surprise at his appearance when he sat himself down on one of the couches in the white-painted gazebo in the centre of the garden, around us the morning air filled with the sound of fountains and cooing doves. He stroked his beard,

'You like it?'

'I do.'

'A young slave girl did it for me. I wouldn't have bothered but she was half-naked and had an amazing pair of breasts.'

He waited until other slaves had laid jars of honey, yoghurt, wafers and slices of melon on the low table between us, after pouring freshly squeezed orange juice into silver chalices, before leaning towards me, leering and winking.

'As she is a slave, is it permitted to, you know?'

I picked up a wafer and dipped it in some honey.

'Rape her, you mean?'

He gave me a look as though butter would not melt in his mouth.

'Rape? If she's willing and I'm willing.'

I turned the wafer to prevent any honey falling off before shoving it into my mouth.

'It is considered impolite to interfere with another person's slaves, Kalet, especially if they belong to royalty.'

He took a slice of melon and proceeded to eat it in a way that got more of it on his beard and robes than in his mouth.

'Do you know why we don't have slaves in Dura's palace.'

He wiped his mouth on the sleeve of his robe.

'Because you and the queen were once slaves yourselves.'

I nodded. 'That is part of the reason, but the idea of lecherous old men who are guests in my house molesting women and young girls disgusts me, as it should you. That is why all my servants are free men and women who are under no obligation to debase themselves on the mere whim of a guest.'

He professed his innocence. 'She likes me.'

'I find that difficult to believe.'

'She was all sweetness and light when she was trimming my beard and hair, smiling the whole time.'

'She is a slave, Kalet, who has to be pleasant and enticing. She is constantly in fear of a flogging, or worse, if she offends anyone, especially a guest. Only an uncouth brute would take advantage of her, and despite your many faults you are not that.'

He puffed out his cheeks and sighed.

'You certainly know how to make a man lose his appetite.'

I picked up another wafer.

'I have a small task which will restore your appetite.'

'Oh?'

'I want you to select six of your best cutthroats for a secret mission that only you and I must know about,' I said, 'and that means no blabbing to Dalir or Eszter about it.'

He picked up his chalice and emptied most of the contents down his throat.

'Two things, lord. I don't employ cutthroats and I never blab.'

I raised an eyebrow at him. 'Very well, then select six of your men who are most accomplished with a knife and send them to the town of Mepsila.'

'Where's that?'

'A town on the Tigris, in the northwest corner of Media.'

He picked up another slice of melon.

'Who do you want dead?'

'The governor of the town, a fat traitor by the name of Cookes. He was the one who seized control of all the post stations along the river as part of his bid to make Atrax ruler of Media.'

He attacked the slice of melon. 'Consider it done. You want the head brought back?'

'What?'

'A gift for the young king here, perhaps?'

'That won't be necessary.'

He looked around at the greenery and doves in the branches of white-stemmed poplars.

'You will kill Atrax?'

'The gods willing, yes.'

'Why did you save his life, then, when he and his sisters were trapped in this very city by Spartacus? You missed an opportunity there.'

He was right. 'I made a mistake, I admit it.'

'What about Atrax's sisters?'

'What about them?'

'You want them dead, too? Loose ends came always back to haunt a man, as you have found out.'

'No, Kalet, I don't want Atrax's sisters murdered.'

He nodded. 'Just the fat governor, then?'

'Just the fat governor.'

After leaving Irbil we made camp a day's march northeast of the city, on the edge of the foothills of the Zagros Mountains, the great chain of mountains and ridges that ran from Lake Urmia in the north to the Persian Gulf in the south. Those unfamiliar with the Parthian Empire might dismiss them as nothing more than bare rock and snowy peaks, bereft of animal and human life. But they would be wrong. In addition to the yellow-hued limestone and dolomite rock faces, they also contained fertile mountain valleys, terraced hills and pastures.

To the south of the fertile Irbil Plain, the land was mostly flat, dry, hot and harsh, the Tigris and Euphrates supplying the water that allowed kingdoms such as Dura, Babylon and Mesene to flourish. But in this part of the Zagros the hills were green and temperatures pleasant. Tall grasses, mulberry and fig trees occupy the hillsides, along with pomegranate orchards where villages clung to the steep inclines.

'The enemy retreats slowly.'

Talib pointed at the hide map laid out on the table, indicating the line of retreat of Atrax's army as it fell back ahead of us. The interior of my tent, though spacious was also warm. It had been another hot day and we had all been sweating in the sun during the march, and now we perspired as we gathered round to examine the map of northeast Media collected from the palace archives. It showed Irbil, the valleys of the Zagros and the position of Lake Urmia to the north.

Klietas served us all with water gathered from the nearby Rawanduz River that flowed from the mountains, the waterway we would have to follow the next day to pursue the enemy.

'The enemy will be able to block the valley,' said Soter, who kept glancing at Gallia beside me.

I smiled. In traditional kingdoms such as Media women did not fight, and they certainly did not participate in councils of war, even if they were royalty. It must have been uncomfortable for a noble from an ancient Median family to be commanded by a foreign-born king and fighting alongside the army of Dura, which for many years had been mocked by Darius, the former King of Media, and his mother, my sister Aliyeh. But he conducted himself with dignity and the same strict adherence to protocol prevented him from speaking out of turn. But he held a powerful and influential position in Media and his support was essential if Akmon was to enjoy a prosperous reign.

'Please continue, Sotor,' I said.

'At its entrance,' he began, 'the valley is wide, but quickly narrows to around two hundred paces around five miles or so from our current position.'

I looked at Soter. 'Is there any way around the valley, lord?'

He shook his head. 'Not without allowing the rebels to escape, majesty.'

'We are not letting them get away,' I told him, before remembering this was Akmon's kingdom.

'Bearing in mind Atrax has many of Media's citizens as captives, lord,' I said to Akmon.

'I agree with you, King Pacorus,' he said solemnly, 'we cannot abandon my people to misery.'

I looked at the map and saw a site marked on it beyond the valley. I pointed at it.

'What is this place?'

'It is called Gird-I Dasht, majesty,' said Soter, 'once a stronghold in the Kingdom of Musasir but now just a post station. It sits on an earth mound and has a mud-brick wall around the buildings, though as far as I can remember it is in state of disrepair. Formerly it controlled the great plain it sits in the middle of.'

'I have never heard of the Musasir,' said Gallia.

Soter smiled. 'They were wiped out nearly seven hundred years ago, majesty, by the Assyrian King Sargon.'

'Just as we will destroy Atrax,' I said.

Chrestus, thus far silent, now voiced his opinion.

'We can use the scorpions to rake whatever the enemy places in front of us in the valley. This will save casualties among our own foot soldiers. The enemy will probably post archers and slingers on the slopes to support their soldiers on the valley floor. We will need to send men to scatter them.'

'*Women*, general, I think,' said Gallia. 'I will lead the Amazons and your legionaries can protect us with their shields.'

Chrestus was unconvinced. 'How many missile troops does Atrax possess?'

'At least a thousand,' Akmon told him.

'Ninety Amazons cannot dislodge a thousand enemy archers and slingers,' Chrestus told Gallia, 'though perhaps if Lord Kalet can supply some of his archers.'

Kalet rubbed his hands. 'Don't you worry, princess, you and your ladies can stay in camp and cook us a nice meal for when we get back after slaughtering the enemy.'

Soter's mouth dropped open at his barefaced effrontery, while Gallia gave him a withering look. She had heard it all before, of course, and took it all in her stride.

'That is a very generous offer, lord,' she said demurely, 'but after your men have slept off their hangovers the day will be late and General Chrestus likes to slaughter his enemies before midday.'

Kalet roared with laughter and even Chrestus allowed himself a wry smile. Soter frowned and Orobaz, who had been silent throughout, did not know what to make of the rowdy, uncouth Kalet.

I looked at each of them in turn, the aristocratic Soter and Orobaz, the hard visage of Chrestus, the impious Kalet, the determined Akmon and Gallia, who looked half her age.

'Tomorrow we will end both Atrax and his rebellion.'

They filed out of the tent, Klietas fussing around to pick up the cups he been filling with water and Chrestus rolling up the map, no doubt to brief his senior officers regarding the plan on the morrow. For him it would be a late night. Gallia embraced me and told me she would be spending the night with the Amazons, as was her usual pre-battle ritual.

'Would you like some wine, highborn?' asked Klietas after she had left.

'No, I will take the evening air.'

'Take it where?'

'Nowhere, it is just a saying.'

'What does it mean, highborn?'

'It means I am going for a walk around the camp.'

'I will get my sling, highborn.'

'Why?'

'It is not safe to wander about alone at night,' he told me.

'I'll take a chance, don't wait up for me.'

'I have polished your boots and helmet, highborn, and put new goose feathers in the crest.'

'Well done. Get some sleep.'

I left him sweeping the carpet, whistling and smiling to himself. Outside men sat around campfires after their evening meal. Parties of sentries were making their way to the ramparts to relieve those standing guard, horsemen watched over their beasts, farriers were fitting horseshoes to hooves, and centurions stalked around like wraiths, looking for infractions on the part of their men. Despite Gallia ribbing Kalet, he and his lords rarely got riotously drunk on the eve of battle. Slaughter was far too serious a business to allow the effects of alcohol to interfere with it.

'Put your back into it.'

My attention was drawn to a centurion standing over one of his men digging a latrine trench, the poor legionary hacking at the soil with his spade. I found it odd he was on his own as opposed to part of a detail. Perhaps he was being punished for some infraction of army rules.

'I want this trench finished by the time I return,' said the centurion menacingly before striding away.

After he had gone the legionary stopped his hacking to stretch his back. He removed his helmet and I was stunned to see a face I had recognised before. I hurried over and stood over him, Marduk resting his helmet and spade on the lip of the trench.

'Your centurions are like wild dogs,' he said half in jest.

'Well-trained dogs, lord,' I replied, a shiver going down my spine in his presence.

I offered my hand to assist him getting out of the trench, but then withdrew it. Was one permitted to touch an immortal? He laughed.

'Is there anything you need, lord?' I asked.

He stretched his body again. 'A new back would be useful.'

He laughed again. 'So, you have saved Akmon and his pretty young wife.'

'A task only half-completed, lord.'

'And tomorrow you go to give battle to Atrax.'

'Yes, lord.'

'He has allies,' he said matter-of-factly, 'you should beware the two eagles. Please pass me my spade.'

I turned to pick up the tool but when I went to hand it to its owner I saw he had gone. I looked all around but there was no sign of Marduk, not a trace. I put down the spade and walked away from the half-finished trench, but then thought such a tool might be useful in the coming battle. I turned but it too had disappeared, just like its owner.

I spent the rest of the evening walking among the men I would be fighting alongside tomorrow, their morale high in the knowledge they were facing an enemy who had already tasted defeat and disappointment at Irbil, a foe that included poorly armed and ill-disciplined hill men. Many were looking forward to battling their legionary counterparts from Pontus, especially when the Exiles and Durans learned they were commanded by Titus Tullus. This was the man who had fought beside them at Ctesiphon but who had now turned traitor to side with the pretender Atrax and his mercenaries. So they sharpened their swords, pledged death before dishonour and dreamed of glory. Chrestus imagined another silver disc added to the Staff of Victory and I returned to my tent trying to make sense of the warning concerning two eagles.

The Rawanduz Valley was green, the river itself a mere twenty paces wide and because the height of summer had just passed, its current slow and its level low, barely two feet at most. The waterway was in the centre of the valley as we advanced east, the gap between the two hillsides half a mile at its entrance but narrowing sharply as we moved upwards on a gentle slope. Kalet and Gallia were leading dismounted horsemen and women respectively, ahead of them centuries of legionaries negotiating the grassy slopes. Once again it was a warm, beautiful day, a slight breeze coming from the north ruffling our banners and providing a modicum of relief for men wearing helmets, mail armour, leather vests and carrying shields and javelins.

In the valley itself Chrestus marshalled his foot soldiers, being able to deploy only three cohorts abreast as the valley suddenly narrowed as Soter had warned.

He was part of the mounted party that followed the cohorts as they marched east, their progress slowed by having to haul scorpion bolt throwers with them. Akmon, magnificent in dragon-skin armour, shining helmet and gold crown, studied Dura's foot soldiers intently, pointing at the cohorts and centuries as they inched forward. Next to him was Joro, large blue plume in his helmet, glancing up at the slopes that were flooded with dismounted archers and legionaries. The valley floor was now around three hundred paces wide and ahead I could see individuals massing some half a mile further up the gorge.

'Our reception party,' I said.

There were also individuals on the slopes either side of the black mass ahead, widely spaced to blanket the hillsides.

'Enemy missile troops,' noted Joro.

Our own troops on the slopes had also seen them and there was flurries of whistle blasts as centurions organised their men into *testudo* formation, men closing ranks to present a wall of shields to the enemy, those behind the front rank forming a roof with their shields. The archers accompanying them, including Gallia, closed up to take cover within each *testudo*.

Because of the incline progress on the slopes was almost non-existent, the valley reverberating with hisses and cracks as the enemy archers and slingers shot at the locked shields of each *testudo*. In reply, our own archers took shots at Atrax's men, a shield in the roof of a *testudo* moving to create a gap through which an arrow could be loosed on a high trajectory against the enemy. Such shots could not be aimed but the enemy had no shields and were very vulnerable, notwithstanding they were widely spaced. That said, they could see the arrows arching in the sky before dropping on them and thus had a chance to dodge the missiles.

With a de facto stalemate on the slopes, Chrestus faced the task of breaking through the mass of warriors now crowded in the narrow neck of land in front of us, around four hundred paces distant. In front of the seething mass of hill men now brandishing their axes and hollering chilling war cries, I discerned a row of slingers standing ahead of the wild barbarians.

'Why does not the enemy place his best soldiers across the bottom of the gorge?' asked Soter.

'He knows, or rather Atrax's commander Tullus does, that we possess scorpions,' I told him. 'That being the case, he will not waste his best soldiers when he can sacrifice the hill men instead. His best men will be well to the rear, safely out of the way. How far to the east is the plain, lord?'

'Five miles, majesty,' answered Joro, 'and the pass is narrow for all that length.'

'It will take the rest of the day to clear the gorge,' Akmon told us, pointing ahead at the files of legionary helmets that had now halted at least four hundred paces from the noisy enemy horde.

'The enemy plays a perceptive game.' Akmon continued. 'Each of King Pacorus' legionaries occupies a space of three feet when he is in close order. A century has a frontage of ten yards, which means a maximum of only three cohorts can attack the enemy, less if we include the problem of the river.'

'You have a keen eye, majesty,' said Joro admiringly.

Clearly being raised in Gordyene had given the new King of Media a thorough education in the organisation and tactics of Roman legionaries, though because of Spartacus' hatred of all things Roman his foot soldiers were called Immortals.

'It will be a challenge for the scorpion crews to hit their targets,' I said.

Orobaz, attired in an expensive scale-armour cuirass, was confused.

'They can hardly miss, majesty.'

'The hill men, yes,' I agreed, 'but they will be aiming at the slingers in front of them. They are the ones that can inflict real damage; the rest are just chaff that can be swept aside easily enough.'

Scorpions were straightforward but effective machines. Resembling a large bow lying parallel to the ground on a wooden bolt carrier, the whole machine is mounted on a wooden stand. Just under the height of a man's chest, the scorpion was a complex piece of equipment, the two arms that shot the two-foot-long iron-tipped bolt being pushed through ropes made of animal sinew, which are then twisted to create hugely powerful tension devices that propel each arm forwards. The arms are then pulled back by means of a bowstring, the bolt is placed on the carrier and then the bowstring is released. A bolt had a range of around five hundred feet and could inflict horrible damage on densely packed groups of foot soldiers. Those bolts now began to hiss through the air, aimed at the slingers but hitting one or more hill men if they missed. The slingers shot back, their lead missiles searching out the crews of the scorpions. It was a deadly cat-and-mouse battle in which we had the advantage, for every scorpion bolt hit at least one man whereas the lead pellets of the enemy only rarely found a target, the hide covered shields of the legionaries protecting the scorpion crews as they worked methodically to search out and hit their prey.

Each century had one scorpion operated by two men and the dozen centuries facing the enemy waited patiently behind their locked shields for the slingers to be killed. In skilled hands a scorpion could shoot three bolts a minute, but the crews were loosing between one and two bolts a minute as they directed their missiles at the slingers. Nevertheless, after five minutes the slingers had been shot down and behind them a few dozen hill men had also been either killed or wounded. But the scorpions had done nothing to dint the bloodlust of the Pontic barbarians who now surged forward in a crescendo of noise to do battle with Chrestus' men.

The river running through the middle of the gorge slowed the advance of those hill men charging through its shallow waters, comrades either side racing ahead of them to hurl themselves at the locked shields of the legionaries.

To run into a hail of javelins.

As they were trained to do, the centurions led their men forward into the attack rather than wait to receive the enemy in a stationary position. The soldiers of Dura screamed their war cries, the first two ranks hurled their javelins at the enemy before drawing their swords to battle the hill men. As they did so the men in the third and fourth ranks paused momentarily to throw their javelins over the heads of the first two ranks, which meant the enemy ran into a rain of iron-tipped missiles. As they were intended to do, once they struck a target the soft, thin iron shafts bent, adding weight to shields if embedded in them or, more likely against unarmoured hill men, piercing flesh easily. The javelin was designed to be used but once, after which it was largely useless because an enemy could not pick it up and throw it back.

But the last thing on the minds of the enemy was retrieving javelins as dozens ran into the storm of *pila* to be cut down. Those following tripped and stumbled over their dead and wounded comrades – to run straight into the legionaries who had thrown them. Using their shields as mobile battering rams, the soldiers of Dura crashed into the faltering enemy to begin stabbing their short swords into defenceless torsos.

'Jab and stab, do not slash and hack.'

I smiled when I remembered the words Lucius Domitus had repeated a thousand times to new recruits at the training posts.

'A *gladius* blade is just under two feet in length, but you only need two or three inches to put an opponent down. Stick the point in him fast and withdraw it just as quick. Don't waste your time and energy trying to shove it into him all the way up to the guard. All that bone, muscle and other bits will only make it harder to pull it out.'

Like dozens of hornets with steel stings, the foot soldiers of Dura moved forward into the disorganised, crumbling horde of hill men, stabbing around, under and over the rims of their shields, *gladius* points sticking torsos, necks, faces and groins. As the impetus slowed due to my men having to step on, over and around the bodies of hill men writhing on the ground with javelins stuck in them, or clutching at stab wounds gushing blood, a fresh javelin storm was unleashed against them as the rear ranks of the centuries moved forward to hurl their missiles at the now-fleeing Pontic barbarians.

Out of the corner of my eye I saw Akmon make a fist as Chrestus' cohorts moved forward, the scorpions being abandoned to be retrieved by the rear-echelon cohorts. I glanced up at the slopes and saw the Pontic archers and slingers also falling back, the *testudos* sheltering our archers inching forward, still shooting the occasional arrow to urge them on their way. Behind us thousands of dismounted horsemen waited patiently for the foot soldiers to clear the gorge of enemy troops to allow them to sweep onto the plain to surround and then destroy the army of Atrax.

As the hillsides became gradually steeper, becoming almost vertical at the narrowest point in the valley, the archers and legionaries withdrew to join the rest of the army, now compacted into a column barely two hundred paces wide but stretching back to the entrance to the valley three miles to the rear. After the initial bout of frenzied bloodletting, the fighting became more sporadic and haphazard as the hill men, now demoralised after suffering hundreds of casualties, became reluctant to tangle with Chrestus' men.

My general, part of his crest missing, and blood smeared on his shield, though not his own, reported to me as the sun reached its highest point in the sky. It was very warm in the confines of the valley and there was no wind. Everyone was sweating, especially Akmon's cataphracts who acted as his bodyguard. Looking magnificent in their scale armour, with tubular steel armour covering their limbs, their horses also covered in thick scale armour, they had nothing to do except hold their lances erect and sweat. Joro could have ordered them to dismount, remove their helmets and lay their long lances on the ground. But these were Media's finest soldiers and in Media appearances were all, and so while Kalet and his men lounged on the ground, chatting and joking, Media's cataphracts stood like stone statues in the valley of death.

Chrestus saluted, clenching his blood-covered sword to his chest.

'Another couple of hours at most and we will be on the plain, majesty. The fight has gone out of them.'

In front of us were neat rows and lines of helmets, with centuries being detached from the main bodies either side of the river to move the dead bodies of hill men and dump them at the foot of the slopes. It was a grisly task but necessary to keep the narrow route through the valley clear, and to remove any bodies in the river itself to preserve the army's water supply.

Soter and Orobaz stared at Chrestus, wondering why a general would fight as a common foot soldier rather than sit on a horse to direct his soldiers.

'We will make camp on the plain and give battle to Atrax tomorrow,' I said.

Chrestus screwed up his face. 'If he's got any sense, he will keep going north rather than offer battle.'

'It doesn't matter,' I told him, 'he can run and you can destroy the foot soldiers he will be forced to leave behind. The rest of us will pursue with the horsemen and hunt him down. Either way, he's a dead man.'

'You are forgetting the civilian captives, lord,' said Akmon. 'In our plans we must consider them, for they are Medians.'

Chrestus half-smiled and shook his head.

'Most likely they are dead already, majesty, or will be as soon as we reach the plain.'

Akmon rounded on him. 'Until I have seen their bodies for myself, general, I will not abandon them.'

'If they are still alive, we will offer the enemy their own lives if they surrender their captives unharmed,' I offered.

'Including Atrax, majesty?' asked Orobaz.

'Yes,' I answered through gritted teeth.

Chrestus puffed out his cheeks and gestured at the ground, which looked like it had been sprinkled with blood.

'If you do that, majesty, he might raise another army and return to Parthia and then we will have to do this all over again.'

'Atrax will not be returning to Parthia,' I told him.

He walked back to his cohorts an unhappy man but Akmon was contented and so was Joro, pleased I had indulged his king regarding his slightly naive desire to save lowly commoners. For his part Soter maintained a dignified silence, though I suspected he was slowing warming to his young king who had shown steel and courage in the defence of Irbil and was obviously genuinely concerned about the welfare of his people. Soter rarely spoke to me directly and I suspected he viewed me with suspicion, probably because the hatred directed at me for years by my sister, her husband and their two sons had made me an ogre in Media, and the cause of the kingdom's misfortune. It did not matter if every one of Media's lords despised me as long as they displayed loyalty towards Akmon.

Chrestus was right about clearing the valley, the sun dipping in the west behind us when his cohorts finally reached flat, open ground. Rather than attempt to block our entry to the vast plain, Atrax and his army withdrew with all speed to the site of the former Musasir stronghold of Gird-I Dasht. Talib and his scouts were sent ahead to reconnoitre the ancient fortress and the plain surrounding it, Gallia joining us after her exertions on the slopes in the valley. She looked remarkably fresh considering she had spent most of the day huddled among sweating, stinking, cursing legionaries in a *testudo*, but she informed me the biggest problem had been trying to keep her footing on the grassy slope rather than worrying about enemy missiles.

She pointed at the mound and crumbling walls on top of it in the distance, shimmering in the late afternoon sun, beyond it the snowy peaks of the Zagros.

'Atrax hides in that stronghold. Now we can besiege him.'

'It will not be much of a siege, majesty,' opined Soter. 'The stronghold is too small to accommodate no more than a few hundred men, its walls are in a state of great disrepair and though there are numerous streams around it, there are no wells on the mound itself.'

'The civilians must be on the mound as well,' lamented Akmon.

Around us the Durans and Exiles, who had suffered hardly any casualties during the day, were now hacking at the earth with their entrenching tools to create a ditch and palisade to encompass our camp for the night. Mules and wagons were also threading their way through the valley to reach the barren plain, which I had to admit was ideal for combat. Our horse archers would be able to isolate, surround and annihilate the enemy's hill men, while other horse archers and our mounted spearmen and cataphracts would be able to counter the enemy's mounted skirmishers and greatly outnumbered horse archers. This would allow the Durans and Exiles to destroy the Pontic legionaries and foot slingers and archers.

By the time over twenty-two thousand soldiers, their animals, wagons, camels and all the non-combatants were safely behind the ramparts of our camp, it was dusk, the sky a mixture of reds, blues and purples in the evening twilight. Evening meals were being prepared, including the one in my command tent, to which I had invited Akmon, Soter, Orobaz, Chrestus and Joro. The King of Media had his own tent, of course, a sumptuous circular affair more lavish than my own, but he had left his cooks and servants in Irbil with his wife, though he did have the one hundred and eighty squires of his cataphracts to assist him in his kingly duties.

My own retinue of servants consisted of Klietas, who in his boyish desire to please and his gratitude at being rescued from a life, a short life, of poverty and hunger, worked like a man possessed. He polished my helmet, sword and even my bow, though I had to tell him it had to be treated with bees' wax, and then only once or twice a year.

'It is not as shiny as others I have seen, highborn.'

He was sitting on a stool polishing my boots, holding one between his knees as he burnished the leather with a soft cloth.

'That is because it has not been treated with lacquer,' I told him.

'Why not, highborn?'

He probably did not know what lacquer was but I indulged him.

'When I made it, there was none available.'

'Your palace does not have any?'

'I was in a place called Italy at the time, far from my home and my father's palace, fighting for a man called Spartacus.'

'The father of King Akmon,' he beamed.

'No, the Spartacus I fought for was from Thrace and he was a gladiator before he became a great warlord. He was the father of the current King of Gordyene.'

He looked at me with enthusiastic eyes, but I might as well have been speaking a foreign language. He had no knowledge of Italy, Thrace or gladiators, so I tried to make the conversation more relevant to him.

'My sword that you have spent so much time cleaning and polishing was a present from the first Spartacus.'

'He must have liked you very much to give you such a gift, highborn.'

'I like to think so.'

'Do you see him often, highborn?'

'He died forty years ago.'

He stopped polishing the boot. 'And yet you still remember him. He must have been a great warrior for a warlord such as yourself to honour him.'

'He certainly was.'

'Was he cruel like his son, highborn?'

His question surprised me. 'Why do you say that?'

'My father was killed fighting King Spartacus when he invaded Media. I remember standing with my mother watching him and the other men of the village leaving with our lord to fight the invaders. None returned.'

His head dropped.

'And your mother?' I asked.

'She died of a broken heart when my father did not return. The idea of my father dying far from home and his body being left to rot tormented her. At least they are together now.'

My heart went out to him and I thought of the countless thousands of other families that had been ripped apart by the wars engineered by my sister and her son Darius. They would not have given a fig about the misery of commoners, of course, but I had spent too long in the company of slaves and commoners over the years not to be acutely aware of the miseries war brought, which is why I detested men like Atrax who viewed it as a sport akin to hunting.

'Leave them,' I told Klietas, 'you are excused serving at the evening meal tonight. Get some rest instead.'

The meal was a subdued affair, Akmon in an earnest and reflective mood picking at his food and only drinking sparingly. Kalet was his usual larger-than-life self but was kept in check by Eszter and Dalir. I was warming to the latter by the day, despite his occasional coarse tongue and forthright manner, which bordered on the impolite. But he adored Eszter and did not drink to excess on social occasions like his father. For their part Soter and Orobaz chatted to each other amicably and Joro sat next to his king brooding. On what I had no idea.

After we had eaten dishes of chicken, goose and goat, washed down with wine and accompanied by radishes, almonds, raisins and bread cooked in Irbil that very morning, I rose and proposed a toast.

'To Akmon, rightful King of Media. May your reign be a long and happy one and may your heirs sit on Irbil's throne for a thousand years.'

Everyone aside from Akmon rose and toasted him with their drinking vessels. He in turn rose and raised his cup to me.

'And to you, King Pacorus, who has on too many occasions saved the empire from internal and external enemies. I thank you, Media thanks you and I hope the gods reward you for your long years of service to Parthia, lord.'

He and the others toasted me, Gallia catching my eye and giving me a knowing smile. It had been the gods that had brought me to Media, and to this barren plain, and I thanked them for it. Tomorrow we would crush Atrax and finally erase the poisonous legacy of my sister and her son from Parthia. Media, the breadbasket of the empire, could then begin the long road to recovery and prosperity. Our victory would also remind Phraates that he might be high king, but the empire was not his plaything. It would also show Claudia that Parthia was the domain of men and not subject to the whims of a coven of witches.

More wine flowed, and the conversation became lighter, Soter chatting with Chrestus about the merits of raising and maintaining a professional force of foot soldiers. Gallia was trying to convince Akmon his wife should have a group of female warriors to be her bodyguard, modelled on the Amazons and his own mother's Vipers. He was not averse to the notion, but stressed Media's treasury was not Dura's and was in effect empty. The only one who was not happy was Joro, his blue eyes narrowing and the worry lines on his face very pronounced as he sat opposite me. At first, I thought it was I who had invoked his displeasure but then I realised he was staring at something behind me. I turned to see Talib who had entered unannounced. All talk died instantly when the others recognised him, an air of concern filling the tent, which became one of alarm when he spoke.

'The Armenians are here.'

Chapter 17

'It changes nothing.'

They all looked at me with surprised expressions. Even Gallia was taken aback.

'How many Armenians?' she asked Talib.

'Piecing all the reports of my scouts together, and taking into account we could not get close to the enemy…'

'A figure Talib,' I demanded, 'that is what we want.'

'At least thirty thousand, majesty.'

There were sharp intakes of breath from Soter and Orobaz, while Chrestus looked thoughtful.

'Our horsemen are in the east,' he said.

I knew what he meant. Dura's professional cataphracts and horse archers were in the east of the empire fighting for Phraates, a decision I now deeply regretted. But what Chrestus was alluding to was that they were highly trained horsemen who could work closely with the legions, and as such acted as a force multiplier on the battlefield. I looked at Soter and Orobaz, both of whom commanded thousands of horse archers but their men only capable of the most basic battlefield tactics. Even Kalet, the gods love him, and his lords, who had fought beside the Durans and Exiles, could not be relied upon to undertake complicated battlefield manoeuvres.

I picked up my cup and sipped at the wine.

'We are greatly outnumbered majesty,' stated Soter.

I put the cup down. 'No, my lord, we are outnumbered by but two-to-one. You may have heard of the Battle of Carrhae.'

'The whole empire has heard of Carrhae, majesty,' he said.

'At Carrhae I fought fifty thousand Romans with ten thousand horsemen and defeated them. Numbers are but part of the equation, Lord Soter, and what I know of the Armenian army it is far from the formidable force created and commanded by Tigranes the Great.'

'We should inform Irbil of this development,' urged Joro, 'just in case.'

I leaned back in my chair. 'In case we are beaten, general?'

His brow creased into a frown.

'A prudent commander considers all possibilities, majesty.'

'You're right,' I told him, 'he does. But I am forgetting myself. This is not Dura but Media. I therefore leave the decision to King Akmon, whose kingdom has been invaded by first rebels and now the Armenians. The decision is yours, Akmon.'

Akmon's grey eyes examined each of us in turn. In those few moments, he must have felt the loneliest man in the world. But that is the nature of kingship. There can be only one standing on top of the pyramid that is a kingdom. With hindsight, I realised my journey on that path had had an easy start. I had been given a piece of land infested with snakes, scorpions, bandit lords, the banished, unwanted and dangerous, all exiled to the barren wasteland that was Dura. I was expected to fail, my fate perhaps to be killed by the hated Agraci, the desert nomads reviled and feared by all decent Parthians. Nothing was expected of me, except perhaps to die a good death. But Akmon ruled one of the most prestigious kingdoms in the empire, a place of great and ancient noble families, long-held customs and high etiquette.

The atmosphere in the tent, before light and convivial, was now heavy with foreboding and uncertainty. Akmon smiled to himself.

'In Gordyene we did not have Greek tutors to teach us how to sing or recite poetry. But my father did hire instructors to teach us how to used a sword and he himself taught me how to shoot a bow and wield an axe, mace and spear.

'I remember one tutor, a gaunt, morose man from Thrace, my father's homeland, who used to tell us stories about ancient battles and famous warriors. His favourite story was about how a handful of Spartans defied the might of the Persian army at a place called Thermopylae in Greece. When the tens of thousands of Persians were arrayed before the Spartans, an emissary was sent to the Greeks from the Persian emperor Xerxes. His message threatened that he had so many archers that when they shot their bows the volume of arrows would blot out the sun. The Spartan King Leonidas sent back his reply: then we shall fight in the shade.'

'A rousing tale, majesty,' commented Soter.

Akmon looked directly at me. 'Tomorrow we will fight in the shade.'

Kalet roared his approval and Joro nodded in agreement.

'I suggest we get a good night's sleep,' I said, 'we will need it.'

Kalet drained his cup, belched and stood. 'What happened to those Spartans?'

'Slaughtered to a man,' Akmon replied flatly.

When they had left the tent, I told Talib to sit down and get some food inside him. He did as he was told, eating greedily the uneaten fare within reach.

'In the morning, send one of your men to Irbil and report what has happened,' I told him. 'He must impress upon Queen Lusin that she must inform Ctesiphon, Hatra and Vanadzor that the Armenians have invaded Parthia.'

325

'They have taken advantage of our best horsemen being away in the east,' said Gallia, drinking from her cup. 'They will be missed tomorrow.'

'Can't help that,' I replied, 'I am not running away when I have a chance to corner and kill Atrax, and slaughter a few Armenians as well.'

'Have you heard the expression: pride comes before a fall?' queried Gallia. 'The prudent thing would be to withdraw back to Irbil and await reinforcements.'

'By which time Atrax and the Armenians will have overrun all Media and perhaps even Atropaiene and Susiana. So much for Armenia being an ally of Phraates.'

'I think Spartacus is responsible for their foray,' she said, 'we did warn him not to invade Armenia.'

I thumped the table, causing Talib to jump.

'No doubt Spartacus has wreaked havoc and his Sarmatian thugs have plundered and pillaged to their hearts' content, and now he is probably marching back to Vanadzor with a smug grin on his face. He is the most selfish person I know.'

Gallia began laughing. 'Oh, Pacorus, you are so moral. You should have been a high priest so you could spend your time lecturing everyone about their lack of integrity.'

'Integrity?' I growled. 'That is a quality singularly lacking in most parts of the world, including Parthia. I blame Phraates for this mess.'

'Some might blame *you*.'

'Me! What have I done?' I protested.

'You refused the high crown when it was offered to you. You have spent your life defending Parthia but you would have done a better job if you had been sitting on Ctesiphon's throne.'

I shook my head. 'We have been over this a thousand times.'

'And yet here we are,' she said, 'once more clearing up the mess of others.'

Talib, who had never heard his king and queen speak thus, kept his eyes down as he ate and drank, occasionally glancing at the two of us.

'Perhaps *you* should have sat on the high throne,' I jested.

'I could not have done any worse than Phraates or indeed Mithridates,' she spat back, 'but of course women are not allowed to aspire to the highest position in the Parthian Empire, more's the pity.'

'The empire would never accept a queen of queens,' I agreed.

'And why is that?' she demanded.

I shrugged. 'Men have always ruled the empire. It is the way of things.'

'Then things should change.'

She rose, walked over to me and kissed me on the cheek.

'I stay with the Amazons tonight. I look forward to learning of your battle plan for tomorrow. You do have a battle plan?'

'Not yet.'

She tutted. 'We are all relying on you, Pacorus, don't let us down. Klietas.'

The boy came scurrying from the tent's sleeping quarters.

'Yes, highborn?'

'Make sure the king does not doze off before he has worked out how to beat the enemy tomorrow.'

He bowed. 'Yes, highborn.'

'Good night, Talib.'

Talib jumped up and bowed his head. 'Good night, majesty.'

'Get me some wine,' I commanded Klietas.

'That will make you sleep, highborn,' he said, trying to be helpful.

'Just get the wine.'

The Gird-I Dasht sits in the middle of the vast Diyana Plain, an undulating fertile piece of terrain that is largely devoid of trees. It is crisscrossed by small streams but not in sufficient number to inhibit horsemen. Our camp was five miles west of the former stronghold, the tents of the Armenians – a blaze of reds, purples, blues and greens – visible on the horizon when the sun showed itself above the snow-capped mountains in the east the next day. It was a fresh, invigorating morning, a breeze blowing from the north making the temperature unusually cool for this time of year.

Out of courtesy to Akmon, it was his kingdom we were in after all, we assembled for a council of war in his pavilion just after dawn. He looked pale and drawn, his eyes bloodshot and he kept biting his bottom lip. He was obviously nervous but I endeavoured to calm his fretfulness.

'The enemy outnumbers us and thinks he has the advantage over us, especially Atrax who believes he has lured us here so we can de defeated.'

'He *has* lured us here,' commented an unhappy Joro, chewing on a piece of bread smeared with butter.

'That may be,' I said, 'but it does not matter. 'He wants a battle and we will give him one, and his Armenian allies will not make a difference.'

Kalet grinned in approval and Orobaz nodded out of politeness. Lord Soter brought his hands together to ponder my words.

'I will make this simple,' I continued. 'Just like the enemy, our army is composed of disparate units that have varying levels of training and discipline, and have no experience of working with each other. However, unlike the enemy we have ten thousand highly trained foot soldiers, each of which is worth ten Armenians.'

'That few?' joked Kalet.

Gallia and Chrestus smiled and Dalir slapped his father on the back. Even Akmon cheered up, if only temporarily. I clicked my fingers to draw the attention of one of the slaves standing ready to refill our chalices with water. Gallia had bridled at the presence of slaves in camp, both Akmon and Soter having brought their own retinues of servants. Even Orobaz had his own slaves to attend him in his tent and to care for his horse. I had to admit I too was uncomfortable with the presence of slaves in camp, but there was little point in antagonising the lords of Media and Hatra. Akmon needed them. *I* needed them.

A slave came over with a tray of wafers. I took a handful and thanked him, Soter smirking at my acknowledgement of a lowborn servant. I arranged some of the wafers in a line on the table.

'Dura's foot soldiers will deploy in a single line of cohorts in the centre of our battle line.'

Chrestus raised an eyebrow. 'That will be a thin line, majesty.'

I nodded. 'The horsemen will be deployed behind the foot soldiers, ready to counterattack against the enemy.'

'You are certain the enemy will launch an attack, majesty?' queried Orobaz, nibbling a grape.

329

'Very certain,' I replied. 'The vast majority of the enemy's foot soldiers are a rabble and they will be easy to rile. My chief scout informs me the enemy has few horse archers, aside from the Median rebels riding with Atrax.'

Soter grimaced in embarrassment.

'That is fortunate,' I said, 'but I am mindful our own horse archers will not be able to call on Dura's ammunition train, so we must be prudent with their use. I intend to deploy the horse archers of Lord Soter and Lord Orobaz on the right.'

The two lords smiled. On the battlefield the right flank was considered the place of honour, which befitted their status. I thought the notion ridiculous but to those obsessed with ideas of honour and protocol it was the very opposite.

'King Artaxias himself is with the enemy army,' said Akmon suddenly.

'Are you sure, majesty?' asked a concerned Joro.

Akmon looked at me. 'I have my own scouts, and they informed me that among the enemy banners they saw a large deep crimson banner bearing a golden star in the centre flanked by two reverse-looking eagles, also in gold.'

'Beware the two eagles,' I said to myself.

'Majesty?' asked Chrestus.

'Nothing,' I snapped. 'It does not matter if Tigranes himself has returned from the dead to lead the Armenians, we will still beat them.'

We toasted Akmon and victory and then left the pavilion to return to our horses. Around us the Durans and Exiles were marching out of camp, together with their scorpions, medical orderlies tramping alongside the centuries they were assigned to. Out of the corner of my eye I spotted Alcaeus deep in conversation with one of his senior staff, both of them wearing leather aprons and bags containing medical supplies slung over their shoulders. I nudged Horns in their direction and called to him.

'A word, Alcaeus.'

He finished speaking to his subordinate and walked over, nodding to Gallia who drew alongside me.

'It might be best if you stayed in camp today,' I told him.

'Best for whom?' he asked. 'Not for the wounded who will not be treated if I am not near them to do administer said treatment. Have you devised a novel way to fight battles that does not result in casualties?'

'I could order you to remain in camp,' I told him, in no mood for his levity and sarcasm.

'You could, and I could choose to ignore you. I will see you after the battle, the gods willing. Take care of yourself, Gallia.'

With that he strolled away, leaving me fuming.

'Sometimes, I wonder why I tolerate him.'

'You tolerate him because he is an old and loyal friend,' said Gallia. 'Something troubles you. What is it?'

'Nothing.'

But she knew me too well and as trumpets blared and the sound of thousands of hobnailed sandals treading the earth filled the air, she stared in silence at me, waiting for me to crumble.

'The other night, Marduk showed himself and warned me about the two eagles. The banner of Artaxias is emblazoned with two eagles.'

'The gods speak in riddles, Pacorus, and they tease us. Perhaps it means nothing.'

'And perhaps he foretells our death.'

She smiled. 'Death roams freely on the battlefield. If we want to protect our friends and family, then order a retreat back through the gorge. The Durans and Exiles can form a rearguard to allow the rest of the army to conduct an orderly withdrawal. Do you want that?'

'No.'

She adjusted her new cuirass. 'Then concentrate on the task in hand. You wish to save lives? Keep a clear head and put aside your emotions.'

It was mid-morning by the time the army was fully deployed on the plain, the twenty cohorts of the Durans and Exiles forming the full extent of our battle line. A cohort in battle array consists of six centuries in line abreast, each one made up of eight ranks, ten legionaries in each rank. The frontage of a century in close order is approximately ten yards, that of a cohort seventy yards, give or take. By the time Chrestus and his officers had organised their cohorts into a continuous, spear-straight line, nearly ten thousand soldiers stood shoulder-to-shoulder over a distance of just over three-quarters of a mile. And attached to every century was a scorpion bolt thrower – one hundred and twenty of the machines ready to unleash death upon the enemy now massing on the other side of no-man's-land.

To the rear of each century stood medical orderlies, a stack of bolts for the scorpions and full water bottles. Further back stood two groups of soldiers, each one numbering two hundred legionaries. They were the colour parties: hand-picked men whose sole task was to protect the religious icons of the Durans and Exiles, the golden griffin and silver lion respectively. They were the army's bravest and most experienced soldiers, veterans of many battles and campaigns, and it was perhaps ironic that on the battlefield they spent all their time away from the action defending the revered totems.

I sat on Horns beside Akmon, behind us Joro and his cataphracts, all sporting blue plumes in their helmets. On my other side was Gallia and behind her Zenobia and the Amazons. On the right and well back from the cohorts of the Exiles that made up the right-centre and right wing of the army, stood Soter and Orobaz with the horse archers of Media and Hatra, six thousand riders in all. Also with Soter was a thousand mounted spearmen raised from the retainers who worked his estates. Media's professional soldiers wore blue tunics and grey leggings but these horsemen wore a variety of colours and though many wore scale-armour cuirasses, others had only a shield and helmet for protection. The shields were round wooden affairs faced with hide painted black and sporting a white dragon emblem. All the horse archers of both Media and Hatra wore tunics and leggings only, with nothing on their heads and only the officers being armed with swords.

The enemy began to mass to our front, Talib and his scouts riding up and down the line to gather as much information as possible about specific formations. But as the morning wore on two things became apparent without the aid of scouts. First, the enemy had more foot soldiers than we did because the foe's line overlapped our own by perhaps half a mile. Second, the enemy horsemen on both flanks extended each wing for a further half-mile at least. It was an impressive spectacle, reinforced by the multi-coloured flags flying among the Armenian horse and foot, and the din of kettledrums, trumpets and foot drummers. Then, as if the enemy's drumming was not bad enough, the sound of kettledrums came from behind.

I turned in the saddle and rolled my eyes when I saw a row of the infernal mounted drummers in the front rank of Soter's mounted spearmen. Gallia saw my annoyance and beamed with delight.

'Perhaps Dura should have a corps of kettledrummers, Pacorus.'

'They fortify the men's courage,' said Akmon, trying to be helpful.

'Over my dead body,' I grumbled.

Chrestus, on foot carrying a shield, walked up as we waited for Talib to report to us.

'The enemy are marshalling archers and slingers in front of their foot soldiers, majesty,' he told me. 'They have chased away our scouts.'

This was confirmed by Talib who arrived moments later, bowing his head and pointing at the enemy.

'The centre of the enemy line is made up of heavily armed foot soldiers, some with long spears, others with shorter ones.'

'The ones with long spears are Armenians,' Akmon told us, 'they fight in a phalanx, like the Greeks of old.'

'Flanking them are lightly armed troops,' said Talib, 'thousands of them, armed with a mixture of spears and axes.'

'What about their horsemen?' I asked.

'A mixture of well-armed and armoured mounted spearmen and horse archers, majesty.'

'No cataphracts?' I enquired.

'None that we have seen,' he told me.

Akmon pointed directly ahead, to a stand of red banners in the distance, behind the enemy's foot soldiers.

'If they are anywhere they will be with Artaxias.'

How I wanted to turn and see Azad at the head of his dragon of Duran cataphracts, and how I resented Phraates at that moment for creating the situation we found ourselves in. No point in dwelling on that now.

Focus.

'Begin shooting with the scorpions,' I told Chrestus.

He saluted, turned and ran back to his cohorts, speaking to one of his officers and moments later a cacophony of trumpets sounding along our battle line. The war cries and taunts of the foe drowned out the sharp snaps of one hundred and twenty bolt throwers shooting at the enemy, but after two or three minutes, parties of enemy foot soldiers on the flanks of the more professional troops deployed in the middle of the opposition's line began to dart forward. The scorpion crews would be shooting two bolts a minute: one hundred and twenty bolts hitting the foe every thirty seconds.

'Come on, come on,' I said to myself.

Two more minutes passed and a further four hundred and eighty bolts struck the enemy line, each one finding a target in the densely packed ranks of the enemy. The arrows and pellets of the enemy archers and slingers deployed in front of the foe's battle line began shooting back, their missiles striking mostly Duran shields, though some would invariably hit flesh and bone. But the scorpions continued to shoot, until there was a mighty cry on the enemy's right flank and thousands of men sprinted forward.

By the speed of their advance it was apparent they were lightly armed soldiers. They resembled a surging mob, which pointed to their lack of discipline. I could not determine their numbers but they were many and they ran at the line of cohorts like a huge wave approaching a harbour wall. For the men standing in the front ranks of the Durans it must have been a terrifying sight. That they did not turn tail and run was down to their training, their morale and an unshakeable faith in their tactics.

Before the wild tide hit them, there were whistle blasts and the first four ranks of each century stepped forward and hurled their javelins, followed seconds later by the subsequent four ranks – each century hurling eighty javelins to create a thick iron rain, which the foremost enemy troops ran into. This did not halt the momentum of those following but it did create an instant barrier of bodies, over which they had to scramble to get at the Durans. The latter, shields locked and swords drawn, began stabbing their blades at those enemy soldiers, disorientated and bleeding, that had survived the javelin storm, only to be mutilated by the swift blows of the Durans.

If the enemy troops had been disciplined professionals they would not have attempted to bludgeon their way through the ranks of the legionaries in front of them, but would rather have attempted to sweep around the end of the line of cohorts. But they were a mixture of the blood-crazed without reason or the terrified who stumbled forward blindly in their confusion.

'Their left flank is attacking,' exclaimed Akmon.

It was the left wing of the enemy's foot soldiers, not the horsemen on the extreme left of their line. I nodded in approval as once more a mass of lightly armed and armoured soldiers raced forward to get to grips with the Exiles on the right of our battle line. The scorpions had done their job to goad the foe and once more the enemy horde ran into a hail of javelins that took the sting out of their charge, the clatter, screams and shouts of men locked in a bloody mêlée filling the air moments later. Another sound suddenly drowned out the din of battle: multiple trumpet blasts signalling the advance of the enemy's heavy foot soldiers.

These troops did not rush, run or break ranks. Instead, slingers and archers in the van provided missile support to silence the accursed scorpions that had tormented them. They maintained their formation and discipline and buckled the centre of our line when the Pontic legionaries hurled their javelins moments before drawing their swords and running forward to fight Chrestus' cohorts.

I turned to Akmon. 'Get your horse archers forward to support our centre.'

Gallia had pre-empted what would happen and had led the Amazons forward to begin shooting over our centre cohorts into the ranks of the enemy. But they were only ninety women and the foe numbered thousands of heavy foot soldiers, against which our outnumbered centuries would struggle to contain. Fortunately, Akmon had also realised the danger and ordered his professional archers to support the Amazons forthwith, and within minutes nearly three hundred and fifty archers were shooting arrows into the enemy ranks.

Those ranks comprised Armenian heavy foot, each man wearing a helmet, either mail or scale armour, carrying a round shield, and armed with a short sword and long spear. They jabbed the latter forward while protecting their torsos with their shields, which meant they out-ranged our legionaries armed with a *gladius*. But their phalanx formation meant there was very little room for individual spearmen to manoeuvre and thus it was relatively easy for my men to use their shields to either brush aside a spear point or use a *scutum* to force it down. Then a Duran or Exile could dash forward to attack an opponent with the point of his sword. My men were winning a host of small victories, but the enemy had replacements that could be fed into the mêlée whereas Chrestus had no reserves.

'Enemy horsemen.'

I turned my eyes away from the desperate battle to the front to see Akmon pointing to the right, to where a large group of riders was sweeping around our right flank.

'Atrax's rebels,' he shouted, bitterness in his voice.

I turned to Soter and Orobaz. 'Now is your time, my lords.'

They needed no second prompting, digging their knees into their horses to gallop over to their waiting men, then leading them forward into the assault. Dragon banners and those showing the white horse's head of Hatra fluttered in the breeze as a thousand mounted spearmen and six thousand horse archers cantered forward to assault the riders who also carried dragon standards. But Soter and Orobaz did not lead their men straight at the enemy horsemen but rather broke into a gallop to head further to the right before wheeling left to ride forward and then swing around the enemy riders. Or at least they would have done had not the enemy wheeled about to withdraw, in turn luring Soter and Orobaz towards them to entice them into a trap. The move and counter-move, akin to a game of feint and counter-feint, resulted in both wings disappearing from both armies.

A lull descended over the battlefield and the sound of combat petered out as men drew breath and pulled back all along the line. The sun was high in the sky, the breeze had dropped substantially and the temperature had risen markedly. Battle stretches every nerve and drains the reserves of muscles and limbs that had previously been feather-light. Shields, spears and swords suddenly became lead weights when battle lust wears off. Medical orderlies behind the centuries distributed water bottles to ease raging thirsts, centurions ordered those in the rear ranks to replace those in the front ranks who had been engaged in hand-to-hand fighting, and everyone steeled themselves for a renewal of hostilities.

The Amazons and Akmon's horse archers had also ceased shooting, Gallia riding to me to report on the situation.

'We are down to one full quiver each,' she told me, 'we need more ammunition.'

I gestured to Talib to attend me. He cantered up and bowed his head.

'Majesty?'

'You and some of your men go and find the horsemen of Media and Hatra. Pass on my compliments and inform them they are needed here, now. Go.'

He galloped off.

'That's what happens when we don't have disciplined troops,' spat Gallia. 'I curse Phraates.'

I smiled, which vanished instantly when a new threat appeared on the left.

Dura's lord and their retainers, standing in a large, widely spaced group, began to move forward without my instruction or indeed that of Kalet who was sitting on his horse near me and Akmon. But he had been on too many battlefields to realise that the horsemen massing in a long line on the left were not a serious threat. He kicked his horse forward and galloped to join his friends and comrades who were now cantering towards the Armenian horsemen.

I looked at Gallia and saw concern etched on her face, not only because Eszter was somewhere within the lightly armed riders heading directly at the enemy, but also because like me she realised

339

the two sides were unevenly matched. Kalet and his men and indeed women were armed with recurve bows, spears, swords, axes and a few maces, though no rider carried a full complement of these weapons. None wore body armour or helmets, a few carried small black shields as used by the Agraci, and their horses were similarly unprotected.

The enemy horsemen, in comparison, were superbly equipped. The multi-coloured banners among their ranks showed symbols dear to the Armenian people: the tree of life, the wheel of eternity and the six-pointed star. The standard showing two gold eagles flanking a gold star was the banner of the Artaxiad dynasty, but these were more ancient, revered emblems and a host of them was now bearing down on Kalet and his lords.

'They will never hold them,' remarked Joro matter-of-factly.

I rounded on him. 'Get your cataphracts ready.'

The general smarted at my tone and looked at Akmon, his liege lord. The king nodded, Joro turned his horse and rode to the line of eighty cataphracts waiting patiently in the sun. He turned his head when a continuous chopping sound filled the air, signalling Kalet and his men had collided with the Armenians.

Whatever his faults, and he had many, Kalet did not want for courage and neither did his followers. They would have seen the well-dressed ranks of the enemy, noticed the helmets, body armour, shields and lances of the thousands of horsemen charging at them, but they did not falter. Their opponents were Armenia's lords, their sons, cousins and retainers, each one attired in scale-armour cuirasses and helmets, carrying round wooden shields faced with hide and armed with lances and swords. The wild frontier men of Dura screamed their war cries and crashed into the enemy, the initial clash unhorsing dozens of them as they were skewered on Armenian lances. Curiously, there was no exchange of arrows before the two bodies of horsemen collided, the Armenian commander probably believing his lancers could easy swat aside the rough-looking riders who looked more like a mounted body of vagrants than soldiers. Thus began a swirling mêlée on the left flank, in the midst of which was our daughter and son-in-law.

A blast of trumpets wrenched my attention away from the mêlée to the centre where the enemy, reorganised and refreshed, again attacked Chrestus' tired cohorts. On the flanks of the line the hordes of Cilician war bands and light spearmen, forced once more to scramble over mounds of their own dead, were held by the disciplined centuries, which could fend off uncoordinated and wild attacks, cutting down unarmoured warriors to create yet more obstacles for those following to clamber over before they could get to grips with the Durans and Exiles.

But in the centre it was a different manner.

I saw the figure of Titus Tullus on a horse, a large yellow crest in his helmet, riding up and down behind his Pontic legionaries, sword in hand and urging them on. In response to his exhortations they were doing just that, fresh bodies grinding forward slowly but inexorably, tired and bloody legionaries giving ground slowly, reluctantly, but at least retaining their cohesion as they did so. The battle line in front of me was being bent inwards to resemble a concave shape. The Armenian heavy spearmen on the flanks of the Pontic legionaries were faring less well, but they too were fresh men who had replaced their battered and bested comrades who had suffered in the initial clash with the Durans and Exiles, and for this reason alone they too were able to inch forward. Slowly but surely, we were losing the battle.

Zenobia sent a rider back to Gallia to report the Amazons had expended nearly all their ammunition, and judging by the desultory volleys coming from the ranks of the Median horse archers, so had Akmon's men. I yelled at Horns to move and rode to the colour party guarding the Durans' gold griffin – two hundred men standing rooted to the spot around a hundred paces from the rear of the buckling cohorts. Their commander stepped from the square and saluted. I pointed at the rear of our battle line.

'Get your men forward and relieve your comrades. If the enemy breaks through the battle is lost.'

He grinned with delight and saluted.

'Yes, majesty.'

Trumpets blew and the whole square broke apart to form two centuries, which ran forward to support the wavering Durans. I rode across to the two hundred men guarding the Exiles' silver lion and relayed the same order, two more centuries racing forward to lend support to the rest of the Exiles. Behind the centuries still battling but giving ground, orderlies were attending to injured men. I saw Alcaeus assisting a man sitting on the ground, blood gushing from a head wound. I nudged Horns over to him. By now the Amazons and Median horse archers, out of arrows, had withdrawn to group around Gallia and Akmon.

'You should get yourself back to camp,' I told him.

He did not look up at me.

'If you are not here to help then I have no time for you.'

He was bandaging the man's wound and oblivious to the impending disaster that was about to engulf him, and all of us. That

342

calamity was but moments away when I heard another trumpet blast and my heart sank.

Behind the Amazons, Media's horse archers and Joro's cataphracts was another body of horsemen, between our army and the camp but a mile distant. The latter was our only sanctuary but now the enemy had placed a body of horsemen between it and us. And not just any horsemen. They were cataphracts, the sun glinting off tubular steel armour on their arms, burnished scale armour cuirasses and open-faced helmets. The latter sported crimson plumes to complement the colour of the eagle banner that flew in the middle of the enemy line, a line that was long in extent. When I caught up with Joro, Gallia and Akmon joining me, he gave me the news that King Artaxias himself was with the enemy cataphracts.

'And not just Artaxias,' said Akmon, pointing at a black banner flying beside the King of Armenia's standard. 'That is Atrax's flag.'

'Then we can kill two birds with one stone,' scoffed Gallia, drawing her sword and resting the blade on her shoulder.

We were finished, that much was apparent. The horsemen of our right wing had disappeared as they duelled with the enemy; our centre was on the verge of caving in; on the left the mêlée was going against Kalet's men as the more heavily armed Armenians pushed them back; and in our rear at least four or five hundred cataphracts marshalled in preparation to launching an attack that would cut through our meagre force of Amazons, horse archers without arrows and eighty cataphracts.

Far better to die doing something useful than meekly waiting for death.

I too drew my sword. 'Then let us kill both of them, as my wife says.'

Joro barked an order to his deputy who ordered the cataphracts to form into a wedge formation, two ranks deep. The commander of the two hundred and fifty Median horse archers began to organise his men to deploy into formation behind them, though what use men without helmets, armour and shields and lacking arrows would be was questionable. Like the Amazons they had swords but against the lances and close-quarter weapons of the cataphracts they would come a poor second. Not that it mattered; the enemy horsemen would cut us to pieces when it came to it. I glanced behind to see the line of Chrestus' cohorts still standing. How long his centre would hold was anyone's guess.

Farewell Chrestus; farewell Alcaeus. We will meet again in the next life.

'They are withdrawing.'

I heard Akmon's voice and saw him pointing his sword at the enemy cataphracts, which had wheeled left and were riding away hard. But to where?

My first thought was they were going to finish off Kalet and his men. But I discounted the idea because if they killed me, Gallia and Akmon they would bring the battle to a swift end and place Atrax on Media's throne. They had seen our banners and knew where we were. They would not abandon the opportunity to strike at the heart of our army. But now they were doing just that. I was even more confused when trumpets being sounded came from the mêlée on our left flank, followed by the Armenian horsemen following their king and withdrawing. What in the name of Shamash was going on?

'I don't understand,' said Akmon, putting into words what we were all thinking.

More confusion followed when the clatter of battle behind us began to die down. I turned Horns and urged him forward, riding through bemused cataphracts who minutes before had pledged to follow their king and sell their lives dearly but now found themselves with no one to fight. Gallia, the wellbeing of Eszter uppermost in her mind, rode over to the left with the Amazons to find her daughter.

Our concave-shaped battle line of cohorts, battered and ragged, many men being treated in the rear by over-worked medical orderlies, still stood and I could hear no sounds of battle. I saw Alcaeus helping a wounded Chrestus and jumped down from Horns to lend a hand.

The general was limping and I saw he had taken a spear point in his right leg. The wound was gushing blood but my experience of such injuries assured me it looked worse than it was. A tourniquet would staunch the flow of blood and a honey coated bandage would assist in its healing.

He gave me a triumphant grin. 'We are lucky bastards, majesty, and that's no lie. The lads were about to break, I could feel it, when all of a sudden they broke contact and are pulling back. What did you do?'

'I am as ignorant as to why the enemy has faltered as you are. It must be divine intervention.'

Alcaeus guffawed. 'Ah, yes, the common explanation of the ignorant and deluded.'

Around us exhausted men removed their helmets and gasped for breath, others rested on their battered and shredded shields and some, utterly spent, collapsed on the ground. Alcaeus frowned at me.

'If you are at a loose end, perhaps you could ride to camp and fetch the carts so I can get the wounded back to the field hospitals.'

He really was incorrigible but entirely correct. But there was no need for me to ride to camp in person because Alcaeus had devised a signal system whereby some of his orderlies were equipped with red flags that they now waved frantically to alert the guards on the palisade – squires and non-combatants equipped with spears and bows. Soon a line of carts would be exiting the camp to pick up the wounded, including Chrestus, who was beginning to look a little pale. Alcaeus was busy applying a tourniquet to his leg after he had instructed the general to sit on the ground. I fetched the water bottle attached to Horns' saddle, removed the cork and handed it to him. He drank some and poured a little over his sweat-beaded head, wincing as Alcaeus examined his wound with a medical probe.

'Nothing in there,' he muttered.

'I've seen them before,' said Chrestus, nodding at riders approaching Akmon and his horsemen. 'It wasn't the gods but mortals who came to our rescue.'

I too saw them and realised a new army had arrived on the Plain of Diyana.

Chapter 18

The score of riders trotting towards Akmon's banner and my griffin standard were expensively attired, the sun reflecting off their magnificent cuirasses of alternating steel and bronze scales. Normally they wore red cloaks, but the day was warm, and they must have been sweating in their armour and the pteruges at their shoulders and thighs, to say nothing of their heavy helmets. I slapped Chrestus on the shoulder, mounted Horns and trotted across to speak to our saviours. Gordyene's King's Guard was a superb force: five hundred lancers armed with ukku swords who also carried bows to add to their potency. Each man carried a round shield sporting a lion motif and the same animal adorned their red saddlecloths. One could not but admire them in their red tunics, black leggings and shiny leather boots. The same could not be said of their commander.

His name was Shamshir, which meant 'sword', and he was one of my nephew's favourites, a man who had a cruel nature but who carried out his orders without question. Tall, dark and ugly, in many ways he was the spirit of Gordyene and its capital made flesh. By the time I had arrived he had removed his helmet and was conversing with Akmon. His cold, dark eyes viewed me with suspicion as he bowed his head to me. Our past encounters had not been happy affairs.

'Greeting, majesty, King Spartacus sends his regards.'

I heard the distinctive sound of trumpet blasts and knew the Immortals were close.

'We have snatched victory from the jaws of defeat,' remarked Akmon, 'where are Atrax and Artaxias?'

'Fled, majesty,' gloated Shamshir, 'like the beaten dogs they are. What sort of king abandons his army?'

'A false one,' said Joro.

'There is only one true King of Media,' said Shamshir, looking at Akmon.

The commander of the King's Guard turned in the saddle to stare at the line of battered cohorts in a concave shape in the heat, most Durans and Exiles still standing resting on their shields now the fighting had ended. Ended for them, anyway. Shamshir turned back to me.

'My lord King Spartacus will deal with the enemy now, majesty, as I can see that your men are at the end of their endurance.'

More riders were appearing and from the left flank came a welcome sight: Gallia, Kalet, Eszter and Dalir, all mercifully unhurt but my daughter wearing a haunted look. She had experienced battle before and at Ctesiphon had been among those who had been temporarily surrounded by a host of enemy horsemen, but something had obviously unnerved her. Kalet reported to me directly.

'If they had not buggered off we would all be dead by now.' He looked at Shamshir. 'Who's this?'

'This is Lord Shamshir, commander of King Spartacus' King's Guard,' I told him, 'whose arrival signalled our change of fortune.'

'We are in your debt, lord,' said Kalet.

This was music to Shamshir's misshapen ears.

'Gordyene's might is always at the disposal of its allies, lord…'

'Lord Kalet,' I informed him.

Shamshir raised an eyebrow at a fellow lord's shabby appearance but said nothing. I also saw him admiring the cuirasses worn by me and Gallia, and which made even his magnificent armour pale into insignificance.

'We should ride to thank my father,' said Akmon.

'He will be delighted to see you, majesty,' smiled Shamshir.

We found the King of Gordyene sitting on a black stallion beside Rasha, behind them the women horse archers of the Vipers and the rest of the King's Guard. Both were watching parties of Immortals disarm enemy soldiers who had surrendered in preference to fighting ten thousand fresh soldiers newly arrived on the battlefield. Rasha, attired in mail armour and helmet, beamed with delight when she saw us, jumping down from her horse to rush over to Akmon, who likewise dismounted to embrace his mother. It was a touching scene and there were tears in Gallia's eyes when she witnessed the reunion of mother and son. Spartacus was less emotional, though even his hard visage cracked a smile when he saw his beloved wife happy. The king's other two sons, Castus and Haytham, slightly behind their father, rolled their eyes in embarrassment at the scene. Both were attired in mail armour and helmets. Castus was a man now, his shoulders broad like his father and his frame stocky unlike his older brother Akmon.

Spartacus jumped down from his horse and told his two sons to do the same, tossing his helmet to Shamshir as he walked past his commander. Mother and son parted to allow Akmon to greet his father. It had been months since the two had last seen each other, in Ctesiphon's throne room, and on that occasion there had been friction between father and son, not least because Spartacus had called Lusin a whore. I was there and remembered his fury when Phraates had declared that his oldest son would be King of Media. As I slid off Horns and Gallia also dismounted, I wondered whether

Akmon would remember the insult to his wife. In the event, he acted like a king, bowing his head to his father and remaining cordial.

'Greetings, father, welcome to Media. I look forward to entertaining you and your officers in my palace.'

All eyes were on the King of Gordyene. Claudia had once described him as a brooding menace who hated the world and everything in it. She was of the opinion he had created a formidable army so that he could use it to inflict misery on others as a way of wreaking vengeance on a world that had meted out injustice to him. What precise injustices a former prince of Hatra given a privileged upbringing and later awarded his own kingdom believed himself to be the victim of I had no idea, but Spartacus certainly suffered from a sense of grievance. But today he was generous, magnanimous even. He walked forward and embraced Akmon.

'It is good to see you, son.'

The meeting between siblings was also friendly and I thought it a good omen for future relations between Media and Gordyene. Much better than if Atrax had triumphed. I looked around at the thousands of demoralised soldiers being corralled into manageable parties by Immortals, the latter using their shields and swords to convince recalcitrant individuals to obey orders.

'They are to be sold as slaves in case you were wondering, uncle.'

The King of Gordyene was in his prime now, his thick neck, muscular frame and square jaw presenting an intimidating impression to the world, much like his army. He did not smile but neither did he sneer. Rather, his expression was one of cool detachment. There was a time when he and I had been close, and I like to think he looked up to me. But we had clashed on numerous occasions and I had taken great exception to him sending his cutthroat Shamshir to plunder the Temple of Ishtar in Babylon, and so now we were related but distant from each other. I think he thought of me as a quaint relic from a bygone era.

'They are to be a gift,' he told me.

'A lavish gift,' I commented, glancing at the thousands of captives being rounded up.

'They will be given to my friend and ally Prince Spadines who deserves them, as compensation for the loss of Van.'

I was disappointed the Sarmatian was not dead but wondered where he was. As if to pre-empt my query, Spartacus provided further details.

'He and his men are currently pursuing the Armenians and the rebel Atrax. They and the bulk of their horsemen unfortunately managed to escape.'

'But father,' said Akmon, 'how is it you and the prince are here at all?'

'I was wondering that,' I added, 'though I have never been gladder to see the lion banner of Gordyene.'

Rasha walked over to embrace me and I kissed her on the cheek.

'You have Governor Kuris to thank for that,' said Spartacus. 'He got a message to me saying Akmon was in peril, so I quit tormenting the Armenians and hastened south.'

He looked around at the ghastly debris of battle: the intertwined bodies, dead horses, men half-dead from their wounds crawling on the ground and the mournful sound of groans from soldiers nearing death.

He smiled. 'Music to my ears. There is nothing more heartening than hearing the death rattle of the enemy. My congratulations, uncle, you have reaped a fine harvest of enemy slain.'

I wondered if he knew this war was down to him, that it was his responsibility there were thousands of dead and dying men on the Diyana Plain. That Phraates had engineered this conflict to muzzle the lion of Gordyene. I was tempted to tell him, but he would probably fly into a rage and declare his intention to march on Ctesiphon. Akmon would undoubtedly inform his father about Phraates' letter to Atrax but that was for another time.

'Where is your camp?' I asked.

'Ten miles to the north.'

He looked at my armour.

'That is a very fine cuirass, uncle, and I see Aunt Gallia has one too.'

I shrugged. 'A gift from a friend. Come, our camp is but a mile south of here. Let us leave this place of dead flesh.'

We walked to our horses and gained our saddles, Spartacus ordering Shamshir to organise parties of King's Guard to provide extra security for the Immortals who had accepted the surrender of more than their number, Rasha ordering Narin, the commander of the Vipers, to remain with the bulk of her women to assist them. So we rode back to camp with an escort of a score of King's Guard, the same number of Vipers, ninety Amazons and Joro's eighty cataphracts. The latter looked very dejected they had been bystanders to the battle, but had they been committed it would have been as part of a noble but futile charge against their Armenian counterparts.

The Durans and Exiles were now limping back to camp, a host of carts containing their wounded also trundling across the plain.

Kalet and his lords had also quit the battlefield after their exertions in the unequal battle with the Armenian horsemen.

Akmon pulled up his horse. 'My people.'

I too suddenly remembered the reason we had marched from Irbil to this vast plain — to rescue the civilians taken during Atrax's betrayal and murder of Parmenion. Spartacus looked bemused as his son turned his horse and directed it towards the grass-covered earth mound in the distance, around two miles away. We all followed, Akmon explaining to his father the reason for the diversion. Gordyene's king was bemused and warned his son the journey might end in disappointment. But he was wrong when we rode up the long ramp cut in the side of the mound to enter what had been hundreds of years before a fortress. The post station — a walled enclosure containing stables, living quarters and storerooms — was well maintained, but the rest of the sprawling site was an overgrown ruin, only traces of mud-brick walls and buildings extant. And occupying the site, sitting or lying on the ground in groups, frightened children clinging to their equally alarmed parents, were Irbil's stolen citizens.

'At least they have been fed and watered,' observed Rasha as people began to move away from the horsemen that had suddenly appeared among them.

'They were to be sold as slaves,' lamented Akmon, 'so it was in the enemy's interests to take care of them, mother.'

'Lucky for you,' said Spartacus.

'Lucky for *them*, father,' Akmon corrected him.

There were no water sources on the mound itself but there were several streams around the Gird-I Dasht and the captives were now herded towards these, Joro going among them to announce their king had won a great battle and they were now going home. Within no time, I saw smiling faces and heard a babble of chatter.

'They can stay in camp tonight,' I said to Akmon, 'and in the morning undertake the journey back through the gorge to Irbil. You have done well, Akmon.'

He seemed morose. 'As long as Atrax lives, Media will have no peace.'

'First's things first,' I emphasised. 'We get your people back to Irbil and then we can think about tracking Atrax down. What are you going to do with the rebels who sided with him?'

'Pardon them.'

I was surprised. 'A more prudent move would be to banish them.' I looked at Spartacus. 'Or to execute them.'

'I will not be doing that,' he said forcefully, 'there has been too much blood spilt in this kingdom already.'

But the gods love chaos and the effusion of blood to alleviate their boredom, and the screams and wails of alarm coming from the streams put a halt to our debate when I saw horse archers putting arrows into the civilians. They were not intentionally trying to butcher innocents; rather, they were trying to clear a path through the scattered groups endeavouring to quench their thirst. But the quickest way to do so was to shoot down anything in their way.

'King's Guard, to me.'

Spartacus drew his sword and without hesitation led his score of horsemen towards the oncoming riders. The latter were the vanguard of more riders coming from the south – the remnants of Median rebels that had been deployed on the left wing of the enemy army during the battle. Soter and Orobaz had been sent against them and I wondered where those two lords and their men were. Behind the attacking horse archers, which numbered around a hundred men, were mounted spearmen carrying shields bearing a white dragon motif. I spied a large group of riders behind them, some way off and difficult to identify. I prayed to Shamash they were not the remainder of the enemy horsemen. Where were the lords of Media and Hatra?

Akmon was gone. I turned to see him galloping over to Joro's cataphracts that had ridden down the ramp to deploy in a wedge formation, two ranks deep, the king placing himself at the tip of it. Behind them came Rasha and her Vipers, galloping to catch up with Spartacus and his sons who were now charging at the enemy horse archers, which immediately wheeled about and shot a volley over the hindquarters of their horses at the King's Guard, several toppling from their saddles and others falling to the ground because their horses had been hit.

Without arrows I was reduced to being a bystander, as were the Amazons that Gallia was mustering behind the cataphracts that had now broken into a canter, Akmon leading them against the mounted spearmen that were bearing down on his father's horsemen. The civilians had scattered in all directions, some being trampled underfoot in the panic and others throwing themselves into the streams, two of which ran east-to-west straight across the cataphracts' path. I sat on the ramp looking down at the unfolding drama, Gallia and the Amazons following Akmon's armour-clad horsemen and Spartacus and the Vipers chasing the enemy horse archers, the female warriors loosing arrows over the heads of the dozen or so King's Guard as they did so.

A prudent commander would have waited for the streams to disrupt the charge of the cataphracts, for mounted spearmen equipped with shields and spears cannot stand against men encased in helmets, scale and tubular armour and riding horses protected by armour comprising thick hide covered with iron scales. The *kontus*, between twelve and eighteen feet long depending on the preference of individual kingdoms, is heavier and longer than a standard spear. In the charge it is gripped by both hands, usually on the right side of the horse, its iron point capable of going straight through a shield and a body when it is driven at an opponent. For the dozens of mounted spearmen galloping towards the blue-plumed cataphracts, their only chance, albeit slim, of defeating Joro's horsemen was to wait for them to negotiate the streams.

But the rebel horsemen merely slowed to splash through the shallow, narrow streams before emerging in a disorganised mass. To be hit head-on by Joro's horsemen. The general was next to his king and I saw him drive his *kontus* through the chest of the enemy rider directly opposite Akmon. There was a rasping sound as forty *kontus* points pierced wood, armour and finally flesh, each cataphract releasing his lance that was embedded in an opponent to draw his sword or perhaps grip a mace or axe to battle the enemy. There was another horrible scraping sound when the second rank of cataphracts joined the mêlée, another forty enemy horsemen being skewered and knocked from their saddles. As the second line began hacking and slashing with their close-quarter weapons, Gallia and the Amazons joined the fray, swords drawn to support the cataphracts. I shouted at Horns to move because I grew alarmed by the increasing numbers of enemy horsemen appearing to the south and splashing through the streams.

In no time at all I was in the mêlée, ducking when a rebel swung his sword at my head and jabbing the point of my *spatha* into his unprotected thigh. He yelped like a frightened puppy, dropped his sword and died when I slashed the sharp edge of my sword across his throat. Other enemy horsemen slashed at me as they passed, though all of them showed a marked reluctance to stand and fight. I saw Gallia alongside Zenobia and a dozen other Amazons.

Gallia turned to look at me and I saw her jaw drop and the Amazons around her look similarly horrified. My sixth sense, honed by four decades of being a soldier, screamed at me that something was wrong. It was. I looked to my left to see a rider approaching, his horse cantering towards me as it threaded a path between duelling horsemen. He wore an evil leer as his mount covered the last few paces between us, in his right hand a spear levelled at my belly. Then he hit me, the iron point driving into my cuirass. I thought I heard Gallia scream above the din of battle and believed it would be the last thing I would hear in this life. But the point shattered and the shaft it was attached to splintered and I felt no pain, not even the force of an object striking me with the energy of a man riding a horse behind it. The horseman, expecting to see me skewered on the end of his spear like a human kebab, looked hurt and disappointed. It had been a perfect strike, but he had been robbed of a kill. He was robbed of his life when his horse drew alongside Horns and I rammed the point of my *spatha* into his neck just above his leather cuirass. He gasped, gurgled and watched with horror as his blood sheeted over the blade of my sword. His eyes then rolled into his head and he fell from his saddle.

Gallia and the Amazons rallied around, many gaping at me and no doubt wondering why I was not dead.

'Stay alert,' snapped Gallia, smiling and laying a hand on my arm.

'Do you think Girra would supply me with a thousand of these cuirasses?' I smiled.

'You should not mock the gods, Pacorus, they can take as well as give.'

Around us the Median rebels were fleeing north, passing the Gird-I Dasht, panicking civilians, cataphracts, Amazons and Spartacus' men to make good their escape. The horse archers the King of Gordyene had charged had skirted the great mound to escape and others of the enemy had likewise given the ancient fortress a wide berth to flee. It was apparent they had fought us only because we were in the way and blocking their escape route.

The reason for their urgency soon manifested itself when Soter and Orobaz appeared, both riding horses lathered in sweat, they themselves looking tired and frustrated. Orobaz raised a hand in salute as he pulled up his horse before me, having identified my griffin banner.

'Greetings, majesty,' he panted, 'your scout and his men found us as the enemy was leading us a merry dance on this seemingly limitless plain. We came as fast as we could.'

'My thanks, lord. You will be pleased to know King Spartacus arrived with his army to tip the scales of battle in our favour. The enemy is beaten and those who can are fleeing Media.'

'Praise be to Shamash,' said Orobaz.

'Praise be, indeed.'

But Gallia's words were to be prophetic and when the enemy had passed, and we rode to seek the banner of Gordyene, a knot tightened in my stomach. My sense of apprehension increased when we drew near to the lion standard of Gordyene and saw a group of men and women standing in a circle, many with their heads in their hands. As if to reinforce the impression of dread, clouds had suddenly appeared overhead. Not light, fluffy buds of white but dark-grey clouds that hung like huge celestial vultures over us all. The gods can indeed take, and they had taken a jewel among women for Rasha, Queen of Gordyene, was dead.

Chapter 19

An arrow had penetrated her heart to kill her instantly. I stood, stunned, as Spartacus scooped up his dead wife in his arms and wept bitter tears, his two sons standing behind him trying their utmost to remain stoic in the face of tragedy and failing miserably. Narin, commander of the Vipers, held one of her young warriors who was on the verge of collapse. Akmon stared, unblinking, at his father cradling his dead mother, while Gallia wept. We had both known Rasha since the first day we had stepped inside Dura's Citadel, when a frightened young Agraci girl in chains had been brought into our presence all those years ago. From that moment Gallia had enjoyed a special bond with the daughter of King Haytham; indeed, she became like a daughter to us both and soon had her own bedroom in the palace. Gallia had given her a bow, the same bow Rasha had carried as she became a teenager, adult, wife and then queen.

Spartacus, holding his wife, turned to Castus and Haytham.

'Remember who you are. You are princes of Gordyene not a pair of milkmaids. Stop your blubbing. You insult your mother with your whining. We will cremate her in the morning and tonight we will stand vigil over her body.'

He wept no more tears now and his face was a mask of granite: hard and unyielding. But he avoided any eye contact with those of us who had known him and Rasha since childhood as a path cleared before him and he walked back to the Gird-I Dasht.

I saw Akmon comforting his two brothers and they in turn embraced him. No ill will between them, it would seem, though the dreadful situation they found themselves in may have merely put aside any resentment between Castus and Haytham and the King of Media.

'Palmyra will weep when it learns of this day.'

Talib stood beside me, distraught at what he had seen. I laid a hand on his shoulder.

'You should be the one to tell Malik, Talib, rather than some words written on papyrus. Leave after the cremation tomorrow. There will be no more fighting now.'

In the hours of daylight still left it was Joro who took the lead in organising the prisoners into parties to scour the battlefield to collect the thousands of wicker shields that lay on the ground, after which they were taken to the Gird-I Dasht to create a vast funeral pyre on which Rasha's body would be cremated the next day. After the pyre had been built the prisoners were confined in the Roman-style camp created by Titus Tullus before the battle. He had disappeared, along with Atrax, Artaxias and the loathsome Laodice. They would all be dealt with in time. But the immediate priority was to pay our respects to Rasha.

Shamshir organised a cordon of King's Guard to ring the remains of the stronghold on the Gird-I Dasht, a long line of visitors waiting patiently in line to file onto the mound and into the small post station office where Rasha had been laid out on a table draped with a red banner emblazoned with a silver lion. Guards stood outside the office but only one person stood sentry over Rasha inside: Spartacus. His brown eyes locked on every person who stepped into the room, creating an air of intimidation to add to the despondency that hung over the mound.

The first to enter were her sons, all three now in a numb state and perhaps unwilling to believe their mother was dead. Castus was a man but Haytham, three years younger, was still a boy, albeit one raised in Vanadzor rather than the gilded palaces of other kingdoms. Akmon had won a great victory that would cement his reign, his right to rule Media and his credibility throughout the empire. But he looked lost and gaunt, his naturally lithe body making him look emaciated. He said nothing to Gallia and me as he walked past us in a daze in the company of his siblings, all of them with their heads down after paying their respects to the body of their mother.

We entered the office next, Gallia choking back tears when she saw Rasha, pale, eyes closed and clothed in a simple red tunic and black leggings, her black hair having been combed and her body washed. I bowed my head to her and then Spartacus, walked forward to kiss Rasha's cold forehead. Her sword had been placed on her chest and her bow was beside her. As Gallia stroked Rasha's hair and whispered something into her ear that I could not hear, I looked at the recurve bow. It been made for the then Agraci princess on the express orders of Gallia and was a masterful weapon, a thing of beauty and power. The arms and setback centre had been fashioned from layers of mulberry and maple with water buffalo horn plating on the inside. Additional horn had been used to stiffen its handle and tips. The latter had been carved into horse's heads and the wood and horn had been bound together by fish glue and tendon strings. The whole bow was covered in lacquer brought from China to keep it waterproof. It seemed a shame that it would be incinerated but it was fitting that the weapons Rasha had used during her life should accompany her to the next one.

Gallia then whipped her dagger from its sheath, gently took hold of a length of Rasha's black hair and placed the blade next to it. She then looked at Spartacus, who did not say anything but after a

362

few seconds nodded his approval. With a deft flick of the wrist Gallia severed a lock of hair and replaced the dagger in its sheath. She then walked over to Spartacus, embraced him, kissed him gently on the cheek and walked briskly from the room, leaving me alone with the King of Gordyene.

I stroked Rasha's white face and walked over to Spartacus and offered him my hand. He took it.

'I wanted to thank you for keeping Akmon safe,' he said flatly. 'From what I hear, he is proving himself a good ruler and Parthia needs good kings.'

'He and Lusin will make Media prosper,' I told him, 'and if they achieve nothing else that alone will be a fine legacy.'

He looked at his wife. 'Others are waiting, uncle.'

Taking my cue, I embraced him and walked from the room to allow others in the long line of mourners to pay their respects. Among them was a distraught Alcaeus who had known Rasha as long as I had, for he had accompanied Gallia and me when we had made the journey from Hatra to take command of Dura all those years ago.

'I have lived too long,' he sighed. 'I have seen too much death and lost too many friends. And now this. The gods are cruel. Earlier I held a soldier, barely out of his teens, as he died from his wounds. I have lost more than I have saved.'

'That is not true, my friend,' I insisted.

'I'm too old for all this, Pacorus. I am going to retire. I feel like butter spread too thinly over a piece of bread.'

'That is your prerogative, my friend, and the gods know you have served your time. All I would ask is that you think about your decision when we get back to Dura.'

'In truth, I have been thinking about it for some time. I wish to go back to Greece.'

I was shocked. 'You wish to leave Dura?'

'I was thinking more of a long holiday. I would like to see Athens again before I die.'

'As long as you return,' I said.

'You can rely on it. Dura is my home now and I wish to enjoy what years I have left living them out in peace. You should try it, Pacorus.'

I thought about his words when I rode back to camp in the company of a silent Gallia. I tortured myself with the idea that I had brought about Rasha's death, or at least had put in motion events that had led to it. Perhaps Alcaeus was right; perhaps I should think about retiring. Despite my reinvigorated body, I was not getting any younger and neither was Gallia, though she would vigorously argue otherwise. Did we not deserve to live out our autumn years in peace? I realised with alarm that of all the kings in Parthia, only Khosrou was older than me.

'Alcaeus is retiring,' I told Gallia, 'he just told me.'

'He has earned it.'

There was a time when Gallia would have turned her horse around and ridden back to our Greek friend and harangued him for voicing such a ridiculous notion. But now she just shrugged.

'He has the right idea.'

The next day thousands of soldiers from Dura, Gordyene and Media lined up on parade to pay their respects to Rasha, her body carried from the room it had spent the night in by a party of Vipers, a tired, unshaven Spartacus leading the way. The remains of the stronghold were crowded with senior officers, lords and others who had been close to Rasha, including Alcaeus who looked old and frail in the harsh early morning sunlight. Talib stood among his scouts, all of them recruited from the Agraci and all of them sharing a bond with the woman who had been of the same blood as they. A distressed Eszter was held by Dalir and flanked by Kalet and Dura's other lords, all of them familiar with the black-haired girl from Palmyra who won the heart of a prince of Hatra and spent much time in the Kingdom of Dura. I was also happy to see Orobaz and many of Hatra's lords, traditionally hostile to the 'barbarian' Agraci who lived in the lands to the west of the Euphrates. But out of respect for their prince, king and queen, they too stood around the tall pyre, upon which Rasha lay on a huge lion banner.

Akmon walked from the group where Joro, Soter and Media's loyal lords stood, a King's Guard handing him a burning torch. Others were handed to Castus, Haytham and Spartacus, the king and his sons taking up position at the four corners of the pyre. The king raised his torch and thrust it into the bone-dry pile of wicker shields. His sons did the same and there was an audible groan from those present as the flames took hold and the fire began to crackle and spit.

'I grieve for you, King Pacorus.'

Where before there was no one on my right side there was now a tall individual wearing a cowl, a long, hooded garment with wide sleeves. The hood was large and obscured the face. Everyone's gaze was directed at the pyre that was now roaring as the flames took hold. The sun illuminated the mysterious stranger's hands that were clasped before him and I saw the signet ring, the same one I had seen in the camp of the immortals.

'Do you, lord? You could have saved her.'

'Did Marduk not tell you it is death to kill one of his high priests?'

I was indignant. 'Rasha did not kill one of his priests.'

'No, it was Spartacus, at Ctesiphon, but the lion of Gordyene's destiny is not to die in this place.'

'So an innocent dies to satisfy some prophecy?'

'When you have finished here, King Pacorus, take a walk on the plain and examine the rotting corpses on the ground. How many of those were innocent men, pressed into service by a king they had never previously seen or by a lord they despised? Innocents are the first to die, it is the way of things.'

'Ishtar saved Haya,' I hissed.

'For which she has been rebuked. But in her defence, she does admire Queen Gallia greatly.'

Rasha's body had disappeared now, the pyre becoming a huge, roaring inferno and the flames becoming pillars of red and orange. I could feel the heat on my face and saw that Spartacus and his sons had retreated a few paces to avoid getting singed.

'It is the fate of the kings of Gordyene to lose their wives,' he told me. 'You yourself have been witness to Surena and Viper and you knew King Balas, did you not?'

'I did. Is it also their fate to die on the battlefield?'

'Surely that is the desire of all warriors, King Pacorus.'

We stood as the fire burned savagely, reducing the body of Rasha to ashes and allowing her soul to leave it and depart to the realm of the immortals.

'Rasha was a good person,' I said pathetically.

A chuckle. 'She will be welcomed among us, King Pacorus, if only because you desire it.'

I laughed, earning me a stern frown from Gallia, who as far as I could fathom was ignorant of my august companion.

'What else do you desire?' he asked.

'Peace, I ache to see an end to war.'

'That will come about only when men no longer walk the earth. But if you speak only of Parthia, then I can help you.'

'Oh?'

'The high crown is yours, should you desire it. The widely held view is that you alone can bring about peace in the empire.'

I was shaken by his offer. I had always believed in Dobbai's prophecy all those years ago that the king who has no crown shall have no crown, and had therefore dedicated my life to serving others who I believed would make good high kings. I had succeeded when Orodes had become king of kings, but only after an ocean of blood had been spilt. My determination to ensure the same did not happen again had made me a fervent supporter of his son Phraates, despite his failings.

'We have a high king,' I said.

A snort of derision. 'Phraates is not an ethical man, King Pacorus. This sombre gathering is testament to that, for without the scheming of Phraates this plain would not now be littered with carrion. So, what do you say?'

I was mightily tempted, I have to admit. To sit on Ctesiphon's throne, knowing I had the support of the Sun God himself, was a powerful inducement to accept his offer. But then I remembered the oath I had taken to Phraates, who would be deposed if I took the high throne, perhaps even poisoned by his trusted adviser, my daughter Claudia. Thus I would break my oath and what sort of man breaks a vow, and why would others follow such a man? Dobbai was right: the gods are cruel. They sought to entrap me by dangling a rich prize before my eyes. Did they think my honour could be purchased so cheaply?

'Parthia already has a king of kings,' I said firmly, 'and I have no appetite to replace him, much less fight another civil war in the empire.'

'So be it,' he said without emotion, 'though in your dotage you may look back on this moment and regret your decision.'

In that moment, I realised I was no better than a temple slave. All my life I had served the gods and Parthia and as I stared at the raging pyre I realised my life had been that of a servant, riding hither and thither to quell the empire's internal and external enemies. And after forty years I was still doing it.

Afterwards, when the troops had been sent back to camp and the mourners on the mound had dispersed, I told Gallia what Shamash had offered me. She sat in a chair in our tent with her eyes closed, Klietas filling our cups with wine and taking away our cuirasses that we had discarded. She did not open them when she spoke.

'You made the right decision. I just want to return to Dura and be away from this place.'

It was a sign that we had become so accustomed to the immortals revealing themselves that she spoke of the Sun God in such a cursory manner.

'And Atrax?'

She opened her eyes, picked up her cup and drank from it. She looked pale and drawn, black rings around her eyes, which were bloodshot as a result of having had no sleep the night before. She looked worn out and surely I presented a similar sorry appearance. I rubbed my leg, which was aching like fury. Gallia saw me wince.

'The gift of eternal youth has been withdrawn, then.'

I nodded.

She drank some more wine. 'Youth, beauty and strength are for the young, which is the way it should be.'

I raised my cup to her. 'You are still beautiful.'

She smiled. 'To you, perhaps, but to the rest of the world I am just another ageing woman whose looks are fading.'

She grabbed some of her hair and examined it.

'Alcaeus told me that people with blonde hair go grey quicker than those with dark hair, but informed me the greying is less noticeable.'

I rubbed my crown. 'At least your hair is still thick. I'm so thin on top I was thinking of borrowing some of Klietas' hair. Klietas, what do you say?'

He ran from the sleeping quarters where he had been hanging our cuirasses on wooden stands.

'Highborn?'

Because he was young he had a mop of thick dark brown hair that tumbled to his shoulders.

'I was wondering if I could borrow some of your hair, seeing as you have so much and mine is diminishing by the day.'

'Of course, highborn,' he picked up a dagger lying on the table.

I shook my head. 'It was a joke, Klietas.'

Gallia examined the youth, who had gained some weight after being fed on a regular basis and looked far healthier than the miserable wretch we had first encountered. He was in the unique

369

position of having physically improved while being trapped in a city under siege.

'So Klietas is coming back to Dura with us,' said Gallia. 'What will he do there?'

'Well, aside from finding himself a princess to marry,' I said, 'I thought he might make a cataphract, one day.'

'You know how to use any other weapon aside from a sling?' Gallia asked him.

'A knife also, highborn,' he replied with an evil glint in his eye.

'Very useful,' she said.

The conversation was interrupted by Kalet, Eszter's father-in-law bowing to us both and noting Klietas, who retreated from our presence when I told him to fetch another cup.

'Excuse the interruption,' said Kalet, 'but the men I sent to kill that fat governor have returned empty handed. It appears the governor and his wife left Mepsila before they arrived and no one knows where they went. They have disappeared.'

'Sit down,' I told him.

He pulled up a chair and flopped down into it. Klietas returned with a cup, filled it and handed it to Kalet.

'Bad business about Rasha,' he said.

'Have you made a count of your losses?' I asked, the death of Rasha too raw to discuss.

'Nearly five hundred dead,' he declared, draining his cup and holding it out to be refilled. Klietas obliged.

'One in ten, the same number in killed and wounded suffered by my foot soldiers,' I lamented.

'The army will be rebuilt,' said Gallia, staring at Klietas, 'Dura's treasury is well stocked and there is no shortage of men and women willing to fight for the red griffin. The fire of freedom will never be extinguished.'

Kalet drank more wine. 'My flame was nearly extinguished, princess, I don't mind telling you. I'm getting too old for charging around Parthia fighting all and sundry.'

'You are right, Kalet,' she agreed, her eyes still on Klietas, 'we have played the same game for too long. It is time to play another.'

I had no inkling what she had in mind and she said no more on the matter, smiling at Kalet and asking after Dalir and Eszter. I did not realise it at the time but looking back her words marked the beginning of a new, darker period in the history of the Amazons. Gallia's bodyguard became her private army, undertaking nefarious missions in what she termed 'Dura's interests'. I did not object; indeed, I had set the precedent by asking Kalet to send a band of assassins to find and kill Cookes, the fat, traitorous governor of Mepsila. It had been a decision taken very much in the heat of the moment, but Gallia had a cooler, more calculating head on her shoulders and allowed more time and effort to be committed to the covert missions of the Amazons. But all this was in the future.

To my great surprise Spartacus and his sons journeyed back with us to Irbil, greeting Lusin fondly on the steps of the city's palace and Castus and Haytham likewise being courteous to their sister-in-law. She in turn was all charm and sympathy, weeping when she was informed Rasha was dead and embracing Spartacus warmly. In truth she was difficult to dislike, her soft voice and large brown eyes being able to charm the birds from the trees. For his part Spartacus displayed none of the prickly temper that had been his hallmark for so long. But it was a tragedy that it had taken the death of his wife to melt the wall of ice that he had built around himself.

The armies were sent home, the wounded Chrestus and the legions returning to Dura and the Immortals journeying north to Gordyene. Happily, the odious Spadines and his Sarmatians had not yet put in an appearance, Spartacus informing me he had orders to pursue the Armenians all the way back to the border, and beyond.

'Not that he obeys orders,' he reflected, running a finger around the rim of his chalice.

After the armies had departed there were no more grand feasts in the banqueting hall to celebrate Media's deliverance. Instead, meals were eaten in Akmon's private quarters, in an intimate dining room near the palace garden. The large mahogany table had been polished so regularly and with such vigour that its surface was like a mirror. While reaching forward to lift my chalice I caught sight of myself in its surface. I looked old again with thinning, greying hair. I took a sip of the wine. It was excellent.

'But not as invigorating as the elixir of the gods,' I mumbled.

Spartacus gave me a quizzical look. 'Uncle?'

I shook my head. 'Nothing.'

'I should ride to Hatra and inform my parents of recent events,' he announced. 'It will be good to see them again.'

He still could not bring himself to say Rasha was dead.

'They will be pleased to see you,' said Gallia.

'The Armenians must pay for their treachery,' spat Haytham. 'We must avenge mother's death.'

He was shorter than his father but had the same muscular build. His hair was black as night, inherited from his mother, his long nose and high forehead giving him a somewhat scholarly appearance. Until he opened his mouth and spewed venom.

'We should lay siege to Artaxata and burn it to the ground.'

He slammed his chalice down on the table.

Spartacus regarded him coolly.

'Apologise to your sister.'

Haytham was shocked. 'Father?'

'Apologise! Now!'

His roar made us all jump, not least Haytham.

'I am sorry, sister,' he muttered.

'I am sorry, *majesty*,' growled Spartacus, 'for Lusin is the Queen of Media.'

'It really isn't necessary,' said Lusin, who was cut dead by a raised hand from the King of Gordyene.

'He must learn proper court procedure if he is to marry well,'

Spartacus glowered at his son, who bowed his head to Lusin and apologised once more, this time as his father had wished.

'You are welcome to visit us at any time,' said Lusin to Haytham, which disarmed the prickly young man somewhat.

Spartacus said nothing about Lusin visiting Vanadzor where she had been held captive after he had raided southern Armenia to pillage the Temple of the Goddess Anahit. Lusin's father had to pay a substantial ransom to get her back, but though Vanadzor's coffers may have been filled with Armenian gold, the episode had led to Akmon falling in love with her. Such is fate.

'Lucius has been working hard on the defences,' said Akmon, changing the subject. 'He thinks it would be better to construct a mud-brick wall to replace the wooden one.'

'Who is Lucius?' asked Castus.

'Lucius Varsas is my quartermaster general,' I told him.

'A Roman,' Spartacus told his son.

Castus' blue eyes narrowed. 'There are no Romans in Gordyene, they are not welcome.'

'Gordyene's experience of Romans is not a happy one, uncle,' said Spartacus, 'and the same Romans who invaded my kingdom fought beside you to restore Phraates. That was a mistake.'

'To restore Phraates or hire Roman soldiers?' Gallia asked him.

'Hindsight is a wonderful thing,' he said, 'and I do not blame you for taking measures to rid Parthia of Tiridates. Rasha was also involved in the plot, as was my mother, but bringing Roman soldiers into the empire was dangerous. It will have whetted their appetite regarding plundering Ctesiphon's riches.'

'The Roman leader Octavian has agreed that the Euphrates will mark the boundary between Rome and Parthia,' I told him, 'subject to Phraates returning the Roman eagles he holds. In return, Octavian will return the high king's son.'

'You really believe the infant is still alive, uncle?'

'The Governor of Syria has assured me he lives,' I answered.

'You believe the word of a Roman, lord?' asked Castus.

'I believed him, yes,' I told him. 'Just because he is a Roman does not mean he should immediately be considered a liar or schemer, in the same way that you cannot consider all Parthians as paragons of virtue.'

'But you have spent your life fighting Romans,' said Haytham.

I sipped at my wine. 'I have spent all my life defending Parthia, Haytham, which has included battling the Romans on occasion, yes. But, and it pains me to say so, I have killed more Parthians than Romans doing so. When you become king, and I pray that day is a long way off, you will find it is better to judge people on their merits rather than their race.'

I looked around at the walls painted light blue, the silver candle stands and the silver chalices encrusted with jewels.

'It was in this palace that the ludicrous policy of Parthian purity was born, but such notions are meaningless.'

'Not to King Darius and your sister Aliyeh, the queen mother,' remarked Haytham.

'Watch your tongue,' Spartacus warned him.

'It is quite all right,' I said. 'My sister and her sons believed themselves to be pure-blood Parthians with an ancient lineage.'

'Which is what they were,' opined Haytham, who had clearly drunk too much wine.

'Indeed, and like my own family could trace their blood line back to the first Parthian king, Arsaces,' I told him, drinking more wine, 'the only problem being that Arsaces himself was descended from nomads of the great steppes. My sister despised above all the Agraci, who are also nomads, not knowing that she too was descended from a tribe of wanderers. I wonder if all the peoples of the world are actually descended from one tribe.'

'The Romans want to make all peoples one tribe, their own,' said Castus, 'that is why we fight them.'

'That is why we keep our quivers full and our sword blades sharp,' I smiled, 'just in case they try.'

'They will,' muttered Spartacus. He looked at Akmon. 'That is why I would like to propose an alliance between Media and Gordyene, to cement the new relationship between our two kingdoms and to stand shoulder-to-shoulder in the face of foreign aggression.'

Akmon was delighted. 'I accept, father.'

375

Gallia raised her chalice. 'Dura will also join the alliance, won't we, Pacorus.'

I looked at Spartacus. 'As long as it is a defensive alliance.'

He nodded.

'Then Dura will be delighted to join, as my wife says.'

It was a cordial evening, Spartacus in a conciliatory mood as he grieved, the angry beast within him having been laid low by the enormity of his loss.

We said our goodbyes the next morning, the sun beating down from a clear sky to herald another beautiful day. The farewell between Spartacus and Akmon was warm and heartfelt, the King of Gordyene also making a great effort to be courteous and affectionate towards Lusin. Castus was friendly enough but Haytham, having drunk too much wine the night before, was sombre and irritable. While they were exchanging goodbyes I pulled Lucius aside. I had asked him to remain in Irbil to oversee the strengthening of the city's defences, having promised I would send his family to him.

'You must impress upon Akmon the need for him to rebuild his army,' I said. 'Increase the palace guard and the number of horse archers and cataphracts. Soter and his lords will be returning to their estates to oversee the gathering in of the harvest. This city is still vulnerable.'

He looked serious. 'Soldiers cannot be created out of thin air, majesty. Perhaps if Dura could loan King Akmon some soldiers?'

'No,' I said firmly, 'his father can supply soldiers. He has enough of them and if they are here then they won't be making war on Armenia or Pontus.'

'Ah, excellent point.'

'I thought so. I have every confidence in you, Lucius.'

The reality was I was leaving him with few resources with which to build a mud-brick wall around Irbil, rebuild the garrison and repel an enemy attack should the Armenians decide to raid Media. I told Spartacus the same when we rode with him from the citadel, a long line of Amazons, King's Guard and camels behind us.

'Akmon needs some of your soldiers to strengthen his garrison until he can rebuild his army.'

'He did not say anything to me.'

'He is proud, like his father,' I said, 'but pride comes before a fall and I worry the Armenians might be back.'

'I will ensure Media is safe, uncle, you have my word.'

At the city gates we said farewell to him and his two sons, around us slaves working feverishly making mud-bricks to build the wall that would surround the city. Spartacus pulled up his horse and pointed at the bare-chested slaves sweating in the sun.

'Here's an idea, uncle. I will leave a thousand enemy captives behind to work on the walls, with five companies of Immortals to act as their guards. That should speed up the construction process. Shamshir.'

The commander of the King's Guard rode forward and saluted.

'Lord?'

'Send some men to ride ahead to catch up with the army. Give General Motofi my regards and tell him five companies of Immortals are to return to the city accompanied by a thousand captives.'

'Yes, lord.'

He returned to his men and a party of four riders galloped north. Spartacus spread his arms.

'Am I not generous?'

Gallia rolled her eyes and I smiled kindly at my nephew, who peered to the west, his eyes suddenly filled with anguish.

'And now we ride to Hatra to inform my parents of recent events. It will be hard on them. Farewell uncle, aunt.'

He raised a hand and dug his knees into his horse, the beast cantering forward, Castus and Haytham and then the King's Guard following. I looked at Gallia.

'I'm done with all this.'

'With what?'

'Fighting. I have lost too many friends and family fighting the empire's enemies over the years. Rasha was the final straw. I want to enjoy my autumn years in peace.'

I nudged Horns forward. 'I have drawn my sword in anger for the last time.'

Epilogue

Zeugma had once been a Parthian city. Straddling the River Euphrates, it had been founded by Seleucus I Nicator, the 'victor', one of Alexander of Macedon's generals. Indeed, Zeugma meant 'crossing' in old Greek and its position on the mighty river blessed it with an abundance of wealth. Standing as it did on the dividing line between east and west, the city's rulers were able to reap a rich reward by charging road tolls on the unending trade caravans that travelled along the Silk Road. The last Parthian king of Zeugma had been Darius, an old, corrupt monarch who liked young boys as well as rich living. When the Romans offered him peace, security and an endless supply of slave boys in exchange for becoming a client king of Rome, he grabbed the opportunity with both hands.

Where once gaudily dressed spearmen patrolled the city's streets, now mail-clad Roman legionaries walked the well-maintained thoroughfares. A Roman governor administered the city and Roman laws prevailed over Parthian rules and customs. On a day-to-day basis this mattered little to the thousands of people who lived and worked in the city, which made it easy for those who had fled Parthia for whatever reason to make Zeugma their home. Those who were rich settled among the large villas built on the cliffs overlooking the blue waters of the Euphrates below. Those villas boasted large atriums – open-roofed central courts – graced with fountains, statues, flowerbeds and miniature citrus trees, around which were galleries filled with upholstered and finely carved furniture. On the walls were exquisite frescoes, and on the floors intricate mosaics.

Cookes rubbed his hands and placed them on the table in expectation of another delicious meal. The dining room of the villa he and his wife had rented for a very reasonable fee had a splendid view of the Euphrates and the Kingdom of Hatra beyond. As well as being obese, an alcoholic and a man of low morals, like all cowards he also had a highly developed sense of self-preservation. At Mepsila he had controlled all the post stations along the Tigris after receiving a large amount of gold from Prince Atrax, but he had also monitored the prince's campaign to win back Media's crown carefully. He ensured he received daily updates regarding the progress of the prince's siege of Irbil, deciding to flee Mepsila when he learned of the approach of a relief force led by none other than King Spartacus himself. He and his wife had planned their escape even before Prince Atrax had left Pontus. They took his gold, crossed the Tigris and headed west to the city of Nisibus and on to Zeugma.

Cookes and his wife thought they would miss Media but in truth they found the rich living of Zeugma highly appealing. They quickly settled into their new home, which boasted fountains in the atrium and mosaics on the floor depicting mythological scenes, such as water fairies laying on grass with springs flowing from their bodies, the bull of Minos and dragons, the latter making them feel at home. There were curiosities, of course, such as the bronze statue of a Roman god named Apollo in the atrium, but these were minor irritants compared to the ease of living he and his wife enjoyed.

He was particularly enamoured of a young slave girl who the chief steward, a rather stern individual, had purchased for his entertainment. In no time at all she was serving him his meals, preparing his bath and massaging his fat body. His wife usually passed out from drinking too much wine in the afternoons, and formally he had joined her in her inebriation. But the new slave girl, with her firm body and attractive face, diverted him from his alcoholic indulgences. His obese frame and shortness of breath made him incapable of performing sexual acts, but Cookes was still very capable of groping young, nubile bodies and licking hands and arms that served and massaged him. And, to complete his happiness, the girl smiled and made no attempt to avoid his lascivious clutches.

'Where is my wife?' he moaned, belching as he shoved a boiled egg into his mouth and washed it down with wine. 'Come here, girl.'

The slave girl, wearing a skimpy tunic that barely concealed her modesty and accentuated the shape of her breasts and pert buttocks, smiled and walked over to stand beside her gross master at the over-sized table. The stench of his body odour was repellent, and she nearly threw up when his chubby fingers began exploring her undergarments. He licked his podgy lips and leered at her, his eyes falling on her breasts as he abused her.

She hastily leaned over to refill his rhyton with wine. Cookes stopped fondling her and reached for the drinking vessel, drinking greedily and spilling wine on the table as he did so.

'Where is Hanita?' he bleated.

'She is coming, master,' said the girl, pointing to a slave boy coming from the corridor leading to the kitchens.

'That's not my wife,' chuckled Cookes, 'he's far too thin. Drank herself into a stupor, I suppose. Fat bitch.'

He began stroking the girl's buttocks. 'Not like you, eh?'

The slave boy placed the large silver tray, which had a silver dome-shaped cover to retain the heat of the dish it held, before Cookes.

'Tonight I will lay with you,' panted Cookes, his lecherous eyes staring at the slave girl's breasts.

'What about your wife, master?'

'What about her?'

'Shall we not ask her, master?'

She reached over and lifted the cover on the silver tray. To reveal the severed head of Hanita resting on a bed of rice and garnished with lettuce. Cookes squealed with horror, his eyes bulging at the sight of his wife's head, her tongue protruding from the mouth and her eyes closed. He did not see the slave boy hand the girl something, but he was aware of her roughly grabbing his chin.

'Queen Gallia sends her regards.'

Haya drew the knife across his neck, severing the windpipe and sending a spurt of blood over the head of Hanita. She continued to saw until the edge of the blade had reached the spine, blood sheeting over his robe, the table and the floor.

The steward, who had been standing by a pillar, walked forward and stared at the bloody mess.

'We should leave. Haya, change your clothes and wash the blood from your hands.'

'It will be a pleasure.'

She spat on the corpulent corpse and walked with Klietas to one of the galleries where they had stored a change of clothes.

'You look very beautiful,' he complimented her.

'Don't get any ideas,' she warned him.

Talib shook his head. Klietas would go far, *if* he managed to keep his head. He had ordered the other slaves of the household to vacate the villa in a covered cart driven by Minu, now his wife following the ceremony held at Palmyra and attended by King Malik, Queen Jamal, King Pacorus and Queen Gallia. His former master Byrd was also in attendance and it was he that had sent word to all his offices to keep an eye out for the fat former governor of Mepsila, who had seemingly vanished from the face of the earth. Byrd was the owner of the large transport guild that operated throughout Syria, Judea, Cilicia, Cappadocia and western Parthia. The men who staffed the offices in those lands and who operated Byrd's camel caravans and boats were told to keep a lookout for Cookes and Hanita. In a short space of time, word reached Palmyra they had taken up residence in Zeugma.

They could have left the slaves at the villa, but to do so would sentence them to death. The Romans were very particular when it came to slaves murdering their masters and mistresses, executing all of those in the household irrespective of whether they had committed the crime or not. This was to deter any slave even considering visiting violence on his or her owner.

Talib met Haya and Klietas in the stables to the rear of the villa, Haya holding the reins of his horse and Klietas waiting at the open gates. The boy's equine skills had improved immensely after his arrival at Dura, the king himself taking a personal interest in the orphan's development.

'You have done well, Haya,' said Talib after vaulting into the saddle, 'I hope this mission has not been too unpleasant.'

She shrugged. 'It was an honour to be chosen by the queen herself. My only regret is that we cannot take both heads back to Dura to show her our handiwork.'

He turned his horse and nudged it forward, all three riding from the villa to head for the bridge across the Euphrates. Minu would be already across the waterway by now, the forged documents of slave ownership in her possession meaning her passage through the Roman checkpoints would be trouble free. Then she and the now freed slaves would be in Hatran territory where they could begin new lives.

During the ride through the crowded streets Klietas wore a dumb grin, oblivious to the dust, heat, horse and camel dung and press of people and beasts. When they arrived at the bridge over the Euphrates, Talib smiled when he caught sight of the covered wagon trundling across the stone structure, having passed through the checkpoint on the western side of the river. He and the others slid off their horses to join the queue, Haya cursing under her breath. Klietas continued to smile at all and sundry.

'Keep calm,' Talib told them, 'they cannot look into your souls.'

A sweating centurion waved them through the cordon with his vine cane, at the other end of the bridge another press of people waited with their beasts to pay tolls to admit them into the Kingdom of Hatra. Such was the volume of traffic between the Roman and Parthian worlds that a pontoon bridge had been built across the Euphrates beside the Greek-built stone structure. This facilitated the movement of camels, mules, carts, wagons and people wishing to enter Roman Zeugma after leaving King Gafarn's domain.

When they had paid the tolls and linked up with Minu and her group of bemused former slaves, Klietas took the opportunity to kiss Haya on the cheek.

'I love you,' he whispered into her ear.

His reward was a slap around the face.

'Don't be an idiot,' she scolded him.

His face throbbed but he did not care. He had found his princess.

*****

It was only when Spartacus had returned to Vanadzor from Hatra did the enormity of his loss hit him. The black stone palace of his capital served only to reinforce his gloom, made worse by seeing his dead wife in every corridor and room. At night he lay alone in his bed, staring up at the ceiling and waiting for dawn to arrive. A lesser man would have crumbled in the face of such misery, but the beast within him, dormant since that dreadful day on the Diyana Plain, reawakened to stir him into action. Rasha had been a brake on his more vindictive and violent plans: a voice of reason that he listened to, even when he ignored the advice of Hovik.

He now sent letters recalling his general and the horsemen he had contributed towards Phraates' 'great muster'. Why would he support a high king who had engineered a rebellion against his son, which had led to the death of his wife? He took his two sons and a small party of King's Guard and rode to the wild region of northern Gordyene, a place of mountains, cave dwellings and a plethora of villages occupied by the Aorsi tribe. In this area of rock, steep-sided valleys and low-hanging clouds the Sarmatians had established a kingdom within a kingdom, which acted as a shield for the rest of Gordyene against the Armenians.

He sent word ahead of their intention to visit Prince Spadines, formerly the ruler of the city of Van but now reduced to living in the same stone hut where he had been born. In truth, though he was most grateful to King Spartacus for giving him land and a city to rule, the Sarmatian was always ill at ease living in a city. He was a brigand at heart, a raider who loved nothing more than leading his men in plunder and rapine. That was why he liked the King of Gordyene so much – he indulged his baser instincts.

Spadines welcomed the king to his humble abode on a cool autumn afternoon, drizzle in the air.

'Welcome, lord,' he gushed, walking forward to embrace the king.

Spartacus returned the gesture, nodding to Spadines' hard-faced henchmen gathered in a semi-circle around their chief.

'We live to avenge the queen's death,' grunted Spadines. 'Come, let us get out of the rain.'

Later, when the rain had passed to leave a cool, damp evening, Spartacus sat with Spadines round a raging fire in the chief's hut, the Sarmatian's wife serving her husband and his guests dumplings filled with mutton, warm bread and thick broth. Spartacus ate sparingly but both Castus and Haytham filled their bellies with gusto. The young sons of Spadines stared in awe at the famous, fierce King of Gordyene who regarded them with cruel eyes but said nothing. He had been disappointed when Artaxias and Atrax had evaded the Aorsi to escape back to Armenia, but what was done was done.

'I wanted to thank, you, lord, for the generous gift you bestowed on me,' said Spadines.

He was alluding to the thousands of slaves gifted to him by Spartacus, the majority of whom had been sold on to slave merchants in Atropaiene and Hyrcania, the reasoning being that men in their prime should be moved as far away from their homelands as possible to both demoralise them and reduce the likelihood they would revolt against their masters in an effort to return home. Some he had kept, which had been given to his subordinates, so their wives could play at being fine ladies with their own slaves.

'Think nothing of it,' said the king, tossing a package wrapped in goatskin to the Sarmatian.

Spadines' eyes lit up as he unwrapped the gift, turning to surprise and then disappointment as he held a blue tunic and a pair of grey leggings. Spartacus grinned.

'I do not understand, lord,' said Spadines.

'Before the snows close the high passes,' the king told him, 'I will send you five hundred of these tunics and leggings, along with banners showing a white dragon on a black background.'

Spadines was now even more confused.

Haytham stopped his gorging. 'The banner of Media?'

Spartacus stared into the fire, the memory of his wife's cremation hitting him like the bludgeoning of a mace.

'In the spring send parties into Armenia to plunder its settlements. Make sure your men are all wearing these clothes and flying a dragon banner. In each village leave a few alive to spread the message that the King of Media has come to wreak revenge on them for killing his mother.'

'I do not understand, lord,' said Spadines.

'The Armenian king will not be able to tolerate such incursions,' Spartacus told him, 'and will retaliate against Media. This will bring about a confrontation between him and Hatra, Dura and Gordyene, all three kingdoms having forged an alliance with Media.'

'We do not need Hatra or Dura to destroy Armenia, father,' said Castus, 'not with our Aorsi allies fighting beside us.'

Spadines raised his cup of ale to the prince.

'No, but we need Dura's siege engines if we are to capture Artaxata,' Spartacus informed his son.

'If Dura was ruled by Queen Gallia, then its army would march beside our own without the need for deception,' sneered Haytham, 'but its king is no friend of Gordyene. In any case, King Pacorus has retired from war.'

'He saved your brother, remember that,' snapped Spartacus.

'He does not like me,' muttered Spadines, clearing his throat and spitting phlegm into the fire.

Spartacus nodded. 'My uncle is a moral man and that morality means he will not wage aggressive war against Parthia's enemies.'

'Weakness,' spat Castus.

Spartacus chuckled. 'I have never heard the army of Dura being described as weak, nor indeed its commander. Do not mistake a reluctance to wage war with cowardice. The army of Dura has never lost a battle. Never. It came close on the Plain of Diyana, though there it was without its cataphracts and professional horse archers. No, the army of Dura is the finest military instrument in the Parthian Empire, and I include my own army in that estimation.'

'King Pacorus will never sanction the capture of the Armenian capital, father,' said Castus.

'He will if he believes Armenia has been waging a war of aggression against Media,' Spartacus retorted, 'a kingdom he has just spilled the blood of his men defending. Anyway, we do not necessarily need to take Artaxata. The fact our army will have siege engines will convince King Artaxias that we have the means to reduce his capital to rubble. That will convince him to offer battle before we reach the city.'

Haytham's eyes lit up. 'The combined armies of Gordyene, Hatra and Dura will crush the Armenians easily, father.'

'Our army will not be present,' growled Spartacus.

His two sons and Spadines stared at him in disbelief.

'I do not understand, lord,' said Spadines for a second time.

Spartacus looked at his trusted ally and then his two sons. 'We will be busy killing everything that moves in Pontus.'

Historical notes

Irbil, variously called Erbil, Arbil or Arbela, is the largest city in northern Iraq, with a population of over 800,000. It is very different from two millennia ago, but its most striking feature is remarkably similar to the stronghold portrayed in 'The Slave King'. Today, Irbil's citadel is a UNESCO (United Nations Educational, Scientific and Cultural) world heritage site, having been formerly a Sumerian, Assyrian, Parthian, Sassanid, Mongol, Christian and Ottoman stronghold. There are currently three ramps leading up to the citadel, on the northern, eastern and southern sides, though in ancient times only the southern ramp existed, which led to a huge, arched gatehouse. This gave access to four main paths within the walled stronghold, which branched out in all directions.

Over centuries the mud-brick buildings gave way to brick and then stone structures and by the 1920s there were 500 houses in the citadel, which had dropped to 247 dwellings and 1600 inhabitants by 1995. By this date most of the buildings in the citadel, having been abandoned, were in a state of great disrepair, leading to a major restoration project being implemented beginning in 2007. The site was cleared of residents so renovation could begin, though one family was allowed to stay in the citadel so as not to break some 8000 years of continuous inhabitation.

Today the citadel gives the appearance of being surrounded by a wall, but in fact the exterior 'wall' is made up of 19th-century house facades built against each other to give a fortified appearance. Inside the citadel the homes of royalty were not expansive due to the confined spaces but usually had two storeys and a basement, the walls being adorned with beautiful paintings and ornate waterfalls found in most backyards. By the 1930s most of the houses in the citadel were of the traditional courtyard type, with 30 being larger palace-like homes.

Irbil and the surrounding area are rich in history. For example, Alexander the Great defeated the Persian ruler Darius on the plain of Gaugamela in 331BC to the west of the city, after which Darius fled east to first Irbil and then the Zagros Mountains but was eventually killed by his own soldiers. Thereafter Alexander assumed the leadership of the Persian Empire, according to legend beginning at a ceremony in the Temple of Ishtar in Irbil's citadel.

Around 35 miles northeast of the sprawling city of Irbil is the Diyana Plain, in the middle of which is the earth mound of Gird-I Dasht, the scene of the battle between Pacorus and the forces of the rebel Atrax and the Armenians in 'The Slave King'. The plain looks almost exactly the same today as it did 2000 years ago when the King of Dura cast his gaze on the massed ranks of the enemy army before giving battle to Prince Atrax and King Artaxias.

Made in the USA
Middletown, DE
09 July 2020

12288256R10219